THE OATH AND THE COVENANT

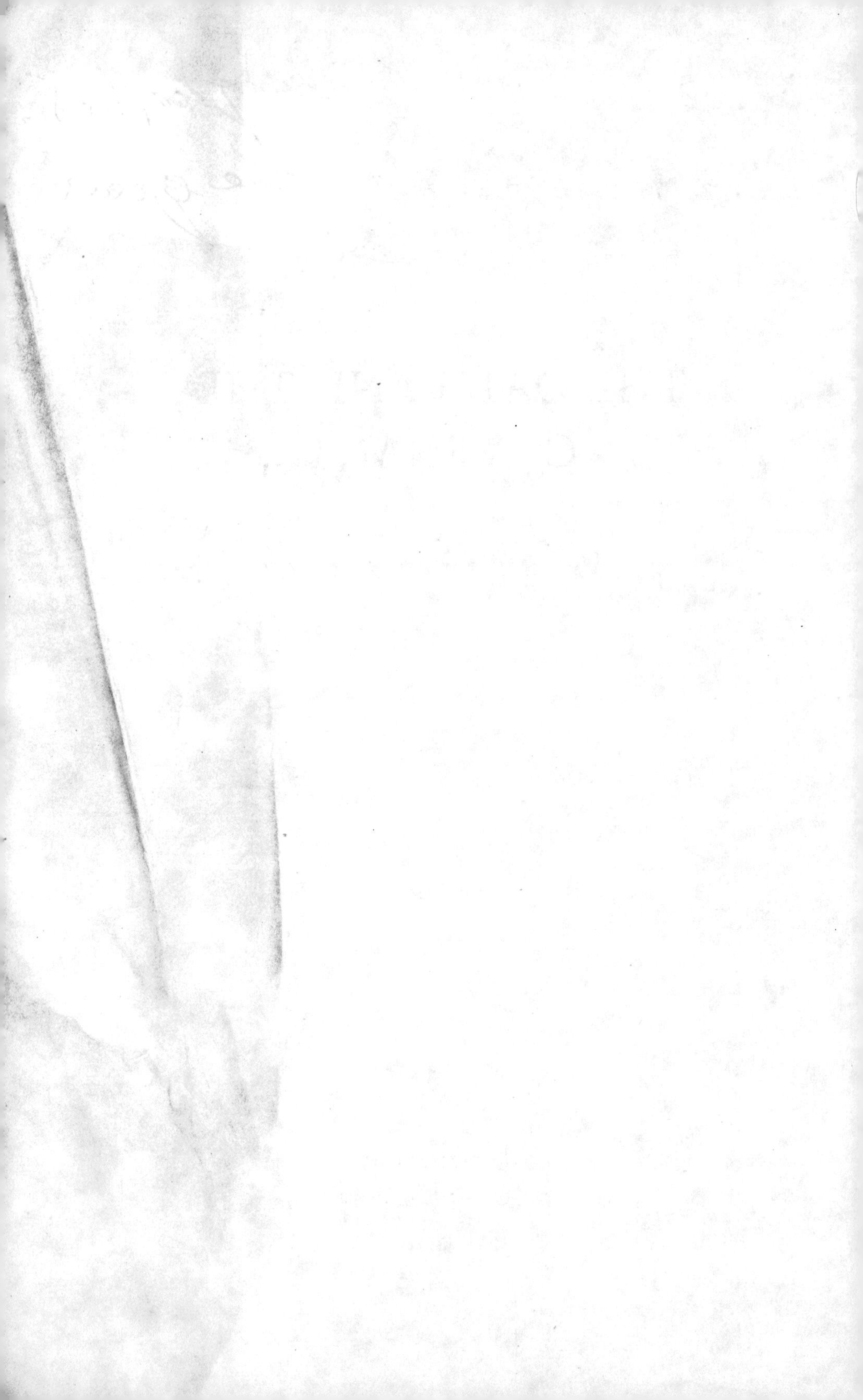

THE OATH AND THE COVENANT

The 'Killing Times' in Scotland

A Historical Novel

Isabelle McCall MacLean

iUniverse, Inc.
New York Lincoln Shanghai

THE OATH AND THE COVENANT

The 'Killing Times' in Scotland

iUniverse books may be ordered through booksellers or by contacting:

iUniverse
2021 Pine Lake Road, Suite 100
Lincoln, NE 68512
www.iuniverse.com
1-800-Authors (1-800-288-4677)

ISBN-13: 978-0-595-39706-8 (pbk)
ISBN-13: 978-0-595-84112-7 (ebk)
ISBN-10: 0-595-39706-9 (pbk)
ISBN-10: 0-595-84112-0 (ebk)

Printed in the United States of America

I DEDICATE THIS BOOK
TO MY BELOVED CHILDREN
JULIANNE
BRADLEY
CARLA JAY
TANIA

Remember to dream a dream
Then work your dream
And never give up
Love
Mom

ACKNOWLEGMENTS

I want to acknowledge my many friends who helped me over the last twenty years to shape this story. Mary MacLellan patiently listened as I composed the first of twenty-seven drafts. Audrey Kirk and Margie Hotten typed that first draft when I had the audacity to think it was ready for publication. Alistair Sumner helped me get it onto a computer and constantly 'recovered' it for me as I learned. Lois Mcdonnell read it and gave me benefit of her input. Iola (Cassie) Wilson edited and sent out query letters by the dozens. My family continually encouraged me although I am sure they tired of 'the book'. Beverley Clements painstakingly edited—with a smile. Diane Manley helped me numerous times to copy it onto a CD, retrieved my lost manuscripts from computer never-never land and in general 'saved me'. Linda Clark was even drawn into it. And, finally, Doral Kemper combed through and corrected spelling errors and made valuable suggestions.

I could not have completed it without all of you—at least not in this life time.

And last but certainly not least, I want to thank my husband, Arvey Drown, for his consistent encouragement—never tiring of telling me 'it's a good story' just keep going…you'll publish one day.

HISTORIC TIME-LINE

Four hundred years after William Wallace, our 'Braveheart', battled to unite the clans of Scotland against English rule, the country was again plunged into civil war. Once more, Scotland's sons and daughters would be called on to spill their blood in defense of their freedom from English rule. However, this fight was for freedom of religion—to worship as *their* hearts and minds dictated, not according to the King's dictate. It was now that the Presbyterian Covenanters were summoned by their love of God and country, to battle valiantly for this right. Their descendants have been taught at the knees of their parents and grandparents, as I have, about the struggles the Covenanters endured...stories oft repeated...mouth to ear...from generation to generation of these, our brave and stoic ancestors and their banishment to the 'Americas'. Some of us agonize, even now, over the inhumane treatment they suffered, and wonder in awe and admiration, at their bravery.

The Oath and The Covenant brings to you some of the struggles they endured and triumphed over during what has become known in the annals of history as "The Killing Times" in Scotland.

To understand the division in thinking between the Stuart/Stewart Kings and the Scottish Presbyterians, from whom the Covenanters evolved, the reader needs to understand first the mind-set of the English kings and then that of the Presbyterians. The Stuarts/Stewarts believed that all true Kings received their mantles immediately from God. This gave them "Right Divine", and when this was adopted into the church, it was termed "Apostolic Succession" which gave the kings exact rule over the state and the church.

On the other hand, the followers of John Knox, the reformer and father of Presbyterianism in Scotland, believed that the function of government did not belong to one person or one class of people; that government belonged to the citizens, and spiritual government belonged to the whole body of the faithful; and that the few who led the government were selected by the people. The Covenanters represented those Presbyterians who held most firmly to these truths and were unwavering in their defense of them, sacrificing their very lives to uphold their beliefs. It is this form of government that is enjoyed by 'free' nations today.

The Presbyterian Kirk of Scotland recorded the following statements:

1) The power of creating that man a King, is from the people.

2) If the King has not the consent of the people, he is a usurper....

We can now understand why Royalty and the common people of Scotland were so polarized.

In 1560, the polarization had its inception when John Knox returned to Scotland from Europe, armed with concepts for reformation in his homeland. From that point onward, this thinking was a thorn in the side of the kings. The Presbyterians' newly acquired belief in their right to worship as they saw fit, grew and was shaped into a firm resolve—being forged in their hearts and in their minds by the atrocities they witnessed and suffered at the hands of the Royalists, followers of the king. The conflict began in earnest when King James VI and his son Charles I attempted to force the Anglican/Episcopal liturgy of the Church of England and its' church government upon the Scottish Presbyterians who, at first tried to compromise, and then resisted.

In 1636, King Charles I ordered the Scottish Privy Council to issue a proclamation to the Scottish churches, commanding them to use a new liturgy, including a newly created prayer book that was sanctioned by the Archbishop of Canterbury and similar to that used in the Church of England. The liturgy and prayer book had not been approved by the Scottish National General Assembly; and it contained Roman Catholic doctrine, causing several ministers to walk out during its reading in this Assembly.

In January 1638, when the Dean of St. Giles Cathedral in Edinburgh, attempted to introduce the new liturgy at Sunday worship, a riot broke out. A popular belief is that that a woman by the name of Jenny Geddes, picked up her stool and threw it at him, decrying him for trying to preach false doctrine, saying, "Will ye read that book at my lug (ear)?" This outburst represented the feelings of the majority of Scots and struck the spark that ignited civil revolt in Scotland.

On 28 February 1638, nobles, lairds, ministers and burgesses "opened a vein and signed in their own blood" the National Covenant in Grayfriars Churchyard in Edinburgh. Copies of the Covenant were circulated throughout Scotland for the common folk to sign locally; and thus the National Covenant became symbolic of Scotland's united opposition to King Charles I's innovations in church liturgy and government. Scotland was inflamed and she exploded into rebellion.

The Covenant they agreed to live and die for ensured them of liberty to worship their God according to their consciences; and they determined to resist to the death the claims of the King and his minions to override the Crown rights of the Redeemer in his Kirk.

In November 1638, soon after the Covenant was signed, a Covenanting Assembly consisting of nobles, gentry, clergy and burgesses met in the Glasgow Cathedral. This assembly determined its authority as a government distinct from civil government. Several motions were carried out to assert the power of the people in opposition to royal authority.

The King's reaction to this was to prepare his army to invade Scotland. The fight was on...for the next fifty years.

Throughout 1638 the Covenanters had gathered arms and an army of 30,000 men, which faced the King's army and successfully forced him to negotiate terms of peace. He agreed to call a free Scottish General Assembly and Parliament to settle the affairs of the Presbyterian Church.

In August 1639, both sides met in Edinburgh, and the General Assembly confirmed the Covenanting Assembly's action by rejecting Episcopacy and restoring Presbyterianism as the form of church government to be used in Scotland. This proposal was rejected by King Charles I, resulting in the Bishops Wars of 1639 and 1640.

In 1641, after the Covenanters invaded England and won an easy victory, a peace treaty was signed at Westminster and the demands of the Covenanters were met.

In 1642, the Scottish Covenanters found allies in the English parliamentarians, who also opposed the attempts by the King to rule by Royal decree without the advice or consent of Parliament.

In 1643, the Covenanters and English parliamentarians entered into the Solemn League and Covenant, which was shaped to defend their religion and liberty against rule by bishops.

In 1644, the Covenanter army joined Cromwell, and defeated the Royalists at the battle of Marston Moor. The combined armies were successful in defeating King Charles I and the war ended in 1646.

In 1649, King Charles I was beheaded. Soon after that Cromwell came into power and he split with the Covenanters because he had no further need for the Solemn League and Covenant.

On 1 January 1651, after the Covenanters had split with Cromwell, they allied themselves with Charles' son, and crowned him King Charles II. He in turn signed and approved the National and Solemn League and Covenants. Cromwell did not take this laying down, and his army invaded Scotland. At the battle of Dunbar, the Covenanters were defeated and after a second defeat at the battle of Worceshire, King Charles II fled to the continent.

From 1651—1660, under Cromwell, there was liberty of worship. Although he suppressed the General Assembly, the synods, presbyteries and Kirk sessions were allowed to meet as usual.

In 1660, Charles II was restored to the throne, when the Cromwellian Protectorate was felled. It was now that Charles reneged on his promise made in 1651 to defend Presbyterianism and to be a friend of the Covenanters. Episcopacy was once again established in Scotland with the Act of Supremacy, which made the King supreme in both church and state. By repealing all acts of parliament carried out between 1640 and 1648, he was able to declare the National and Solemn League and Covenants as unlawful oaths and he declared that the government of the church was now the prerogative of the Crown.

In 1662, the Scottish Privy Council issued a decree that all parish ministers were required to be approved by the local patron or landlord and the bishop. In this manner, the King was able to install his own ministers who replaced the Presbyterian ministers whom he ejected. The Presbyterian ministers (some records state this number was 262, and others state it was slightly over 400 ministers) who were ousted continued to preach to their congregations in open fields and glens and these meetings were called Conventicles.

In 1664 the Bishops were habitually giving the Royalists lists of parishioners' names who were not in attendance at their Sunday sermons. Subsequently, the soldiers were given legal authority to hunt down all who refused to conform to these Curates' demands and either shoot the Covenanters on the spot or bring them into court for sentencing. The sentences, more often than not, demanded dismembering of the body—placing the head of the Covenanter on a post with the hands nailed together in praying fashion under the chin. The other body parts were buried separately, effectively stopping their family and others mourning at the gravesite of a possible martyr. This barbarism was usually reserved for those who were considered the leaders of the so-called rebels or 'phanatics'.

What the Royalists could hardly control, though, was the loyalty the parishioners felt for their ousted ministers. The Covenanters would rather gather in a glen, out in the open, exposed to all kinds of weather, just to hear what they esteemed to be the true word of God; rather than listen to the Anglican/Episcopalian ministers preach what they, the Presbyterians, deemed as religious heresy.

The conflict escalated into bloody civil war as the Covenanters hid their ministers and each other from the English army and the enlisted Highland Host—these fiends who chased them from glen to glen, burning their houses, destroying their animals and crops and ravaging their women if their demands for capitulation to the King's policies were rejected. The English soldiers were obeying their King and defending their country's religion; the Highland Host, which was composed of Highlanders and Irishmen, was earning its promised loot and money.

In 1666, one thousand Covenanters marched on Edinburgh, but were defeated. This resulted in many of them being imprisoned and those who escaped were fined when they did not attend their parish churches. To enforce the King's decrees, his soldiers were billeted with those who refused to promise to keep away from Conventicles or refused to divulge the whereabouts of other Covenanters.

In 1679, the Archbishop of St. Andrews was killed by a group of Covenanters. This was carried out in retaliation for the inhumane persecution he had heaped upon them. An army led by John Graham of Claverhouse, Viscount Dundee, was determined to persecute the Covenanters for this action, but he was defeated at Drumclog Muir, much to his agonizing shame. However, Claverhouse and the Duke of Monmouth did defeat the Covenanters at the Battle of Bothwell Bridge and following this defeat, the Covenanters suffered inhumane persecution at the hands of the Royalists.

In 1685, Charles II died. His brother James VII, succeeded him.

In 1687, James issued a Proclamation of Indulgence, which allowed Presbyterians to worship according to their own belief, as long as they only worshiped in private houses; the laws against Conventicles remained unchanged. Most of the Presbyterian Covenanter ministers accepted this Indulgence; however, a smaller and stricter group of Presbyterians, led by James Cameron would not adhere to the Indulgence. This little group, called Cameronians, was mercilessly hunted down, shot on sight or hanged for treason.

In 1688, James VII of Scotland (James II of England) was forced to flee to France, declaring his abdication when William of Orange landed with an army, supported by the English Protestant nobility. William was a Presbyterian, who realized that his best supporters were Scotsmen.

In 1690, William abolished Episcopacy in the Church of Scotland, and the surviving ejected ministers who had been ousted in 1662 were restored to their parishes. Episcopalian ministers were forced to swear an oath of allegiance to the

King and accept Presbyterian Church government. He also abolished patrons and bishops.

The Covenanters had won a long and bloody battle for the right to worship according to their own consciences and to conduct their own church government, free from state control. This freedom was sorely won—a freedom that we in the 'free' countries enjoy—but should not ever take for granted.

The Oath and The Covenant is a novel based upon the foregoing historical facts. It was inspired by the declaration of the faith and belief of my ancestor, John Whitelaw; he became known as the Martyr of Monkland, a Covenanter. While he stood at the gallows with the noose around his neck, waiting to be hanged on November 28, 1683, at the Market Cross in Edinburgh, he fearlessly declared his beliefs.

The transcript of his dying address was recorded and published in *The Scots Worthies* and in *A Cloud of Witnesses.* These books can be obtained through inter-library loan.

GLOSSARY OF TERMS

1. arisaidh—a long shawl worn over a woman's head and shoulders
2. awa'—away
3. bairn—small child
4. bile—boil
5. bubbly—crying
6. coorie—snuggle
7. dinna—don't
8. frae—from
9. guid—good
10. hame—home
11. heid—head
12. ken—understand
13. kertch—a woman's head covering
14. laddie—boy
15. lassie—girl
16. leine—man's shirt; woman's chemise

17. och aye—okay, alright then, oh well
18. phanatics—fanatics
19. puir—poor
20. uin—one
21. wi'—with
22. weesht—quiet
23. ye—you
24. yer—your

Chapter 1

Scotland—1679

Beneath the moonless cloak of night, eight men carefully made their way to Tigh Sona, the home of John Whitelaw of Monkland. The deep, green slime of the bog would swallow anyone foolish enough to cross it at night; unless, of course, you were a friend of Whitelaw and knew its' secrets. Mercifully, many an enemy soldier and his horse floundered in this bog and were lost while attempting a nocturnal raid upon Tigh Sona.

The dark morass guarded the inhabitants of this humble Scottish cottage against the Royalists, the Highland Host, and any traitors to the Solemn League and Covenant.

"Aye?" John Whitelaw's voice boomed a response to the timid tapping at the cottage door. And then, "Lizzie, get back th' now!" Da cautioned me in a whisper.

I quickly slid behind his weaver's loom, where a deep pallet of straw, laid upon young tree poles that had been lashed together, offered my brother, sister and me a comfortable night's sleep. Within seconds I had slipped out of my leine and slid under the blanket in my shift. I rearranged the wool that was hanging from the loom so I could peek through and watch—and learn.

The door opened slowly and Davie Prescott cautiously stepped into the dimly lit cottage. There was a note of relief in Da's voice when he recognized his friend. "Aye! Cum' in, man! Dinna stand out there chillin' yer bones!" The night was damp and cold, typical for early May.

John Whitelaw's gruffness fooled no one. His rough exterior hid a matchless love for his fellow man and those who had not benefited, were few. However, when he determined that he was going to go in a certain direction, all the king's men couldn't drag him off his course. Sometimes this was good and eventually a happy thing; but sometimes his stubbornness brought some serious problems down on his head.

Davie smiled...but his usual twinkling eyes, which always accompanied his smile, were dull and sad.

"What's the matter wi' ye?" Da looked at him more closely. "Yer wife—she's well and a'?"

"Ach, aye! She's well enough, John...but..."

"Speak up, man! What's troublin' ye?" John demanded.

Davie swallowed hard and continued hesitantly, "When the others arrive I'll be makin' a....". Davie's words trailed off as John responded to another knock at the door. It was a few more of the Covenanter ministers who were meeting here, tonight.

They crowded into our one room cottage, gratefully placing their damp cloaks and tams in the waiting arms of my mother, Christie Whitelaw, who hung them near the fire in the hearth. "So's ye'll have them to warm ye on yer way hame!" she said softly, in her usual hospitable way.

"Christie!" Reverend Cargill exclaimed, his lined face relaxing into a smile, "Dae ye know how good it is tae look upon that bonny face o' yer's?"

Ma blushed, brushing aside the compliment with a wave of her hand.

"Aye...ye take the breath away from a man, ye know that?" Mr. Balfour added, causing Ma's eyebrows to shoot toward the ceiling. Mr. Balfour was certainly not given to compliments; in fact, I had heard Ma wonder out loud if he thought that women, and wives in particular, were only a necessary evil.

My mother's beauty was legend among the country folk. Golden curly hair circled her head like a halo; coal black lashes and brows framed green eyes that tempted even the most straight-laced man to look deeper; and her complexion shamed the finest of porcelain. Ma could hold a man mesmerized as long as she allowed.

Da, however, managed to subtly remind the wayward man whose wife she was...bringing him back to reality with a loud clearing of his throat. In spite of Ma's outward attractiveness, her real beauty sprung from an inner fountain of gentleness and meekness...not to be foolishly confused with weakness. And she was always very properly dressed; her hair done up in a bun and covered with a kertch which was either tied under her chin or at the nape of her neck. As I was a young single woman, I didn't have to wear a kertch yet.

The rebel ministers of the Presbyterian Kirk seated themselves around the peat-fire that burned warmly in the center of the floor, sending its smoke spiraling upwards, toward a small opening in the thatched roof. However, no matter how hard Ma tried to wave the smoke toward the ceiling with her apron, some smoke always managed to escape, routinely blackening Tigh Sona's walls, thus allowing it to join the bevy of Scottish 'black houses' that dotted the hills and glens.

All of these ministers were known as strong leaders and were loved for their dedication to the Covenant, which was a solemn oath taken to defend our right to worship God according to the dictates of our own hearts.

As it was common knowledge that the ousted Presbyterian ministers often gathered in our small cottage, we Whitelaws became hunted and persecuted along with the ministers who were forced to hide in the hill caves. It was during these meetings that I would feign sleep and quietly listen as they related their hair-raising experiences of escaping capture. That the ministers held each other in high regard was so reassuringly evident in the unspoken respect that flavored each word they spoke to each other.

Tonight, a grave and brooding concern permeated the atmosphere of the small room as the meeting began.

I wiggled down on the straw pallet, gently moving the sleeping and limp forms of my younger sister and brother. "Good grief! They're getting heavy," I thought as I positioned myself to eavesdrop on what promised to be another very interesting evening. How could I have known what the next few hours would bring?

These were well-educated men and although I was only fourteen years old, I had honed my literary skills listening to them present and defend their views in our beautiful Scottish brogue, evening after evening.

"Let us give thanks!" said Da, opening the meeting.

Their heads bowed in prayer. Mr. Balfour was voice, expressing their feelings of humility and gratitude for truth and pleading for the strength to stand by it. He prayed for discernment—that they would know the truth of all things and be able to act upon it. He prayed for the deliverance of our people, especially for those being held in the gruesome dungeons of Bass Rock Prison and Blackness Castle.

"Amen!" All had agreed to the supplication.

"My brothers!" The words burst from Davie as if they had been shot from a cannon. "I've a statement to make!"

The force of his words caught everyone's attention and heads and eyes snapped towards him.

Davie's face, though gnarled around an overly large nose, was always kindly. He hunched his shoulders and moved closer to the fire, nervously wringing his hands. "I've accepted the Indulgence—I've taken the oath to the King!" he said quietly, then waited patiently for the shock waves, that were crashing over each of the men, to subside. "Davie! What're ye doin' that for?" was asked time and time again in a dozen different ways.

Davie sat still, staring at the fire, as if he could find the answer amidst the small blue flames shooting upward from the peat. When silence eventually reigned, he continued. With his fingers pushing back and forth—back and forth—through his long matted hair, he said "I've no more stomach for the fightin'. My boy was put into the iron boot last week...". His broad shoulders slumped forward again. "He'll never walk again." The words caught in his throat.

My hand flew to my mouth, stifling a cry of pity. Adam was my friend. We had grown up together. His laughing eyes and freckle-spattered face rushed into my mind. Now, he was crippled—for life!

"Ach, he's only fourteen—a laddie still!" Da cried and his mouth twisted, revealing the anguish he was feeling.

The ministers shook their heads in genuine sympathy. They knew all too well what it meant to be put into the iron boot...a torture device that encased the leg from foot to knee in a metal legging. The inhumane instrument was activated by a wooden mallet which struck the iron wedge that was jammed between the knee and the metal "boot". Each blow forced the wedge in tighter and tighter until it crushed the kneecap with excruciating pain.

The family of the victim was further violated when forced to witness the monstrous torture of their loved one. All of this inhumanity was carried out against the Covenanters in order to coerce them into revealing the hiding places of the ousted ministers.

I watched Ma quietly move from the shadows of our small cottage, where she had stood with her arms folded inside her arisaidh to keep warm. She quietly moved to stand behind Davie and placed a comforting hand on his shoulder, and at her touch, he reached up and covered her hand with his. "I'll accept the Indulgence," Davie restated quietly, but adamantly.

Davie, and so many other ministers like him had been forced to submit to the Royalists' oppression, a means by which King Charles II and his supporters attempted to bring about an acceptance, by all Presbyterians, of the King as head of the Church *and* State—it was known as the *Indulgence.*

The Covenanters, whom the Royalists called rebels or 'phanatics' or whigs, defied the King and fought to maintain the right of moral and religious conscience, in that we demanded and defended our freedom to worship according to the dictates of our own hearts, which did not preclude giving due respect to the

King. But we did not deem him, the King, as the 'Head' of the Church—that was Christ's rightful throne.

Davie's words tumbled out. "I'm as salt that's lost its savour. I'm not a front rank man any longer. I can only live my life in the second and third ranks of this war."

He paused briefly and then slammed his fist down on his knee. "But I will not bring any more grief to my family!" Davie choked the words out as he wiped his heavy wool jacket sleeve across tearing eyes.

It seemed that all Covenanters had to be brought to the brink of this decision at one time or other and this decision exacted painful soul searching and prayerful wrestling with the Spirit, begging to know right from wrong. Then came humble pleading for the strength to live by the answer.

This struggle was not reserved for adults alone. No—no! Many youths of my age and younger had been tortured as a means of forcing them to tell the Royalists where their parents were hiding. Some broke down and confessed; but more often than not they stood firm, choosing rather to bear the physical pain than the humiliation of becoming a traitor.

Adam had borne the pain.

"Oh, God..." I cried out in my mind. The thought was terrorizing. The possibility of being tortured was very real—not just a young girl's imagined fantasy—but a very real possibility. To be tortured was bad enough, but to be tortured and then fail to keep the Covenant—that was *my* fear. The fear that I might not measure up as a true Covenanter and stand strong for the beliefs with which I had been raised. The shame in failure would be worse than any torture I might be treated to—or at least I thought so at the moment.

I shuddered at the thought of Adam's knee being crushed...slowly crushed in the iron boot, as the wooden mallet drove the iron wedge tighter and tighter against his leg, slowly splintering the bone—the thought was unbearable. "Please, please—don't let me be tortured!!" I silently pleaded with God. "I'll do anything You want of me—just don't let me be tortured!"

Mr. Cargill's pleading voice brought me back to the present. "Davie, Davie! Ye'll surely shine in Heaven but ye'll shine nae mair in Scotland!" he cried in an attempt to change Davie's mind.

"Davie! Remember when ye stood toe to toe wi' Archbishop Sharp demanding yer right to preach out of the Bible, as you understood it? And not according to what he wanted ye tae say? Dae ye mind tellin' him that if ye should listen tae him about what to preach that ye'd be his ambassador and not Christ's?" asked Mr. Balfour angrily.

"Aye, I remember well. And I also remember how he instructed his 'goons to put the thumbkins on me!" Davie stuck out his mangled thumbs. "They've threatened—that if I don't take the Oath, my daughter will know the thumbscrews as well. There's four o' the Highland Host devils billeted in my house th' now! They're watchin' my every move! One wrong move—anything—and the wee lassie's in for it!" Grief twisted his face. "I canna abide it! I canna abide it! I'll take the Oath to the King! I *am* going to accept the Indulgence!"

"Do the Royalists know you are here tonight? And dae they know of yer decision, Davie?" Da asked quietly.

"I managed to gie 'em the slip when I came out tonight. And no—not yet. I wanted to tell ye mysel'...first. My wife doesn't even know!" Davie answered.

The others said no more.

Davie shriveled into himself. He knew what they were thinking. He had signed the Covenant. A man cannot make a covenant with God—a heart-felt promise—a promise to God!—and then backslide on it! God will not be mocked! Not without eternal consequences.

"Ye're a good man, Davie. Ye'll be missed!" confessed Mr. Cargill.

"Aye, Davie! Aye!" the others agreed, but disappointment had etched itself in the lines on their faces. Flickering shadows, mercilessly tossed about by the fire's flames, only deepened those lines. Old faces...old before their time...drawn and weary—peered into the fire as if it held some magic answer for them.

To whom, in all Scotland, could we turn? There was no one! The English and many of our own countrymen had stolen our civil and ecclesiastical liberties from us, reducing us to hunted fugitives in our own country.

It was 1679 and brother was pitted against brother and father against son. The country was in the throes of a bloody civil war. Slowly, insidiously, our enemy, King Charles II and his Royalists were winning...by terrorizing men like Davie into compliance. Covenanters in England and Ireland were not restricted in their worship at all—why was it so different for Scotland?.

Intense bitterness was felt toward King Charles II because of his broken promises and his desire to rob the Scots of the sacred gift of liberty, which they held most precious—even over life itself. To worship according to the dictates of their hearts—a birthright gifted by God Himself, no man had a right to repudiate. Scots felt very deeply that he who cares little for civil freedom will care as little for religious liberty. And he who will not struggle for the one will not fight for the other. God had entrusted freedom to us as citizens—to be preserved for the sake of our freedom as Christians—for the profession of true religion cannot be maintained without it.

We believed with our entire beings that he who surrenders this freedom to the willful and proud acts of a tyrant is recreant—and will be held accountable in the Heavenly courts.

Such were the doctrines with which I, Lizzie Whitelaw, was raised...reared by poor people in lowly stations, who held firmly to elevated principles and maintained a high level of character, well laced and bound up with a valiant integrity.

Davie squatted on his haunches and peered into the faces of the men around him. "Forgive me! God forgive me!" Anguish gripped each word he spoke and the silence in the room beat like war drums in my ears. Davie pushed himself to his feet, his movements were laborious and slow; he was a beaten man.

Ma stepped out of the shadows once more, but this time she held Davie's gray cloak in her outstretched arms and he turned, allowing her to drape it over his shoulders.

"Oh, here's yer blue bonnet," she reminded him. He pulled the tam onto his head, making sure the white cockade was on the left, standing up—telling everyone that he was a Covenanter. His movements were slow and deliberate as he raised his hand to its' edge and saluted his friends—tears glistening in his eyes. Ma reached up and touched his cheek gently but a deep sadness dulled her eyes. Not a word was spoken. There was nothing left to say.

A blast of cold air signaled Davie's departure. No one looked up; they just huddled closer to the fire. Da was first to speak. "We've lost a good man," he whispered as he ran his fingers through his thick red hair. A moment passed before Da continued angrily, "We are trapped! It's either give over to the Royalists or be killed, or worse...our wives and children will suffer for our actions!"

"We're goin' tae fight our way out o' this...and still keep the ways of Christ." It was a statement—not a question. "I see no good comin' from just lying down and letting Bluidy Clavers massacre us," Mr. Balfour answered. "We're entitled to defend ourselves and we are entitled to our beliefs!" he concluded emphatically.

"Aye," Da slowly conceded, though obviously not wanting to continue the bloodshed.

"Aye!" persisted Mr. Balfour, his squinty eyes narrowing at this hint of opposition. I could tell by the set of his jaw and how he squared his shoulders, that he was ready to fight anyone, at any time, to maintain his point of view. His pitch black hair and beard gave him the appearance of a formidable opponent. He was short but broad and strong.

During happier and lighter times he told us that his family all had short legs because they were descended from generations of Orkney fishermen, who, from time beginning were always crammed into the fishing boats...and that's why their legs became shorter and shorter. I had asked Da if that was true but his only answer was a crooked smile as he said, "Could be, could be", leaving me none the wiser.

"This is becoming a grave issue among us—whether or not to fight—and I'm afraid it'll split the body of Covenanters wide open," Mr. Cargill interjected.

"Well," Rev. Cameron jumped into the discussion, "we'd better come to a decision and quick! Claverhouse is rattling his sword and will win by default—'cause we'll be goin' in a dozen different directions at once. We'll defeat ourselves with no help from him!"

Crack!!!

The startling sound of a musket shot shattered the still night air.

"No! Please! No! Wait!" Pleading, desperate words were screamed into the dark night, echoing through the countryside.

Crack!! A second shot.

Then silence.

"That was Davie's voice!" Ma cried out.

Da jumped up quickly and pulled her to him, holding her face against his shoulder. "Weeshtt!" he whispered.

I was hardly breathing as I watched the men wait, their unblinking eyes never leaving the door. Finally, the sound of horses galloping away told us the Royalists were not going to attempt to cross the bog...at least not this night.

"Our friend is out there dyin'!" cried Rev. Renwick, the youngest of the ministers, as he struggled against John Balfour's grip on his arm.

"Renwick! Use yer head, man! Ye can bury him in the morning! Ye'll only get yersel' shot, too. Ye know that!" Mr. Balfour's face was so close to that of the young minister's that he had to pull back to get out of range of the spraying saliva that accompanied the desperate words. "They more than likely have left one or two of their dragoons to watch for us—they know we'll try to go to Davie."

"What if Davie's still alive? What if they've just left him for dead?" Rev. Renwick insisted. He glared at the others but their faces told him what he already knew...that the Royalists would not have left until their bloody work was finished. No, they would not leave had they not been sure their work was complete.

"God, please! God help us!" Da pleaded quietly.

"We'd be wise to move into the hill caves right now." Mr. Balfour whispered hoarsely. "Ye can't tell wi' these 'goons. Some o' them are daft enough to be tryin' to slip across the bog this very minute. And no doubt they've got orders to set the house on fire again, Whitelaw. Ach, I'm awfu' sorry to bring this on ye!"

"But we have more to discuss!" David Hackston almost shouted his demand to be heard.

"Quiet, David! Are ye wantin' tae bring them down on our necks? If they knew we were all in here, there's nothing on this earth that would keep them away. Why they'd even take the chance of drownin' in that bog to get at us, and ye know it!" Mr. Cargill warned.

"But we have trouble! Serious trouble!" Hackston insisted.

Da, ignoring David's insistence, said to Ma, "Get the bairns ready, Christie." But she was already at our bed, beckoning at me to get up and dress.

Da turned to the others and asked, "Will ye help get the bairns up tae the hill caves? And David, we'll listen tae yer news then…when we're in the cave. And too, gie me a hand wi' takin' this loom and wool out back in the trees and my golf ball makin' bits and pieces—that needs to go as well," Da asked in his attempt to protect his means of income for our family.

"Aye."

"Aye! Of course!" came the immediate answers.

I had left the comfort of my bed where my sister and brother and I had been tucked into each other's backs like three spoons.

Ma bent over them, whispering gently, "Come away, my sleepy ones!" Her smiling face and voice was so gentle and kind. I wondered how she could sound so calm in the face of this repeated agony.

Jenny and Iain stirred for a moment and immediately snuggled further into their warm bed. She bent closer, humming a familiar Gaelic tune. Soon, their arms reached up to her. Their trust and the warmth of their love must have touched Ma's heart for I could see a tear gather in the corner of her eye.

"Lizzie!" Da shouted.

"Aye, Da!" I answered as I wrapped the arisaidh over my leine.

"You, Lizzie! Get the sheep and make sure they are away from the cottage…" Da ordered.

"…and the hens—don't forget the hen's, Lizzie!" Ma added.

"Aye—aye!" I answered as I slipped through the opening into the byre.

We only had four Soay sheep and a half dozen hens. "Weesht! Ye daft things!" I scolded as the hens began squawking. "Dae ye want tae end up in the 'goons soup pot? Then stop yer noise." I pushed them into the crate and asked one of the ministers to carry it for me.

The other ministers who weren't carrying out the loom and wool, helped carry the few belongings we had managed to gather since the last time our cottage was razed by the Royalists. They put all they could carry in the folds of their plaids.

Ma and I each pulled our arisaidh around our waist, making large pockets in which to carry food stuffs and other items to save from the inevitable fire that would destroy our pitiful little pile of belongings once more.

Once outside I whistled and my sheep dog, Haggis, came running obediently. She instinctively knew what she was supposed to do and so faithfully followed me as I made my way up to the cave in the hill, herding the sheep behind me.

The peacefulness of the glen belied the grim troubles of past years and actually increased the tugging at our heart strings each time we were forced to the shelter of the caves. We loved our beloved Scotland and here we were, fugitives in our own land, running for our lives. Within minutes we were, again, well on our way to the hillside caves.

"Christie!" Mr. Cargill whispered, "This little brood o' yers is as stout hearted as their parents."

Ma acknowledged the compliment with an "Ach, weel...", but she was pleased and we knew it.

Da basked in the glow of the compliment as well, and added, "Our Lizzie, here, has had an old head put on her young shoulders—she's had to accept danger all of her life." With that stated, he reached out and ruffled my hair that was as red as his own.

We were all thankful, though, that these events hadn't suppressed Jenny's bubbly, good nature. This little ray of sunshine, a pure delight to everyone around her, lighted up the darkest day. Da called her his "pocket full of sunbeams".

Mr. Renwick had Jenny cradled like a baby in his strong arms. She seemed content to be carried and I knew she was probably being her coquettish self and smiling up into his face.

Our wee, fair-haired Iain was feeling very special as he rode on Da's shoulders; his little hands clutching handfuls of Da's red hair to steady himself.

Clouds, that had hidden the moon, soon drifted away leaving the path to the cave washed in bright moonlight. The family of us and the ministers all huddled into the safety of it's darkness and before long even the chill had evaporated from the night air.

Da and Ma sat at the mouth of the cave where they would be able to see Tigh Sona in the morning light. They pulled Jenny and Iain close to them and covered them with the warm woolen blankets Da had woven.

"It's itchin' me, Da!" Jenny complained as the blanket's roughness rubbed against her young cheek.

"Ye just weesht, now, Jenny," Ma scolded, "yer lucky tae have a nice warm blanket."

I managed to get the sheep to lay down at the back of the cave and stayed with them, plucking at their wool. "Might as well get started on gathering the wool again," I thought to myself. These particular sheep shed like a dog so we were always plucking their wool for spinning into yarn. The finest wool was taken from their throats and chests and the stronger fibers were plucked from their sides. Most of our yarn was either brown or tan except for the one black sheep we had—she gave us some coveted black wool that Ma spun into yarn and then knitted into stockings and sold, helping to add to our income. And our precious sheep also gave us milk which we turned into cheese.

But it was always a sad day when we had to butcher one of them for food; I had to be really hungry before I could eat the mutton. Every part of the sheep was used; the hides for the leather pampooties we wore on our feet; and even the stomach was used when Ma made haggis—the mixture of oatmeal and the sheep's organs all chopped up, along with onions and seasonings were stuffed into the stomach sack and boiled. Yes, these animals were very important to our survival.

The ministers tugged their plaids closer to their bodies, pulled their blue bonnets farther down on their heads and sat closer together for warmth.

Ma had knitted Da's bonnet and he looked so handsome in it. When I called it a tam, he would be very insulted as these 'blue bonnets' were what all Covenanter men wore. Ma had made the cockade from a piece of sturdy white ribbon about a foot long and an inch wide; she attached the ends at right angles, forming it into a cross; then sewed it in place on the left side. Da was so proud of his 'blue bonnet'.

As I looked at the ministers, watching them pull their plaids around their shoulders, I recalled how Da had woven the cloth for some of them. He made two lengths of tartan, about eighteen feet long by two and a half feet wide. Then he would sew them together, making the requested plaid. This, the men wrapped around their waists and leaving some to go over their shoulder and hang down the back, being very careful that the fringe did not dangle below the calf of their legs. It was held to their waists with a belt and if there was time, the men gathered the material around them in folds or pleats, making it look very attractive.

Finally, Mr. Balfour invited David Hackston to "tell us yer news, David."

David finally had their attention. Grunts of agreement and nods indicated that he should carry on and "tell his news".

"This morning I was riding with Balfour, here," began David as he nodded toward him, "...and about ten others. We were looking for William Carmichael—tryin' tae have a meet wi' him." He shook his head angrily before continuing. "Ye know this lunatic must be stopped. He's thrashing little children just to find out if their parents attended any of our meetings; roasting old men on a spit until he wrings out an Oath to the King. And Archbishop Sharp—it's him that's given Carmichael the authority tae carry this out—in the name of restoring order—ha!" David said bitterly.

Thousands of Covenanters had suffered at the hands of Archbishop Sharp as he carried out the King's orders to bring the Covenanters to their knees and accept the Oath. His demoniacal methods were driven into reality by William Carmichael, one of his minions, who carried out the heinous deeds.

"Yer not tellin' us anything we don't already know, David!" grumbled Mr. Renwick.

Ignoring the remark, David Hackston launched into his report. "We crossed the fields up and down for hours, searching the hills and every place that we knew he had ever visited, but couldn'a find Carmichael.

"Around midday we talked of giving up our search, when Robert Black's servant came runnin' up tae us to say thatArchbishop Sharp's coach was in Ceres. This wasn't far from where we were at that moment. This news surprised us—here we were looking for the servant and the master is put into our hands." David peered into the intent, shadowy faces around him before continuing. "We began thinking that it was Providence who had put Sharp into our hands and we should finish him right there and then...and relieve the country of his tyranny."

"The others wanted me to take command of our party—but I declined," he continued. "It wasn't right, seeing as how I had a personal difference with the Archbishop and that could be looked on as me carryin' out a personal revenge." He stopped for breath...no one spoke, but waited for him to continue.

"By this time we'd ridden up to a little village 'round Magus and the Archbishop's coach had just left—we could see it in the distance. One of our faster riders gained on it and looked in to see if Sharp was, in fact, in the coach." David sucked in a deep breath and then said quietly, "He was and our rider hailed us forward. We could hear Sharp begin crying to his coachman, "Drive, man! Drive!'"

"The others pursued at full speed while I kept my distance. The Archbishop's servant, who was riding beside the driver, turned and tried to aim his musket at us, but two of our men dismounted him and took it from him. Meanwhile, the coach is speeding furiously away, with the driver shooting at us!"

"Geordy rides up beside the coach and cries out to Sharp, "A Judas, that's what ye are! And yer gonna be taken!"

"Sharp screams at his coachman, 'Drive! Drive! Drive!' But our man rode up to the driver and shouted at him to stop! There was a struggle; our man pulled the driver from the coach and straightway cut the traces of the coach to stop it." Stunned silence met David's pause.

He continued, "Sharp had his daughter in the coach with him. John, here," David nodded at Mr. Balfour, "ordered him out of the coach so that no harm could come to his daughter. He refused. Then the captain of our group fired a shot at Sharp."

"His daughter shrieked and then wept bitterly. We thought that Sharp was dead but as we were riding away we heard his daughter cry out that he was still alive! Her father was laying in her lap, his blood staining her gray dress."

"We turned back and pulled Sharp out of the coach—he cried for mercy all the while! Our captain said, 'Mercy? You ask for mercy? You? when you've dipped your hands up to the wrists in the blood of those innocents whose only crime was to acclaim Christ as the Head of their Church! You sold your soul a long time ago…and for what? A few shiny baubles and some fancy robes!'"

I recalled seeing the gold encrusted robes that the Archbishop always draped around his person and the many luxuries he enjoyed as he creamed off the best from the common people's tithes. His daughter was known for the elegant dresses she wore and especially the beautiful beaver skin robe she flaunted—one made from pelts brought over from America.

"Gentlemen, save my life, and I will save yours," Sharp cried out." Mr. Hackston's voice brought me back to the present. "Our Captain replied, 'You haven't power either to save us, or to kill us, that is God's alone! What of the Covenanters who cried out to you? Begging for mercy! Did you give it? No! You did not! You are an enemy to Christ and his Kingdom! You have wrung your hands in the blood of his saints. And their blood cries out to heaven for vengeance and we will, this day, satisfy that cry!'"

Ma reached for Da's hand as he shook his head slowly from side to side.

David continued, "Sharp dumped his purse onto the ground screaming, 'Money! Here's money!'"

"'Your money can perish wi' ye! I will give ye only time to pray! Make your peace with God!' our Captain said. Another one of our company stepped forward and said, 'Look at him! He's not repentant of any of the innocent lives he's taken! We'll suffer a terrible judgment if we don't stop him…now! To let him go only means that more Covenanters will be put to death. We cannot let him live!'"

"He fired his pistol at Sharp but missed again. Another rode up and wounded him with a sword. 'I am gone!' Sharp cried, but still he was not mortally wounded. Again the Captain urged him to prepare for death and pray, but Sharp seemed not to have any faith that the Lord would save him. 'For God's sake, save my life, save my life!' He continued to beg and offered us even more money. He even promised to lay down his Episcopal function as Archbishop."

"'You've been without mercy and need not expect mercy,' said our Captain. 'We cannot spare your life,' and again we pressed him to prepare to meet God and pray."

"His daughter tried to position herself between her father and us. Andrew protected her by securing her in the coach. Instead of praying, Sharp then spotted me at some little distance and crept towards me on his hands and knees crying, 'Sir, I know you are a gentleman; you will protect me.' To which I answered, 'Sir, I shall never lay a hand on you.' And I rode a little way off. 'Please spare the life of an old man!' he begged."

"'He refuses to prepare to meet his God!' said our Captain." David paused, obviously uncomfortable with his story. He took a deep breath and said quietly, "Our Captain ran his sword through Sharp...another followed suit...and another until we were assured he was dead. The Captain relieved Sharp's party of their arms and the papers he was carrying; the contents of which are in this pouch." David was finally silent.

It was later that we learned that Archbishop Sharp's papers were decrees to imprison and confiscate property of all "rebel Covenanter phanatics"; and that this property was ordered to revert directly to officials within the Episcopal Church.

Da looked into the shadowy faces of the ministers. "There'll be no fishin' the fat out of the fire now," he prophesied solemnly.

"Aye, it's war now, whether we like it or not, John Whitelaw. This'll give Carmichael a license for killin'. There's no recourse left to us. None! We can only fight our way out." Mr. Balfour's eyes flashed angrily.

We were all too familiar with William Carmichael's ways. As a Laird, his greed, self-indulgence and lasciviousness had catapulted him headlong into financial ruin. And Archbishop Sharp, the avowed enemy of the Covenanters, rescued him from total disaster by placing him in the office of Sheriff in Fifeshire.

He and others like him wallowed in the power that Archbishop Sharp bestowed upon them. All of this to discover and punish the Covenanters, by any means necessary. The sheriffs used their authority to loot, ravage and burn the houses of their prey...confiscate cattle and horses and burn crops and torture and maim and kill all whom they arrested. This brutality was carried out under the protection of the King, the government *and* Archbishop Sharp.

"We can only pray for deliverance...and wait," Da sighed.

"...and arm ourselves in defense!" Mr. Balfour demanded in a hoarse whisper. "As long as I'm able, I'll defend our cause...I refuse to lie down and let Claverhouse massacre us!"

Jenny and Iain, who had dozed off to sleep, stirred and we all felt soothed as Ma lulled them back to sleep, crooning soft words of a lullaby.

Low toned "ayes" finally rippled around the cave, responding positively to the call to arms. Mr. Balfour's eyes narrowed with determination. He was right! He knew he was right!

CHAPTER 2

Da touched the back of my mother's neck. She smiled and leaned into his hand, moving her head slightly from one side to the other, allowing the moonlight to wash her with its' soft glow. His love for Ma softened the lines in his face for a moment.

"Christie," he whispered, "dae ye think that maybe, just maybe, mind ye, that Davie Prescott's right after all?" Pausing, as if he was asking himself, he said thoughtfully, "Is this really the right way?" Jenny and Iain's sleeping forms caught his eye and he shook his head sadly. Da searched the sky, looking for the streaks of light that would herald the dawn...the dawn, when once more, we were sure, we would see our home in flames.

Eleven times my parents had rebuilt the little cottage. Eleven times Claverhouse and his dragoons returned to loot what few belongings we had been able to gather since the last razing. To see our little home go up in flames again hurt the same as having a bone broken again—in the same place—before it had time to heal.

Da groaned under the burden. His agony urged Ma to hold his hand tighter. A serene, peaceful look swept over Da's face and I knew what he was thinking. He had told us the story so often, but it seemed when he was most troubled, the vision would return, bringing peace to his mind.

'The Dream', as we now called it, occurred to my Da one night following an hour of terrible torture by Wallace Lauderdale and his dragoons. Although Lauderdale was of a good Scottish family, he had aligned himself with the English and was now a Royalist captain who was terrorizing the western Lowland counties of Scotland. Crops, cattle and women were at his dragoons' mercy as they sated their animal appetites...when and where it pleased them.

During the occupation of Scotland by the English Army and the Highland Host, Lauderdale and four of his dragoons had been billeted at the cottage of my Grandda Gray—Ma's father.

Grandda told me that it was a long time ago—just after my parents had been married—and that during one of Ma's visits to him and Granny, Wallace Lauderdale first laid eyes on Ma. His immediate and obvious fascination with her became popular gossip among the country folk. However, in some remarkable way, Ma had escaped all of Lauderdale's advances, but her rejection of him had eventually caused his fascination to turn into a white-hot anger. No longer did his face light up when he was in her presence. Instead, it was obvious that a slow simmering rage had replaced whatever decent feelings he had initially experienced.

Rather than walk away like a gentleman, his twisted mind devised ways to punish her and the most effective was to abuse and terrorize those whom she loved. More than once, James Gray, my Grandda, had been threatened with torture over some incident that, if he hadn't been her father, would have been overlooked. Fortunately, Grandda had so far managed to side-step Lauderdale and his madness.

Punishing Da for not attending the church in the village where an Episcopal curate preached, was one method with which Lauderdale chose to torment my parents. His plan was apparent to everyone—he was hoping that Da would give him a legitimate reason to kill him...thus leaving Ma free.

Da's life had become a continual round of narrow escapes and this had carried on year after year.

One day, not long ago, the soldiers arrived unexpectedly at Tigh Sona,. Da was working at the loom and Ma and I were in the byre, attending to our chores—feeding the chickens and animals. Fortunately, Jenny and Iain were away visiting Grandda and Granny and not at home.

Lauderdale announced himself in his usual way by having one of his dragoons kick the door open. He pushed himself into the cottage and immediately demanded that Da take the Test, which was to sign the Oath to King Charles II, agreeing that for all time he would be loyal to the King; that he would not hide any of the Covenanters and would turn over to the authorities any one known to him to harbor or to be such a rebel.

Da remained motionless at the loom. Stubbornly quiet, offended and seething over such an intrusion of his home and moral rights. He also knew that his time had come. There was no escape this time. He was outnumbered five to one.

Lauderdale swung his eyes around the room. Da knew he was looking for Ma. He succeeded in finding her at the far end of the cottage as she came in from the byre and openly leered at her, stretching his thin lips over yellowed teeth. Lauderdale didn't even try to hide his rage that had coiled crazily around his lust. Ma stood in front of me, shielding me from the soldiers. Da was infuriated. He glared at Lauderdale, his eyes flashing with anger, which made Lauderdale snort out a fiendish laugh. It was obvious he was enjoying wallowing in his power over my Da.

"Let's see what the lady's husband is made of!" Lauderdale barked the words. His face suddenly twisted into an ugly grimace. Bushy eyebrows knotted together, and his mouth puckered tightly as he rasped, "We'll use the sticks!"

Perspiration beaded on Da's forehead, a fact that was not missed by Lauderdale.

"Right you are, Mr. Whitelaw, to sweat! You are nothing but a fanatic and rebel and deserve this...and more!" he whined into Da's ear. Lauderdale stepped closer to Da and bent down until they were almost nose to nose.

"Will you take the Test?" he bellowed, his foul breath forcing Da to lean away from him. Not waiting for an answer, Lauderdale shouted, "Hold out your filthy rebel hands!"

Da slowly pushed his tightly fisted hands out in front of him.

"Open them, rebel!" Lauderdale was roaring like a madman.

Da straightened out his white knuckled fingers; his eyes never left Ma and me.

"Ma!" I screamed as one of the Highlanders pulled Ma away and left me standing alone.

"Don't move!" Ma demanded in a whisper. I had no doubt she meant it and that rooted me to the spot, although it took all of my effort to obey as I watched her struggle in the soldier's grip. I wanted to claw at the soldier's face—hurt him before he could hurt my Ma!

"Let her go...!" Da began, but his attention was forcibly brought back to himself when the soldiers wrenched his hands open. Long, thin, splintered pieces of wood were jammed between his fingers. Lauderdale made a grand show of striking the flint into his tinderbox and with an exaggerated flourish, lit the wooden pieces.

The soldier had a fight on his hands keeping Ma still. She strained against his brute strength...biting, kicking, yelling until the soldier forced her arms behind her back and held them there with one hand and almost smothered her, covering her mouth with the other. Her eyes were stretched wide with terror—her screams stifled—tears streamed from her eyes over the soldier's hand.

I was terrified at what I was witnessing. Frantically, my eyes swung from Ma to Da and back again. The fire quickly traveled down the strips of wood, until the heat burned the hair on Da's fingers; the flames licked at his skin...again and again...a trickle of blood appeared on his chin as he bit into his bottom lip.

"I'll wager when the one at the end burns down—he'll scream like a woman!" one of the soldiers said with a laugh. The other soldiers took him up on the wager and as Da agonized, they made sport of his torture.

My knees wouldn't hold me up any longer. I folded onto the floor, my hand holding back the screams that welled up in my throat. When I came out of my faint, the cottage was filled with the smell of burning flesh.

Da was wracked with pain; and Lauderdale's obvious lunatic delight in watching him suffer this excruciating torture was shocking, disgusting...and yet strangely revealing. "You, Lauderdale, are the devil himself!" Da shouted. "Ye hear! The devil, himself, has found a place tae rest—in *YOU*! Dae ye hear me! Look at ye—Satan—that's who ye are!"

Da told us later that in that brief moment he learned an eternal truth! As sudden as a flash of lightning he understood that life was nothing more or less than a struggle between good and evil. Two mighty powers in a continual battle for supremacy.

Da had chosen the good! And was fighting for his choice...at this very moment he was paying a high price for it! He knew it! But there was no doubt in his mind! Exquisite joy absorbed his pain. He now understood how the early Christians were able to walk into the arenas filled with lions—walking to their certain deaths—singing.

"I know that my Redeemer lives...." A song of praise for the Savior burst from Da's lips, taking the soldiers...and me, by surprise. They slowly backed away from him, their mouths hanging open. "He lives to give me rich supply..." Da's beautiful tenor voice boomed forth.

"He's mad! He's raving daft!" the soldiers yelled, dropping his hands as if they were hot coals. They scrambled to get out of the cottage, jamming their bulk into the open doorway.

Even Lauderdale was startled. And when he saw that he, alone, was left to face this wild-eyed, red-haired giant, his courage and bravado left him. He, too, turned on his heel and fled out of the door. Within seconds he was astride his horse, lessening the distance between him and his men.

"Run, ye coward! Run!" screamed Ma at his disappearing back. Ma lost no time in flying to my father's side. I numbly followed her—too deep in shock to even speak. She helped him to the little burn that bubbled past the cottage where they squatted down and Ma held his hands in the cool water.

"Oh John! John, my Jo!" Ma wept; her tears splashing into the water. The sight of his charred and blackened fingers made her cry out loud. I sat quietly on the bank, hugging my knees to my chest and rocked back and forth, trying to ease the pain that had me in its grip.

After some moments Ma spoke the obvious, "John, we need tae mend those hands." Reluctantly she moved away from him and ran into the house. Within seconds she reappeared, carrying a little pot of honey.

Da held his hands out. White finger bone glistened where the charred skin had washed away. I retched, then bit down hard on my lip, fighting for control over a heaving stomach.

Ma smoothed the soft honey over Da's hands, a continual prayer on her lips. "Oh, God. Please stop the pain—oh, please God!" Tenderly, she wrapped his hands in slan-lus (plantain leaves) and secured them with pieces of linen. Slowly, the pain lines eased in Da's face, giving us some relief as well.

"Look at me, lass," Da said sternly, looking deeply into Ma's eyes. "No more tears, ye hear me?"

"Aye," she whispered but her shoulders still heaved with stifled sobs.

"Easy, lass. Easy." Da whispered more gently and pressed his cheek against the top of her head. They were one in the pain—both hurt. Ma looked intently into Da's eyes and I know that she found courage there. I watched as her magnificent love enveloped him and pushed out the world.

The healing had begun.

Once again in the cottage, Ma and I tucked Da into the bed. He allowed himself to sink gratefully into the big feather pillow. Quickly Ma produced a bowl of broth and proceeded to feed him as she would a child.

"Ye think soup'll fix everything, don't ye lass?" Da smiled weakly. But he didn't refuse her offering. Ma continued to cluck around my father, attending to his every need and even inventing some. Eventually, he fell into a fitful sleep.

Da told us later that during that night he was startled awake by an incredibly bright light gathering at the foot of his bed. He was speechless with fright. As the light gradually took the shape of a man, Da told us that his fear left him...no, it dissolved in the glow of love that now filled the room.

The power and majesty radiating from the apparition brought Da to tears. He could not gaze directly at him, but a fleeting glimpse into his eyes revealed such loving compassion...a depth of compassion that defied description. In those brief seconds, Da said he was given a gift—the divine gift of understanding.

No words were spoken, Da told us, but it seemed that pure intelligence seemed to flow through him, giving him an understanding that had eluded him until then. He confessed that he had been overcome with emotion and grateful tears had flowed down his cheeks.

As suddenly as it had appeared, the light gathered about the personage and he was gone. Da said that he was left alone in the darkened room to ponder, to meditate, to commune with his God; to search the room again and again for the healing, shimmering whiteness; to remember that surge of love that had pulsated throughout his entire being; to feel the renewed strength that flowed through his body. He told us that suddenly he remembered the burns and looked down at his hands! The pain was gone! Only a strange pulsating sensation remained. He didn't dare take the bandages off. What if this was only a dream? "No! No!" he chided himself. "Don't lose faith now!"

I remember that I woke at this point and raised myself on my elbow to watch my father—I was unaware of the unusual experience he'd just undergone. A look of pure joy was on his face and I thought it was because he was looking at my mother. I wondered if I would ever know that kind of love.

Later he told us that the joy in his heart had been nearly unbearable at that moment. I remembered the tears that came to my eyes as I watched my father look down at Ma, his beautiful Christie. He touched her arm and she stirred, then woke with a start.

"Yer a'right, John?" she asked with her eyes full of worry.

"Aye, darlin'!" he said softly. "I've somethin' tae tell ye!" and I, too, listened—uninvited.

Ma sat still, absorbing his every word as he recounted the sacred experience. "John, what does it all mean?" she asked in a reverent whisper.

"I believe that we must know, in some small way, the same pain and humility He suffered on the cross. It is pain that refines the gold of our souls. The dross must be separated and cast out...and that takes a high heat!" Da explained.

I watched Ma's quivering fingers unwrap the bandages and with a small cry, she let them fall to the floor. They moved closer to the dying embers of the peat fire and Da held out his hands for further inspection. There, where the bare bone glistened only hours before, new pink skin had appeared. Ma's hand flew to her mouth as she stared in wonder at Da's hands. I could stand it no longer and tumbled out of bed to look and stand all amazed, with my parents, at the miracle that had been given us.

A musket shot brought me back to the present...to the dark cave. My eyes searched the glen for our small house, now visible in the gray dawn. The burning of our cottage was always announced by a musket shot. Next, smoke puffed into the sky; then flames danced upward and our home was burning, again.

Again! Oh, the wound was opened, again. And there was not a soul in all Scotland to whom we could turn for justice.

The Royalists continued to wage their war, an army drilled in skill and discipline, pitted against the Covenanters, untrained and raw, who fought with only courage and good conscience, defending their rights and their homes.

Ma groaned out loud. Da reached for her hand and held it tightly. She was crying—quietly, so as not to hurt him—but he knew.

"I understand Christie. A woman's hearth is her country; my pain is similar—only it's for my Scotland."

Another black pall of smoke burst into flames. Together we watched the fire consume Tigh Sona once more.

"Don't bother making a door, this time, John. I can do just fine with skins over the door. You've struggled so hard with every one of those doors...just to see it go up in flames...I can't stand it another time," Ma said.

"Christie, they can burn the walls and doors of Tigh Sona again and again—but they'll never destroy the spirit o' Tigh Sona! It is freedom and love! the spirit o' Scotland!"

"Aye! So it is, John...my Jo!

Chapter 3

Tigh Sona rose from the ashes once more. Sod, straw, rock and mud were shaped into walls and roof. Jenny and I toiled to mix straw with mud, which we carried in buckets to where our parents labored tirelessly, plastering it over the rocks and logs. They let us feel that every handful was the most important for the entire house and we thrived under their encouragement. Even wee Iain shouldered his share of the work and before we knew it, Ma was hanging animal skins over the doorway and window.

Once again, our home became the familiar refuge for the Covenanters, as it's humble walls offered shelter from the elements, relief from hunger, and safety from the enemy—as safe as possible, that is. And under it's roof, the plan for opposition to an edict, recently issued by King Charles II, was formed.

My Grandda explained to us what was happening, in his eloquent way of speaking. "The King's declaration is a presumptuous act! It is imposing upon Scotland an 'holy anniversary day'; to be kept yearly upon the 29th of May, as a day of rejoicing and thanksgiving for King Charles II's birth and restoration to the throne!"

"How ambitious! How grandiose! How dare he?" Grandda's voice rose to a fever pitch. His extensive vocabulary had been acquired during his studies at the University of Aberdeen. He took care that our lessons always included "speaking properly". As a result, there were times when only Ma, Grandda and me knew what he was talking about.

But he always commanded attention and got it—even if others had to scramble afterward to learn the meaning of some of his words.

The Covenanters objected to this intrusion upon the Lord's prerogative for holy days. Besides this, they resented the glory being given to a King whom they perceived as destroying the interest of Christ in the land.

On May 29th, eighty Covenanters gathered at the market-cross in the small burgh of Rutherglen. They extinguished the bonfires set for the Royalist celebration and affixed a copy of their declaration to the market-cross. Their public burning of the "Holy Day Declaration" was to evidence the Covenanters' dislike of and their testimony against the Royalists who had "unjustly, perfidiously, and presumptuously burned our sacred covenants".

Thus we objected to yet another of the King's attempts to overthrow the Reformation began by John Knox more than an hundred years ago.

It was plain to see that the Covenanters were "digging in" and this, in spite of suffering imprisonment, fines, forfeitures, banishments, torture and death at the hands of the Royalists. They stood ready to add their witness and testimony to those who had before suffered a martyr's death.

'Bloody Grahame', as Grahame of Claverhouse was known, (among other derogatory names) was infuriated with the Covenanters' response to the Holy Day Declaration.

James Blair, chancellor to the assize, was angry as well. He raged through the streets like one possessed, threatening and abusing the inhabitants of Rutherglen, demanding to know the whereabouts of the Covenanters who had burned the Declaration. He swore that he would "run his sword through their souls when he got hold of them!"

Through informers, Claverhouse and Blair learned of the field meeting or conventicle, as it was called, to be held the next day at Drumclog, it being the Sabbath. Claverhouse had been given great powers and liberty to "kill and destroy all those he found in-arms or at any field meeting; to deal with them as traitors; and to discover, seize, and, upon resistance, to kill all who had any part in the burning at Rutherglen."

The "burning", along with the murder of Archbishop Sharp, set the stage for the escalation of the bloody civil war in Scotland. So desperate for retaliation was Claverhouse, that he took as prisoner, Mr. King, an ejected Covenanter minister, along with more than a dozen other Covenanters who had not even been at the Rutherglen 'burning'.

It was Spring. The Sabbath was sunny and warm and the Covenanters had gathered to worship the God of their fathers...not to fight. They had chosen a place far from the cities...a place where the long, dark heath waved gently in the breeze. If a disturbance occurred, it was only to the heather cock or other small birds nesting thereabouts.

The Covenanters were armed for self-defense; those without guns or swords brought stout sticks and stones—anything to protect themselves. Too many times bands of the Highland Host and Royalists had made raids upon their field-meetings, professing to be putting down treason when in reality they were waging war against religion.

Indeed, the Royalists' continual battering had left the face of Scotland bruised, and bleeding. Rev. Thomas Douglas was preaching the sermon that morning, attacking the evils of tyranny with such eloquence that as we listened, our hearts were set aflame with the sufferings and wrongs perpetrated upon us and upon our church.

At this precise moment, one of our four watchmen who were standing sentry at the four corners of our glen, fired his musket and ran toward the congregation shouting "Clavers' on the march! He's yonder wi' a great army! "The congregation looked to Rev. Douglas for direction. "I have finished," he said to them adamantly. "You've got the theory—now for the practice; you know your duty! Self defense is always lawful!" He raised his eyes to heaven and prayed aloud, "Lord, spare the green and take the ripe."

Ma looked up at my father. Without speaking a word, her eyes betrayed the fear gripping her heart. "I've no choice, Christie!" Da replied defensively to her unasked question. "Ye know I don't like it! But neither can I let the butcher, Clavers, take you and the bairns." This was as close to pleading for her approval as I had ever heard.

"How will you fight? Look at your hands—its only been a short time—they are still tender!" The skin on Da's fingers shone where the new pink flesh had knit together over the bones.

"Christie! I'll not argue wi' ye!" he answered impatiently.

Without a word, Ma took the kertch from around her head and with strength springing from her intense anger, tore it in two. Silently, she wrapped his hands in the firm linen cloth, tying the ends securely around his wrists. "That should help a wee bit," she said, avoiding his eyes, and she pulled her arisaidh over her head.

"Yer a bonny lass—ye know that, don't ye!" he grinned, grateful for her support. "I'll be back afore ye know it!"

Squaring his shoulders, he turned and walked toward the battle.

The officers collected the men belonging to their respective districts and led them to the muir—positioning them so the bog lay between them and Claverhouse. Sir Robert of Hamilton ordered the foot soldiers into the center where they fell into three ranks. A Company of horse soldiers stood waiting on the left. Another Company was sent to higher ground—for protection from a surprise Royalist attack to their flanks. In all, there were 40 horses and about 150 foot soldiers. Those who didn't have weapons picked up sticks and rocks.

The aged men, along with the women and children, retired slowly from the battlefield. Reluctantly, we left our men folk to fight this battle. The old men pulled the flat, blue bonnets from their heads and with the breeze gently blowing their gray locks, began singing the well-known Covenanter tune "The Martyrs." The stirring words floated down to our men on the muir, filling them with courage.

Three cheers—loud and strong—went up in response. The pitifully small and outnumbered group of men was transformed into the most ferocious army that Colonel Claverhouse had yet to meet.

"Look!" I cried out.

We stopped our retreat up the hillside and looked across the muir to where I was pointing. Claverhouse and his troops were slowly winding down the opposite dark mountainside.

"Those are the slaves and bloody executioners that the king uses to complete our miseries," Grandda whispered angrily.

James Gray was not pleased to be considered too old to fight. But this did not deter him from stretching out his arms to invite his family to stand close to him.

"Grandda! Hold me up! I wanna see m'Da! Iain begged.

Grandda responded by swinging the little boy onto his shoulders. Granny tried to comfort Ma. "Pray, Christie! Pray with all yer heart for him!" I sensed that her counsel came from experience.

'Wee' Jenny and I stood together, our hands twisted tightly together, as if we were holding on to life itself—and in a way we were. Our eyes desperately searched the ranks of men below for John Whitelaw, our beloved Da.

"Grandda," I called for his attention. "Why does Claverhouse hate us so much? Isn't he a Scot as well? Just who is he?"

Grandda looked down at me and heaved a sigh, "Well, lassie, as far as I know he is John Graham, the eldest son of Sir William Graham and I'm told their family descended from King Robert III and it was he who had given the estate of Claverhouse to them. Seemingly he was educated at St. Andrews University and served King Louis XIV with other Scots in France and Holland. He evidently distinguished himself in 1674 at the battle of Seneff, where he is said to have saved the life of the Prince of Orange. Then he was sent as a cavalry leader to Scotland, last year, with orders to enforce conformity to the established church."

"But what has made him so mean to us, Grandda" I wanted to make sense of it all.

"Well, now this is only my opinion, Lizzie—its not gospel—just my own thinking. In 1674 he married a daughter of one of our more fiercely Covenanting families and I heard that set his military career back quite badly. I think he is trying to show that he is not partial to us in any way—even though his in-laws are Covenanters—just my own thinking—mind you."

Unexpectedly, Jenny Gray, my Granny, began a high-pitched clicking sound with her tongue. Soon, the other women followed suit; an age-old custom meant to encourage their men and a way of letting them know they were near. The men cheered an enthusiastic response.

The enemy, with it's bugles sounding a defiant blast and its' kettledrums beating out their war cry, bellowed back Claverhouse's challenge.

An expectant, anxious pause followed the shouted challenges, creating an air of suspense.

We watched an officer lead fifteen people from Claverhouse's ranks to a knoll on their left. "It's Mr. King!" Grandda said excitedly, as he recognized the black clad figure of the minister. "And those others must be the men whom Claver's arrested yesterday."

"What's that devil up tae?" another man wanted to know.

They didn't have long to wait for an answer. Claverhouse's words rang through the glen as he shouted in a thunderous voice to the officer, "Let them be shot through the head if they should attempt to escape."

Claverhouse then turned his attention to the Covenanter Army and viewed them carefully. Soon, a messenger rode toward the Covenanters, the Royalist flag fluttering over his head. Sir Robert, always a gentleman, held a flag sacred and allowed the messenger to approach, asking for the message. The messenger nervously replied, "I come in the name of his sacred majesty, and of Colonel Grahame of Claverhouse, to offer you a pardon, on condition that you lay down your arms, and deliver up your ringleaders."

Sir Robert answered, "Tell your officer that we are fully aware of the deception he practices. He is not clothed with any powers to negotiate, nor was he sent out to bargain with us to attempt reconciliation. The government, against whom we have risen, refuses to redress our grievances, or to restore to us our liberties. Had the tyrant, the King, wished to render us justice, he would not have sent such a ferocious assassin as Claverhouse." He looked past the messenger to where

Claverhouse was astride his horse and continued, "Let him, however, show his powers, and we shall not refuse to bargain; and we shall lay down our arms to bargain, provided that he also lay down his. You have my answer."

"It is perfectly hopeless!" a young minister, by the name of Burley, said as he rode up beside Sir Robert. "Let me add a word. By your leave General!" Sir Robert nodded his agreement.

Burley shouted angrily after the flag-bearer, "Get up to that bloody dragoon, Clavers, and tell him that we will spare his life, and the lives of his troops, on condition that he, your Clavers, lay down his arms and the arms of his troops." He paused, before continuing, "We will do more! As we have no prisons on these wild mountains, we will even let him go on his honor, on condition that he will swear to never again lift arms against the religion and the liberties of Scotland!"

A loud burst of applause rose from the Covenanters' ranks and the words of Psalm 76 echoed throughout the glen as the men of the Covenant sang out their agreement with Burley:

"There, arrows of the bow He brake;
The shield, the sword, the war.
More glorious Thou art than hills of prey,
More excellent art Thou by far.
Those that were stout of heart are spoil'd,
They slept their sleep outright:
And none of those their hands did find,
That were the men of might.
At thy rebuke, O God of Jacob
Both the chariot and horse
are cast into a dead sleep!"

Claverhouse received the report with savage fury. "Their blood be on their own heads! *'No Quarter'* be the word for the day!" he roared.

His dragoons echoed his command. "NO QUARTER!" Their war cry seemed to bounce from hill to hill until it filled the glen.

Burley shouted back to Clavers, "Then be it so! Even let there be 'No Quarter', at least from my men!" Then he pleaded aloud, "God, send me a meeting with that chief under the white plume—Clavers! My country would bless my memory, if my sword could give his villainous carcass to the crows."

Claverhouse's horse reared back at the angry pull on its reins. The Covenanters watched with unflinching firmness as the foe approached and at the moment their enemy halted to fire, the whole of the Covenanter foot company dropped to the heath. Not one man remained down when the order was given to rise and return the fire.

The first rank fired, then kneeled down, while the second fired. They made each bullet count. As often as the lazy, rolling smoke was carried over the enemy's heads, a shower of bullets fell on Claverhouse' ranks. Many a Royalist tumbled to the heath. The firing was incessant. At times it was as one blazing sheet of flame along the line of the Covenanters. Claverhouse screamed savagely at his men.

"We've got him! We've got him!" Grandda cried excitedly. "He's crazed with the fear of defeat."

The women of the Covenant were aghast at the sight of Claverhouse striking out at those of his own men who dared to flinch and tried to flee. He could be heard screaming, "In the name of God! Cross the bog, and charge them on their flanks, till we get over this morass. If this fails, we are lost!"

"Spearmen to the front!" Sir Robert's deep-toned voice lofted to our ears. The frustration of having to helplessly stand by, drove the old men to beat their bonnets against their legs in time to their heartfelt curses.

"Kneel and place your spears to receive the enemy's cavalry, and you, my gallant fellows: Fire! God and our Country is our word!" shouted Sir Robert, as he and other officers flew from rank to rank. He held their flag high over his head; its whiteness emblazoned in gold with "God and Our Country," as it fluttered in the breeze. The Covenanters continued to fire with great steadiness.

Suddenly, a company of Covenanters burst across the bog; swords in hand—they attacked.

"See! Look! Watch the Laird of Torfoot!" Grandda cried out excitedly to the rest of us who were unwilling onlookers. Our eyes obediently searched where Grandda was pointing. "Now there's a warrior for you!" He smiled proudly.

Granny glanced at her husband disapprovingly. The Laird waved his sword at the weapon of an enemy captain. The captain's pistols fired, but the bullet glanced off the Laird's sword. A raging battle ensued with hellish ferocity where men reeled and fell with life's blood gushing in torrents on the heath.

I looked up at Grandda, questioning what I was seeing. He wiped tears of pride from his eyes as he placed his arm around my shoulders and said in a low voice. "Lass, you'll never understand." He paused a moment before adding thoughtfully, "I pray to God that you'll never have to know battle!" He shook his gray head and pulled my head against him, while he muttered, "It doesn't bear thinkin' about!"

Suddenly Grandda yelled and pointed, "Look!" as he directed our attention to the left of the field. The Covenanters, Cleland and the fierce Burley had charged, with a terrible shout, the strong Royalist Company that had been sent to flank them—to which the dragoons screamed their reply, "No Quarter!".

"Be 'No Quarter' to you then, ye murderous 'goons," cried Burley and with one blow he cut their leader through the steel cap, scattering his brains on the men following him. Burley's every blow cut down one of the enemy. Both Royalists and Covenanters were now in the swamp. They had dismounted and the dreadful work of death was carried out in hand-to-hand combat.

Suddenly, a trumpet sounded behind the Covenanter lines. All eyes looked to where Captain Nisbet and his friend, Woodburn of Mains, sat astride their horses. Nisbet had brought no reinforcements but proved to be an army all by himself.

With a loud cheer and a flourish of his sword he rushed to Burley's side, shouting "Jump the ditch! Charge the enemy!" The two of them struggled through the marsh, their men following as best they could. Once on the other side of the bog, they formed into lines and marched on the enemy's right flank. At that same moment, Sir Robert and David Hackston brought forward the whole line of infantry.

"God and our Country!" echoed and re-echoed throughout our ranks.

"No Quarter!" answered Claverhouse' fierce dragoons.

"There!" I shouted and pointed to the Laird of Torfoot who was galloping towards the knoll where Mr. King and the prisoners were standing. We watched and cheered as the Laird quickly severed the ropes, which bound their arms.

As quickly as the Covenanters were released they snatched up the weapons of their fallen foe and moved forward to charge Claverhouse' ranks.

"Are we gonna win, Grandda?" I cried excitedly.

"Going," he corrected me out of habit, his eyes never leaving the battlefield "God willin', we will, pet."

Claverhouse had formed a hollow square with himself in the center; his men fought, gallantly defending their commander. Whenever the Covenanters broke through his lines, Claverhouse speedily filled the gap with more of his men. Three times he fell from his horse and rolled headlong onto the ground while rushing from rank to rank and as often, remounted, and carried on.

"I will take him!" many of the Covenanters begged their officer. "No!" cried Burley. "It's impossible to take aim at him! I'd sooner shoot ten heather cocks on the wing than one flying Clavers!" At just that moment, Burley saw an opening and pushed into the hollow square. He charged Claverhouse, but his impatience caused his sword to land on the head of Claverhouse' horse, bringing the animal to the ground. Burley's men rushed at the fallen Claverhouse, but the faithful dragoons threw themselves over their commander and drove Burley and his men back.

Claverhouse was instantly on a fresh horse. His bugle man recalled the dragoons who were driving back Burley's Covenanters. Within minutes he had collected his troops and readied them to make one last desperate attack. Claverhouse charged the Covenanters' infantry with such force that they reeled...but only for a moment.

Sir Robert snatched the blue and white flag of the Covenant and placed himself in the forefront of the battle. The Covenanters shouted "God and Our Country!" and rallied under their flag, again fighting heroically.

Claverhouse fought every bit as bravely. His attack was aimed at the Covenanters' officers. Claverhouse's sword struck the helmet of David Hackston, whose sword was entangled in the body of a dragoon. Hackston's men carried him into the rear where they revived him.

"Watch the Laird of Torfoot!" Grandda called to the onlookers. "He's at them again!"

Claverhouse was ready for them. As the Laird rode towards him, poised to take him, Claverhouse rose in his saddle and struck at the Laird's steel helmet with all the force he could muster. The Laird resisted the blow. Claverhouse lunged down on the Laird a second time. This blow glanced off the Laird's Ferrara sword and Claverhouse's sword shattered to pieces.

The Laird and Claverhouse rushed headlong at each other again, pistols cocked and ready to fire. Claverhouse's pistol misfired, being soaked with blood. The Laird's pistol found it's mark but the wound was not deadly. Their horses reared and the two men were sent rolling to the heath where they clawed for a grip on each other. The combatants were buried under their own men, each eager to save his respective officer.

Gawn, the Laird's faithful aid, dragged him out from under his horse and within moments the Laird was again rushing toward Claverhouse, who had been pulled from the melee by his faithful underlings.

My young mind felt sorely assaulted at the sight and I began to cry softly. On the battle field below me was spread an immense moving mass of humanity, heaped up together in the greatest confusion. Covenanters and Royalists, struggled in a bloody tangle. The men shrieked and groaned and shouted; horses neighed and pranced and swords rung on steel helmets.

My eyes absorbed the horror, lastingly imprinting it upon my memory.

"Da! Where are you? Where are you?" I whimpered over and over as I desperately searched the battlefield.

Ma pulled us close to her as the cacophony of the battle wrung sobs and tears from us. Grandda and Granny had sunk to the ground, arms around each other, not able to bear any more. Only Ma remained erect—head high. Her eyes had never left the battlefield as she maintained her constant vigil of keeping Da in her sight; his bright, carrot colored hair disappearing and reappearing as he fell and rose up again to fight.

A bugle sounded! It blared out the loud notes of a retreat. Claverhouse's men carried him away and helped him throw himself onto a horse. Bareheaded, without a sword, he fled in the first ranks of his retreating army. His troops galloped behind him in the greatest of confusion.

The Reverend John King could be heard, laughing and calling at Claverhouse's retreating back, "Why don't you stay to hear the afternoon sermon?"

The Laird's men closed in with Burley's men and took a number of Royalist prisoners. Other Covenanters pursued the fleeing Royalists. Claverhouse halted only when he reached the top of Calder Hill. He stopped to look behind him for a moment, and digging the rowels of his spurs into the horse's sides, drew blood in his panic to escape. He was headed for Glasgow…a defeated Colonel.

A deathly pall settled over the now quiet countryside, except for the sound of the wind that blew the smoke from the battlefield.

No bird made its song; no animal uttered a sound; no man spoke. A tangle of death, struggling life, horses and weapons littered the Muir of Drumclog.

Grandda struggled to his feet. "That, my children," he began, "was in defense of our lives! For the regaining of our liberty and religion! How great is the love of liberty when it carries men forward to endure the most cruel of hardships and disgusting of spectacles—war. Your freedom to worship as you please has been hard won today! Never abuse it!"

His words burned into my mind; I would never forget them.

Grandda walked toward the muir and the exhausted men of the Covenant. His strong voice shattered the silence as he shouted his praise for them and their victory.

Chapter 4

Ma clutched my hand and pulled me toward the battlefield. "Help me find yer Da!" she demanded. I hesitated, and pulled my hand from her grasp. My whole being recoiled at the thought of walking through the dead and dying. "He may be dying, Lizzie!" she said, looking deeply into my eyes, pleading with me.

My feet sunk into the blood soaked ground, making it squirt over my pampooties; I wanted to cover my eyes, but my need to stop my ears against the moans of the wounded was more. Carefully, almost apologetically, I stepped over the bodies. Ma frantically turned man after man over looking for Da. All I could do was step behind her. We searched and searched amid the bloody carnage and finally, there he was, sitting on the side of the hill, exhausted, his head in his hands.

"You're wounded!" Ma cried.

"Aye, but I'm alive!" was his weak reply.

"Help me get your Da onto dry ground," she demanded. His great bulk took our combined strength to pull him to a standing position. We held him steady until he mustered the energy to move one foot…and then another…allowing us to lead him away from the blood-soaked battlefield. After what seemed an eternity, we eased him down on the heath at Granny's feet—where Jenny and Iain were clinging to her dress, horrified at what they were witnessing.

The wound in Da's shoulder had soaked his leine. Ma worked quickly, pulling the heavy cloth away from his skin before it dried. She tugged at wee Jenny's shift and then at mine, shredding them into bandages to dress our father's wounds.

I watched other families as they searched for and found their soldier. Mother, father, children—arms entwined—moved slowly from the disgusting site of carnage. The reality of death had draped its frightening cloud over all of us.

In all, fifteen of the Covenanters were wounded and only one, John Martin, was killed.

"Incredible!" Grandda exclaimed at the news but then, quickly and sadly shook his head. Even the loss of one man was cause for us to grieve.

Once again on higher ground I shuddered as I looked back upon the once beautiful muir, which had so quickly been turned into a battlefield. Then I peered into the faces of those around me. They were smiling! How could they?

As if reading my thoughts, Ma whispered into my ear, "Give thanks, Lizzie, that one o' those," she nodded toward the bodies of the dead Royalists on the muir, "isn't yer Da's."

"Aye—but they're someone's Da!" I replied angrily.

Ma's arms encircled me, letting me know she understood my bewilderment and anger. "Aye, Lizzie, you're right." Then she glanced at Da and said, "This one's got more o' you about her than just your red hair."

"Aye, I know," Da said sympathetically. "She's in for a lot o' heartache, and I can't keep her from it, either. I don't even know how tae help mysel' at times!"

The gloaming that was creeping into the glen matched the sadness that was enveloping me. This Sabbath day, which had begun so fair, now found the men and women of the Covenant bound even more tightly together...having been victorious in this, their first battle. The aged men made their way from soldier to soldier, thanking them...praising them...telling them how skilful they'd been in battle, while trying to cheer the family who had lost its' husband and father.

It wasn't long, though, before it began to dawn on everyone that our position was now more precarious than ever. If, before today, the Covenanters had to endure brutalities, torture, being chased like fugitives—and this for no lawful reason—what could we expect at the hands of the Royalists, now? We certainly could not return to our homes—at least not tonight. Our protection and strength lay in unity—remaining together in a group—our numbers being our only protection. Not only would we have to withstand the fury of Claverhouse, but the hostility of the King's court in London was now added to our burden.

"We must remain undivided in order to preserve our lives," Grandda concluded. Grandda became spokesman for the decision-makers. "We'll camp over Calder Hill tonight," he announced to the group. "The Duke and Duchess are away in London so we can put up for the night in their fields—they would want us to. The horses can graze there as well."

Da had to be helped into the wagon by all of us…he was so big and heavy. Even little Iain helped, or thought he was helping, by holding onto Da's foot. When he was seated by Ma, I lifted Jenny and Iain into the back where they could dangle their legs over the back edge. I was about to climb in myself when Da suddenly called out to Grandda.

"James Gray!"

"Aye, son?" the old patriarch answered from where he was sitting in his wagon.

"D'ye see Sir Robert, yonder?" Da pointed to the gallant soldier, sitting proudly erect on his horse.

"Aye."

"I'm uneasy wi' him in command. What dae ye think?" Da asked.

"He does seem a wee bit puffed up. But, ach, he's all right, ye ken! It'll wear off."

Grandda listened to the boisterous laughter for another moment before reluctantly nodding his head in agreement. "Alright. What do you have in mind?" He turned to Da and waited for an answer.

"I would like tae see Christie and the bairns and Ma, there," Da nodded at Granny, "with my cousins in Glasgow. I don't know what's goin' tae come out of this whole thing and I'd feel better knowin' that they were out o' harm's way."

"Well, it'll be dark enough soon—should be able to slip into the city—soldiers would have no way of knowin' we were at Drumclog…" Grandda was thinking out loud, "…as long as you keep that red head of yours out of sight! You would be a dead give away with all those rags wrapped about you…soldiers would shoot you on the spot! Maybe you should stay with these…" he suggested, nodding at the rest of the Covenanters who were moving toward Calder Hill.

"Aye, I think you're right. Will ye take them, then?" Da asked.

"Aye. You know I will!" was the quick answer. "Iain! Get on up here wi' Grandda. That's a good wee boy…up ye come!" Iain had scramble down from our wagon and in a blink of an eye was being lifted up onto the seat between Grandda and Grandma. The whole situation was under Grandda's control, which felt very comforting to me and much to Da's obvious relief.

Da gave Ma a wink which she received with a shake of her head, and as she opened her mouth to object, Da raised a finger to his mouth, silently telling her there would be no discussion on the subject. "I'll see you at hame, lassie. God speed—and I love you." And with that he eased himself out of the wagon and hit the ground with stifled groans.

"I'll explain as we go," Grandda said sternly, stemming any questions Granny and Ma were about to ask. Our little group separated from the main body of Covenanters and struck out for Glasgow. I sat beside Ma and fell asleep; I don't know how I could, but when I woke we were approaching the soot blackened city of Glasgow.

"Pull up, Christie! Pull up!" Grandda demanded.

When the two wagons were abreast of each other, Grandda instructed Ma, "We'll cross the bridge…go 'round the University grounds and we're home free!"

"Aye, Da. I'll follow ye," Ma answered.

"Quiet, now. Don't be drawing any attention to ourselves," Grandda whispered. "And let me do the talking if soldiers stop us," he continued to instruct us.

The events of the day and the long night's drive had left us all very docile, willing to be led to a cup of broth and a bed, which we were sure of having at Da's cousin's house. Granny, however, kept casting doubtful glances at Grandda, punctuating them every once in a while with a loud "humph".

Not a soldier in sight! We crossed the bridge—only a few students were there, meandering around the university buildings.

We drove through some fields and finally—finally—we stopped at the familiar door of Charles and Peggy Wilkie. It opened almost before Grandda knocked. Charles stood in the doorway, tall, slim and handsome. Without hesitation he pulled us inside.

Peggy, small and delicate, with the kindest of smiles, became what Grandda called "a whirling dervish of activity". The kettle was filled with fresh water and placed on the hob over the fire. More peat was laid beside the unsteady flame now flickering in the grate. Great chunks of cheese appeared on a plate; and the magic pan was placed over the flame.

We children always thought of it as magic because of the incomparable scones and bannock it produced. This idea was happily encouraged by Peggy, a woman of middle age and childless.

"We've heard," Charles said simply, before anyone spoke. "We thought ye might o' been there." The news obviously had already traveled far and wide.

Everyone began talking at once. Ma and Granny described the horrendous events. Grandda and 'Charlie', as he was called, quietly put their heads together, Grandda giving this man, who was only five years younger than himself, a first hand telling of the battle.

I pulled a three-legged stool closer to the fire, watching, listening, and rocking back and forth. A warm, comforting arm around my shoulders interrupted my worries. "Cum' here tae yer old Grandda, wee uin." He had lapsed back into his familiar soft way of speaking while pulling me onto his lap. “Cum’ on, now. Just ye put yer wee puddin’ head down on this shoulder…”

No sooner had he said the words than I melted into tears. My Grandda! How I loved him! Always, always he knew where I hurt and why. And there was always the comfort of his shoulder as he told me how I was better than I thought I was…and making me believe it. My love for him made my heart ache.

“Is the wee uin alright, James?” Granny asked.

“She’s on my lap, isn’t she?” Grandda answered confidently, making everyone laugh…including me.

The first streaks of dawn had arrived shortly after we did; and with the dawn came the sound of soldiers’ boots clattering on the cobble stone street. Claverhouse’s unmistakable voice was barking commands—first here and then there—never in one place longer than a moment.

“Stay here!” Grandda ordered as he stepped out of the cottage. “I’ll see what they’re up to!”

“I’m comin’ too!” I announced and ran after him before anyone could stop me. I knew I was safe with my Grandda.

Once out on the street, we made our way to the Gallowgate. The soldiers were building barricades of sod, rocks, pieces of confiscated furniture—anything to afford protection from the “rebels”. Grandda casually asked one of the young soldiers what he was ‘up tae’.

“The rebels are on the march! There’s five thousand of them!” the soldier replied without stopping his work.

“Umm…and I’m the man in the moon,” Grandda said as he winked at me and we both smiled, remembering yesterday and our little Covenanter Army of two hundred men.

“And who told you there were five thousand Covenanters?” he continued aloud.

“Claverhouse! He told us! They outnumbered us five to one yesterday!” The soldier tossed the answer over his shoulder as he carried a large plank toward the market cross.

Grandda squeezed my hand, stopping me from calling the man a liar. “And, of course, Claverhouse would never lie about such a thing, now, would he?”

The soldier stopped what he was doing and turned back to scrutinized Grandda’s face, trying to determine whether or not he was being mocked. Only when the soldier relaxed and shrugged his shoulders, dismissing his suspicions, did I breathe.

Then, seemingly, as an after thought, the soldier called out, "Better you're in your house today, old man! Safest place for you!"

"Cheeky beggar! That's what you are!" Grandda growled and shook his fist at the soldier's retreating back, but the effect was lost in the hubbub of barricade building.

The soldiers also formed a barricade in the center of the town square. They laid carts on their sides and covered them with large pieces of wood while the town clock chimed ten bells into the morning air.

Suddenly, a shout announced the approach of the "rebels".

Grandda scrambled to the top of a two foot high rock wall and while grasping the trunk of a tree, stretched his neck until he caught sight of Sir Robert who was leading the Covenanters toward the city.

"Where's the man's head?" Grandda asked out loud as he tried to puzzle out Sir Robert's strategy. Grandda, curiosity overriding his good sense, remained on the wall with his arms still wrapped around the tree trunk. I hopped up behind him and hung onto his jacket. We watched the Covenanters ride over the hill and heard them approach the city with great shouts of courage to each other.

Sir Robert led his men into an impossible situation—even I could see that. The proud look on his face plainly said that he had forgotten who had allowed us our victory yesterday.

"He thinks that he's invincible! That he's the one who won the battle yesterday!" Grandda shouted angrily. "God help us, we're lost!"

The Covenanters' shot was no hazard to the Royalists who remained behind their barricades. Our men showed an abundance of courage in spite of such a disadvantage; their horses were of no use, open as they were to the Royalists' fire from the closes and doorways of the houses. Our countrymen gave a good accounting of themselves, and were able to rout one nest of Royalists and send them scurrying for cover under the tollbooth stairs.

One, two, three Covenanters were brought to the ground by Royalist's bullets. Another fell—and another. Grandda and I recognized Walter Paterson—a choice young man from Cambusnethan parish, his youthful face now twisted in agony. If only they had had trained and wise leaders, the Covenanters would have had more than an even chance of chasing the Royalist soldiers out of Glasgow that day.

Grandda remained motionless. I, too, was as still as death. Life hung in a balance around me—again. "I can't believe what I'm seeing," Grandda whispered hoarsely, over and over again. But the six bodies strewn over the cobblestones screamed the truth—Scotland was at war!

Retreat sounded—Sir Robert led the way. The Covenanters drew up a little way from the Gallowgate port—obviously expecting the Royalists to now venture out from behind their barricades and engage in the fair play of field battle. But no! The Royalists were content to remain with whole skins and did not move from their entrenchment.

The Covenanters waited for some time in the field and not until it became apparent that the Royalists were not coming out to fight, did they swing around and ride toward Hamilton.

Grandda turned his attention to the dead bodies of his brothers in the Gospel. "The waste, oh, the waste!" he cried as he moved toward them. His voice trembled with sadness and regret. "This, Lizzie, was caused by the pride and impatience of one man, Sir Robert. Don't forget this lesson as long as ye live...that pride is one of the deadliest sins!"

My head bobbed up and down in agreement. I could find no words to speak. Just yesterday I had foolishly thought I had seen all of the death that I would ever see in my life. But here I was again...and what troubled me more than seeing the bodies of the Covenanters was that I wasn't as shocked...and could actually look at them. What was happening to me?

"Ach, you poor wee boy!" Grandda sobbed as he picked up the body of Walter Paterson.

"Drop that!" Claverhouse demanded. He was on top of Grandda, waving his sword wildly about his head.

"But he's needing burying!" answered Grandda, incredulous that Claverhouse did not recognize the obvious.

"Drop that!" Claverhouse shouted again, not even giving the young man the respect of being called a man. Quickly he brandished his sword and pushed the point of it against Grandda's chest.

"As ye can see, I'm not armed." Grandda appealed quietly to the gentleman in Claverhouse.

"Your obvious love for this rebel tells me that you are one of them!" Claverhouse screamed back, the white plume on his hat shaking as he exploded in anger.

"It's only decency to bury anyone," Grandda defended himself.

"These will not have burial—they don't warrant it! Let the butchers' dogs devour them!" Claverhouse raved madly. "...and you as well!" His face twisted fiendishly as he lunged at Grandda's heart, his sword bursting the organ.

"Oh, God! Not now! Not...yet!" Grandda had breathed his last words.

"He was outside the law! He was harboring a rebel!!" Claverhouse roared, justifying his butchery. "Do not bury them!" he shouted at his dragoons. "They deserve only the dogs!"

I gasped and slid down onto the road, my back tight against the rock wall. Claverhouse and his dragoons didn't even see me. I had crumpled in a small heap beside the wall, where only minutes before my Grandda and I had been standing. Pain—the all too familiar pain stabbed through my heart and gripped me once more as I stared at the lifeless form of Grandda—my beloved Grandda, his precious blood staining the cobblestones. How I hated the Royalists—the English—and how could Claverhouse, a Scotsman, lead the Royalists against his own people!! Anger, a deep raging anger, rescued me from the overwhelming sorrow and sense of loss I was experiencing.

Word of Claverhouse's inhumane brutality spread like a peat fire from house to house until it reached the ears of Charles Wilkie. When Grandda and I had not returned, it became obvious that we must be in trouble, prompting Charlie to run toward the town square.

Not listening to Charlie's advice to 'stay put', Granny caught up her arisaidh, pulled it around her head and shoulders and ran out into the street as well. Ma and Peggy followed suit...wee Jenny and Iain were not about to be left behind either.

I heard their voices in the distance, calling "James, Lizzie!" over and over again until they reached the town square. When they stopped calling out our names, I knew they were where they could see Grandda and me, but I still couldn't speak or even acknowledge them.

Suddenly, a terrible scream ripped through the morning air. It was Granny. She flew to Grandda's side. And suddenly, Ma was crouching beside me, trying to cradle me in her arms.

Men...decent men, disputed angrily with the soldiers, their sensibilities being assaulted, not only by Claverhouse's butchering of Grandda, but by his further determination to leave the bodies of the Covenanters to the dogs. Only by sheer armed force and brutality were the soldiers able to prevent them from carrying away the dead for burial.

No matter how incensed they were, the people of Glasgow were not successful in prevailing upon the soldiers to release the bodies. The controversy became so white hot that even the dogs, lurking around the fringes of the crowd, didn't dare move toward the bodies. Charles was felled with the butt of a musket when he defied the soldiers and bent over Grandda, searching for any sign of life.

Peggy screamed abuse at the soldier as she shoved him away from her husband and half pulled, half carried Charles to the edge of the square. Stunned, I watched him lean heavily on her, allowing himself to be led home.

Granny stood quietly by, as near to her husband's body as the soldiers would allow. Ma, wee Jenny and Iain pressed close to me. Grief clutched us in its painful grip once again and Ma began to sob quietly.

We kept a silent vigil until dusk began to fall, when finally, one courageous woman, with one eye on the soldiers, moved cautiously toward her dead husband.

A connivance! The soldiers turned their backs, pretending not to see.

Within minutes, other women were struggling to lift the bodies of their men folk; a man stepped forward to help but he was beaten back with the butt of a musket. It became obvious that the soldiers would allow only the women to perform this service.

Ma lifted her father's shoulders, her mother—his feet. I held on to a stiffening arm—my Grandda—my beloved Grandda! Iain and wee Jenny, crying loudly, ran alongside. With tears streaming down their pale faces, they struggled to lift up the other arm that was dragging on the road.

The town square soon emptied, leaving only the dogs to lap up the drying pools of blood.

Peggy came running down the road to help lighten our load with her strength. Finally, we arrived at the Wilkie house and Charles helped us lift Grandda's body onto the table. Burial linens were produced and the work of preparing the body for burial began. Peggy sent Charles to locate posts for a bier on which to carry Grandda to the cemetery.

Grandda's body was so heavy that it was difficult to handle but when he was finally laid out on the table, Granny washed his face tenderly as her tears dropped softly onto it. Ma, the strongest of us all, lifted, pulled, pushed—perspiration making her face glow in the firelight.

Finally, washed, combed, and dressed, Grandda was prepared for his last rites.

I had remained constantly at Ma's side and had washed, buttoned, and lifted as much as my strength allowed. I was not scared to touch him, in fact, the ache eased a little as I handled my Grandda's body and I was able to silently pour out my love for him.

Ma hadn't wanted me to help, thinking that it would be too difficult for me, but as I worked side by side with her in this, the last service she would ever be able to give her father, I sensed that she was suddenly seeing me as a woman and not as a child. Our work for Grandda was done and now we turned to one another, gently embracing each other, trying to heal this terrible wound in our hearts.

Suddenly, the door burst open with a crash! Soldiers—cursing—drunken—laughing, stumbled to where Grandda was lying peacefully on the table. From out on the street, a high pitched maniacal voice screamed at the soldiers to, "Rid us of these rebels and phanatics...NOW...and forever! or it'll be you that feels the point of my sword!"

Granny screamed and threw herself across her husband's body as the soldiers moved toward him.

"Outta the way, ye old relic!" one of the soldiers barked, taunting her in her widowhood. And with absolutely no pity for her in her grief, laughed while she cried out with all of the love in her heart, "James, oh, my James, my own one!"

Another soldier sneered, pointed his short barrel carbine at Granny's head and growled, "She gets it if there's any trouble from the rest of you!" The look on his face didn't match the terrorizing words he spoke and for the briefest moment, I detected a reluctance in the soldier to carry out the orders being shouted at him by his commander in the street.

We stopped in our tracks—wee Jenny and Iain didn't move a muscle. These men who had been known to throw women into snake pits and were able to be so fiendish as to stab a pregnant woman in her side with a dirk, were not to be disobeyed. Only a gasp was heard from Peggy as the soldiers ripped the linens from Grandda's body, leaving him almost naked.

Iain cried, rubbing his little fists into his eyes and wee Jenny pulled him to her, defiantly staring up at the soldiers.

Then they were gone—as quickly as they had come.

"God in Heaven! Oh, God in Heaven!" Peggy cried out as she reached for her linen bed sheets. Granny, in shock, walked unsteadily toward her husband's body once more. Peggy held out the sheet. "Come on, Jenny! We have to get him buried! No tellin' what these 'goons will do now."

Once more they wrapped their beloved James in linens. Ma bent into her task again and lifted her father's shoulders while I lifted his arms to allow the sheet to be wound around the body. No one spoke—we had all been shocked into our own silent thoughts—again.

Charles opened the door, gasping for breath. He was clutching bier posts. "Soldiers—did they come?" he asked between gasps.

"Aye," was the simple answer. The older women never looked up from their work.

Charles swore. Peggy reminded him that the children were present and that Covenanters don't swear. Without another word he dragged the bier posts into the room and began lashing the posts together with the leather strips that were draped over his shoulders.

As soon as Grandda's body was decently covered, they laid it on the bier. Peggy dug into a trunk and found a black cloth—a mortcloth—to cover the body for its trip to the church burial ground.

Once on the moon lit road, Peggy and Ma argued with Charles as he took hold of the front bier posts. "Charlie, don't," begged Ma, "please don't take the chance!" Even little Jenny tried pulling on his sleeve, but it was to no avail. He gripped the posts defiantly and lifted, taking most of the weight. The women took hold of the other end and we began our trek to the Churchyard.

We were brought to an abrupt halt by the sound of running boots. A sudden flash of metal and Charles collapsed; the bier clattered to the ground as blood rushed onto the cobblestones from the wound at the back of his head.

"Only the women!" shouted the soldier. "Only the women!" And they dragged Charles to the side of the street.

"Go on, Peggy. Just get the job done!" Charles shouted at his wife who had turned to help him.

Reluctantly, the women picked up the bier once again. I now had to carry my full share of the weight, too.

"Iain, Jenny—stay with your Uncle Charles!" Ma demanded.

They gave no argument but obeyed quickly.

Loud, raucous laughter filled the street. Another pack of soldiers drunkenly bumped into each other as they staggered past the women who were trying to carry the dead to their resting place. Cries echoed through the street as the soldiers ripped the mortcloths with their swords and pulled the biers out from under the bodies of the dead Covenanters. The soldiers seemed to be puppets, responding to the cries of one man who was continually urging them into heinous acts toward those trying so hard to be respectful of their dead.

I cringed under the sour, whiskey soaked breath of one soldier as he clumsily groped for the pieces of mortcloth covering my Grandda. He missed and fell to the ground only to rise up again, cursing obscenely. Only Ma's restraining hand on my arm kept me from striking out at him.

"Don't be foolish!" Ma whispered.

It was the captain of these men who lay sprawled drunkenly on the cobblestone and the one who had prodded his men into such inhumane acts. As soon as he had struggled to his feet, he unsheathed his sword and with the point, snatched up the mortcloth and swung it in the air, bringing a roar of approval from his men. Ma tightened her grip on the bier, but it was to no avail; his men easily wrenched it from her hands, dumped Grandda's body on the ground and cut the leather straps with their swords.

Having finished their fiendish work, the soldiers stumbled off down the street, leaving behind their Captain...Wallace Lauderdale. Before leaving himself, he turned on his heel in order to view his devilish work once more. He spun around toward Ma, who unfortunately had turned toward him at the same time; Lauderdale stopped—surprised and suddenly sober—he stared into her face, his eyes revealing the long ago tender feelings he had held for her. However, within seconds, he had recovered and his face contorted into a sneer that revealed his malicious joy in destroying the happiness of the source of his hurt, anger and desire for revenge—my mother, Christian Grey Whitelaw.

"A beauty we 'ave here, boys!" he said, calling his men back to his side.

"Take her, Captain!" one of his men shouted.

"No, this one's different!" he answered, holding Ma motionless with his pig-like eyes. "I will have her. But not now," he said, as he pushed long strands of greasy yellow hair out of his insipid, sallow and almost hairless face. Ma shuddered and turned away: he was a very ugly, distasteful man.

I stopped breathing...looking quickly from the Captain to Ma, remaining motionless, until he reluctantly turned and left. His men followed somewhat dejectedly; they had been cheated out of satisfying their passion for voyeurism.

My need to breathe overrode the scream welling up in my throat, and I gulped air into my lungs.

Granny, emotionally spent by now, silently pulled her tartan arisaidh from around her shoulders—ignoring the social custom of a woman never appearing in public without her head being covered with the arisaidh. She folded it lengthwise and drew it under her husband's shoulders. Ma took hold of the other end. Peggy followed suit—and I lifted with her.

We struggled toward the cemetery. The weight of Grandda's body pulled at my arms until the muscles burned unbearably.

The sound of boots again!

"No! No! Please...no!" Granny wailed as the soldiers cut the tartan shawl with their swords.

Again they left, laughing fiendishly.

Peggy spread her arisaidh on the ground. We lifted the body onto it. Granny covered Grandda with the remaining pieces of her shawl.

"Ma," my Ma said quietly, "Ma, I think we should just take him to the alms house over there. The soldiers aren't going to let us bury him tonight."

No answer was forthcoming. We stood still in the middle of the road, waiting for Granny to speak.

Ma," she pleaded again, "Ma, I want Da to have a proper burial, as well, but they won't let us. Not right now." She waited another moment for her mother's answer. Only silence was the answer. My Ma knew she was right and she didn't want to subject me or her aunt or her mother or herself to any more danger.

Without any further discussion and using the last bit of strength we could muster, we pulled Grandda's body into the almshouse and covered him as much as the pieces of tartan would allow. There, Grandda would wait for a proper burial, along with the others who had fallen today.

My heart felt as though it had broken, the pain was so severe. But the last two days, in concert with all I had seen throughout my life, entrenched the resolve to do whatever was necessary to find somewhere to live in peace. I wondered if wars happened in that great black hole—America—to where people were banished and were swallowed up and never returned.

That night the conversation was subdued, even dispirited; however, much of it centered around Captain Wallace Lauderdale. Uncle Charles wondered at how such a fine young lad could turn into the monster that Wallace had become, as he had known him and his family most of his life. Uncle Charles remembered that he had seemed to be a normal lad, but something must have 'twisted' him along the way—perhaps when he was fighting in France with Claverhouse.

Granny disagreed. She remembered him being rejected by all of the lassies...he was so ugly and the odor about his person was so offensive that it 'brought tears to your eyes'; and the girls were so repulsed by him that they even clapped a handkerchief over their noses when he tried to stand close to them.

Ma shuddered and agreed, remembering out loud his advances toward her and then, how he turned from worshipping her and the ground she walked on, to being consumed with a downright mean spirit.

"But he wasn't the only one that pursued you, Christie, and not the only one you rejected before ye settled on John Whitelaw," Granny said quietly. "And the others haven't turned on you and yours. He is twisted, I tell ye—he is twisted—I agree with Charlie." Granny heaved a sigh that seemed to come from the very core of her being, shaking her little body. Her grief was so intense that it invaded and increased the weight of my own grief. My shoulders felt the load and I bent over, not able to sit up straight any longer.

Ma said sadly, "I sorely regret the day that I met up with him again at your house, Ma—that day, just after John and I had married, and he and a couple of his cohort Highland Host was billeted wi' ye."

Finally, she turned to me and whispered, "Come away, now, Lizzie, cum' on the now and have a wee rest, that's my pet. You've had too much—too, too, much." The crooning sounds of her words soothed me somewhat, and I allowed sleep to take over, gratefully escaping into it.

Chapter 5

"Ma, I want to stay wi' ye," my mother was explaining, but I must get back to Tigh Sona—John will be making his way back and he is wounded—not badly—but it will need tending to. I am so sorry Ma, so sorry—I miss Da so much, too." She threw her arms around Granny who sobbed so hard that again, I thought her frail body would shake apart.

"Granny—I'll come back as soon as I can and I'll stay wi' ye," I promised through the sadness that repeatedly welled up in me, although thankfully, the tears had stopped flowing.

"Oh, lassie, oh lassie—I dinna think I'll bide long wi' out him," she said between sobs. "I'll no bide long wi' out him."

There was a ring of truth in her words and I could not bear one more shred of grief. "Don't say that, Granny. Please, don't say that! I couldn't live without ye. You watch, we'll be back for ye and ye'll stay wi' us—right Ma?" I looked for support.

"Of course, Granny'll stay wi' us. We wouldn't have it any other way. Ma, as soon as I see how everything is at the croft and that it is safe—well, as safe as I can be sure of—we'll come and get you. Please, take that worry offa me and stay here wi' Charlie and Peggy. Promise, Ma? Besides Ma, ye need to bury Da."

"Oh, aye...aye...I know that—I just don't want to do it without ye." Granny sounded so tired. I had never heard her sound like that before and that alone, was heart rending.

Eventually we took our leave amidst many warnings to be careful and God's blessings, and soon Ma, Jenny, Iain and me found ourselves on the road back to Tigh Sona. Although Ma was very quiet, I knew that worry was riddling her every thought and it showed on her face. It was certain that Da wouldn't put us in jeopardy in any way, which meant that he would not openly return home—at least not until this religious strife was settled. He must now join the other Covenanters, to be hunted in his own hills like a fugitive—and by Englishmen and his own Countrymen! Shame—a terrible shame!

Ma was driving the wagon very slowly, not pushing our horse in any way. In fact, it allowed Iain and Jenny to bound up the hillside ahead of Ma and me. A gray mist filled every little nook and cranny of the hills and in the glen the trees etched themselves in black against the colorless sky; even the birds' songs sounded dampened. The only happy note was Iain's laughter, as he played with Jenny, and even that sounded colorless as well. The day appeared as sad as my heart.

But suddenly and wondrously, the clouds parted and a shaft of golden light mercifully fell over us. The hillside shimmered in the glow. Ma and I slipped down from the wagon and Ma sat down on her heels, her long woolen leine falling in folds around her bare feet as she stretched out her arms, waiting for the young ones to come to her. "Look!" she whispered as we huddled together in the middle of the road. "Look! God has given us a gift!"

The golden beams of light touched each drop of dew, turning it into a jewel of amber hue. The yellow gorse and purple heather sparkled under the heavenly shower of sunbeams. The air was laden with the sweet scent of sunshine on rain washed grass and tight buds of heather. The joyous trilling of a heathercock wound its way through the symphony of colour. Our little world sparkled in its golden, jewel bedecked dress, breathing its exquisite perfume, looking so majestic, so royal.

Ma filled her lungs with the pure ecstasy of it all.

"Breathe, children! Open your eyes! Remember this—it is a gift from the Lord! Be thankful—ever so thankful! He sent us this beauty to help us heal our hurts!"

I glanced at Iain and chuckled for the first time in days. His eyes were stretched wide in childlike obedience and Jenny had inhaled until she looked like a Ptarmigan, puffed up and ready to burst.

Wordlessly, I drank in the beauty and welcomed the peace that was enveloping us. Ma held out her hands, inviting us to pray with her. We stood in a little circle, holding each others' hands and Ma bowed her head and prayed. "Oh, God! Help me to not be swallowed up by sorrow. Help me to not be caught in the trap of fear. Oh, Lord, strengthen me to continue in thy service. Grant me the gift of thy Holy Spirit that I might discern right from wrong; that I might forgive my enemies; that I might learn holy conduct from thy Son."

She continued, "Oh, God, please protect my husband and mother. Please let right win. Oh, Father, I implore thee by all that is Holy to protect these, my children, and lead them in Thy light."

She raised her head and met Iain's adoring eyes, where she found a treasure of pure love. For a moment, I felt I had glimpsed heaven.

Ma swept Iain up in her arms, and holding him tightly, spun around and around. His delighted laughter rang throughout the glen. A moment—only a moment more of reprieve before the clouds gathered together again, closing the rent in the veil between heaven and earth. The gray returned, but not before the warmth had penetrated our hearts and souls.

"Ma," I said gently, "Ma, you are so beautiful! I love you so much!"

"Aye, me too, Ma! Me too!" Jenny and Iain were not to be out done.

Ma and I exchanged smiles over the heads of the young ones.

In the midst of this happiness a sudden worry nagged me. "Ma, shouldn't we try to cross the bog before night falls?"

"Aye, you're right, Lizzie," Ma agreed. She rose with what seemed renewed strength and a lightness of heart. "Come along then! Into the wagon—the lot o' ye. Blackie—up to the top o' the hill!" she cried as she gently laid the reins on Blackie's back.

With squeals of laughter, we shouted Blackie on—not stopping until Tigh Sona was in view.

"There it is!" Jenny shouted excitedly, pointing to the small cottage snuggled in the walled glen. "Will Da be there?"

Not knowing the answer seemed to plunge Ma into anxiety once more. "Be careful!" she shouted angrily at Iain. "You just wait for the rest of us before you tackle that bog! And just you wait until I get Blackie loose form these ropes."

Jenny and Iain looked at her, saddened as the gaiety had once again vanished from Ma's face. She winced at their sidelong glances of disappointment. "Oh, God! Here I've only just prayed to You and I'm already letting fear take hold of me!" she cried.

"God did not place the spirit of fear in man," she repeated the scripture over and over, reasoning that if He didn't—then it must be of the evil one. "Please, Lord, cast this fear out of me!" she prayed aloud. Before long, her face softened into the familiar, gentle smile and she was peaceful once again. We all relaxed and walked happily by her side.

"Jenny," Ma called, "are you a big enough lassie to lead us over the bog?"

"Oh, aye, Ma. I can do it! Just watch!" Jenny answered enthusiastically.

"Now, remember that the rest of us aren't mountain sheep like yourself. Take pity on us!" Ma teased her.

Jenny's honest little face lit up with the compliment, exaggerating her steps into slow motion, much to Iain's annoyance.

Soon his plaintive cry of, "Ma!!" was tattling on her. "Jenny, now don't be aggravating your brother. Get a wiggle on—but be careful! Honestly, Jenny, you can try the patience of a saint! Ye know that?"

I smiled. In spite of the last few days' events, it was good to hear the familiar sounds and words. Carefully, so carefully, we picked our way over the bog, our feet finding the firmness of the boulders that nature had camouflaged with lichen. And Blackie followed us, knowing exactly where to step.

Tigh Sona looked smaller. Each time we rebuilt it, it seemed to shrink just a bit...or maybe I was just growing bigger. We stood back as Ma went through the ritual of cautiously pulling away the animal skins from the doorway. "Just to give the wee beasties time to escape," she would say.

We were never disappointed. Always, two or three field mice scampered out. I squealed; Jenny called me a 'fraidy cat'; and Iain hopped from one foot to the other in pure delight.

Ma worked quickly and soon had a warm peat fire burning in the grate. The milk and cheese that had been lowered into the coolness of the well were pulled up and set upon the table and before long, scones were browning on the griddle.

Ma smiled as she listened to me trying to coerce Jenny into pulling back the blankets on our bed—"to check for wee beasties, pleeese Jenny!" I wailed.

Jenny smiled triumphantly as she reveled in her moment of power before carrying out my request.

The trill of a heathercock caught Ma's attention and mine. That's strange, a heathercock singing at night? I straightened up.

"Wheesht!" Ma quieted us. Again, the heathercock sang out. "Don't move!" she ordered, moving quickly to the doorway. Carefully, Ma pulled the skins aside, and closed them, aside and closed them...again, aside and closed them. The silence was filled with suspense.

"It's me!" Da's unmistakable voice filtered through the dusk to us.

Ma spun around to face us, demanding in a hoarse whisper, "Don't you make a sound! It's yer Da! Just you let him slip in quietly!" She moved to the fire and sat down on a stool, pulling another up beside her. Da slid past the animal skins, hardly moving them. A big, happy grin lit his rugged face. "Ach, will ye just look at the family of ye! Yer beautiful! That's what ye are! Beautiful!" Tears glistened in his eyes but he raised a finger to his mouth, telling us to whisper.

As he sat down on the stool, Iain and Jenny, faces beaming, wrapped their arms around his neck, burying their heads in his shoulders. He winced, but stopped Ma from taking them away.

Remaining on my stool, I crossed my arms over my stomach and rocked to and fro, smiling, waiting for the young ones to make room for me. Finally, it was my turn and I, too, buried my head in his shoulder; Da's coat smelled of the heather and the wind. I laid my cheek against its rough twill and waited for Da to drop a kiss onto my forehead.

"Yer a bonny, bonny lass, my little Coileach-fraoich!" he crooned tenderly in Gaelic.

"Da!! You always call me that!" I whined.

"And that's because you have the red head of the cock of the heather and...it is a beautiful bird!" he answered.

Then, holding me away from him, he scrutinized my face and with a look of surprise exclaimed, "Ma! When did my little girl become this beautiful, young lady?"

I glowed. To not be called a girl—but a young lady!

"Oh, Da!" I said shyly.

"The cakes are burning!" Jenny cried, only to be met with a chorus of "Sshhh-hhshs".

"Come, let's eat!" smiled Ma. Da, with bowed head, lead us in thanking the Lord for the food and for our lives. After supper, we began to get ready for bed but Da called after me. "Hen," one of his pet names for me, "I think ye should sit in on this news," he invited. I couldn't have been more honored than if Lady Hamilton had asked me to tea.

Jenny and Iain objected. I did not, nor did I have to enter into discussion on the subject. The whole bedtime ritual was carried out with so much dignity on my part that my young sister could only retaliate with wails of aggravation from Jenny, "Ma! Lizzie's smiling!"

I shook my head calmly and with dignity, perhaps with just a hint of superiority, but nothing anyone other than a younger sister would detect.

"Ohhhh!" Jenny sounded wounded. Eventually, Iain and she settled down and I pulled my stool closer to the fire.

"Ach, look at that, Ma!" Da exclaimed sadly as he gazed at me. "Just look at that young face of hers—radiating such innocence!" Da shook his head sadly and then told us how sad he was over Grandda's death. Ma began to cry softly.

Ma and I described the soldiers' brutality, tears coming o our eyes as we recalled the ordeal. "Da?" I asked for his attention. He waited for me to continue. "Da," I began again. "There's something happening inside me I don't understand." I looked at my father for encouragement.

"What are ye meanin', pet?" he questioned softly.

"Well, ye know we aren't strangers to the sights that sicken." I was having difficulty getting started.

"Aye," was his patient reply.

"Well, this morn', when we left Glasgow, there were two men, hanging from a tree." I stopped for a moment, then blurted out, "Da, this time I didn't even get sick to m' stomach when I saw them up there. I didn't feel anything. Later on, we passed a post with a man's head atop o' it and his hands nailed together just below his chin, like he was praying. I looked and just kept walking. Jenny and Iain didn't even look. They just kept running along the road. And Ma said nothing, either. What's happening to me Da? To us?" I implored.

Da shook his head from side to side, agonizing. "Christie, she's only fourteen!" He pleaded with his wife for help. "What have we given her?"

Ma folded her hands in her lap, unable to answer but no doubt was thinking that the three children who had died between my birth and Jenny's birth were better off right now, on the other side of the veil, than with us.

"Elizabeth Whitelaw," Da said as he turned toward me, "my first born, the delight o' my heart. I would give my life to know that you could be spared this brutalizing of heart and mind. That's what's happening to ye, hen. Ye've been brutalized. The whole country has been brutalized! When a young lassie such as yersel' can pass by something like that and not be horrified, it tells us what's happening to our country. That alone is enough to make me want to pick up a sword and fight for peace." He paused, shook his head, and gave a bitter laugh. "Fight for peace...how ridiculous!"

Ma and I waited for him to continue.

"I have a choice to make; but I need yer help. It concerns all of us. It's my opinion that the battle at Drumclog Muir is only the beginning of a long and bloody civil war. The Royalists are marshalling their troops now—thousands of men, including some unwilling Scottish nobles who would lose their estates if they don't comply—to put down the "revolution", as Clavers calls it. Many of them agree that we should be able to worship according to our own ways, to be allowed to meet in houses—as Presbyterians are allowed to do in England and Ireland."

Da sat quietly gazing into the peat fire for a moment before continuing. "I believe wi' all my heart in the freedom to worship God as a body sees fit. But I do not want to take up weapons to kill for that right. On the other hand, why should I allow someone else to kill me, or worse, kill my family, trying to take this right away from me? There's James Gray, losing his life to that Butcher Clavers and just for wantin' tae bury a man. The Covenanters are planning to meet the Royalists at Bothwell Bridge. But we are split over whether we should rewrite the Covenant and whether or not to include that we are still loyal to the King. King Charles took the oath to keep the Solemn Covenant and has broken it. What good would it do to get a dozen of his signatures? It means nothing to him and he has proven that. How can we be loyal to a king who isn't loyal to us and won't defend us? Others believe we should let the King know that we are loyal to him, but expect his loyalty in return."

He took a deep breath and said, "What I'm afraid of is that we've beaten ourselves with our indecision. The enemy will only have to go through the motions. Victory is already theirs." Da's shoulders slumped forward with the weight of his concern and decision. "This is what I'm faced wi'. I can take the lot o' you and go tae England and leave this mess. We'll be relatively safe there...if I keep m' head down and mind my own business. Or I can be at Bothwell. It sickens me—the thought of killing but, there it is. Looks like I have no choice and it seems that my three brothers aren't having the same misgivings as I am, about killing the enemy."

"Did you see Thomas and James and William? How are they and how are their families?" Ma wanted to know.

"Christie—this is important!" Da refused to answer and gave Ma a dark look before adding, "They're ready to chase the Royalists out of Scotland, once and for all! This is the way the talk is going. One group is in favor of this and another in favor of that." He stopped to heave a great sigh before continuing. "If we stay in Scotland, the tide of revolution will pull us along with it, whether we like it or not, and there'll be no turning back. Right now, there is no law protecting us. We're defenseless against the government.

"We can't leave Scotland, John." Ma said. "You know that."

I looked from my father to my mother, wishing that I was in bed with my brother and sister. This was too much for me.

"If we stay in Scotland, I cannot guarantee yer safety. I can promise to do all that's in my power to protect ye. I can't even live wi' ye—at least not during the day—and then it'll be risky slippin' in and out o' here at night," Da warned.

Ma and I nodded our agreement.

"Then ye're willin' to stay here, is that right, Christie?" Da asked, wanting to confirm what he thought she said.

Ma turned toward me, asking "Well, Lizzie?"

"Aye," I answered nervously, "Aye...or...Da—what would America be like for us?". Both of my parents just stared at me without answering my question...and continued speaking to each other as though I hadn't even spoken.

"We'll stay with it, John," Ma gave her answer.

"Aye. Then the next thing I'll have to think about is how to get food into the house. I won't be able tae carry on wi' my golf ball and golf club makin' or the weavin', cause they'll be bursting in here looking for me and I don't dare let them catch me here.". "But I've had a wee bit o' luck in findin' these beauties. Look!"

A smile lit up his eyes as he reached into his pocket and produced six fresh water pearls. "I can get a good price for them in Edinburgh."

"You used to go down to the streams for those when you were young!" Ma chuckled.

"Aye...and they're worth a lot more money now. Remember the black one that fellow in Aberdeen found and gave to the King. Well King Charlie had it made into a ring and now his whole court is daft over these misshapen beauties."

I gently pushed the little pearls around the palm of Da's hand with my finger. "Da, yer a wonder!" I said, showering my father with sincere praise. "Will ye show me how to find them?"

"Lizzie, I want you to have this one," and Da pointed to the largest pearl, ignoring my question. "I can't gie ye much, but if you hang onto that little beauty...well, it's like gold in your purse."

"Oh, Da!! I'll keep it forever!" I cried and threw my arms around his neck.

"Little darlin', that isn't the idea—this is for you to use when you need it and I am not there to help you!" He was smiling at my innocence but was ensuring that I would be wise.

Ma broke in with, "But John, you can't go to Edinburgh, not with that head full of red hair. The Royalists will have you in the tollbooth prison the minute you set foot in the city. We have to do something to cover your hair," Ma worried.

"Other than shave it off, what dae ye suggest?" Da was apprehensive.

"I know if I boil potato skins and put the water on your hair, it'll turn it darker," she offered.

"Not tae me, yer not!" Da moved away from Ma with a grin.

"Now, John. Just think about it! You'll see I'm right!" she coaxed. An intimate smile flitted between my mother and father that did not include me, so, as quietly as possible I slipped into bed, seemingly unnoticed by my parents.

I crawled in beside Jenny, pulling the wall curtain closed after me. Only my mother's silvery voice could be heard, coaxing—teasing Da. Low, inaudible whispers, followed by the sound of the other bed curtain being pulled closed, told me it was time to put the pillow over my head...again.

Then there was no sound.

Only happy echoes lingered for the moment in Tigh Sona.

CHAPTER 6

It was always an event when John Whitelaw, my Da, returned to his family and fireside. It was so eagerly anticipated and longingly prayed for by us that no monarch ever received a more joyous welcome.

Da's imitation of the trill of the heathercock was the signal for which we were constantly on the alert, and when it did float toward us, it was always near the close of day. Then the long wait began—waiting for night to cast its protective cover over his arrival.

The excitement that Da's visit created was unparalleled by any other occasion. Patiently waiting by the fire, our eyes remained focused on the doorway while Ma nervously bustled around our small cottage, never seeming to have enough time to make everything just right for her "man comin' hame".

Soon, darkness would fill the quiet glen. No one made a sound. We just waited.

"Ma!" Iain cried out when the doorway skins moved, eliciting a shower of "shshshs's" from Jenny and me. The skins moved again—ever so slightly—long fingers slowly wrapped around the edge of the skin—no one even dared breathe—a foot slid past the door post—and then the smile that warmed the whole room, appeared. Da was home and we were all one again!

Trying to smother our giggles made us laugh all the more.

And Da was of no help as he made faces for us. Good-natured scolding from Ma went unheeded. Oh, the comfort and joy of being just the family of us as we gathered 'round the warm fire, mesmerized by Da's stories that were so well laced with wit and humor.

He regaled us with his adventures of fishing pearls from bubbling streams and rushing rivers; and his escapades in finding buyers for the pearls kept us hanging on every word. However, the hair raising escapes from the Royalists—which reminded him that Ma needed to darken his hair again with the potato water—worried and saddened me. Da had learned to keep those tales for Ma's ears only.

The hard earned coins were always presented to Ma with great pomp and ceremony, much to the delight of we three children. Da would bow low before her, as he would before a queen, and offered his treasure for her scrutiny and pleasure. Ma received it, often misty eyed, as she struggled to choke back the tears that sprung from a heart full of love for her husband. She would then fall into the game and assume a lofty and superior air by first inspecting the coins with great care and curiosity, knowing full well the suspense brought all of us to the edge of our stools. At long last, with grandiose words and gestures, she would accept them, much to our delight.

During those precious moments, Tigh Sona lived up to its name, "Home of peaceful love".

By dawn of the next day, Da was always gone. But the bond of his love could still be felt, tying our little family firmly together. And always, there was another little pearl in the small leather bag I had made to hold my treasure.

Ma was now able to barter for food with the coins, being very careful not to bring attention to herself. Often, she shared with others who had been stripped of their goods by the Royalist dragoons and left without food. She especially made sure that our closest neighbors, Angus and Maggie Winters had some food, as well.

One evening, Da arrived unannounced and stayed only a few moments. He told us he was going to the gathering of the Covenanters at Bothwell Bridge. Under no circumstances were we to try to follow him. He looked at me sternly and said, "And that means you, lassie! Dae ye hear me?"

"Aye, Da," I answered meekly, trying to figure out how to get to Bothwell.

"I know what's goin' on in that wee puddin' head o' yers and I want ye to promise me and yer Ma, that you'll not follow me."

"Aye, Da," I reluctantly agreed.

"Say ye promise!" Da insisted.

"Ah, Da! Very well, I promise!"

"As soon as it's over, I'll come back and make sure ye know about every step I took—*I* promise! Will you agree, now?" Da asked. I agreed—and promised reluctantly, knowing that now I was left with no alternative other than to do as we agreed.

"Ye'll tell me everything, Da? And not get peeved when I ask questions?" I bartered.

"Now, Lizzie, ye know ye can drive a man tae drink wi' yer questions!" He stood in front of me, hands on his hips. Slowly his face relaxed into a smile. "Ye have a deal." Ma turned her back to us but not before I caught the look of pure delight on her face.

Da picked Iain up and hugged him, telling him he was the "man o' the house, now". Jenny waited for her turn, her arms stretched upward. Da's eyes filled with tears as he cuddled her to him and stroked her soft auburn hair. Then he gently set her back down on the floor, obviously reluctant to let her go.

Next, Da turned to me and held me firmly by the shoulders. He bent down until he was able to look at me eye to eye. "Lizzie—Lizzie—how I love you! Remember everything ye've been taught, hen, about choosing right from wrong, and then to have the courage to act upon it!"

"Aye, Da! Oh, aye, I will!" I cried. We threw our arms around each other and I clung to him until he gently pulled away from me.

"Christie..." he began.

"Don't John," Ma cried. "I'll see you as soon as the battle's o'er—and that's that!"

"Aye, ye will—ye will at that!" he said and kissed her long and hard.

"Awa' wi' ye, man! The fightin's going tae be over afore ye even get there!" Ma forced a smile and pushed him towards the door.

He stopped to look at us one more time before ducking around the door skins.

"Oh, John, John, my Jo," Ma whispered.

And he was gone.

CHAPTER 7

JOHN WHITELAW'S BATTLE AT BOTHWELL BRIDGE

On June 29th, 1679, the Countrymen, as the Covenanters were often called, were considering alternatives to gain their objectives. They met at Bothwell Bridge, attempting to agree upon a strategy to resolve the problem of whether or not to fight. However, they were divided upon several issues...too many issues.

A majority of the Covenanters decided upon and wrote a supplication; and this majority also agreed that David Hume, the Laird of Kaitloch, and John Welsh should present it to the Duke of Monmouth, the General of the Royalist Army, who was known to be a peacemaker, approachable and fair. Also, some did say that he was a son of King Charles II, at least the King recognized him as a son.

The supplication requested that, "They, the Covenanters might be allowed the free exercise of religion, to attend gospel ordinances dispensed by their own faithful Presbyterian ministers, without molestation; that a free parliament, and a free general assembly, without the clogs of oaths and declarations, should be allowed to meet, for settling affairs both in church and state; and that all those who now are, or have been in arms, should be indemnified."

However, those of the Covenanters who disagreed with this action, did so out of lack of trust of any agreement that might come out of a conference with the Royalists. While they waited for David Hume and the others to return with the outcome of negotiations, many of the noblemen, who were also now destitute fugitives in the hills, spoke to the blue bonneted men.

For example, the Laird of Torfoot, the same as many other nobles, had lost nearly everything when his estate had been confiscated because he had sheltered some Covenanters and had sided with them.

His wife and babes were stripped by Claverhouse's Life Guards of every remnant of earthly comfort which could be hauled away; and he, himself was doomed as an outlaw, to be taken, executed on the spot—without trial—by these military assassins.

All speeches that day echoed the same theme. What right had any man to do hurt to another? To punish so cruelly. No law was broken. No one harmed. Only a desire to worship God with the spirit of freedom given to every man ever born on this earth. Yet, for all their desire for peace, the Covenanters would not compromise their beliefs...that Christ stood as Head of the Church and could instruct each man individually, according to his faith. And that an intermediary, such as a priest or Episcopalian Bishop, was not necessary, nor acceptable to them.

A call for attention interrupted the sermon. "A trooper advances at full speed!" the watchman cried.

The men remained motionless while their eyes searched the mountainside. The rider approached, waving his blue bonnet above his head. It was David Hackston. He rode into the midst of them, his message tumbling out between gasps for breath. "Claverhouse, Livingston, Dalziel, Monmouth!—they're on the march—listen!"

It was true! The marching boots sounded like distant rolls of thunder. "What of the negotiations?" John Whitelaw cried out to David Hackstone.

"There's still no answer. Our men haven't returned yet. We can't wait any longer—we must prepare to defend ourselves." David stood up in his stirrups, cupping his hands around his mouth as he shouted. "Fall into your ranks. We can hold them back if the Bridge remains ours."

"Choose our officers!" came back the cry.

Sir Robert Hamilton assumed the role of General. A dearth of military leadership resulted in the men milling about, not knowing where to station themselves. In disgust, many simply left the field.

John shuddered because his instincts told him that this was going to be a bloody and losing battle for the Covenanters.

"John!" he heard his brother call him.

"Aye!" he answered.

"I've told Sir Robert that the four o' us would help barricade the bridge while the rest get organized," James Whitelaw instructed his younger brother.

"Where's Matthew and Robert?" John asked, inquiring about his other brothers' whereabouts.

"They're headin' for the Bridge," James answered, reigning his horse in that direction.

A man standing nearby handed John the reins to his horse saying, "God's speed, Whitelaw!" John sprung into the saddle and with a quick salute to his brother in the Gospel, was soon abreast of James. As they approached the Bridge, three riders were crossing at full gallop: it was David Hume, the Laird of Kaitloch and John Walsh. They raced past the Whitelaws, heading toward the main body of Covenanters.

They dismounted at the bridge and could now hear the distant thunder of marching boots growing louder with every passing second.

Under Burley, two hundred of the Covenanter foot soldiers positioned themselves at the Bridge and along the river. Captain Nisbet's dragoons lined the banks of the river, which was not fordable and whoever maintained the Bridge was guaranteed victory.

The Duke of Monmouth, leading his Royalist troops, advanced onto the muir. On the right, a fury breathing Claverhouse led his Life Guards, anxious to erase the disgrace of his defeat at Drumclog. Dalziel placed his men on a knoll to the side of the Bridge. Lord Livingston led the vanguard of the Royalist troops.

The Covenanters at the Bridge were mainly Kippen and Galloway men. The Whitelaw brothers, who were from The Stand in Monkland, stood shoulder to shoulder with them, facing the overwhelming odds of the enemy's numbers. They gripped their large claymores with both hands, waiting for battle.

Bothwell Bridge had been strongly secured by a barricade of rocks and wood. The Covenanters' little battery of cannon was planted on the bank in order to have a clear sweep of the Bridge. John and his brothers watched the Royalists' piper advance at the front of this enemy column and snickered at the sight of a Highlander leading the English. "Puir misguided soul—look at that farce of a sight!"

A tall, black haired man, was bravely leading the Royalists and Highlanders into battle; he played tunes of battle and glory, encouraging those behind him. But the piper was lost in a sudden surge of men who, in vain, tried to push their way through the barricade.

Each attempt the Royalist, Livingston, made to force his troops across the Bridge was met with defeat. For one hour the Covenanters kept their foe in check. Livingston wisely sent another strong column to storm the Bridge.

A line of Royalists advanced with all the military glory of brave men—the horses pranced—their armor gleamed...and the Covenanters' battery fired upon them. In one moment there was a mangled mass of mortality before them. Limbs and bodies of humans and horses commingled in one huge heap, while others were blown in pieces into the distance.

One more column attempted to cross above the Bridge but some men from Burley's troops threw them into disorder, and drove them back.

While the Covenanters on the Bridge were in the heat of the battle, Sir Robert was laboring to bring the differing divisions of the main body of Covenanters into action. However, in vain he called on Colonel Cleland's troop—in vain he ordered Henderson's to fall in—in vain he called on Colonel Fleming's men.

Hackston flew from troop to troop—all was in confusion; he, also in vain besought, entreated, and threatened. The Covenanters' disputes and fiery misguided zeal had contracted a deep and deadly guilt.

The Whig turned his arm in fierce hate, that day, against his own vitals.

The ministers, Cargill, King, Kid, and Douglas pleaded with the main body of Covenanters. Finally, Cargill stood and preached concord. He called aloud for mutual forbearance. "Behold the banners of the enemy!" he cried. "Are ye deaf to their fire, and to our own brethren? Our brothers and fathers are falling beneath their sword. They need our help—*now!* See the flag of the Covenant. See the motto in letters of gold—CHRIST'S CROWN AND THE COVENANT. Hear the voice of your weeping country. Hear the wailing of the bleeding Kirk. Banish discord. Let us, as a band of brothers, present a bold front to the Royalists. Follow me, all ye who love your country and the Covenant. If I am to die, I will die in the forefront of the battle!" cried Cargill.

All of the ministers and officers followed him—amidst a flourish of trumpets—but a greater number remained to listen to the harangues of the factious.

The Laird of Torfoot was on the Bridge and found that his men and himself were down to their last round of ammunition. He sent for more powder. When the barrels arrived they were found to be full of raisins. Was this treachery or a fatal error?

David Hackston called his officers around him. "What must be done?" he asked in agony of despair.

"Conquer or die!" they answered him. "We have our swords yet. Lead the men back to their places, and let the ensign bear down the blue and white colors. Our God and Our country be the word!"

Hackston and his men rushed forward against the enemy once more. The officers ran to their respective corps—trying to cheer their men, who were now dispirited. Their ammunition was nearly expended, and they seemed anxious to save what little remained. They fought only with their limited range carbines. The cannons could not be loaded any more, a situation the enemy soon perceived.

A troop of horsemen approached the Bridge. It was that of the Royalist Life Guards. John recognized Claverhouse's plumed helmet as they approached in rapid march. A solid column of infantry followed.

"John Whitelaw!" the Laird of Torfoot called out. "Take my request to Captain Nisbet to join his troop to mine."

Quickly, John left the Bridge and delivered the request. Nisbet responded immediately and John returned to the Bridge in time to join in the charge against the Life Guards. Their swords rang out as they struck the Royalists' steel caps. Many brave men fell on both sides. The Covenanters hewed down the foe. The Royalists began to reel, which kept the whole column stationary and prevented them from taking the bridge.

John could hear Claverhouse's dreadful voice—more like the yell of a savage than the commanding voice of an officer—pushing his men forward. Again, the Covenanters hewed them down.

A third mass of Royalists was pushed up. The exhausted Covenanters fled the Bridge. "James! Behind ye!" John shouted. Before James could ward off the blow, a Royalist sword came down on his head. John rushed toward his brother, only to be thrown against the unrelenting stones of the side of the Bridge. He spun around, his sword ready. But one of Claverhouse's dragoons rushed headlong at him, sending him flying over the side of the Bridge into the water below.

Only the Laird of Torfoot, the brave Nisbet, Paton and Hackston remained on the Bridge. They glanced at each other in silence and on an unspoken signal, galloped in front of their retreating men and rallied them.

A short distance away, Sir Robert Hamilton was standing almost entirely alone now with the blue and white colors floating near him.

The other officers desperately cried out, "See yonder our brave leader—see our colors flying about him! God and Our Country, men! For God and our Country!."

Spurred on by brave Sir Robert, their men faced about and with a fierce roar charged Claverhouse once more.

"Torfoot!" cried Nisbet, "I dare you to the fore-front of the battle!" and they rushed forward at full gallop. Their men, seeing this, followed at full speed; their inspired strength broke the enemy line as they bore down each file they met and cut their way through the Royalist ranks. But the Royalists had now lengthened their front and their superior numbers rose against the Covenanters and drove them back.

The Royalists finally took the Bridge—Bothwell Bridge.

Livingston and Dalziel were overtaking the Covenanters on the flank with bloody and disastrous results. A band of Claverhouse's dragoons had managed to get between Torfoot and Nisbet and Burley's infantry.

"My friends," shouted Hackston to his officers, "we are the last on the field. We can do no more. We must retreat. Let us attempt, at least, to bring aid to those deluded men behind us. They have brought ruin on themselves and on us. Not Monmouth, but our own divisions, have scattered us."

At that moment one of the Life Guards aimed a blow at Hackston. Torfoot's sword received it—and a stroke from Nisbet laid the Royalist's hand and sword in the dust. He fainted and tumbled from his saddle. They reined their horses, and galloped to the main body of Covenanters.

What a terrible scene presented itself!

The misguided men had their eyes now fully opened to their fatal errors. The enemy was bringing up its whole force against them. Torfoot and some of the other officers gathered on a knoll and faced about to watch the battle rage below them.

They witnessed Sir Robert of Hamilton do everything that a brave soldier could do with factious men against an overpowering foe. Burley and his troops were in close conflict with Claverhouse's dragoons where he, himself, dismounted three dragoons with his own hand. Although he could not turn the tide of battle, he did his utmost to cover the retreat of the now frightened Covenanters.

Before the men on the knoll could rejoin Burley, a party led by Kennoway, one of Claverhouse's officers, attacked them. "I pray to God this was Grahame himself" one of the Covenanters was heard to shout.

"He's mine!" demanded Torfoot as he advanced toward Kennoway. Several thrusts were parried before Torfoot dismounted him. The Royalist party was soon disposed of and the officers turned their attention to the battle below.

Dalziel and Livingston were riding over the field like furious madmen, cutting down every countryman in their way.

Monmouth galloped from rank to rank and called on his men to give quarter but Claverhouse countermanded the order. In his attempt to wipe away the disgrace of Drumclog, he created heinous and fearful havoc.

"Let us find Clavers!" cried Haugh-head, one of the Covenanter officers.

"No use! The gallant colonel takes care to have a solid guard of his rogues about him at all times!" replied Captain Paton, sarcastically. "I've kept my eye on him, but he's continually surrounded by a mass of his guards."

At that moment, the Laird and others realized that it was Sir Robert who was disentangling himself from the men who had tumbled over him in the melee. He emerged with his face and hands and clothes covered with gore. Although he had been dismounted, he was fiercely fighting on foot and within seconds they rushed to his aid and drove back Dalziel's scattered bands.

"My friends," said Sir Robert, as they mounted him on a stray horse, "the day is lost! But you Paton, you Brownlee of Torfoot, and you Haugh-head, let not that flag fall into the hands of these incarnate devils. We have lost the battle, but, by the grace of God, neither Dalziel nor Clavers' shall say he took our colors. My ensign has done his duty. He is down. This sword has saved it twice. I leave it to your care. Look—you see its' perilous situation," he cried, pointing with his sword to the spot. Paton and others collected the scattered troops and flew toward the banner.

The standard bearer was almost dead, but was still fearlessly grasping the flag staff that was being held upright by the mass of men who had thrown themselves in fierce contest around it...a twisted tangle of flesh, both dead and dying.

Its' well known blue and white colors, and its motto, CHRIST'S CROWN AND COVENANT in brilliant gold letters, inspired the Covenanters with a reverent, pulsating enthusiasm. They gave a loud cheer to the wounded ensign, and rushed into the combat. The redemption of that flag cost the Royalists many who fell beneath the Covenanters' broad swords. With horrible expletives dying on their lips, they gave up their souls to their Judge.

"There he is!" cried Torfoot as he recognized the ferocious dragoon of Claverhouse's. It was none other than Tam Halliday, who, more than once in his raids had plundered the Laird's halls, snatching the very bread from his weeping babes. Halliday seized the white staff of the flag and had only just shouted a great oath of victory when the Laird's Ferrara sword struck his, Halliday's sword, with such force that it shivered into pieces.

"You'll remember your evil ways, this day!" the Laird shouted viciously at Halliday and struck him again, this time laying him out cold on the heath.

The Covenanters fought like raging lions. The Laird wrenched the standard out of the grip of yet another Royalist. It was torn and tattered but he wrapped it around his own body and with others, cut their way through the enemy, while carrying the exhausted Sir Robert off the field. They retreated once again to the knoll and looked back down upon the dreadful spectacle below.

It was no longer a battle, but a massacre.

"I cannot leave the field!" said the undaunted Paton. "With your permission, General, I shall try to save some of our men from those hellhounds!" He looked around at the exhausted men. "Who will join me?"

"I will be your leader!" cried Sir Robert.

"Look! There's Clavers'!" Paton shouted. The bloody man was at that moment nearly alone, hacking to pieces some poor fellows already on their knees, disarmed and imploring him to spare their lives. He had just finished his usual oath against their "feelings of humanity" when Paton presented himself. Claverhouse instantly let go of his prey and slunk back into the midst of his troopers. Having formed them around him, he advanced.

Those Covenanters left on the field formed and made a furious onset. At their first charge, Claverhouse's troop reeled and Claverhouse was dismounted. But at that moment, Dalziel attacked on the flank and rear. Countrymen fell like grass before the mower.

The bugle men sounded a retreat.

Once more in the melee, Torfoot fell in with the General and Paton; all were covered with wounds. They now directed their flight in the rear of their broken troops. By the direction of the General, the Laird of Torfoot had unfurled the standard. He carried it off the field, flying it at the sword's point. But that honor cost him much. He was assailed by three fierce dragoons; five more followed close in the rear. He called to Paton, who, in a moment, was by Torfoot's side.

The Laird threw the standard to Sir Robert and he and Paton rushed once more at the enemy. The Royalists fell beneath their swords; but Torfoot's faithful horse, which had carried him through his dangers, was mortally wounded and took the Laird down with him as he fell, throwing his master among the fallen enemy. Torfoot fainted.

He opened his eyes on misery, to find himself in the presence of Monmouth—as a prisoner—with other wretched creatures, awaiting in awful suspense their ultimate destiny.

* * * *

John regained consciousness—a chaotic clamor of battle sounds ringing in his ears. Screams—blood curdling screams of his dying and wounded friends pushed him into action. He tried to leap to his feet, but his head reeled and he fell backwards, once again onto the wet earth.

"Yer not wantin' tae be out there, rebel," a soft Gaelic voice told him.

John turned to see a muddy Highlander smiling at him. He looked vaguely familiar. It was the black hair—or was it the beard? John stared at him and shook his head, as if clearing his brain, and stared at him again.

The Highlander laughed at him. "MacLeod's the name...Rory MacLeod," he offered genially, as though there wasn't a war raging about them.

"I'm Whitelaw of Monkland—John Whitelaw." It was John's turn to laugh. "Well, we've gotten that out of the way, what now?"

"Ye suppose we ought to try to capture one another?" MacLeod asked, smiling broadly.

"Wouldn't take much tae take me out right now!" John admitted.

"Aye, I know," MacLeod agreed calmly. "Although, the way you came over the side of that bridge...your neck should be broken. You must be as strong as two short planks...or is it that you're as thick as two short planks?" The laughter in the Highlander's eyes put John at ease.

"Ahh, right! Right!" John narrowed his eyes, remembering. He recalled falling over the edge of the bridge...but everything else was a blank. This big Highlander must have pulled him out of the river and dragged him up on this bank. "Why?" John asked, looking deeply into his rescuers eyes.

"Ach, I dunno. Seemed like a waste to let ye drown," was his simple answer. MacLeod continued closely examining something...John wasn't sure just what was holding his interest, so moved closer to see for himself.

"One o' you rebels did this tae my pipes." MacLeod growled at John as he held up his bagpipes to reveal that the chanter had been neatly sliced in half. "Do ye have any idea how precious these pipes are—do ye?" Rory roared at his new companion.

John shrugged his shoulders, feeling helpless under the barrage of venom-filled words that were being pelted at him.

"Whitelaw, don't aggravate me by playing the dunce!! These pipes belonged to my Uncle who was the piper for the Clan MacLeod. Dae ye know what an honor that is?? Dae ye?? Kings pay a high price to have a piper play for them at court."

John shrugged his shoulders again, although he did know, he wasn't taking a chance to even speak to this big highlander—not in the temper he was in at the moment.

"Do you know how much time it takes to make a set of pipes? Do you?" His voice was raising to a 'battle' pitch. "The ironwood is imported from Africa and after it has been dried out for two years—two years, mind you—then, and only then does the pipe maker carefully select the straightest limbs and begins to bore through the center, making sure that the hole is only 9/16th of an inch—nothing less or more—and that's just the beginning—the sound has to be perfect—the holes in the chanter have to be placed just right to bring forth the sound of bells ringing when the fingers strike it—that takes years to get it right!! Then they are turned leaving a design on the outside—see these lines and beads and how they are spaced—well that tells me who made this set—a great pipe maker, he was—

but he's dead now—so tell, me, Whitelaw—how in the devil am I going to match up another chanter to the drones—the man's dead!!" he shouted, his voice still at a fever pitch, cracked under the emotion.

For a moment, John watched Rory carefully, expecting him to break out in tears at any moment.

"Ohh!!" Rory wailed, "what a loss!!" but no tears appeared, much to John's relief.

In a stumbling effort to console Rory, John offered, "Would ye like me tae tell ye how to make golf balls and clubs...?" But all he got for his attempts at comforting his rescuer was a roaring threat that, "If these weren't so precious to me and my family, I'd wrap them around that rebel neck of yours!"

Then the light went on for John. "Yer the piper! I thought I'd seen ye before!" he cried out innocently.

Rory MacLeod peered closely at John's red hair showing through the mud. "And you! You were with the other three carrot tops—must have been your brothers!"

"Aye! That's us!" John said excitedly. However, reality set in at the mention of his brothers. John's face clouded in a frown and he struggled to get up. But, at that exact moment, a voice boomed from the Bridge, startling John and knocking him back down onto the ground.

"He's got red hair—there were four of them...only three are here!" an English Royalist cried out.

"Then I'm wagering that it was John Whitelaw that's got away! Clavers' won't be amused to know that he got away!"

"And Lauderdale will have our hides as well!" was the rejoiner.

"Then he's probably lying out on the field," another added hopefully.

"Naw, not him. He's got away again—a slippery one, that! But as far as I know—yer right—he's out there—dead. I'm not gonna lose my skin over the likes o' him. So...s'that our story?"

"You're right, that's our story, mate," was the answer.

Rory MacLeod looked long and hard at John, with a growing respect lighting up his eyes. Finally, he raised his eyebrows in a silent salute and then nodded his head in approval, causing John to feel easier with this big man—who was supposed to be his enemy.

John was now able to take his eyes from his companion to scrutinize his surroundings. He and MacLeod were fortunately concealed behind some bush growing close to the underside of the Bridge. He moved around where he could get a clearer view. The sight revolted him!

Bodies of both Covenanters and Royalists were strewn up and down the banks of the river.

Approaching voices caused John and Rory to flatten themselves behind the bush. The voices grew louder and louder. Soon, it became obvious that Royalist soldiers were looking for wounded rebels to take prisoner or shoot on the spot.

"What dae we do now, MacLeod?" John asked when the danger had passed.

"What dae we do now, Whitelaw?" Rory replied sarcastically in a falsetto voice. "How the...how'm I supposed to know? I didn't want to be here in the first place!"

"Nor I!" John shot back in an angry whisper.

Rory MacLeod stared at him in silence for a moment. "I don't know why, but I believe ye!" he said sullenly.

"Look," John began to reason, "if yer gonna take me prisoner...let's get at it instead o' playing cat and mouse wi' each other!"

"I don't want ye—just what in heaven's name would I do wi' *you*! I just want tae fix my pipes and get back tae my studies!" MacLeod stated emphatically.

"That's all I'm wantin' as well! Well, to go hame—at least! What studies?" asked John curiously.

"I'm in medical school at the University of Glasgow and they dragged us out here—to fight; and someone told them I was a piper—so nothing for it but I had to lead them in this battle—or else! And I'm supposed to be studying how to save lives!" Rory barked back at him.

"Look, MacLeod, I'm in no mood for yer sass! My brothers are lying dead...right above me...and..." John's words trailed off.

Rory stared at John intently for several moments before speaking. "The blood thirsty devils are at work, right now." He jerked his head toward the battlefield. "I could walk out there, no problem, but they'd put a carbine in my hand and expect me to kill anything that moved. Take a look for yourself!"

John maneuvered himself to where he had a view of the field. Rory was right. Claverhouse was cutting down men to the right and to the left of him, while many of them were even on their knees, begging for their lives. His dragoons were stripping the Covenanters of their clothing and leaving them all but naked before forcing them to lie down on the blood soaked heath. There, the Royalists murdered the Countrymen in cold blood.

"That's been going on for more than two hours." Rory informed John. "It's disgusting! I'll not align myself with that kind of butchery!"

Their eyes never left the field while they spoke to each other. Loud shouts, commanding the Royalist soldiers to tie their prisoners two by two were screamed across the battlefield.

"We're better off here, waiting until the field is cleared. Then we can make a run for it," Rory suggested.

"Aye—yer right," agreed John as he leaned back against the stone foundation of the Bridge. "But I'm not running for it! I'll follow this bunch—at a distance—to see if I can cut away any of the prisoners."

"I'm goin' the other way!" stated Rory.

"What's that?" asked John.

"The opposite direction to you, Whitelaw, that's what!"

"Oh..."

They sat still for a long time, watching the butchery and brutality Claverhouse was carrying out against the Covenanters. When night began to fall, great shouts of "Get up—you rebel" cut through the air. The prisoners were being dragged to their feet to begin the march.

"Where're they takin' them?" Rory asked.

"Probably into Edinburgh," John answered. "Ach, look at that!" he said disgustedly.

Rory looked to where John was pointing and shuddered as well. Claverhouse had two of his dragoons drag a man with a wounded and bleeding leg to his feet while he whipped his back shouting, "Walk, Whig! Walk!"

Eventually, the battlefield was emptied of all prisoners. Only the dead were left and already the human scavengers were picking at the dead bodies, searching for anything that could be sold for money.

Rory was quiet a long time before he spoke. "John, I'm not a religious man—didn't hear much about it in the Highlands—but what Clavers' and the likes of him are doing isn't right! What are your plans? How do you figure you can help them?"

"Not sure—I just know I'm gonna try!"

"How are ye? Can ye move?" Rory asked.

"Aye, I think so." answered John, as he carefully moved his head from one side to the other. However, he winced with the pain in his shoulder as he pulled himself to his feet and was glad for the cover of darkness. "It's dark enough, they won't see us th' now."

"Aye."

John Whitelaw and Rory MacLeod, one a Lowlander and the other a Highlander, emerged cautiously from under the bridge.

"First, I'm gonna look for my brothers," John announced.

"You wait here. It'll be safer if I take a look," said Rory firmly as he turned to climb the bank up to the bridge.

John waited.

"They're here, John." Rory called down to him, his voice suddenly less gruff. "There's nothing ye can do..." he said as he climbed down the bank and, taking John firmly by the arm, led him away from the bloody scene.

"Cum' on, John! Yer right! There *is* something we can do for those poor devils ahead of us. Let's go!"

John held back, wanting to go to his brothers. He looked Rory in the eye, seeking the truth. "I need to bury them—at least that much, McLeod!" he pleaded with the much stronger man.

"John," Rory said quietly as he firmly led the unwilling man away from the Bridge, "it'll do you no good to see it—trust me—let's just try to help the others. I'll try to get back and bury them—I promise—if I can."

It was a promise he managed to keep.

John reluctantly let himself be led away. The battlefield was a sea of blood that oozed over their shoes with each step that they took.

"Over this way!" Rory said. "It'll take longer but we won't have to walk through this!"

Once on higher and drier ground, they made up for lost time. Darkness had closed in and made it hard to see how far the prisoners were in front of them but conversely, it was just as hard for the Royalists to see them.

"What's that?" John put a restraining hand on Rory's shoulder. They listened. It sounded inhuman, like the groans and cries one might expect to hear in hell.

"It's them—the prisoners," said Rory. He sounded almost apologetic. "I am ashamed that I let them brow beat me into leading them as their piper—I've never regretted anything more in my life!"

They pushed forward, sometimes walking, sometimes running, dodging from tree to tree. "There!" John said, pointing into the darkness. "See those four prisoners at the rear?" John asked.

"Aye," answered Rory, squinting at the shadowy figures. "There's only one guard on them—I'll take the guard and you loose the prisoners."

"Won't the others hear ye?" Rory asked.

"Cum' on, Hielan' man! Ye know what I'm talkin' about!" John taunted the big Highlander.

"Aye. I'm afraid I do." Rory agreed, resigned to the plan.

They slipped quietly through the trees until the exhausted marchers—guards and prisoners—were only a few feet ahead of them. John touched Rory's sleeve, silently pointing at the last man in the line who was dressed in the Royalist uniform. Rory responded by giving a quick nod of his head. John crept forward, silently coming up behind the soldier and with his hand clamped tightly over the guard's mouth, John plunged his knife into his victim's heart...he felt it slide into the man's body and for a brief moment, realized a power he had never experienced before. With enormous strength, John held him in a death grip until the soldier stopped fighting and only then did John let him slip quietly to the ground. "It was you or me, 'goon!" John whispered into the dead man's ear.

"Appleby—any trouble back there?" another guard shouted.

"No! No trouble—they wouldn't dare!" Rory answered with a perfect English accent while he quickly cut the Countrymen's ropes, freeing their wrists and ankles.

Leaning on and pulling each other, the four freed prisoners staggered toward the trees, then disappeared into the darkness.

There was no sense of victory in carrying out their grim work. John and Rory worked systematically, taking turns in felling the guards and freeing the prisoners.

They managed to cut loose twenty-three men before a guard came riding back to discover what was happening.

"Prisoners escaped! Prisoners escaped!" he shouted over and over into the black night as he galloped to report to his leaders.

John and Rory slipped into the trees and listened to the commotion from a distance. Several guards were sent to protect the rear of the inhumane procession and with them vanished the opportunity to release more prisoners. As the freed men evaporated into the blackness of the night, John and Rory found themselves alone. "Shall we follow them to Edinburgh?" asked Rory.

"Aye, that way we might be able to cut loose a few more," was the ready answer.

They didn't arrive in Edinburgh for two days; it was dawn when they slipped into the soot-blackened city. John pulled a tattered bonnet over his red hair so as not to bring attention to himself. Positioned across from the Greyfriar's Kirk, they watched as the prisoners were herded into the cramped quarters of the churchyard. This was the beginning of one of the most brutal incarcerations ever inflicted upon man by man. The prisoners suffered from exposure to the elements and from hunger for months on end, many dying, thus being mercifully released from their torture.

John and Rory, always together, surreptitiously assisted the prisoners in whatever way they could, most often by sneaking food to them and carrying messages back and forth between them and their families. Regardless of their own endless bantering and chiding, they were always there, protecting each other's back.

When John was able to return home and relate the story of his escape—over and over again—he always concluded with, "Aye, Lizzie, the Lord hadn't left me entirely alone. In the midst of affliction he had provided me a brother—Rory MacLeod. I tell ye, lass, brothers could've not been closer than we were."

CHAPTER 8

(FOUR YEARS LATER—1683)

Ma's movements seemed nervous. She worked quickly to prepare our supper. An anxious glance was tossed at me as she flitted between the hearth and the table. "Lizzie, will ye keep those two quiet? Supper won't be long, now; the stew's just about ready and Lizzie…." Her words trailed off as she stirred the stew.

The aroma of the fresh baked scones filled the cottage, tantalizing Jenny and Iain. Putting a quieting arm around each of them and pulling them to my side, I whispered, "Hush! The more noise you make, the longer Ma'll take!"

I smiled at the facial expressions of my younger sister and brother. Their eyes never left Ma as she cut generous pieces of cheese onto the large pewter plate.

Iain whimpered. "I know you're starvin' Iain." I tried to console him by holding him in my arms and rocking gently back and forth. Thin, sandy red hair seemed to make his little face even paler. The difficult times we were living in had taken their toll, causing him to be small and frail for his six years.

I loved to watch my mother. She was so gentle, yet strong, and as ever, beautiful—but seemingly unaware of her beauty. As she lifted scones from griddle to plate, a honey-golden curl fell onto her forehead. She looked like a young girl, as in vain, she tried to brush it back into place.

The moment passed too fast—that fleeting moment when I glimpsed what Ma must have looked like when she was young—maybe around my age. I wasn't as beautiful as Ma so I always strained to catch any similarities. How I wished I looked like my Ma! Instead I inherited Da's flaming red hair—but I did get Ma's eyes.

Ma turned once more to the blazing peat fire. Dancing flames cast unfair shadows that deepened the furrows on her brow and emphasized the long lines beside her mouth. I was still for a few moments, until I became conscious of something pressing upon my senses—coaxing for my attention. The music of the day had sounded too many sour notes.

Something was wrong!

"Ma, why do ye keep lookin' outside?" I asked. I had been blessed with an intuition that warned me of danger far in advance of the actual happening. Most folks said I had second sight and was blessed to have this gift; however, it was a burden most of the time because I had learned to keep the warning to myself, not wanting others to have to endure the wait for the axe to fall, as well.

Fear—ugly and all too familiar—was tightening its' hold on me again. "Where's Da?" I demanded. "He's outside, waiting for dark so's he can come in, isn't he? Oh, Ma, do you think the dragoons followed him here?"

"They haven't so far, have they?" Her answer was sharp and not like her. What a quandary! We wanted more than anything to see our Da, but there was always the fear that the enemy had followed him and we knew that there was no possibility of reprieve if they caught him.

"Ma?" I begged for another answer but her face told me the truth. "No, not again! Oh, not again but...I will see my Da!" I cried to myself, fearing for my father's life.

That was all we had known for the last four years—agonizing fear—ever since the Battle of Bothwell Bridge. The Highland Host hunted by day and by night for my father, chasing him from glen to glen and into the hill caves. But they never caught him. No! not John Whitelaw! He had made a fool of the King's Army.

Da never left us without food or money to buy it. This, he seemed almost passionate about—that his family would not go hungry. Besides the weaving that Ma learned to do and the pearls that Da fished out of the stream, he made golf clubs and golf balls.

This he would do when he slipped into our small haven under cover of night. These balls were very much sought after as the nobility had taken up the game of golf. Da had learned to take bull hide and cut it into oval strips and then would sew them together into the shape of a ball. Then Ma would boil down a top hat full of feathers for Da to force into the bull hide ball. He did this by poking the wet feathers into the ball and then tamping them in tighter and tighter with an iron rod that was flat on one end. He then placed the flattened end of the rod against his chest and pulled the ball toward him, crushing more and more feathers into the ball with the other end of the rod, making it hard and round. When all of feathers had been pushed into the small ball, Da sewed up the opening, creating a perfectly round golf ball. Da told us that these golf balls sold for a high price and only the nobility could afford the game as a ball only lasted for three or four hits.

He made the golf clubs from hedgewood that grew near the bank of the streams. The root grew out of the bank at right angles and then turned upward toward the sun, making a perfect club. Da carefully extracted the best of these roots with limbs that were about an inch thick and as straight as possible and then polished the wood until it gleamed. When he sold one of these sets, Ma was able to lay in more staples, which she always shared with our neighbors, especially those who had been ravaged by the dragoons.

Ma looked up from the plate of steaming scones she had set on the table. Her face was sad as she eased herself wearily into the big chair and stretched out loving arms toward us.

Jenny and Iain scrambled onto her lap like eager young pups. Looking over their heads at me, she said, "Lizzie, I'm sorry. How I wish you didn't have to deal with all of this. You're so young to have an old head forced onto yer shoulders. It's not fair, pet!"

"I'm not that young, Ma! I'm almost eighteen! Most of the lassies are married at my age!" I was impatient. Not impatient with my mother; it was the "old head put on my young shoulders" bit that kept grating on me. "Wish I'd a penny for every time that's said to me!" I grumbled to myself. "Wish they'd let me grow up!"

For the moment, supper was forgotten as Jenny and Iain greedily wallowed in our mother's affection. Suddenly, Ma stiffened. She grasped Jenny and Iain by the arms and held them tightly as they slid from her lap when she stood up.

"Quiet!" she whispered, a finger pressed to her lips. We listened—not daring to breathe.

The unmistakable sound of horses at full gallop propelled her into motion. She flew to the huge weaving loom and pulled it away from the wall, motioning for us to hurry over to her.

"Ah, Ma!" Jenny moaned. "Let us stay out, just this time. Please Ma!" she begged.

I didn't blame Jenny. It was always the same men—the same words—the same threats. This wasn't new to us.

"That's enough!" The tone of Ma's voice put a stop to our whining. "Now, get in there...or are you all daft?" Her voice was rising, which meant that a stinging slap was soon to find it's mark on our backsides. We rolled into the pile of wool behind the weaving loom. I detested the odor of raw wool. "Rotten lard! That's what it smelled like!"

"Ma! Please! I'm old enough to hold my own with them. Please let me stand beside ye." I begged.

"Lizzie, that's exactly the problem. You are old enough," she paused before adding, "and pretty enough to catch their eye. Those soldiers would have you before ye could blink. Now, don't you worry. I can handle them."

"They might not get over the bog," I said hopefully.

"They've finally figured that out. We can't depend on the bog keeping them away anymore." Ma's voice was once again quiet and controlled. She continued to whisper reassurances as she tucked the wool around us, urging us to hurry. We wiggled uncomfortably as twigs and burrs in the uncarded wool stuck into our skin. "I hate this! I hate it! The smell is putrid, Ma!" I grumbled.

"Just think about how beautiful your skin will be with all of this good sheep oil on it—look at mine!" she said with a wink and a forced smile. It was true—Ma's skin was beautiful and everyone said that when women carded and spun wool that the sheep oil kept their skin smooth.

"Ah, Ma..." I continued to whine.

"Wheesht!" Ma chided. "I'm going to pull the loom in front of you. You'll be safe, you'll see." I knew that she was consoling herself. "I want you to be still—not one peep—no matter what happens." She paused briefly. The silence was effective. "Did you hear me? Not so much as a peep." To ensure that we would keep our promises, she added, "You want harm com'n to your Da and me? Well, do you?"

Jenny and Iain shook their heads and I said reluctantly, "Aw, Ma. Don't start that! I'll make sure they're quiet."

Hiding with the young ones was embarrassing. I really wanted to be with my mother, not cowering in here. Both Ma and Da insisted that I would be of more use keeping the young ones out of sight when the soldiers came to search for Da.

This time Ma seemed to linger longer than usual...making sure we could breathe properly, tucking in bits of wool. Finally she whispered, "I love each one of you more than life itself. Always remember that, no matter what happens!" Then she added quietly, "God bless you—always, please."

I listened to her footsteps move toward the door. It squeaked open. "John! They'll soon be here!" she whispered hoarsely through cupped hands.

Muffled, but unmistakable, the voice of our father faintly floated through the air saying, "Aye, I know!" which brought a surprised cry of "Da!" from the depths of our hiding place.

"Lizzie!" Ma shouted. "Keep Iain still!"

"Aye, Ma!" I put an arm around Iain, coaxing him to 'coorie in'.

"Jenny," I said, "put your fingers in your ears. I'll tell you when they're gone." Still holding tightly to Iain, I managed to push away some of the wool and wiggle around until I could see through an unfinished part of the blanket on the loom that Ma was weaving for our bed.

I watched Ma hide our supper behind the stack of dried brown peat we used for our fire.

The sound of horses galloping toward our cottage grew louder and louder, bringing a mounting terror with each hoof beat.

The Royalists had managed to cross the bog! Curses, mingled with the thunder of their horses' hoofs suddenly exploded at our door followed by a shower of splinters, as our precious new wooden door was kicked open once more.

Five soldiers barged into our small cottage; three were Royalists and the other two were of the Highland Host, kilted in their dark green and black tartan.

"Where is he, Christie?" a soldier demanded as his eyes swept around the room.

That voice—I had heard it before, but where and why is he calling my mother by her first name as if he knows her?

"Speak up! We want John Whitelaw!" another demanded.

"Where have you hidden him?"

Three of the soldiers pulled out their swords and thrust them savagely upward into the thatched roof, while the one that seemed to be in charge just glared at my mother. Soon the cottage was filled with bits of straw floating to the floor.

"Dumb oxes!" I thought as I watched them make sure my Da wasn't hiding in the roof. That proved they didn't know what he looked like if they thought he could hide in the roof straw.

Ma clamped her lips together tightly.

"You *are* Mrs. Whitelaw, are you not?" one soldier asked as he moved toward the loom. I held my breath and put a firm hand over Iain's mouth.

Ma cried out in a clear strong voice, diverting his attention, "Aye, that I am!"

"Well, now! Let's see what being Mrs. John Whitelaw is going to do for you. That is, of course, if you insist on protecting him," sneered the soldier who was moving toward the loom. The next ensuing few seconds of silence were unbearable. Finally, the soldier turned from the loom so as to hear Ma's answer.

Ma never took her eyes from the one in charge. He growled out a laugh and said, "I am pleased to see that you haven't forgotten me, Christian Gray!"

My brain strained to remember where I had heard that voice before. Of course! The memory burst upon my senses when he called Ma by her maiden name. It was the same soldier who had treated us so brutally when we were trying to bury Grandda. It was Captain Lauderdale!

"You didn't really think that I would ever forget you, did you? It's been a long time, Christie, but the years have treated you well." He reached out and touched her cheek and then let his hand slip over her neck, lingering on her bare skin and then gently cupped her breast. "I'm sure you have thought of me—one way or the other," he said, almost hopefully. For a brief moment he had let his guard down and appeared surprisingly weak in front of his men and me.

Ma shuddered at his touch and snapped, "Don't!" and jerked away from him. "Wallace Lauderdale, you never enter my thoughts! You are nothing but filth!" Ma spat her words at the Captain, sending her venom into the soft underbelly of this otherwise brutal man.

The soldiers were immobilized by her words and I, too, knew that only disaster would follow that outburst. Quietly, in a voice that betrayed his hurt—a hurt that was quickly turning again into a cold rage, Captain Lauderdale said, "You will forever regret that you came to feel that way."

His face turned hard, like rock...grey granite...before he continued. "Now, you will learn what happens to Scotch wenches when they do not obey. You must obey—that's what women are supposed to do—or haven't you learned that yet?" He stamped his booted foot hard on the dirt floor, looking like a spoiled child and interrupting his own tirade. "Obey the king—the English King—take the Oath! And obey ***me***!! With each word the pitch of his voice became higher and higher until he was screeching, much like the fish wives I had heard at the market when they fought among themselves. His soldiers seemed almost embarrassed at his performance and in unison stared at the floor.

"Duncan, see those eggs?" Captain Lauderdale, seemingly oblivious to Ma's anger and his soldiers' discomfort, pointed calmly to the basket of eggs. "Take two and drop them into that pot of boiling water."

"Aye, Captain." Duncan seemed relieved to have something to do and jumped to his task.

Plop—plop—I heard the eggs being dropped into the water. The silence was cruel. The only sound, now, was the water bubbling around the eggs.

Finally, after what seemed an eternity, the Captain spoke. His voice purred with superiority and condescension. "That'll do Duncan; roll them into the peat fire."

The metal spoon scraped against the pot as Duncan scooped the eggs out of the steaming water. Ma gasped! She knew what was coming. And so did I! Iain wriggled, reminding me that my job was to keep him quiet. I did this, although my every raging instinct demanded that I go to my mother's defense.

Duncan rolled the eggs into the red, hot embers of the peat fire while Ma stood still, silently defiant. One of the soldiers laughed loudly, grabbed Ma's hair and turned her head toward the fire. The others displayed insane pleasure in watching her stare at the eggs as they slowly turned black...watching her eyes widening with fear.

Every pulse in my body was beating wildly.

"That's enough—they're ready. Hold her arms up!" the Captain shouted; then he laughed—a high pitched animal-like screech. "Just a moment. We wouldn't want her to miss the full benefit..." He grabbed the front of Ma's stay and ripped it apart, leaving her breasts exposed.

Duncan's gloved hands picked up the eggs. Just then Iain began fighting and I clamped my hand even more tightly over his mouth. To keep his legs from kicking, I tucked them under my own. What was the matter with Iain? Didn't he know that his very life was in danger?

Soldiers, on either side of Ma, yanked her arms into the air, almost pulling them out of their sockets. Pain twisted her beautiful face. And then, the one called 'Duncan', stepped toward her; the blackened eggs in his outstretched gloved hands.

"Tell us where John Whitelaw is hiding! Save yourself this agony, woman! Where is he?" Lauderdale demanded. But Ma's only response was to clamp her teeth over her bottom lip.

"Once more! Where is he? You will obey me and answer!" he screamed. Without waiting for an answer, Lauderdale snatched the blackened eggs from Duncan and rammed them into Ma's bared armpits. The two soldiers, standing beside her, immediately brought her arms down, pinning them to her sides...locking in the torturous eggs. A long, piercing scream ripped through the room! I held Iain tightly and hugged Jenny to me with my other arm.

"Oh, Ma! Ma!" I cried silently as I watched her sway slightly; then her dress billowed around her as she crumpled limply to the floor.

Suddenly, my father, wild eyed and angry, his bushy red hair making him look even more ferocious, was pushed into the cottage by two soldiers.

"He's mad!" one of the soldiers complained, "fought like a bloody madman, trying to get in here!"

Da's eyes were blazing! "Does it tak' five o' ye tae hold down one lassie?"

"Run, Christie...run!" he shouted, swinging at the soldiers. But there was no response. Ma had fainted.

"Take him! Or I'll make sure you'll swing instead of him!" Lauderdale yelled at his men.

"Ahrgg!" Da roared as two of the soldiers slammed him against the wall and another ran a sword through his shoulder.

"Da! Da!" The words struggled to be shouted. My father was wounded. He clutched his shoulder...the bloodstain on his leine grew under his hand. The soldiers threw him to the floor and poised their swords above his heart and throat!

"Don't kill him! I want to see this one hang!" Lauderdale shouted. "Get him onto the horse!" He paused, then added, "No! Wait! Tie the two of them onto their horse. Never let it be said that I came between a man and his wife."

His soldiers laughed slavishly at his witless humor. The two Highlanders bent down, and clutching Da by his leine, they cursed and moaned under his weight, demanding help to lift him onto the horse.

"I can walk!" I heard Ma say weakly, but still with defiance, as Captain Lauderdale picked her up. "Take your filthy hands off of *me*!"

I could no longer see what was happening, but I didn't dare move. They were all outside, now. Where were they taking Ma and Da?

"Put her up there behind him!" I heard the Captain order. "Use this, tie them together. She won't let him fall!"

Once again boots thumped against the floor and I watched two of the soldiers return into the cottage. I clung to Jenny and Iain—hardly breathing—just watching as the soldiers poked around the cottage, sneering at our poverty. We were so poor that even they couldn't find any loot...they who scavenged so well. With a snort of disgust, the would-be pillagers disappeared out of the door as well, taking with them our beloved Ma and Da—the hub of our very existence—all that was dear and secure!

Ma! Da!

CHAPTER 9

I listened...not daring to breathe, but my mind was racing. Iain was still now. He's asleep! No time to waste. Jenny's still as well. I must get out of here! Defying my cramped muscles, I turned around until I was on all fours, and cautiously crawled out of the wool.

The silence in the cottage penetrated my senses and slowly, very slowly I peeked around the loom, my eyes sweeping around the now empty cottage. "Jenny! Iain! You can come out now," I whispered to them before I scrambled to the open doorway to peer across the bog. I strained to see down the road. There was no one in sight!

"Ma! Da! Oh, where have they taken you?" I ran down the path that led to the bog. Nothing...no one. The soldiers had managed to cross it. "Oh, God! Help me," I pleaded. "I have to think. Da was wounded...so was Ma. I must follow them...must help them. Iain and Jenny...can't leave them here. Think! Think!"

I hurried back into the cottage and closed the door behind me. Fighting to control my panic, I called as calmly as I could, "Jenny! Iain! Come out now! We're going to the Winters'. Hurry!"

My plan was made. First I would take them to our neighbors, Angus and Maggie Winters. Then I'd try to find Ma and Da. No time to waste! "Hurry, you two!" I yelled impatiently.

Jenny slowly pulled herself around the loom, her young legs wobbling under her. She was strangely quiet. "Lizzie, look at wee Iain." Her voice was hardly above a whisper.

Searching her face for a clue was futile, for it was totally expressionless; I tried to comprehend it as I walked toward the pile of raw wool. Impatient to get on with my plan, I pulled it away from my brother, "Iain...!" I began to scold, but he lay motionless, his little face turned towards me.

The truth hit me...suddenly...not giving me time to get used to it.

"Oh—no! NO!" I stepped backward and covered my eyes with my hands.

Jenny tugged at my hand. "Lizzie," she whispered, "is he...?" I forced myself to look at my brother again. Around his mouth were dark red outlines...of my fingers. I had smothered him! I had killed my brother!

My thoughts raced in every direction...punishing me...my stomach taking each blow.

Voices! I could hear voices from outside!

Jenny threw her arms around my waist and buried her head against me. Terrified, we clung to each other, waiting for the door to open. The voices sounded vaguely familiar, taking the edge off my fear. In spite of this small reassurance, we stood in terrorized silence, watching the door latch slowly move. Choking on stifled screams, we clung to each other as the door creaked open. Terror catapulted us into hysterics. Our screams tumbled out in one long, continuous wail.

"Lizzie! Jenny! It's me! It's me! Maggie Winters! Don't be afraid!" she pleaded. "Look! Look at me! I'll not hurt you!" She held my face in her rough hands, forcing me to look at her. Slowly the reassuring words and familiar voice penetrated my mind and I collapsed into her arms.

Then I noticed Katy McAdam and two other fisher wives standing in horrified silence in the doorway. "How many times will we have to see this?" Katy said angrily, pulling her brown arisaidh tighter around her shoulders, "The weeping bairns, the black eggs, no Ma and Da...". Their faces looked grim, the muscles working in their cheeks as they fought to hold back tears.

"Where's wee Iain?" Maggie asked softly.

Jenny and I turned to stare at the loom. Maggie nodded her head toward the loom. "Katy, take a look. See what's up."

Katy moved obediently toward the loom, hesitated, and then pulled it out of the way. Her hand flew to her mouth.

"Ach, no! Dear Lord! No!"

She quickly pulled the arisaidh from her shoulders in a vain attempt to shield us from the truth and covered Iain's little body.

"He's dead...isn't he?" Jenny stated flatly.

No one answered her. I certainly couldn't. Instead I threw my arms around Maggie once more, sobbing great deep sobs, grateful for the comfort of her big, soft body. She wisely let me cry myself out, never "shshing" me or telling me to stop. Eventually, I could cry no more.

"Right!" Maggie sighed patiently, gently pulling away from me. "Katy, you lift Jenny here, and Lizzie, you climb onto my back and we'll be takin' ye tae my house." With astonishing strength, Maggie moved easily under my weight, through the door and into the cool night air.

"I must be heavy for you, Mrs. Winters." I heard myself whimper in a voice no one would take seriously as an objection. How grateful! How very grateful I was to turn this moment over to Maggie.

"After haulin' that man o' mine and his fish from boat to shore all these years? Naw, lass, yer as light as a feather. Just ye hold on tight to old Maggie, d'ye hear?"

Effortlessly, the big, genial fisher wife carried me away from the cottage, closely followed by Katy who carried Jenny. Katy McAdam was shorter than Maggie, but much wider and was able to tuck Jenny into her arisaidh.

The other two fisher wives, Elizabeth McCall and Euphemia Jack remained at the cottage to "lay out" Iain, a task that had become all too common during these "Killing Times". We had only gone a few steps when Mrs. Jack came running out of the cottage with a pair of brogues in her hand. "Lizzie might be needin' these!"

"Oh, aye—indeed I will, thank you!" I exclaimed, not knowing at the moment how precious those shoes would become.

I glanced back at Jenny and thought, "How small you look, Jenny! You don't look like your eight years!" I wondered if it was because Katy was carrying her like a baby in her arms.

I tightened my grip around Maggie's neck—I had almost slipped. "Hang on, Lizzie!" I chided myself. "You're no good to anyone if you get hurt, too! And you're all that our family has right now!" The full impact of my responsibility made me groan.

"Yer alright, back there, hen?" Maggie asked.

"Aye," I answered.

Maggie looked neither to the left nor the right, but followed a direct course to her cottage that was about a half-mile away. Broom, grasses and sand dunes either gave way or were trampled underfoot; the chilly night air seemed to hurry her along. "We're almost home, wee uin. I'll fix ye both a bite tae eat afore ye can blink yer eyes twice."

Although I knew I wouldn't be able to eat, I hugged Maggie in response. She was a welcome and safe port in this ugly and brutal emotional storm.

"There now, what did I tell ye!" Maggie said brightly as her cottage came into view. "Here ye are, safe and sound," she announced a few moments later, somewhat breathless, as she let me slide to the ground.

"Oiy, Mr. Winters—will ye be lettin' us in?" she called out as she led me toward the small, thatched roof cottage and pushed the door open.

Mr. Winters was kneeling by the fire, poking at it, coaxing it into a brighter flame. A lifetime of hard work had toughened every fiber and sinew in his body. Without speaking, he pulled a stool over to the fire and indicated that I should sit down. Taking my feet in his big, callused hands he gently rubbed them until the chill left my body and I stopped shivering. Maggie put another piece of peat on the fire and positioned the pot "so it'll bile faster" she explained.

We heard Katy's voice getting louder as she approached the door. "See here, Jenny, we've made it!" Katy was gasping for breath, which made Maggie break into a grin that showed her few remaining yellowed teeth. Winking at Katy, she said, "Gettin' old, are ye, lass? I can remember when ye could keep up wi' me, no bother!"

"Aw, away an' bile yer heid, woman!" Katy spat out her retort. Although younger than Maggie, Katy was no match for the older woman's strength and endurance. Perspiration was standing out on her forehead, making her hair stick to it in little curls. "Where can I set this wee bairn down? M' arms are gonna fa' off!"

Angus Winters stood up with arms outstretched, ready to take Jenny. Katy handed her over to him, then shook her arms to "get th' feelin' back in them".

Something about the look on Jenny's face set off a warning signal in my head. "What's wrong with her, Mrs. Winters?" I asked. Not waiting for an answer, I began calling Jenny in a quiet voice. Then a little louder, "Jenny!" Still there wasn't an answer. I moved closer to Angus and tried to take Jenny into my own arms.

"Easy! wee uin." Maggie put her arm around me, but I wasn't to be pacified and pushed her away in a panic. "Jenny! Oh, please Jenny, answer me!" I pleaded. Then changing my tone, I said sternly, "This isn't a game, Jenny. I'm not playing with you! Answer me…now!"

Maggie's quick mind correctly assessed the situation and as usual, she took command. "Angus, here…sit down!" She pulled a large chair closer to the fire. "The shock's been too much for the puir wee thing. Now, Lizzie, don't ye be worryin', your sister'll be fine. Her wee brain can't take in all that's happened, so it won't let anything in. Mind old Willie, Angus," Maggie rattled on without taking a breath, "when he thought he saw a ghost? He just sat for nearly a fortnight afore he spoke to us. Dae ye mind?" Maggie asked for Angus' agreement.

"Aye," answered Angus dryly, "and we've not been able to shut him up since."

"She'll come around, Lizzie." Maggie ignored Angus' sarcasm. "We'll keep her warm and fed—but most important, she needs to be held close."

"I know when it happened to her, Mrs. Winters," I volunteered, as if confession could repair the damage.

"Don't upset yersel' just now. There'll be plenty of time for that. I want ye tae eat first."

I wanted to have my say first but knew it was no use. I might as well save my breath to cool my porridge. It was common knowledge in the village that you couldn't win an argument with Maggie. I sat down again on the stool. My fingers curled around its smooth edge. Angus had made it from the vertebra of a whale that had washed up on the shore and it was worn smooth with years of use.

Maggie hovered over Jenny. "Angus," she ordered, "sit her up so's she won't choke on this." Angus raised Jenny's head and shoulders as Maggie held a spoonful of warm soup to her lips. "It's all right, wee uin," she cooed, "yer safe, th' noo." Gently, Maggie coaxed her mouth open and poured in a bit of the warm liquid, only to watch it dribble out again.

I caught a knowing glance flit between Maggie and Angus and my heart pounded with the realization that there was something seriously wrong with Jenny.

"I'll be goin' back tae the Whitelaw's—see if I can help Lizzie and 'Phemie," Katy announced. "Ye don't need me the now, dae ye, Maggie?"

"Off wi' ye, lass. And thank ye." Maggie smiled warmly at her friend.

I set aside my bowl of soup and knelt beside Maggie as she patiently coaxed Jenny with soft, cooing sounds. I followed her example. Over and over again, we coaxed my sister to respond. After what seemed an eternity, Jenny began to cry. "The tears'll have tae come out afore th' food'll go in," Maggie stated wisely and began to hum a little lullaby as she stroked Jenny's forehead.

I felt agitated at the sound of the lullaby. I wanted to go! There was no time to waste, now that Jenny was on the mend...our family needed to be together—*I* needed my family together...my whole world had crumbled.

Jenny was allowed to cry it out—at her own pace and in her own time. Angus held her as the horror of the past few hours sputtered out between sobs.

I didn't want to hear it...with all of my heart and soul I didn't want to hear it! I refused to think of Iain—I couldn't—it would finish me! I forced myself to think of my next move, which was to get the loan of a horse, or failing that I could walk, but...to where? Where did they take Ma and Da?

Finally, Jenny accepted the soup. Maggie and Angus smiled triumphantly at each other and Jenny readily basked in the warmth of their affection. "Mind when she was born, Lizzie? How she immediately cooried into my arms—she's not a stranger to me, and she knows it." Maggie seemed to take it as a medal of honor—Jenny's trust in her. Of course, we all trusted Maggie—she had that uncanny sense of knowing when she was needed but never interfered. The country folk called her the 'countryside's treasure'.

"Mr. Winters, where did the soldiers take Ma and Da?" I asked. "I'm going to look for them. I can help them…I know I can!"

"Lizzie, I won't try to stop ye. But I'll not let ye go tonight. Yer Da would never forgive me! Ye know how dangerous the road to Edinburgh is! Grown men don't travel it at night for fear of those highway bandits. What chance dae ye think ye'd have?"

Anger and impatience welled up in me. I wanted to argue. "Mr. Winters, don't ye see…" I began, but I could see, by the set of his jaw and the determined look in his clear blue eyes, that I wouldn't be traveling tonight and I might as well "content myself" to the fact, as Maggie had put it.

"Lizzie," asked Angus, "did ye get a look at any of the men or did you hear their names?"

"Aye, Ma called the one who was giving the orders 'Wallace Lauderdale' and he called one of his men 'Duncan' when he told him to boil the eggs." The thought of Ma's ordeal made me cringe and I wrapped my arms around myself and rocked back and forth on the stool.

"Ach, no! They didna' dae that tae her!" Angus exclaimed, and then growled, "They're nothing but tools o' the devil!"

"Will the Royalists ever let up on us? When is this all going to end?" I pleaded to know.

I wanted an answer. My pent up questions tumbled out, one on top of the other, until Maggie put a stop to them saying, "Weescht, now, Lizzie, don't be upsettin' yersel' any more th' night! Ye know what's happened. Ye've heard the stories over and over."

"Aye," I agreed. "But why're they chasing Da and not everyone else who was at Bothwell Bridge?"

"They've caught most of the others, that's why! Yer Da's managed to keep out of their reach these past four years! I'll tell ye, he's no one's fool!" Maggie said emphatically.

"Here—she's asleep." Angus handed Jenny over to Maggie, who laid her on a sheep skin rug on the floor and tucked a blanket around her. He reached for my hand and gently patted it. "It's the Covenant, Lizzie. Aye, many a guid man has laid down his life for the Covenant."

"And woman!" Maggie added emphatically.

"Aye. Many a guid man and woman has laid down their lives for the Covenant," Angus repeated patiently. "But Lizzie," Angus rubbed his beard thoughtfully before continuing, "we know why Lauderdale had it in for yer Ma—and how you've all suffered because of it—but your Ma is a good woman and would not give into Lauderdale or his demands."

"Oh, aye, we know all about it!" he answered my look of surprise. "We know how he can be ranked among the most wicked. He was responsible for putting the thumbkins on Davie Prescott—mangled his thumbs so badly he'll never be able to work properly. He tied two women—one old and one was only a young lassie—to stakes in the sea while the tide was out and as the tide began to come in again, he told them he would release them if they would take the Oath to the King. When they refused, he left them there, to drown in the incoming tide—all the while yelling at them to take the Oath and he would release them. They drowned. He's used the iron boot more than anyone else has. I've seen him take an old man and tie him to a spit and roast him over a fire, trying to make him tell where his son was hiding. Wallace Lauderdale is a monster…no tellin' what he'll do…." his voice trailed off as he glanced at Maggie, who was shaking her head.

Chapter 10

"Here's a cup o' broth," Maggie interrupted Angus' silent journey into his memories. Angus glared at her. He looked as if he wasn't sure if she was interrupting or genuinely making him more comfortable. A full minute passed before he grunted out a "thank ye".

Maggie turned to me and winked. I felt myself smile weakly at her attempt to make the situation lighter. But I couldn't join in her efforts.

Angus continued telling me stories of the Covenanters and their valiant effort to maintain their civil and religious rights. I could only shuddered at the atrocities—and to think that this murderous man had my parents in his grasp. "Oh, dear God—please help them!" I pleaded silently.

"It's all right, hen. We don't need to go on" Maggie said, glaring at Angus, "—we've heard enough." Maggie was patting my arm. I just stared, not really seeing her, as my own trial played out once more in my mind. And then, mercifully, I remembered the many times we had sat around a peat fire, just the family of us, as I had done with the Winters tonight and Da would again tell us stories and our favorite was the 'Dream', the one he had after Lauderdale had burned his fingers. To think that we might never have that joy of being together again, cut through my heart making me gasp.

"Are ye alright, hen?" was Maggie's immediate response to my gasp, but before I could answer, she was telling me how I felt.

"Of course yer not alright—what am I askin' for? Forgive a silly old woman. You've come through a lot in your young life..."

"Please, Mrs. Winters...please don't say I've had an old head put on young shoulders, please don't!" I pleaded.

"Naw, lass, I won't do that tae ye...but you know, when people say that about ye, they're just paying you a compliment—saying you are wise for your age. But what would we expect? Ye haven't even had a chance to be a child or play like a child or even take time to find a beau like ye should be doin' right now. All of you young uins should be at ceilidh enjoying yersel's, finding your mates...not running for your lives!"

"Where did Lauderdale and his men take Ma and Da, Mr. Winters?" I forced my thoughts to the present.

Angus puffed on his pipe, tamping the precious tobacco into the bowl, and gazed at me for a moment before saying softly, "You've grown into a beauty, Lizzie. Even prettier than yer Ma...and yer Granny!" He stopped to chuckle to himself and gave Maggie a teasing sidelong glance. "Ye've got yer Da's red hair, alright! No mistakin' who ye belong tae!" Another long moment passed while the smoke from his pipe wreathed his head. "And yer Ma passed on tae ye that lovely complexion of hers, along with those green eyes!"

"Aye, Mr. Winters, I know." I said, trying to curb my impatience. I wanted to be on my way, not talk about my hair and skin!

"Mr. Winters, where did they take them? How am I going to find them? Please, help me!" I pleaded, trying to stay this side of being cheeky.

"I'll not be able to talk ye out of it, then?" Angus heaved a weary sigh. "Yer a Whitelaw, alright." He took a deep breath and said, "They'll be taking them to Edinburgh, to the Old Tollbooth Prison...but think carefully afore ye go running off half-cocked! That's a dangerous road 'tween here and Edinburgh." He was thoughtful for a moment. "Suppose ye'll be needin' a horse—to catch up tae them, right?"

"Aye, Mr. Winters." I reined in my impatience with both hands, knowing that Angus Winters had one speed and marched to that drum beat, no matter what.

"Aye," he repeated thoughtfully. "Well, seems to me we can get along without our old nag for a few days. What dae ye think, Maggie?"

"I think ye should quit tormentin' the lassie and let her be on her way—with Noddy! That's what I think!"

I gave Maggie a silent cheer but as I swung around to smile my thanks at her, my eyes caught the sleeping form of Jenny. Her deep auburn hair was fanned out on the sheep skin, framing a tear stained, pretty little face.

How small she looked, curled up under the brown blanket snugly tucked up under her dimpled chin. I quietly went over to her, kneeled down and touched her hair. As I bent down to kiss her cheek, I smelled the odor of the raw wool still clinging to her hair. The memory was so vivid that it made me gasp, tearing through me with an unrelenting vengeance that was so unforgiving.

"What are ye going tae do for money, lass?" Maggie wanted to know. "We have a little we could let you have—yer Ma, having looked after us so often wi' food—we couldna' let you go empty handed."

I asked Angus to 'close yer eyes, please' and reached under my shift and retrieved the little leather pouch of fresh water pearls. "See, Da gave me these—one every time he came home." I emptied the pouch into my palm and held them out for inspection.

"Those are real beauties—is that how yer Da kept the food coming into the house?" Maggie wanted to know.

"Aye! He would sell them and give Ma the money or would bring food in himself and he made those golf balls and some clubs and that brought in good money," I said proudly.

"He brought me brogues—real brogues, not pampooties—these shoes," I said, holding them up. "My Da can do anything!"

"Aye, he was clever and he especially loved you," Angus agreed gently.

"He said that the pearls were to be used if ever he wasn't near to help me—or," and I felt myself blush, "...or for my dowry."

"I've nae doubt ye'll be wise in the use of them, and yer Da's tae be blessed for his wisdom as well," Angus stated loudly, as if saying it in his thundering voice would make it so.

"Well, it must be close to dawn," continued Angus, bringing me back from the brink of another flood of tears at the thought of my beloved father. "Safest time for ye tae travel. Those scoundrels go to sleep about now—they are nothing but pirates, ye know, riding up and down the road, waiting to rob people!" Angus moved with difficulty but finally reached the door. He took his blue bonnet from the peg and pulled it over his shaggy, gray hair while beckoning me to follow him.

"Angus! Watch yer puir heid, man!" Maggie cried out.

"Aye, woman, aye!" he growled as he ducked to avoid hitting his head on the top of the doorframe.

Once outside, Angus led me to where his faithful old Noddy, a dappled grey, was tethered. Angus bent over and laced his fingers together. I slipped my bare foot into the proffered stirrup and was lifted onto Noddy's old, swayed back.

"Follow the Glasgow-Edinburgh Road," were the simple instructions. "God go wi' ye!"

"Wait!" It was Maggie. "Here's a few oatcakes...and a wee bit o' haggis. And yer shoes, don't be forgettin' them and this cloak—it'll be a little big, but it will keep ye warm. Ye'll be needin' them in town!"

My polite objections were silenced with a wave of her hand.

"Thank you, so much!" I said, and bent down to drop a kiss on each of their foreheads. "You've been so good to me. I'll tell them you have Jenny. I know that'll ease Ma and Da's minds." A pain shot through me as I remembered about Iain...guilt, shame, fear...too much...I can't think about it, I can't tell Ma and Da...not yet! "I'll take good care of Noddy. We'll be back soon." I forced a smile of confidence that I did not feel.

"Old Noddy, here, knows his way home from anywhere. Just tell him 'go home' and away he'll trot, won't ye, old fella?" Angus gave Noddy an affectionate rub on his flank, before quickly adding, "...that is if you have to stay any length of time and want him to go home."

I nodded my understanding.

"Then, God be with ye—remember, ye'll always have a home tae come to—right here!" I glanced back at them, they both had tears running down their cheeks and were standing with arms entwined, clinging to each other.

Noddy patiently plodded toward the road. As I turned to give the Winters' a final wave, my cloak flew open in a sudden gust of wind. For the first time in my life I felt completely unprotected and totally left to my own wits—and at the mercy of the elements. The thought of a loving God had left my mind as the chill of the grey dawn cut through me. It was so cold...and I was so alone.

CHAPTER 11

"Edinburgh! That must be Edinburgh!" I bent over to pat Noddy's neck and tell him he was so clever to get us here.

"There's the Castle that Grandda told me about," I muttered to myself. The black outline of Edinburgh Castle was etched against the pink sky of the setting sun.

"Hold it, Noddy! Let's give you a rest, and me as well." I slid from the horse's back, grateful that the long, ride was over. "Cum' on, Noddy, ol boy! Such a good boy!" I tugged at the reins, leading him to a patch of green grass and a cool stream.

I'd never seen so many people! They were rushing in every direction at once. "Watch where ye're goin' with that nag," a man shouted at me.

"Ahhhh...we're not hurtin' you!" I yelled back. Having had only a few snatches of sleep while Noddy stopped to graze at the side of the road, left me in a cranky humor. "...and I especially don't like being shouted at for no good reason!" I grumbled, a little more quietly, at his retreating back.

"'Scuse me, sir. Where is the Old Tollbooth Prison?" I asked a more friendly looking man.

"Just at the top of the road, Miss." He waved his hand in the general direction of the Castle and kept on walking, leaving me none the wiser.

It'll soon be dark, I thought. I have to find Ma and Da, and I'll need sleep soon! My body felt numb but my mind was racing ahead. The prison...I must find the prison.

"Where is the Old Tollbooth Prison, please?" I asked a young man who was very well dressed and looked only a little older than myself.

"Just up the High Street," he answered without stopping.

After taking a few steps, he stopped, slowly turned around and asked, "But what are you wanting at the prison?" He looked puzzled.

"I have to find my Ma and Da," I said. The young man looked at me so sympathetically that I had to swallow hard to keep from crying for myself. "Don't cry, Lizzie, don't cry!" I chided myself as I bit down hard on my quivering lip.

"Where're you from, lassie?" The young man asked gently.

"North of Glasgow."

"That's your horse?" He pointed at Noddy, who was grazing contentedly.

I nodded.

"Look, Miss, you don't want to go to the Tollbooth Prison tonight. There's going to be a hanging tomorrow morning and they won't allow visitors in tonight."

"Please, I must try! My Ma and Da are in there. Please help me!" I pleaded, looking into his brown speckled green eyes.

His face softened and a smile played around the corners of his mouth. "Well, what is it you want me to do?"

"Just help me get into the prison. The soldiers tortured my Ma and wounded my Da and tied them onto a horse and brought them here!" The words tumbled out. "I must help them!" I cried.

"Quite frankly, I don't know what you think you can do to help them." He paused to look into my eyes as if he might find the answer there, and then gave a little shrug of his shoulders before adding, "Getting you in won't be much of a problem. It's getting you out again that'll be the trick. You'll be on your own then. You understand that?"

"Aye." I would have agreed to almost anything.

He ran his fingers through his thick dark brown hair and looked thoughtfully up at the Castle and at the setting sun. "Hmmm...by the way, my name's Michael—Michael Stewart," he said, not giving me any clue as to his thoughts. Suddenly, he grabbed my hand. "We haven't a minute to lose then. Come on! We'll head for the High Street!" he ordered as he pulled me in that direction.

We ran...and ran! I thought my heart would burst! Stores and people melted into a blur; but finally, mercifully, he stopped and I clutched at my throat, gulping for air.

"Here it is!" he gasped. I was staring at huge, wooden, double doors hanging on large brass hinges that were coated with years of grime. A soldier, who was leaning against one of the doors, smiled at me; a lewd grin that made me shudder.

"Any visitors allowed tonight?" my young escort asked. The soldier took another long look at me. "No. But I'm sure something can always be arranged," he said, pushing himself slowly away from the door to stand erect. "Who're lookin' for?" His voice sounded familiar—where had I heard it before?

Before I could say John and Christie Whitelaw, my new friend wisely interrupted with, "Taylor Lawson…our cousin."

The soldier bobbed his head at me, asking, "You—ye're this one's brother?"

"Aye." The lie was told so simply. "My name's Michael Stewart and this is…" he looked at me, hesitating ever so slightly.

"Lizzie." I said quickly.

"What are you taking in to this 'cousin'?" the soldier asked me. "Food? Money?"

"Yes!" my 'brother' interceded. "She's taking a little gift to him. Our father is sending this." Michael produced a ring from his pocket—a small fresh water pearl mounted in silver. It was similar to the pearls Da had brought home.

The soldier snatched it and inspected it closely. It was well known that the soldiers could be bought with 'favors' of one kind or another. "This could bring a few merks!" I heard him mutter to himself. "Uh…why don't you leave this with me…I'll make sure your cousin gets it—in the morning."

Michael nodded. The agreement was made.

The soldier smiled at me, pocketed the pearl ring and reached for the door handle. The door squealed as the soldier pulled it open—allowing a foul smelling stench to escape. I took a step backward, covering my mouth and gagging at the same time.

"Well, do you want to go in or not?" the soldier barked.

"Aye. Aye, I do. But where….?" I stammered, not knowing where to go, once inside.

The soldier answered by shoving me into the dark hall where the dampness hung like a curtain in the air. The door banged shut, startling me. I turned, grabbed at the large door latch, and desperately tried to open the door—wanting out—wanting my new friend—"Michael!" I screamed.

"Once that's shut—it's shut for good!"

I spun around, squinting into the dimness. A small candle flickered somewhere near the staircase. It cast eerie shadows over a woman who was sitting on the stairs. She pushed her stringy, dirty hair from her eyes to get a better look at me. "What're ye in fer?" she asked, sniffing and wiping her nose on the tattered sleeve of her dress that once was possibly a pretty blue.

"I'm visiting—my cousin." I stammered.

"Humph! That's what they all say!" She glared at me, narrowing her cat-like eyes. "Ye just want to drum up some more business for yersel'…right?" Not waiting for my answer, she continued. "I know yer kind! Always wantin' more and more while the likes o' me has to live off a' the crumbs ye leave."

I stared at her, dumbfounded. What *was* she talking about?

"Ye just bloody well leave my men alone! Dae ye hear?" she whispered, her voice low, guttural and very threatening.

"Oiy! What's goin' on down there? Is that you, Agnes?" a soldier shouted from the top of the stairs.

"Aye, it's me!" Agnes shouted back, then she moved toward me and breathed her words into my face, "and he's one o' them." She jabbed her thumb toward the soldier. "Stay away from 'im or I'll have the teeth out o' yer head!"

"Aye! By all means I'll leave him alone—nothing to fear from me!" I finally understood and agreed without hesitating. "Absolutely! He's all yer's Agnes!"

I walked toward the staircase; put my foot on the bottom step, paused, and looked Agnes in the eye, displaying courage I didn't feel. Then I continued my climb toward the towering soldier at the top of the stairs.

"Who let ye in here?" he roared at me.

"The soldier at the door." I answered as calmly as possible.

"And I'll bet Duncan took every last penny you had…right?" he sneered the question.

I shrugged my shoulders and wobbled my head in a way that could be taken as a 'yes' or a 'no'. A fervent prayer was in my heart. "Oh, God, please! You've helped me get this far. Let me get to Ma, please!"

"Who're ye visitin'" the soldier demanded.

"Taylor Lawson." I lied so easily.

He was thoughtful for a moment. "Can't bring him to mind." He looked me over from head to toe, obviously suspicious and finally stared menacingly into my eyes. I tried to not waiver as I bravely met his gaze. Then, as if the mental struggle was too much for him, he shrugged his shoulders and said, "Ach! What does it matter? No one in their right mind would want to go in there, anyway!"

He spun on his heel and motioned for me to follow him to the wide door. From a large ring of keys attached to his belt, he chose one and wiggled it into the lock. It clicked and he pushed the door open. Another wave of nauseating stench overpowered me, but this time it was even more putrid.

Clutching at my nose, I stepped into a huge, square, dimly lit room. From wall-to-wall, it was crawling with people. Dirty, ragged bodies, rooting around like animals, trying to find a place to sleep—without mattresses or blankets—on a bare, filthy floor.

A large figure of a man loomed in front of me. His wild mass of black hair and beard made him look ferocious. I stepped back—but the door at my back was locked.

"Who are ye looking for?" he asked with a surprisingly soft Highland Gaelic accent.

"I want my Ma!" I meant to sound defiant, but the words sounded childish in my ears.

"And who might yer Ma be, lassie?" he asked.

The familiar accent weakened my defenses—he sounded so much like Grandda. "Tay...No! Christie Whitelaw." I didn't need to lie any longer! I just wanted to find my mother.

Without warning the big man grabbed my shoulders and shook me. "Ye little fool! What are ye doin' here?" he growled.

"I told ye! I want my Ma!" My patience was at an end. "Where's my Ma!" I pushed his hands away and tried to look around the room but the prisoners had begun to crowd around us.

I felt a tug at my dress; then a grimy hand touched my hair; another tug—this time at my petticoat! A hand with a missing finger pinched my cheek. My arms were swinging wildly, trying to keep the sea of drooling, slimy smiles at bay.

Suddenly, my feet left the floor! I was hoisted into the air and with a thump, found myself dangled over a huge shoulder. The big man with the mass of black hair held my legs in a vice like grip against his chest.

"Put me down!" I screamed, thrashing against his back with my fists. Only a quick and smarting smack to my backside stopped me before I was lowered to the floor to the accompaniment of loud, humiliating guffaws which filled the room.

"Now, be still!" the big man with the beard whispered in my ear, as he pinned my arms down at my sides. "I'm not about to hurt ye. And if ye just turn yer head that way...," he nodded toward the wall.

I turned my head but my eyes never left his. "Look, lassie, for cryin' out loud! It's yer Ma." He smiled gently.

"Ma?" I turned slowly, hardly trusting this big man. All I could see was a curled-up form against the wall. "Ma?" I asked again?

Huddled as close as possible to the wall, was my mother. Her honey-gold hair had fallen out of the neat bun she always wore; blood stains circled her waist; the sleeves of her blouse hung by only a few threads. She didn't move.

"Ma!" I cried out as I made a move toward her.

"Don't!" the big man whispered hoarsely. "She's exhausted…let her be!" And he grabbed my hands and held them in his. Before I could kick at him, he pinned my foot down with all of his weight—until I cried out for release.

"Then settle down! Right now!" was his whispered bargain.

"It's my Ma and I can do as I please!" I whispered back, following his lead. Again my words sounded childish as they echoed in my ears. I stopped fighting and as my arms relaxed, he released his grip on me.

"That's better!" he said.

"I'm not a child! You don't need to talk to me like that!" I was offended by his tone but he just smiled an infuriating all-knowing smile.

Then panic seized me. "She's not…?"

"No, no! But she's had a bad shock today. She…"

"You should have seen what happened to her day before yesterday!" I interrupted angrily.

"Look, lassie, I'm not the enemy here!" He shook his head impatiently, then held me at arm's length while he scrutinized me more closely. Apparently satisfied, he said gently, "I know ye want to talk to her, but sleep will help her more than anything else right now."

"My Da! Is he…?"

"He's in the East Wing. He's not here."

"What's going to happen?" I asked impatiently.

"First, I should introduce myself," he said in an educated voice. "My name is Rory MacLeod. I met your Da at the Battle of Bothwell Bridge. We saved each others' necks a couple of times." He paused, waiting for my reply.

"Are you the Rory who fished Da out o' the river?" I asked.

"Aye. The one and only!"

"My name's Elizabeth Whitelaw. But I'm usually called "Lizzie," I offered somewhat sheepishly.

"Aye, I know more about you than you think!" he said with a smile. "Your Da told me about you…about how spunky ye were—and I see that he was right, I might add. How old are you now, Lizzie?" Rory asked.

"I'm eighteen—almost!" I answered and seeing as he felt free to ask me, I asked him his age as well.

"I am twenty-four—almost twenty-five," he said, mocking me but sobered quickly, adding "and not likely to see twenty-six if I don't get out of this prison soon! The bloody fleas will have eaten me alive!"

So many questions raced through my mind. Why was Rory here? What had happened to Ma? Why was Da in the East Wing—whatever that meant? As if reading my mind, Rory said, "It's hard to know where to begin and by the looks of you, some sleep wouldn't hurt you either."

Just then, a loud voice announced that the pitifully small candle at the doorway was to be snuffed out, eliciting a discontented murmur that roared through the room. Darkness enveloped me—total and absolute. It all happened so fast—I suddenly felt very alone. "Rory?" I whispered. "Are you still there—here?" I corrected myself.

"Aye...here or there, which ever pleases you."

I felt his hand on my shoulder. "Lizzie, this is bloody awkward." He paused before continuing. "Look, I'll have to sleep beside you, otherwise that bunch of she-cats'll have the dress offa you and the teeth outta your head before you know what's hit you."

I didn't say anything. I didn't know what to say. I was grateful for the blackness because Rory couldn't possibly see that I was blushing. My eyes were beginning to adjust to the dark and I unbuttoned my cloak and rolled it up, intending to use it as a pillow.

"You'd better lie on it or it'll be stolen by morning." Rory advised.

"What are you going to sleep on?" I asked.

He didn't answer me.

Ma was lying on a plaid. I put two and two together. "Rory, you gave my Ma your plaid, didn't you?"

"Well, you wouldn't want her lying on the bare floor, would you?" he asked defensively.

"Thank you."

"I told you before, your Da and I are friends." He paused and then added, "You'd better lie down and get some rest yourself."

"Aye, but will you tell me what's happened to Ma?" I asked as I spread my cloak over the bare floor.

"Ach, Lizzie, I don't want to be the bearer of that kind of news."

"Stop yer gabbin' you two! Or I'll come over and put a foot in yer trap! D'ye hear?" someone snarled into the darkness.

"Does he mean us?" I whispered.

"Aye," Rory whispered back. "It'll be alright—sshh."

I felt Rory take a deep breath as he sat up and roared, "Ye just try it, MacCallum, and ye'll be walkin' peg-leg for the rest o' yer life!"

A tense silence filled the room. I could taste the anticipation that rippled through the darkness. It was apparent that these two had tangled before. Very slowly, Rory lowered himself back down beside me, tensed, ready for battle.

I didn't dare speak. Perhaps...should I be afraid of this angry man? No—he was a friend of Da's. Besides, I felt myself drawn to him—not like a friend—more like—oh, I don't know! It's all so confusing—too many things happening at once.

My eyelids suddenly felt very heavy. My last thought before I succumbed to sleep was that of Rory and how his anger had erected a safe wall around the three of us and his gentleness made it a comfortable place to be.

CHAPTER 12

"Lizzie! Lizzie!" The words tugged at me—pulled at me—the voice—that voice was so familiar! I blinked into the dim light that was struggling through dust and grime encrusted windows.

"Where...?" I began. With great difficulty I focused on a tear stained, swollen and begrimed face. Only the green eyes looked familiar! "Ma?" I asked, not really believing it was her.

She nodded her head and smiled weakly.

"Oh, Ma! What've they done to you?" I cried and flung my arms around her. She winced in pain. Too late, I remembered her burned armpits. I sat back to look at her. She looked shrunken...and broken...as if her spirit had been whipped. Embarrassed under my gaze, Ma tried to pull the torn pieces of her dress together over the exposed ripped undergarments and bruised shoulders.

"Oh, Ma! Ma!" I put my arms around her, ever so gently and held her, just as she had comforted me so many times. My mind was in a whirl. How was I to get her out of here?

I glanced quickly at those around me; the snores, grunts and groans from the sleeping bodies sounded hideous; hands and arms flailed the air in an attempt to ward off the fleas and lice. Suddenly I became aware of my own bites and squirmed, reaching down my back to scratch. As I twisted and wiggled, trying to catch the offending flea, I bumped Rory's shoulder.

"Oh! No!" In my confusion, I made a move to get away from him and then remembered that he was my only defense in this nightmarish hole.

"Lizzie," Ma whispered, "He's all right. You're safe with him. He and your Da were friends—remember him telling us about Rory MacLeod?"

"Aye..." I hesitated to tell her that I already knew because I didn't want her to stop talking—I loved hearing her voice.

She nodded her head at the still sleeping Rory. "Well, that's him," she whispered.

"Sshhh, the two o' ye!" Rory put an arm over me and pushed me down. Ma eased herself onto her side to face me. We grinned impishly at each other...for a brief moment we were back home again, enjoying a wee giggle together and teasing Da.

"What happened, Ma?"

"Lizzie, I don't know how to begin to tell you, pet," she whispered. "First, tell me about Iain and Jenny."

"They're fine." The lie slipped out easily. "The Winters' are taking care of them 'til we get back."

"Ach, no!" I muttered as I remembered leaving Noddy all on his own, down by the stream.

Ma looked at me with a question in her eyes.

"Aw, Ma," I began. "I borrowed Angus' horse and I've left him tethered down the street."

"Don't worry about Noddy," Ma smiled. "That horse could find his way home blindfolded!"

"I hope so!" I muttered again. We lay silent for a few minutes, lost in our own thoughts. Then I noticed that Ma had tears rising in her eyes. "Lizzie..." she began, but faltered. "...I can't bring myself to tell you."

Rory stirred and raised himself up on one elbow. He addressed my mother, "Mrs. Whitelaw, don't upset yersel'. I'll tell her...that is, if ye want me to."

"Aye, Rory, please. There's only a few hours left and she must know."

I didn't move. My eyes were fixed on Ma's face.

Rory's mouth was close to my ear; his warm breath against my face made me blush...I felt strange...in a way completely new to me...I didn't know what to do with these feelings. I was grateful when he began speaking.

"Lizzie," he began. "Lauderdale's bunch brought yer Ma and Da in here just before dawn, yesterday." He paused, searching for the right words. "Yer Da was put into the East Wing and yer Ma, here. Later on, in the morning," he continued, "a court was held downstairs. They took down about half of these ones, here," I felt his head move as he looked around the room, "your Ma and me included." He paused again—which I was beginning to find annoying.

"Get on with it!" I said impatiently.

"Lizzie!" Ma sounded shocked at the way I had spoken to Rory.

"You, lassie, hold yer tongue, if ye know what's good for ye!" he snapped back at me.

"Ach, the two o' you deserve one another," Ma said under her breath, taking the neutral and higher ground.

I felt Rory draw in a deep breath. "Once the Turnkey had herded us into the courtroom, the judge came in and sat down, and banged his gavel for order.

"I looked all over for yer Da but he wasn't there!" Ma interjected.

"Aye, I know!" Rory said sympathetically. "As I said, the court was called to order and everyone stood while the judge took his seat at the bench. He looked ominous in his wig and robes. As soon as he was seated, he struck the table in front of him three times, declaring the Court in session. I didn't like him right off...looked like a pompous coward hiding behind those robes."

"He told the Clerk to ask those who agreed to take the Oath of Allegiance to the King to step forward. Eleven men and two women stepped up to the bench. The judge told them to give their names to the Clerk before they took the Oath.

Someone shouted, "Traitor!"

The Judge stood up and jabbed the air with his gavel. "Order in the Court!" he screamed. "One more comment and you'll all spend time in Dunnottar Prison!"

"That quieted them in a hurry!" Rory said sarcastically. Then he continued. "The Judge told the Bailiff to take the Oath takers to his chambers. He was probably afraid of a riot. He sentenced a couple of whores to a dunking in the Lieth River before he got to the Covenanters. I'll try to remember exactly what the Judge said. He began like this:"

"This day being the 30th May 1683*, this Court doth carry out this decree against the following persons who are guilty of harboring rebels and traitors, or joining with them and refusing to take the Oath of Allegiance, which His Majesty's laws justly require from all subjects.

"The following persons are guilty of one or other of the said crimes; Alexander Richie, James Wilkie, John Mclean, William McLean, John Cunningham, Thomas Brown..."

"There were about sixty names, Lizzie, and he called my name out at the very last." Ma said quietly. There was a far away look in her eyes that told me that she was reliving the whole ordeal.

"The Judge said," Rory continued, "...and these persons who have obstinately refused to take the Oath are hereby banished to His Majesty's plantations abroad, discharging them forever, to return to this Kingdom under the pain of death, and to have the following stigma and mark, that they may be known as banished persons if they return to the Kingdom; that the men have one of their ears cut off by the hand of the hangman and that the women be branded by the same hand on the cheek with an iron with the letter "C," after which they will be put aboard a ship, the Henry and Francis, for transportation to the Americas. A surgeon will travel with them also, to see to their care. They will be transported to the plantation of East New Jersey in America."

"Banished! Oh, Lizzie!" Ma cried. "Banished! Never to return to Scotland. My children? What of my children?"

My head was spinning. I couldn't comprehend it all. I put my hand against her cheek and she held it in hers, pressing it to her lips.

"They might as well have hung me!" she said bitterly. "I'm as good as dead without my family."

I was silent. This wasn't happening! There must be a way out! Plan, I must make a plan! "Think one thing at a time, Lizzie! One thing at a time!" I scolded myself silently, trying to bring my racing mind under control.

Rory's voice caught my attention. "That's not all, Lizzie, there's more," he said quietly. "The Judge then dismissed them. While they were leaving the room, I spotted that monster, Lauderdale, whispering to the Judge. I couldn't hear what he was saying but the Judge yelled at the Bailiff to bring your Ma to his bench." Rory took a deep breath.

"The Bailiff reached into the crowd and grabbed her, none too gently I may add, and marched her over to the Judge.

'Are you Christian Whitelaw, wife of the rebel and Covenanter, John Whitelaw?' he asked your Ma. Your Ma nodded her head."

"Aye, Lizzie, I couldn't imagine what else they could do to me." Ma said.

"Then the Judge leaned over and said, right into your Ma's face, 'You are being banished and branded on the cheek for your rebellion and law breaking. Further, as an example to other wives who want to hide their lawbreaking husbands from the authorities, you will be required to witness the execution of your husband...while being held in the stocks—in front of the gallows!'"

"Your Ma wrenched her arm free from the Bailiff's grasp and spun around to face Wallace Lauderdale. She looked so furious that it took that greasy buzzard by surprise and he stepped backward...but your Ma was too quick for him. She swiped at his face...her fingernails ripped three long gashes across his left eye and cheek. I think he might lose the eye...but that's not near enough to even the score."

I felt stunned and speechless. Agony was piled on top of agony. Da was to be hanged. It was too much to take in all at once.

"Lizzie," Ma's defiant voice broke into my thoughts. "What else could they do to me?"

"Aye, she gave him a right good uin'!" a voice said from above us. We looked up into a semicircle of faces. The same faces that had frightened me the day before, now just looked pitiful...defenseless and beaten. How long they had been listening was anyone's guess and it was plain to see that Rory wasn't amused by their intrusion.

He sat up and pulled me up beside him and then leaned over to speak to Ma. "Mrs. Whitelaw, what can I get for you?"

"A bowl of water, please, Rory," she asked. "If this is to be the last time John sees me, at least I can show him a clean face." She paused briefly, then added, "You can tell Lizzie the rest while I'm washing myself."

We watched in silence as Rory went to the door and banged on it until the guard opened it. "I want to buy some water!" Rory growled at him. "It'll cost you, MacLeod!"

"Doesn't it always?" was Rory's quick response.

The guard sneered his answer in a bullying tone. "Watch it, MacLeod! It won't be long a'fore yer outta merks and then what will ye bargain wi'?" He slammed the door in Rory's face.

Within a few minutes, the door was opened again and the precious little bowl of water was handed over to Rory, who carefully held it in one hand and covered the top with the other, being careful not to spill so much as a drop. He returned with it, saying, "Sorry it's not a larger bowl, but it's the best I can do."

"You had to buy the water?" I asked, hardly believing what had just transpired.

"Aye, we have to pay for our food and water and those poor souls against the wall are in here without money—they won't last long," Rory said sadly.

"Except Agnes, she doesn't have to pay!" The comment was accompanied with mirthless snickers.

"Aha, so that's what that was all about!" I now understood why Agnes had warned me. She was protecting her 'income'.

Ma ripped away a piece of her sleeve and dipped it into the cold water. Carefully, patiently, a small patch at a time, she removed the grime until her white skin shone through once again. Always so spotlessly clean...having to wash herself in a cup! I was angry! I clenched my fists, wanting to hit something...anything. Why were these folks just accepting it all—not fighting back—just accepting what was happening! I realized at that moment that the anger helped sooth the agony. I determined to stay angry!

Rory covered my fist with his hand. Its warmth was soothing...too soothing. I pulled away from him.

"Carry on, Rory" Ma said, "But hurry—you'll have to get her out of here soon."

"Aye."

Rory spoke quickly. "Well, the Judge bellowed, 'Leave the Court!' and cracked his gavel on the desk with each word. Then he shouted, 'Bring in the other prisoners!'"

"I tried to get a glimpse of your Da," Ma said, "but the Bailiff dragged me from the court room...but not before I heard the Judge say "John Whitelaw, Arthur Bruce and John Cochrane..."

"They closed the door behind me and I couldn't hear any more but Rory was still in the court room, he'll tell you what happened next." Ma's words faded into a whisper.

I looked at Rory who appeared to be lost in thought. "Rory?" I urged.

He looked up and into my eyes. I looked away quickly...suddenly feeling shy. He shook his head and began again.

"Well, Lizzie, your Da was brought up to the witness stand and Judge Dempster bellowed at him: 'John Whitelaw, of the shire of Lanark, sometimes of Stand, you are hereby indicted before the Justiciary for being at Bothwell. Your confession will hereby be read to you: John Whitelaw, declares he thinks the Battle of Bothwell Bridge lawful, that rising being in defense of the Gospel. He thinks himself and these three nations, Scotland, Ireland and England, bound by the Covenant. That it is beyond him to tell whether the king be a lawful king or not. He confessed that he was with the rebels at the Battle of Bothwell Bridge. He refuses to say God save the King. He declares he can write, but will not sign the Oath.'

'Your confession and refusal to take the Oath of Allegiance has been considered carefully in this court and I, James Johnston Dempster, pronounce sentence that the said John Whitelaw be taken to the Merket Cross of Edinburgh on the morrow, being the last day of May 1683* and between the hours of two and four o'clock in the afternoon be hanged on the gibbet until he be dead, and all his lands, heritages, goods and gear to be forfeited to our sovereign Lord the King's use.'

I looked from Rory to my Ma. I tried to speak, but my throat had closed. Da! Oh, Da! A pain squeezed my chest. I can't breathe! Then a warm blackness enveloped me. Far in the distance I heard Ma's worried voice saying, "She's fainted, Rory!"

Being slapped on my face to bring me out of my faint just made me feel angry and I wanted to hit back or scream.

"Don't scream or you'll be charged with being refractory and then you'll know all about it!" Rory whispered as he covered my mouth with his hand.

"Oh, Ma! Da!" I whimpered when he finally took his hand from my mouth.

"Lizzie. We have to face this, like it or not!" Ma's voice steadied me.

"But what can we do?" I cried. "I can't let you go, Ma! We can't give up, Ma! Not without a fight!"

"There's no way around it, pet." She hung her head and repeated, as if trying to convince herself, "Aye, there's no way around it. If there was—don't you think I'd take it?"

"Ma!" I shouted. "Don't give up!" That frightened me more than anything else I had heard so far this morning. I held her by the shoulders, wanting to shake her. "Ma! Da hasn't given up! I know he hasn't! Fight, Ma! Fight!"

"Easy does it, lassie. Your Ma's had all the fight taken out of her, for the moment," said Rory.

He leaned toward me, saying, "Lizzie, you have to get out of here before they see who you're visiting and then you'll be sent off to America as well...you know...for helping your Da."

I shook my head, "No! I won't leave her!"

"Come on. I'll take you downstairs," he insisted.

"But I can't leave Ma now!" I argued.

"Lizzie," Ma intervened, "you can't do anything for me...or your Da. You'll do more good by looking after wee Iain and our Jenny...and Granny—she'll need you now, as well" She held my hand tightly in hers. "Please, Lizzie," her voice pleaded with me, "help me go through this, by at least knowing that my children are safe. The Winters' will help you...you know that. Please see it through my eyes, pet. If you stay with me, there's an even chance you won't even live to see next year. But if you're with the Winters...well, then at least I can know that the three of you are safe. Do you know how much that means to me?"

"Three...." I began angrily.

Rory interrupted by thrusting out his hand to help me up. The gesture stopped me from blurting out my secret. Reluctantly, I rose to my feet. "Ma...somehow I'm going to do something. We'll live through this mess—all of us!" I promised.

"Come along, lassie, let's go," Rory coaxed softly. He led me to the door and banged on it until the Turnkey opened it.

"Let me take her down the stairs," Rory demanded. "She's a visitor."

The Turnkey grinned at Rory, "Some visitor, MacLeod. How do ye manage it?" He looked me up and down, then growled, "Ach, well, go ahead. Mind yer back in two minutes or I'll have the army after yer hide!"

We walked to the top of the stairs and were about to step down when the door to the street banged open and several soldiers bounded up the stairs, pushing us to the side, yelling at the Turnkey to open the door. Suddenly, I felt a tug on my hand and the next moment I was flying down the stairs with Rory half pulling and half carrying me.

"What on earth…?" I stammered, when I found myself out on the street in the blinding sunshine.

Rory was yanking my arm again. "We haven't any time to waste. In for a penny—in for a pound—I can't turn back now!"

"Where're we going?" I gasped, trying to keep up with his long strides. "What are you doing?"

"I don't know! I hadn't planned on escaping!" he tossed at me over his shoulder.

"Rory, stop! I can't go any farther! My shoe is untied!"

He groaned. "You'll get me killed, ye wee bubbly bairn!" and pushed me into a dark close. "Tie it for cryin' out loud!"

My fingers were shaking so much that I kept fumbling with the short ties. Suddenly, a great clatter of boots against the cobblestones thundered in my ears.

"Rory…?"

It's the guards," he said. "They're looking for me!"

He turned his back to the open doorway and swept me up in his arms, burying his head against my shoulder. We stood still, holding onto each other until the clatter of the boots passed and faded into the distance. That same feeling swept over me again. I felt safe. For a brief moment, his strength was once again a fortress against my terrifying world.

"Lizzie!" he said, pushing me away from him, "I think I have a plan. I've no family left now, my Ma and Da are gone—over a year ago," he explained. "There's nothing keeping me here. If I can manage to get on the same ship as your Ma, I can keep an eye out for her. The trick is getting on board with both ears still intact."

"Take me with you, Rory," I demanded, surprising him as well as myself.

He thought for a little while and, completely ignoring my request said, "Aye, it's about time for a change. Maybe I'll have a better chance in the Americas." He held me at arms' length, looking at me without seeing me. The excitement of adventure shone in his blue eyes. "Lizzie, I've heard tell that the Captain of the

Henry and Francis is having a devil of a time getting a crew. Seems that no one wants to sail with him...let's say his reputation has preceded him." His grip on my shoulders tightened. "Now, think about this. A new kilt—I'll trim my beard—clean up! Do you think I could pass for a surgeon?"

"A surgeon?" What a strange question I thought. "What do you know about barbering?" I asked skeptically.

"That's just the problem right now. A barber doesn't know what a surgeon has to know, yet they do surgery anyway. I've spent a couple years in Edinburgh's Medical School—learning surgery, not barbering!...before I was yanked into the army! and that was against the law as well! But there is such a fight going on right now between the barbers and surgeons, that it's hardly worth the study."

"Rory, what if someone recognizes you! They'll throw you into Bass Rock Prison and you'll die for sure. No one ever gets out of there!" I said.

"Look, what've I got to lose? I'll get this beard of mine cleaned up and then I'll see what I can do with the ship's Captain." He smiled at me as if I was a little child.

"Are you alright, now? Sorry for calling you a cry baby!" he smiled apologetically, then abruptly changed the subject. "Can you make your way back to your brother and sister?" It was obvious that he was anxious to have me on my way and he on his.

"Don't patronize me, Rory MacLeod. I am not a child!" I almost shouted. "And furthermore, I'm not going home. I'm staying with my Ma!" I was adamant. "Jenny'll be fine with the Winters...and I'm going to the Americas with Ma!"

I couldn't believe I said that—I was actually demanding to go to America—that big black hole that swallowed up everyone who stepped foot into her—except Mr. Winters' nephew who was a sailor and brought back tobacco for him.

"What about your wee brother?" His question interrupted my self-talk.

"Look, Rory, just help me get onto that ship, will you?" I ignored his question. He rubbed his chin and paced in a small circle, and then, once more around the imaginary circle before he stopped in front of me. "You're pulling me in deeper and deeper, ye know that? Lizzie, do ye realize that I may be leading ye straight to yer death...our death? Do ye know how many ships don't make it to America—they are just devoured in storms. And how Many folks just plain die of disease on board—before setting foot on shore...and then there are the savages when we get there. Lizzie, do you know what you're asking for?"

"I've nothing to lose either, Rory." I said evenly. He knew I meant it—and studied my face, looking for a reason to say "No".

After a few moments of thought, he shrugged and muttered, "I can see there's no changing your mind." He took a deep breath and added, "We'll have to dangle then! Can ye keep up with me?" he asked.

"No, I can't." I admitted. "You go on and I'll make my own way to the ship. But wait...here..." I pulled the little leather pouch from my bodice and poured the precious pearls into the palm of my hand. "Take some—you'll need the money to buy your kilt and medicines..."

His eyes glistened with tears as he asked, "Your Da...he gave these to you?"

"Aye, how do you know?" I asked, surprised.

"Could be I was there when he fished them out of the streams. He loved you so much, Lizzie..." he said softly.

"He '*loves*' me—he's not gone yet!" I said angrily.

"Alright, then, have it your way." He sounded defeated. "I have no idea how all of this is going to turn out...I wish I could promise you something, Lizzie." He paused in front of me and shook a finger under my nose, "You...my lady...stay out of trouble!"

I smiled at my victory and looked steadily back into his eyes, pleased that I had graduated from "bubbly bairn" to "lady".

"Ach...that's probably too much to ask!" he grinned and with a wave of his hand was off down the High Street.

*the actual documented date is 28 November 1683

CHAPTER 13

Alone again!

How was I going to let the Winters know that I wasn't coming back? Further more, how was I going to get Noddy back to them? I fervently hoped that Ma was right and that Noddy had already started for his home. I struggled to form a plan in my mind.

Cautiously, I stepped from the doorway of the close and peeked into the High Street. So, this is what it looks like—Michael Stewart had whisked me up the street to the prison with such speed that I didn't see anything and, of course, Rory had just pulled me down the hill and I didn't see anything again.

The street was full of people; vendors hawking their wares, shouting each other down in price.

"Duck!" A woman with a baby slung over one hip pushed me ahead of her, back into the close. A torrent of dirty water poured over the doorway, splashing us and leaving a sour smell on the cobblestones.

"Watch yersel', lassie. Ye can't trust those biddies up there." She looked up at the brown brick building and shook her fist at a woman hanging out of a window two stories above us. "They's not tae throw their slop outta the windows but, no one tries tae stop them either." And she was gone, baby bouncing on her hip.

I stepped onto the street, casting nervous glances at the windows above me and at the bustling women who impatiently pushed me out of their way.

Soon I was caught up in the stream of pedestrians and found myself walking quickly toward the place where I had left Noddy. At least my body knew what to do, even if I didn't.

My mind was in a whirl, constantly struggling with the thought of my father being hanged. "Oh, it can't be! It can't be! Someone is making it up!" I said aloud, oblivious to those around me. "That's it! It's all a mistake! It has to be a mistake." My emotions spun painfully inside me.

Before I knew it I was standing in front of Noddy, who was tethered to the tree. Someone must have looked after him and I wondered if it had been Michael. Noddy whinnied when he saw me and let me pat his dirt caked nose.

"Noddy, you're supposed to be a very smart horse…" I paused. A note…I'll fasten a note to Noddy's rein! Mr. Winters said that all Noddy had to hear was the word "home" and away he would go. Oh, Mr. Winters, I hope that you were telling the truth 'cause that's just what I'm going to have to do now. Having made my decision, I turned my mind to writing the note.

On what? With what?

"My shift! I'll use my shift!" I exclaimed to no one in particular. I sat down on the grass and reached for the hem of my undergarment. "Daft thing won't tear!" I grumbled and yanked on it again. "There!" It gave way, resulting in a ragged piece of cloth being clutched in my fist. I smoothed it out, making it ready for my message.

A slender stick lay close by. "I'll dip the stick in the mud…" I said out loud. Carefully, I etched muddy words on the white cloth: "Ma banished/Da hanged tomorrow. Please take care of Jenny. Lizzie". I took out two pearls and placed them in the center of the cloth and knotted it tightly.

"Cum' here, Noddy," I called and reached for the reins.

"Just you stand still and let me knot these reins so you won't trip on them. How's that, old boy?" I said, hoping the horse would understand I didn't want to abandon him.

"There," I patted his head, successfully tucking the note inside the knotted rein. Putting my arms around the old horse's neck, I whispered into his ear, "Noddy, you go home, now!" I hugged him and stepped back. "Go home, Noddy!" I shouted again and slapped him on the rump. He obediently turned toward the road, stopped once to look at me, and headed back over the road we had traveled just a few hours ago.

Standing with my hands on my hips, I peered up at the Castle. How many times had my Grandda and Da told me stories about this very Castle and here was I, actually looking at it.

"Oh, Da! They can't…" I couldn't say the word. "Not you, Da! Who've you harmed? I've seen you walk miles to help others."

Once again I found myself on the High Street, walking toward the prison. "Just once more, please God," I asked out loud, "just let me see my Da one more time."

"Think about him," I told myself. "Remember what he looked like when he would come slipping into the cottage at night. Remember his smile." Da's face loomed in my mind, the twinkle in his clear blue eyes and how his "laugh lines", as he called them, crinkled every time he smiled. The mental picture eased the ache in my heart.

I must see him, at least one more time. But seeing him in the prison was out of the question. I can't go to the Merket Cross where he was to be hanged...that was out of the question, too. Leaning against one of the stone buildings, I tried to think it through!

Finally a plan slowly formed in my mind. "Why not, Lizzie?" I asked myself. "Your Da and your Ma are going to be there. Can't you stand by them at the Merket Cross?"

The whole idea of seeing my father hanged weakened me so, that I nearly collapsed there on the street. "Oh, please, I'm not strong enough!"

"My Ma will need me." That thought strengthened me enough so that I could push myself away from the wall and look up to the sky. The sun was overhead and the judge had said something about two o'clock. What had Rory told me to do—I struggled to remember.

"I'll go now," I decided, "in case I can get to see Da sooner."

"The Merket Cross—where is it?" I asked a ragged looking youth.

"Follow me! Ye know there's a hangin' there today, don't ye?" he asked.

"Aye, I know," I answered wearily. Suddenly I felt quite old.

"They're croppin' ears and brandin' as well! Here," he invited, "tak' some o' these." Two rotten potatoes were thrust into my hand.

"What do I do with these?" I asked disdainfully.

"Ye pelt the hangman when he's done his job! Ye've never been tae a hangin' afore?" he asked unbelievably.

"No. No, I haven't." The words choked me. I coughed to clear my throat.

"Well, hurry yersel' or ye'll miss it!" and he darted off into the crowd.

I watched him disappear into the throng of people that was winding its way to the top of the street. "Move yersel'!" a wiry little man growled as he pushed me out of his way.

"Either walk or get offa' the road!" someone else barked. People pushed me aside as they rushed ahead, carrying rotten vegetables in their hands.

"I must…I must…" I said over and over, forcing my legs to move, willing my feet to take each step. I looked down at the rotting vegetables in my hand. "Eeagh! Get away!"

Putrid brown slime slid down my fingers, revolting me; I shuddered as I heaved them into the road but my hands were still covered with the sour mess. I flattened them against the rough stones of the building I was leaning against and rubbed and rubbed, frantically trying to erase the whole day.

"Walk, Lizzie, walk!" I forced myself to continue up the street. Eventually, I came to the Tollbooth Prison doors, and stopped, stepped back and looked up at the windows high above the street. "Da's up there…so close…only a door and few stairs between us."

At that moment, the prison doors opened and a soldier walked out. The sight of the uniform brought me back to reality. "Get away from here! You've got to get onto the ship with Ma!" I chided myself.

"The ship—Rory—it must be at least four hours since he left me." I felt so alone. "No! No time for self-pity. You'll not get anywhere feeling sorry for yourself!"

"I wish my cloak was warmer!" I whimpered as I clutched it to my body, trying to ward off the icy chill—but the chill was not coming from the wind—the chill was coming from the very core of my being.

The ever increasing crowd swept me along with it and without warning, I was at the dreaded Merket Cross. The hangman's gibbet looked so sinister! So big and threatening! And the rope, it swung so menacingly in the wind!

"I can't! I can't!" Covering my eyes, I turned to run but stumbled when the toe of my shoe caught on a cobblestone.

"Get outta the way! Get outta the way!" A soldier pulled me up by the collar of my cloak. "Get outta here! The wagons are coming!"

Five wagons, each pulled by a team of horses, rattled over the cobblestones and blocked the High Street, which stopped the crowd from emptying into the Merket Cross.

The stream of yelling and cursing humanity was now forced to go around the wagons. Once more, I was shoved forward by the sheer momentum of the crowd until it almost crushed me against the side of one of the wagons.

"Here they come!" the crowd called out, its voice filled with awe as it parted and made way for the prisoners to pass.

"Lizzie, get up here!" A familiar voice.

"Rory? Is that you? You look so…so…" his beard was now neatly trimmed and he was clean and officious looking in his kilt and jacket.

"Here," he cried as he jumped out of the wagon. I had no objection when he put his hands around my waist and lifted me up onto the wagon seat.

"What in heaven's name are you doing here," he demanded to know as he jumped back into the wagon. His face looked like a black thunder cloud.

I couldn't answer because I had just caught a glimpse of my mother being led to the stocks.

"Kneel down!" the soldier yelled at her. Ma slowly went to her knees. "Put your head here and your arms there!" She rested her head and wrists in the grooves that had been hewn out of the rough wood. The top half of the stocks was lowered, securing her neck and arms; the soldier slid the wooden peg into place, locking her into the crude device.

Rory moved closer, and put a protective arm around m shoulders. I winced as the soldier hit Ma on the buttocks and laughed crudely. Ma's head drooped in humiliation.

"Lizzie, I brought this for your Ma—to cover herself with." He handed me a long piece of cloth that she would be able to wrap around her bosom and regain some dignity.

"Thank you, Rory." I was touched by his thoughtfulness. No wonder Da said he was like a brother to him.

A buzz of voices murmuring, "Move...get outta the way!" brought our attention to the hangman who was pushing aside the crowd as he stomped toward the gibbet.

"He looks like a bloomin' rooster!" a man said and laughed out loud. "Bloomin' rooster! Bloomin' rooster!" the crowd chanted while the hangman climbed the ten steps to the platform of the gibbet.

"You know, Lizzie, they're right!" Rory sneered. "Just look at him wi' his black hood over his wee green velvet suit."

I could only nod my agreement. My attention was riveted on the gallows. Two cross pieces held a large beam from which a stout rope swung in the breeze—swinging as if it was happily waiting to do its gruesome task. The hangman tugged at the rope, making sure it would do its job. My father was standing up on a horse drawn cart beneath the rope, balancing himself as the horse moved with each roar from the crowd.

"Oh, Rory!" I cried at the sight and buried my face in my hands, only to look up just as the hangman turned his attention to Ma. I was close enough to see his eyes; when they narrowed and I knew he was smiling behind his mask.

"Turnkey..." A well-modulated voice made itself heard above the din. It belonged to a man who was standing beside Ma. "I am Captain Adams. These people are my cargo. I want them in those wagons as soon as they receive their mark."

Then he added, "I understand that this woman is among my quota as well?"

"Aye, this is Christian Whitelaw." I saw Ma's body jerk from still another humiliating slap to her backside.

"Where's yer doctor? I can't let 'em go 'til I see him...ye remember what the judge said."

Rory 'humphd' in my ear disdainfully. "Just look at that drunken geezer enjoy his little moment of power!"

"He's there—behind you." The Captain pointed at Rory, who had only moments before taken his arm from around me. "And that's his assistant next to him." The Captain had pointed at me!

Rory hadn't told me. He pushed his elbow against my side and whispered out of the side of his mouth, "You're on the ship, if you play it right!"

I tried to sit straighter, to look like whatever an assistant looked like. Suddenly, I panicked. "The Turnkey knows me!"

For a terrorizing moment, he began to turn toward me, but before he could get a closer look, the Captain demanded his attention again. "Turnkey," Captain Adams sounded exasperated, "the Doctor will take responsibility for getting these people to the ship. I won't be staying for this!"

A hush fell over the crowd as the hangman climbed down from the gibbet and stood beside the chopping block. It was a round stump of wood with a groove cut out of one side.

White hot coals lay burning in the small grate; the ends of several branding irons had been laid across them. Between the fire and the chopping block was a large bucket.

Ma was only six feet away from the block, branding irons and the gibbet. The crowd gasped as the hangman picked up a large cleaver and tested the edge for sharpness.

Satisfied with its edge, he swung toward the Turnkey and shouted, "First!"

Horrified, I watched a man being led toward the chopping block. His hands were tied behind his back and his head was forced down on the block, the groove holding his chin immobile. A soldier pressed down on the man's shoulders with all of his might. The hangman gripped the man's ear with one hand and swung the cleaver with the other, slicing the prisoner's ear off. He then held the blood dripping ear for the crowd to see and with a flourish, tossed it like so much garbage into the bucket. With another flourish the hangman grasped the handle of a branding iron and applied the hot tip to the raw and bleeding flesh, where the ear had been, just moments before.

A scream of agony pierced our ears.

"Oh, God! Please let Ma faint before it's her turn!" I prayed over and over.

"Next!" shouted the hangman.

I covered my ears and screwed my eyes shut but the shrieks of the women as their cheeks were branded with a "C" ripped through the air; the men's guttural deep throated, animal-like roars pierced my senses—penetrated my mind. I knew that I would hear their screams over and over for the rest of my life.

Another scream.

I knew it was Ma! I opened my eyes to see the hangman step back from her, the branding iron in his hand was still smoking.

Ma was branded. My beautiful mother—her face mutilated—was branded.

Rory held on to me, using his might to keep me still. "Let me go! Let me go!" I fought to get free, pushing against his arms. I wanted to run to my mother! He put his mouth close to my ear and whispered gently, "Coorie in, Lizzie! Coorie in!" while keeping me immobile against his body. His big hand held my face against his shoulder.

"Lizzie...it's your Da," he said quietly, with a catch in his voice and added, "Don't look, lass."

I fought his hand away and sat up straight, "You're right! It is *my* Da!" I said defiantly, wiping the tears from my face.

Soldiers stood erectly on either side of the gallows, watching carefully as Da stood beneath the rope. He too was standing tall with his head held high.

The crowd fell quiet.

The hangman seemed anxious to get on with his work and held the rope, impatiently waiting for the cart to be moved into position. Finally, he placed the looped end of the rope over Da's head, letting it rest on his shoulders. The blood stain on his shirt reminded me of the horrible scene in our home when the soldier wounded him. Was it only three days ago?

"John Whitelaw," shouted the hangman, "do you have any last words?"

"Aye, I do," said Da in a strong, clear voice. "Men and brethren. I see my joy now begun that will never have an end. I heartily forgive those who have done me harm. As a dying man, I beseech my wife and children..." he looked straight at me.

My heart skipped a beat. How did Da find me? I sat up straight, my lips forming the words, "Da, I love you!" over and over. He smiled.

"Oh, Rory! He smiled at me!" I sat up even straighter.

Da continued, "...to seek Him in earnest, because only through Christ can we be reconciled to God the Father. Make religion your main work and make the Lord your only choice and His love your delight; for if it be not so, you will soon faint in your own hour of trial."

"Aye, Da! I'll do it! I'll do it!" I was nodding my head up and down as fast as I could.

Rory put his arm around me again and I looked up just in time to see him give Da a quick salute. Da nodded his head and smiled again.

The beating of the drums thundered louder and louder, deliberately drowning out the rest of his words. But Da's voice thundered above the drum rolls. "And now I leave my wife and children to the Lord, who has promised to be a Husband to the widow and a Father to the fatherless. Farewell my beloved ones." His smile wrapped itself around my Ma, holding her close.

"Oh, John, John, my Jo!" Ma's voice could be heard above the drums as well, crying to her beloved husband.

Then Da lifted his eyes to the heavens and prayed, "Welcome Father, Son and Holy Ghost, into whose hands I commit my spirit. Amen."

"NOW!" bellowed the hangman. The soldier slapped the rump of the horse, yelling, "Giddyap!" forcing it to bolt, yanking the cart floor from beneath Da's feet. Da's weight dropped him quickly, stretching the rope and mercifully, his death came quickly, releasing him from the horrors of this day.

"John Whitelaw of Monkland is now a martyr for the Covenant," Rory whispered and he bowed his head respectfully.

The crowd was still—but only for a moment. A rotten potato, hurtling through the air, splattered on its' target. The hangman walked away through the crowd, accepting the ritual of being peppered with rotten vegetables and foul words.

"Da spoke the truth, Rory," I said as I relished his dying words that were still ringing in my ears. Before he could answer there was an explosion of musket fire. The crowd froze—but, again, only for a spilt second. Then, as if by some secret signal, it dispersed; the people scattered in every direction, disappearing into the walls like cockroaches in a sudden light.

"Load the prisoners into the wagons—make room!—get outta th' way!" the Turnkey shouted as he shoved away those in his way.

"Lizzie, wait here and don't move, now. Do you hear? I'll be right back." Rory jumped from the wagon and I watched as he bobbed and weaved through the soldiers. Within seconds, he was tugging at the pegs, releasing Ma from the stocks.

He lifted her limp body up in his arms and carried her back to the wagon. As I watched, I began to pray, "Oh, God..." but I didn't have any more strength, for praying or for anything.

Rory sat Ma on the seat beside me and I wrapped my arms around her. "Ma, its me, Lizzie," I whispered in her ear, but she was so dazed that I am sure she didn't hear me. I wrapped the warm cloth around her, thankful that my mother was at least alive and sitting beside me.

"Twelve to a wagon...twelve to a wagon," the Turnkey shouted as he herded the prisoners into the waiting wagons. I cradled Ma, trying to rock back and forth with her as if she was a child. "It'll be alright. It'll be alright, now." I crooned. My new role that had been so cruelly thrust upon me felt so strange and unfamiliar.

A hand touched my arm. "Good luck tae ye, lass." I looked down into the youthful face of Michael Stewart, my friend who had helped me get into the prison. "You found your Ma?" he asked kindly.

"Aye," I said, looking down at him.

The youth's face blanched. "That wasn't your Da? Ach, naw! It couldna be..." he stammered.

"Aye." I answered calmly. "Aye. That was my Da. Those words that he spoke? They're the truth, you know!" I looked into Michael's eyes, smiling proudly and fighting back the tears. "Aye, that's my Da," I repeated.

"Lizzie, I...." he stammered.

"And this is my Ma." I tightened my arm around her before turning back to my friend. "Aye, they don't make them any better than my Ma, you know!" I smiled at him and suddenly remembered about the pearl ring. I wasn't going to be able to replace it! "I'm sorry about the ring...I...but...here, I want you to have this," I said as I reached for the leather pouch.

He interrupted me saying, "It was for a good cause. My privilege. *My* pleasure, Lizzie!" Suddenly, the wagon lurched forward. Rory had leapt into the wagon and was now leading the other wagons to the ship.

"All the best, Lizzie! All the best!" Michael called after me.

"Aye, to you as well." I called back but the wagons rattled so noisily on the cobblestone streets that I feared my words were lost.

I turned to look at our mutilated passengers, huddled against each other. They were writhing in their pain—each their own way. My heart ached for them.

"We'll soon be there!" I called out, forcing cheerfulness and thinking of the waiting ship at the dock in Leith Harbor.

"What am I saying?" I questioned myself, as I examined the words I had just spoken. "That they should content themselves because...they can now leave

Scotland, the country they love and their beloved children and parents and wives and husbands?

"Ach, Lizzie!" I said aloud, realizing that I had embarrassed myself. Just then I felt Ma's hand, lightly patting my arm.

Chapter 14

"Is that the "Henry and Francis'?" I asked, pointing at a ship that was rolling lazily with the waves.

"Aye, that's her alright! Home for the next six weeks." Rory didn't sound too enamoured with the idea.

"Captain Adams looks like he might be a difficult man," I observed. His arms were folded arrogantly across his chest as he oversaw the activities of his crew. He seemed to enjoy hearing the sailors groan as they hefted and carried the crates of supplies on aboard.

Captain Adams' head snapped around as Rory's 'whoa—whoa' brought the horses to a halt. "Make ready to take the prisoners aboard!" he barked at his crew, who looked anything but happy.

Rory jumped down and approached the Captain. "Are you ready to deal with these poor wretches, Dr. MacLeod?" he shouted.

"Aye, that I am!" Rory answered.

"Dr. MacLeod?" Ma whispered weakly.

"Just go along with it, Ma. I'll explain later." I hoped she wouldn't start a fuss. The first lesson I can remember being taught by my mother was the importance of always telling the truth...the absolute truth, no shades of grey.

"But that's a lie, Lizzie. He shouldn't...." Ma persisted.

"Ma! Shhh. Please don't give him away!" I pleaded.

Rory was still talking with the Captain. "As you know, Captain, I have enlisted the help of a capable assistant...Miss Elizabeth Whitelaw." Rory pointed in my direction. The Captain's eyes swept over me, steely blue and cold...and bloodshot.

"She's not marked," he growled and peered intently at me. It was difficult to determine what he was thinking. His emotions were so well hidden behind his granite-like features.

"She's not a prisoner...she's a very capable young woman who is willing to assist me, especially as a mid-wife," Rory countered.

This last bit of information left the Captain standing with his mouth slightly agape and before he could ask any more questions Rory spun around, returning to our wagon to lift us down. The rest of the prisoners followed suit—helping each other.

Excruciating pain twisted their faces as they shuffled past the Captain and "Dr." MacLeod. It was also evident that many of them recognized Rory, even with his beard and wild mop of hair cleaned and trimmed. Their misery seemed to be lightened somewhat by their curiosity.

The sixty prisoners were led up the gangplank toward the open hatchway. Members of the crew bawled at them to 'get below!'. One by one, slowly and hesitantly, they descended the ladder into the hold. Too quickly, it was our turn. "Will I ever again know the sweet scent of the heather?" Ma whimpered as we descended into the dark, dank hold.

The dim interior was totally cheerless. There were only two small candles that managed to flicker out uncertain light as they swayed from hooks in the beams above us. I was sure that I saw a mouse—a very large mouse run behind some barrels. Oooh! dear God—don't let it be a rat!

"C'mon, move yersel,'" someone growled and pushed me aside.

"And where do you think you're off to in such a hurry?" I snapped back, but the words were lost in the hubbub.

"This tub is sinking! Look at the water comin' in!"

"I need the doctor!" someone shouted.

"Me, as well!" another shouted, and another. Everyone was demanding attention, now!

Rory's booming voice ordered them to be quiet. "I'll attend to th' lot o' ye as fast as I can. Now, where's Mrs. Whitelaw and Lizzie?"

Ma, ignoring her own pain, slowly raised one arm.

Rory's head craned above the rest until he spotted us and began to worm his way through the bodies to reach us...we were jammed together like kippers in a barrel! "I'll need your help as well, Mrs. Whitelaw. Lizzie and I won't be able to handle this all by ourselves."

"Rory, are you really a doctor?" she asked, "and if you aren't, do you know what a chance you're taking with these lives?"

"Sshh!" he whispered, "Lower your voice!" but it was too late, the others had overheard.

"Aye, Rory, what're ye up tae?" someone asked.

He was at the center of attention. They waited patiently for an explanation. "Well," he cleared his throat and began. "When I heard that Adams was to be the Captain of this crossin', I knew that he wouldn't be spending a penny more than he had to—which meant that maybe, and only maybe, mind you would ye be gettin' a proper doctor. So I offered him terms that the greedy..." he glanced at Ma and made an obvious effort not to swear before continuing, "...uh...that he couldn't turn down. I'm to have a free hand in doctorin' you, which means that in addition to helping you heal your wounds, I'll make sure that ye get out of this hold as often as possible."

Rory paused for a moment before he straightened his shoulders and then continued confidently, "As for my doctorin'...I attended the Edinburgh Medical School for two years and was just about to write my anatomy exam (that sets me apart from a barber—in case you're wondering) when I was dragged into the Royalist Army as a piper...and that was against a law written by Queen Mary—that a surgeon was not to be called into the army."

He took a deep breath and put his hand up, stopping a question from being asked, then continued. "Also, I studied under my father before that, who was a surgeon. He contracted the fever when he went into Dunnottar Castle to treat the Covenanters imprisoned there and while he was fighting to survive the fever, our entire estate was confiscated because he was then caught hiding and treating some of your Countrymen. The shock was too great for my Ma and she died soon after my father had passed away. So, although I never proclaimed being a part of your religious beliefs, I have suffered some loss for your cause, as well. The only thing I have of my father's is this medicine bag," Rory said, as he held the bag up for everyone to see—"and my pipes".

He swung a large oblong leather case from his back and patted it tenderly, as one might pat a bairn. "These bagpipes belonged to my mother's father and I treasure them—they even survived Bothwell Brig...well...with a sliced chanter—but that's replaced now! And that's how I ended up in the Tollbooth—I was buying a chanter when a Royalist spotted me and identified me as being a friend of John Whitelaw—which I would *not* deny. Now, are ye satisfied? That's how I landed in wi' the likes o' you!"

"Now," he continued, a note of impatience creeping into his voice, "tomorrow, another sixty or seventy poor souls are to be packed in here, as well. So, if you'd rather just keep bletherin'..." he glared at the upturned faces around him,

"I can leave you to Captain Adams...or you can accept me as the doctor. Make up your minds! And in addition to that, this so-called crew is made up mostly of convicts that signed on to get out of prison—you may recognized some of them. Captain Adams is known for his lack of generosity, to put it mildly, and if we all land on the shores of America—well, it'll be a miracle."

He took a much needed deep breath and continued, "Now, what do you want—because I can go right now if that's what you want—make up your minds!"

"Ach, no, Rory. We was just wonderin', that's a'! Don't git yer knickers in a twist!" The men tried to josh him out of his anger.

"Aw g'wan wi' ye—how could he get his knickers in a twist—he's in his kilt!" Weak attempts at laughter broke the tension.

"What's in it fer you, Rory?" The question was tossed out from the depths of the ship's hold.

"I've not much to lose and...the rest isn't any of your business!" he barked back.

"I'll help," Ma said, somewhat meekly. "Just give me a wee bit o' time to get something on my burns." she gingerly touched her cheek and then pointed to her underarms. "We'll both help! Right, lass?" She turned to me, looking for approval.

Apparently she did not understand yet how it came about that I was able to sail with them.

Rory smiled, visibly relieved. "I'll get the medicines," he announced, and quickly pulled himself up the steep ladder to the deck of the ship. We watched him disappear and like little children waiting for their mother to return, didn't move until we saw his stocking covered hairy legs and kilt reappear at the top of the hatchway.

He was carrying two pails of water with two pouches under one arm and some rolls of cloth under another. I reached up and took one of the pails. He handed the other to Ma. She winced as she tried to move her arm upward, but said nothing. And, shamefully, Rory nor I gave her the medical attention she needed so badly, so engrossed were we in the job that faced us.

"I want you to clean around the wounds as best you can, then sprinkle the burns with this silver nitrate." He handed us each a pouch, ordering us to, "Watch me and then do the same, then cover the burn with a plantain leaf and wrap this cloth around their head to keep it in place. I've brought some fever few herb and my father had acquired some ginger that he dried and ground into a powder—for stomach ailments, and some other herbs."

"Aye, Doctor." Ma said obediently.

"You can at least ask us nicely!" I rebelled at being ordered around by him and was out of patience myself.

He slowly turned toward me—glaring a hole right through me. I was beginning to recognize his 'thunder cloud' look and learned it was my signal to keep quiet. "If ye think I'll have time to send an engraved invitation every time I want ye to do something, well, that's just not on, Lizzie!" he barked.

I felt embarrassed at being caught at acting like a rebellious child. "What is it you want me to do?" I asked, still somewhat defiant, not being able to give in completely.

Rory peered angrily at me through knotted eyebrows for a moment and then called to the group for silence. "Right—now listen. If possible, try to find a place to sit down." The hold vibrated with groans as they pushed and shoved each other, trying to find their own space. Eventually, everyone was on the floor of the hold—body overlapping body.

"Your burns and any other open wounds must be attended to right away. If they aren't, you stand a good chance of gettin' the fever. Another thing! If we're to survive this crossin' we must establish some kind of order or we'll all die…from chaos alone, never mind fever!"

"Rory, where are the other sixty gonna sit when they come on board tomorrow?" one of the men asked.

"I have no idea, but we'll come up wi' something. Just let me get on with this job right now," Rory answered, rather curtly. Impatiently, he turned around, only to trip over a tangle of feet. Hitting the deck with a thump, he yelped "Bloody…" but, with great control, stopped it there. Quiet reigned in the hold.

Finally, Rory announced loudly, "The hardest thing about being a Covenanter…which I'm not…well, maybe I am—somewhat…is NOT swearing!"

Covenanters didn't swear.

"Yer doin' well, son! Yer just fine!" was to become a familiar chorus as Rory learned to "curb his tongue". I smiled to myself, taking pleasure in seeing him humbled as well.

"Well, seein' as I'm down here, I'll start wi' you," Rory quipped good naturedly. And then, "Don't wet the burn," he instructed me as he busily attended to his own patient. "Just clean around it."

I looked around, not knowing where to begin. A voice behind me said, "Ye can start wi' me, lass. Don't be shy!"

It was a young woman, about the same age as myself. I knelt down beside her and dipped the cloth into the pail. "Ach, now, I don't want to hurt you. Just stop me if I do," I told her. Gently, I wiped away the dirt from around the "C' brand on her cheek. Tears blurred my vision—I cried for the loss of an unblemished face. She was so young...looked Irish...such lovely blue eyes and black hair. Her name was Mary Gilfillan, she informed me.

"Yer goin' tae have to be braver than that, Lizzie!" Mary chided guietly.

"The doctor will heal it!" I promised, as I ignored her advise.

"Hurry up, will ye?" ordered the woman next to Mary. "I'm not wantin' the fever either!"

"Plantain will heal that burn up nice and fast!" one woman said. "I always put the pure bee's honey on an open wound," another added. Everyone offered their own particular "remedy", as all conversation revolved, at this moment in time, around the healing of burns. Not only healing the burns, but managing to do it without scars. Tried and true remedies were pulled out of memory banks and exchanged.

"Lizzie," Rory called.

"Aye?" I answered.

"When you're through there, I need yer help in the cabin—to bring down more medicines," he said, and disappeared up the ladder to the deck. Glad for the chance to get out of the hold, I scrambled up the ladder as soon as I was free. Rory's cabin was small and he was sitting in the only chair. He looked worried. "Lizzie, we haven't near enough medicines!" he confided.

"What can we do about it?"

"All that skin flint will let me buy is silver nitrate," he nodded disgustedly toward Captain Adam, who was out on the deck. "However, I was able to get some silver paper from my father's medicine chest, along with some silver coin to treat the water. I know he would want me to help these folks. I went to my cousin's house where I had left some of my belongings and to let what's left of our family know where I was going." He sighed deeply, then added, "But when I heard those biddies talking about their herbs and potions...well, I suddenly felt extremely inadequate."

The truth was coming out. I waited for Rory to continue. It quickly became obvious to me that there was more on its way. "Ye know, Lizzie, for a minute there I lost my nerve," he admitted.

"What about?"

"Well, I suddenly realized that I could be signing my own death warrant by signing on this ship and that I was a prisoner as well, along with everyone else. I have a choice. I don't have to go. No one is forcing me...unless they catch me again and then I would probably swing for it!"

"I know," I sympathized. "If it wasn't for my Ma, I wouldn't be daft enough to try this either!"

We smiled lamely at each other.

"Make your mind up, laddie, then forever hold your peace!" Rory counseled himself audibly.

"Aye, that's kind of what I said to myself, too," I confessed. "But it was easier for me, 'cause of Ma."

Rory looked into my eyes and smiled. "Aye, I think I know what ye mean." He opened the door and we stepped onto the deck.

"Doctor! Help!" a voice from the hold called out in pain.

"Aye! I'm coming." At that moment, Rory crossed over to the point of no return. He looked at me, asking "Ye comin'?"

"Aye, I'm with you." I, too, stepped over the line, never to look back.

"Then, lassie, we've work to do." He took my hand and I let him lead me to the hatch and back down into the hold.

The men reacted to our treatment differently from the women. They seemed to comprehend the seriousness of their situation more quickly than did the women. Additionally, their wounds were more painful, leaving them subdued and quietly angry. It goes without saying that each person dealt with their own pain differently than the next one.

Some wanted to have a "wee" laugh, others needed soothing words. Still others hardly wanted me to touch them at all. Finally, the last patient was washed and his wound dusted with the silver nitrate and a plantain leaf was wrapped in place.

"Mrs. Whitelaw..." Rory began but Ma interrupted.

"Rory, you can call me "Christie", if you wish; it'll be easier and it is going to be such a long trip."

He nodded. "Very well, then—Christie—you'd better let me clean your face as well. Here, hold still." Gently, ever so gently, he washed away the accumulated grime, tears and blood.

"Oh, Ma!" I cried silently, as I thought about her mutilated body. She had so many wounds. How was I going to keep her from getting infection and the fever?

"Rory," Ma began, "I want Lizzie to see to my arms and waist." I moved closer to her, intending to start right then but Rory thought differently.

"I want you to take yer Ma up tae my cabin and tend to her there. She's had enough humiliation over these wounds." He led us up the stairs to the hatchway, only to have the barrel of a musket shoved in his face. Disgusted and tired, he pushed the gun away. "Are you totally witless, man? I'm the Doctor. Now go about your business and don't do that again! Ever!"

Rory charged out of the hold and with his feet planted firmly on the deck, he looked down at the sailor, who was a good six inches shorter, and said loudly, "You agree, don't you sailor?"

"Aye, aye...sir!" was the immediate answer and sailor and musket quickly disappeared.

Rory smiled. "Well, that took care of that!" he said, pleased with having won at least one battle.

However, as we made our way to Rory's cabin, Captain Adams stopped us. "A word, Doctor, if I may." His politeness was a facade, camouflaging an explosive anger. "I understand that one of my crew and you—uh, just had words, we might say."

"Aye," Rory said, as he turned to face the Captain.

"I had given an order to shoot anyone leaving the hold. The prisoners will not be allowed on deck at any time. They will receive one meal per day, sufficient rations for anyone not doing any work. The prisoners will be expected to clean their quarters daily and all human waste will be thrown overboard by the men you appoint for that duty. Only they will they be allowed on deck and only for the space of time it takes to complete the task."

I waited, looking from one man to the other.

Captain Adams lit his pipe, never taking his eyes from Rory and continued, "I will see that barrels are provided for such use. Those prisoners who will be coming aboard in the morning must remain in chains and shackles, as they are considered dangerous." He then gestured at Ma, as if she were a dumb animal. "I see this woman is marked. She must remain in the hold for the entire journey. No exceptions—for any reason—I'm afraid. Those are the rules of my ship. Do we understand each other, Doctor?"

His tone had been that which one would use when speaking to a wayward child and not a peer.

We watched Rory, waiting for his reply and we didn't have to wait long.

"Captain Adams," Rory began, "I can and do appreciate your position. However, when I was retained by yourself and the ship's owner, Mr. Barclay, we agreed, did we not, to certain of my stipulations. One being that I would have the necessary latitude to carry out my duties as the ship's doctor."

"And exactly how much latitude are we speaking of, Doctor?" the Captain asked. "Is Miss Whitelaw included in your 'latitude'," he asked, leering at me with obvious approval.

"Sir, I will not interfere with your Mastery of this ship, nor will I put you or your crew in jeopardy in any way. However, as the Doctor, I will expect the necessary freedom to bring about the cure of these brutalized people. Further, as you know, Miss Whitelaw is my assistant and I have also appointed her mother, Mrs. Whitelaw, to assist as well. You will agree the situation warrants it. At various and sundry times I will ask one or both of them to retrieve necessary medications from my cabin and I would like to think that neither they, nor I, will be forced to look down the barrel of a loaded musket every time we emerge from the hold."

"Sounds like Rory really did go to school," Ma whispered in my ear.

Rory was gaining momentum and his education and background was obvious. We watched, more curious than afraid, as the Captain and Rory verbally jockeyed for dominance.

"This is going to be a very interesting journey, Doctor," the Captain observed.

"I'm not finished, Captain. If you are changing the terms of our agreement, please let me know now and I will leave the ship and you will have time to retain another doctor in my stead."

"Don't leave me!" I cried silently. The thought was unbearable!

"No, Doctor, that won't be necessary," said the Captain. "I think we understand each other." The Captain raised an eyebrow, "By the way, Doctor, do you play chess?"

"I've been known to win a game, now and then. Why?" Rory answered cautiously.

"Hmmff," the Captain snorted and walked away. "Oh, good day, Doctor…ladies," he tossed over his shoulder absentmindedly.

"Interesting man," I noted. "One can never quite guess what he's thinking or his next move." I felt guilty finding him intriguing, when it was obvious he was going to be our common enemy for the next six weeks.

Once inside the cabin, Ma lowered herself slowly into the comfort of the cabin's only chair. "So, you've been more than a piper and soldier in your life, laddie!" Ma stated, obviously waiting for an explanation.

Rory laughed politely, but no explanation was forthcoming. The cabin was so small 'there wasn't room to swing a cat!' as Ma observed. A narrow bunk was attached to the wall and a small writing table stood next to it.

Rory opened his wooden medicine chest, which he had placed on the table and stared at the array of bottles.

"Rory, are you sure you know what you're doin'?" Ma asked.

"Aye," he had slipped back into the informal speech that we were used to. "I'll fight for these poor wretches better than any full-fledged doctor could, besides, the only thing standing between me and my certificate is the writing of the anatomy exam—and I know that I would pass it—if I had the chance to write it."

Ma said nothing more.

"Can you manage to help me carry some more silver nitrate and silver paper down to the hold?" Then, catching himself, he said, "What am I thinking of...you came up here to tend to yourself. Here, ye've been to the very gates of hell and back and I'm asking ye to fetch and carry for me. Look, I'll bring you some water and just you take your time and do whatever you have to do." Rory apologized to Ma and left the cabin.

"Ma, what do you think of Rory?"

"How?"

"Well, do you think he can be trusted?"

"Aye...your Da trusted him. I don't know the ins and outs of the whole story, but I know they ran together after Bothwell Brig...yer Da saved his life a time or two. I think that's what he's doing...repaying yer Da by caring for us."

Rory returned a few minutes later with a basin of water and handed Ma a clean cloth. Before I could pick up the cloth to help Ma, she dismissed me with, "I can manage just fine. Away ye go and help the others."

I knew she wanted this precious time alone. Perhaps, to grieve for Da. I hoped it was the beginning of her healing—both mind and body—but it was too soon. What was I thinking?

Rory glanced quickly from me to Ma, but said nothing. I bent down and picked up some of the medical supplies.

"Aye, away ye go—the two o' ye." Ma said with a smile.

Rory smiled his appreciation. We left Ma to her privacy...such a precious commodity.

"You're sure ye can manage, Lizzie?" Rory handed me more supplies to carry.

"Aye, I'm sure." But I groaned under the load which made both of us laugh. We walked slowly toward the hatchway, breathing deeply. "I wish we could take this air down with us," I said. "The air in the hold is already foul and we're not yet under way!"

Rory put his bag of medicines down. He took hold of my shoulders and studied my face. "What's goin' on inside that pretty head of yours?" His eyes looked sad and he spoke slowly. "Your young years should be reason enough to be spared all of this pain and hurt, Lizzie." He cupped my face in his hands. "Only this morning you watched your Da..."

"Rory," I interrupted, "right now I just want to work." I paused before adding, "...and not think."

I was filled with grief and didn't know where to begin letting it go. The thought of releasing all of my pent up pain actually frightened me.

I pulled my face away from his hands and said, "Cum' on," forcing a brightness I didn't feel, "we have work to do. Whose turn is it to work on Alistair MacCrimmon?"

"Alright, you've a right to handle it your way," he conceded. "Now, what's this about Alistair? Is he being awkward?"

Relieved to be onto a safe subject, I quipped, "Awkward is putting it mildly, Rory. He's outright miserable. He doesn't have to say a word. You can feel the anger just radiating from him!"

Rory chuckled, "Aye, he can be like that at times. Here, watch yer step..." and we helped each other carry the supplies down the ladder.

"Doctor!" A woman, with an irritatingly grating, high pitched voice, met us at the bottom of the ladder, demanding, "Where is Mrs. Whitelaw?"

"She's probably restin', right Rory?" someone else said sarcastically.

"She'll be paying a high price for this sleep!" cackled another.

I looked around the hold and couldn't believe what I was witnessing. The men were exchanging knowing glances with each other and the women were whispering and snickering—especially the prostitutes that had been banished with the Covenanters. My eyes filled with angry tears.

"Lizzie," Rory said gently, "I want you to go up the stairs and into my cabin and you and your Ma stay there as long as you want. In fact, tell your Ma that I said to stay the night and have a good sleep. And you might as well, too. And what do you think of the idea of going ashore to pick some plantain leaves—just tell the Captain I asked you to do it. Take your time, lassie."

Then he bent over me and asked, "Do you think you can use some of your pearls for the medicines."

I nodded my agreement but mentally calculated that I only had eight left. To part with these precious pearls—a gift from my father—was becoming extremely difficult.

He waited until I had climbed through the hatchway and thought that I was out of earshot. But instead, I crouched down small as possible and hid by the open hatchway, waiting to hear what he was going to say. Night had shrouded the ship in darkness and I hoped that no one could see me.

"Right," he started, "let's understand something. Your comfort and perhaps even your very lives depend upon how well I can negotiate for it with the Captain. It is common knowledge that out of the one hundred and twenty prisoners that'll be in this hold by tomorrow, about ninety o' ye will be alive when we arrive in America. We have the added worry of your wounds getting infected, so that ups the numbers considerably."

"How long will the crossin' tak' Rory?" someone interrupted.

"About six weeks, depending on the weather." he answered calmly.

"But there isn't enough room in here for a hundred and twenty o' us."

I waited. "Why were they talking about the other prisoners? Ma's honor had been questioned. If he isn't going to do something, then I will!" I mentally poised myself for the confrontation.

Rory continued speaking. "This is the worst of it. The sixty prisoners from Leith...well, some of them have to make the crossin' in shackles and chains. Now, if you're already complaining, we'll be at each other's throats within a week and dead in two, and..." he continued, "besides that, there is the probability of an outbreak of fever, and some of you will get sea sick and wish you were dead. Those who are well will have to help those who are sick."

He took a breath before continuing. "And see those two barrels? That's for our waste. The men will see to the emptying of them every day. At this point, none of you, with the exception of Mrs. Whitelaw and her daughter, Lizzie, are allowed on deck. I hope to get exercise privileges for everyone, but it certainly won't happen if we are heard quarreling with one another!"

His words were greeted with silence. I crept close and looked into the hold. They were bobbing their heads up and down in agreement. Without warning, Rory spun around to face the women who had been maligning Ma. "And you!" he thundered, wagging a threatening finger at them, "stop those clacking tongues about Christie Whitelaw! Just one more word and you'll rue the day you were ever born. Mark my words!"

"Ease up, MacLeod!" An equally threatening voice was heard, "That's my missus yer talkin' to."

"Then it'll be yoursel' I'll be pasting if she speaks out of turn again!" Rory said coolly.

Their eyes locked. "There can only be one giving orders right now and that dubious privilege has fallen to me. Does anyone disagree? Because if ye do, say so now and I'll be on my way."

"That's blackmail, Rory," I thought.

Only silence met his challenge. "Right, then we leave everything as it stands?" he asked.

"Aye!" It was unanimous.

"Now, I'll go to the galley and see what's being made for your supper. It's been a long and miserable day for all of us."

I scrambled toward the cabin and burst through the door, out of breath. Ma was startled. "What's chasin' ye, lass?" she asked when she had recovered her wits.

I didn't answer.

Ma glanced at me, almost shyly. "Strange. But ye reminded me of yer Da, bursting in here like that, all breathless and your red hair looking so wild."

"Ma, I'm away to pick some plantain leaves and buy some herbs. I won't be long." I didn't wait for her answer and just quietly closed the cabin door and left the ship.

CHAPTER 15

The next morning we were wakened by the sound of angry voices.

"Strange, I can remember being happy to wake up and leave my nightmare behind. Now I wake up to a nightmare," Ma moaned. "Oh, my poor body!" she cried as she carefully lifted one arm and then the other, inspecting the burns in her armpits. "They look awful!" she cried.

And they did, as scabs were beginning to form over the brand on her cheek and under her arms.

"Ma! Don't get up! I can help Rory!" Before I could finish speaking, there was a loud knock at the door.

"What a sight the two o' you make!" Rory laughed. He ducked through the doorway, so as to not hit his head. His face looked tired and drawn. "They're bringing the other prisoners aboard. Hear that?" He nodded his head toward the sound of metal, scraping against the deck. "Some of those poor devils have their wrists and ankles rubbed raw from the shackles. We'll have our hands full, ladies, trying to keep infection from killing them all off!"

"Where did you sleep last night?" Ma asked.

"In the hold wi' th' others."

"Thank you," Ma said simply. Then she asked, "Rory, what does my face look like? It feels hot and swollen."

"Your face is beautiful as ever!" he said easily, "but let's get it washed and we'll put some more silver nitrate on it…no, let's put a piece of the silver paper on it."

"Where did you get the pieces of silver paper, Rory?" Ma asked.

"They were in my father's medicine bag. Before he died, a friend of his brought them from Egypt—they use them there for treating burns and my father had good results with them as well. I want to put one on you, Christie."

"Aye, I'll try anything to heal this." She touched her cheek gingerly, wincing as she did so. "I'm so stiff and sore!" she cried as she struggled to stand up. "If I eat something, maybe that'll help," she muttered, trying to get her balance.

"Well, can you pretend that this is a warm scone, just off the griddle, and that this is the freshest cheese in all of Scotland?" Rory laughed as he offered us some of last night's leftover dried bread and hardened cheese. "And if you can, tell me how you did it, alright?"

"Away wi' ye, Rory!" Ma and I giggled in spite of our aches and pains.

"Well, enough of this love makin'!" Rory grinned at me. "Hurry yersel. I need you in the hold. We have to do what we did yesterday, all over again, and twice as many."

I groaned.

"Rory!" Ma called out, but he was gone. "Lizzie," she turned to me, "what does my face look like?"

"It looks sore, Ma."

"But what does it look like?" she insisted.

"It looks sore, Ma!" I repeated impatiently, not wanting to tell her the truth. I didn't have the courage to tell her the truth or the maturity to understand what she was feeling. I only knew that my beautiful mother was scarred for life.

"You're my Ma! It doesn't matter what you look like!" I tried to evade her question.

"It matters to me," she said, looking down at the floor.

"Ma, you always look beautiful to us!" Such a little word—us—but it brought back a flood of memories, of Da telling Ma how beautiful she was. How he was the envy of every man in Scotland and Jenny, Iain and I would giggle, watching her blush.

"Lizzie, where's Jenny and Iain?" Ma's whispered question brought me back to the present.

"They're with Angus and Maggie Winters." I forced myself to repeat the lie I had told her in the prison. She must have forgotten. I knew Ma couldn't handle the news of Iain's death right now.

"You mean old Maggie and Angus took them in?"

"Aye."

"God bless them!"

Then Ma was silent. I was thankful she didn't mention Da's death. We still hadn't talked about it, but I was sure that her mind never left the sight of him on the gibbet and swinging from that rope. Hearing her cry out to him with all the love and anguish in her soul, "My John, my Jo!" will remain with me forever.

Mercifully, Ma interrupted my thoughts and with a weak smile, said, "Well, hen, let's eat up and face our day's work! And let's get that silver paper on my cheek, that's a good wee girl."

I nodded my head, tucking my lie about Iain away into a corner of my heart. I made a silent promise, "One day I'll tell you the truth…one day, Ma. But not just now."

I placed the silver paper on Ma's cheek and we tried to make a dent in the cheese but gave up, not wanting to break out teeth. It was good to hear a giggle out of my Ma once in a while; but I knew her heart wasn't in it. Time—it would take time.

Rory was bent over his patient, Geordie Cameron, intent upon cleaning his "ear", or more correctly, where his ear used to be when we descended into the hold again.

"Is it a good ship?" Geordie wanted to know.

"Aye, the "Henry and Francis" seems quite sturdy. Must be a fast sailing ship?" Geordie asked longingly. He was a fisherman and loved the sea. To be cooped up in this hold and not be up top, enjoying the air and sea, was an added punishment for him.

"Captain says she's a real veteran—she's made many an Atlantic crossing." Rory answered, keeping the conversational ball in the air.

"Feels like the winds are favorable, and the sea must be fairly calm, right?" Geordie pulled for more gossip.

"Oh, aye," Rory agreed, "I don't know anything about ships and the sea, but I think we must be traveling at a good clip."

"Aye, aye, that we are," Geordie agreed quietly. Geordie was an exception, the overall atmosphere in the hold was far from calm. The crowded conditions made sure of that! I shuddered each time an argument broke out over whose foot was in whose space.

"Keep offa me—this is my place!" had become an oft repeated war cry.

However, it was so forgivable after hearing their stories about their survival. About twelve of the prisoners had suffered being imprisoned in Edinburgh Tollbooth, but when the officials heard that the Earl of Argyle was fighting for their release, they decided to send "the prisoners for religion" to Dunnottar Castle, a recently acquired state prison which rivaled Bass Rock Prison for security and torture.

Evidently, the doors of the Edinburgh jails were opened and the surprised inmates, two hundred and forty in number including women were led hurriedly down to Leith by soldiers. They were not allowed to tell family or friends that they were leaving and were packed into open boats and landed at Burntisland. Then they were crowded into two rooms of the Burntisland Tollbooth and kept there for two days and nights without food or water. However, any who would swear the Oath of Allegiance to the King were sent back to Edinburgh—and forty complied. The rest were willing to take the Oath of Allegiance, but they firmly refused to accept the Oath of Supremacy, as it involved the acknowledgment of an avowed Papist, the King, to be the head of the Church.

With their hands tied with strong cords behind their backs, the prisoners were driven on from Burntisland to Freuchie near Falkland, constantly surrounded by unfeeling and cruel soldiers who heaped all kinds of monstrous abuse upon them. Old women and invalids who lagged behind were beaten and threatened with death for going so slowly.

The Covenanters begged to be allowed to hire horses at their own expense but were refused. They were driven from Freuchie to the Tay and were ferried to Dundee where they were allowed refreshment "at their own expense". They were then marched through Forfar and Brechin to the North Esk bridge, and here were forced to stand or crouch all night long. At four o'clock the next morning they were marched to Dunnottar.

This notorious fortress stands on the top of a rock four acres in extent and 160 feet high, overhanging the sea, and is separated from the mainland by a deep but dry chasm. It is about 15 miles south of Aberdeen and these prison vaults held the grimmest of tales. It was here that the Covenanters were handed over to the tender mercies of the governor—a master fiend.

He thrust 167 men and women into a dark, dank dungeon, 54 3/4 feet long by 15 1/2 feet wide. The floor was ankle deep in mire and mud. Only one window looked out on the moaning ocean and this alone could not allow enough air into the vault to satisfy even their most meager needs. They were so tightly packed together that they could not move without leaning on each other. To their horror they soon learned the use for the apertures that were cut into the walls. If prisoners cried out or complained, they were deemed refractory and the offender was stood with his arms extended and his fingers, gripping the crevices, were secured by wedges that were pounded into the crevices. In this cruel manner many mercifully died, but others, who lived, were deprived of the use of their limbs for the rest of their lives—being wracked by rheumatism and other diseases.

In addition to these apertures, there was a row of hooks which ran along the roof and, again, if a prisoner was deemed refractory by the jailer, he was suspended from the hooks by his wrists while a stool, full of iron spikes, was placed beneath his feet, offering him the alternative of either this painful suspension, or puncturing the soles of his feet if he sought relief by placing them on the stool.

Still others took courage from the story about those few who escaped the Canongate Tollbooth and had witnessed the hand of the Lord. Their favorite story was of the twenty-five prisoners in two big upper rooms in that jail and not one of them expected to see the light of day again, until they were taken to the Merket Cross to be hanged. But being men of God, they prayed for help in planning a mass escape. It was not a very well kept secret as friends in Edinburgh and even as far away as Glasgow knew the time and how it was to be executed and added their prayers for its success.

One cell was on the floor above the other and those in the lower cell, on a certain night, were to begin to saw through the iron bars of their window which had no glass. Those in the cell above were to get part of their flooring ready to take up easily when all the iron window bars were cut. The plan was for the prisoners in the upper cell to pull up the floor and drop into the lower cell and they would all escape together.

About nine o'clock one night, the first window bar was sawn through. But to the horror of all concerned and before anyone could catch it, down fell the errant bar into the narrow street below, landing with a great clatter to where a sentry was standing!

They all waited and watched and prayed. Nothing happened—the sentry hadn't come running up with the bar in his hand—nothing was said. On top of this, although their window was almost parallel with that of the garrison commander, Lord Linlithgow, who lived on the other side of the street, they had neither been heard nor seen. Their prayers had been answered.

Next morning at about nine o'clock a friend was allowed in to visit them. They asked him to go out on the street and see if the window with its missing iron bar was noticeable to passers-by. Down on the street, he not only was able to retrieve the window bar but was able to get it sent into the prisoners. They then were able to replace it and continued sawing through the remaining bars without incident.

When all was ready, the signal was given to those prisoners in the cell above them that it was time to lift up the loose part of their floor, and one by one they dropped into the lower room. Quickly and quietly all twenty-five prisoners escaped through the barless window and into the street, to disappear into the night. Many of them were countrymen who did not know their way about Edinburgh, but all found safe haven. One of them, an Englishman, had the faith or guided simplicity, to go forward and knock at the door of a house where he had seen a light in a window. It happened to be the home of the Bishop! To the serving maid who came to the door he frankly told who he was. She took him in and hid him until she got him safely away to some Covenanter friends. Only one of the twenty-five was ever recaptured.

A terrible row broke out in the circles of Edinburgh officialdom! The magistrates of the city were called together and roundly and soundly blamed! They were warned that if it happened again, they would be imprisoned.

This was one of the favorite stories and was often told and retold as the Covenanters compared this escape with that of Peter's from the insane fury of King Herod.

Stories were wonderful but I had to deal with the present. "Ach, cum' on now," I constantly pleaded, bargaining for a little more space for the sick to stretch out. Over and over again, Ma and I repeatedly cleansed the weeping wounds of the prisoners. It seemed, at times, that it was going to be an impossible task to keep infection at bay. But slowly, ever so slowly, our efforts were rewarded. The wounds began to form new pink scar tissue.

We were winning!

Rory had instructed the shackled prisoners to keep flexing their muscles so as to avoid cramping and he coaxed them into pushing against their leg and arm irons in hopes of preventing their muscles from atrophying. Those of the prisoners who were well enough, massaged their aching limbs—anything to keep the blood circulating and avoiding the punishing and unforgiving cramping.

Recently, Rory could even be heard whistling, softly. It had a soothing effect upon those around him, most of the time.

"Let's hear 'Westering Home'," someone would ask.

"No! That one makes me homesick!" another would object.

The familiar tunes we had heard all our lives now became so very important to us. It was all we had. Music and stories. And this, only in our memories. One's ability to remember events, detail by minute, correct detail, was constantly challenged.

"Ach, away wi' ye! the Bruce fought at Bannockburn in 1375 not 1378! Any dim-wit knows that!" And the fight was on. To sing a song, note perfect, also became an all-consuming challenge.

"Sheilagh Kirk, now tell me, was I on key or not?"

Sheilagh was recognized as the final word. Her voice and pitch was acknowledged by all as indisputably perfect.

Anything! Anything to make the time pass and keep the nightmares from invading the waking hours. Slowly we adjusted as best we could to the cattle-like conditions.

All, that is, except Alistair MacCrimmon. He was a life-long friend of Rory's; a man of about thirty years who 'had been snatched from the bosom of his young family'; Wallace Lauderdale was also the author of his horror.

Time after time we shared our personal experiences that had altered our lives so horribly—and learned that most of our tragedies were due to Captain Lauderdale and his dragoons.

Alistair's wife, Mary, and their five small children had been left in Scotland, all alone, to fend for themselves. Alistair could not bear the pain of the terminal separation; so he had very quietly turned his face to the wall of the hold and was patiently waiting for death to release him from his agony. The sadness that enveloped him was so intense that it reached out and infected the rest of us. His plight began to take precedence over even our own miseries and it wasn't long before the competition was on, as to who was going to be able to coax him to at least turn around and eat something.

In spite of all our loving efforts, his will to die seemed stronger than our combined will for him to live. "Lizzie," Ma whispered in my ear, "have ye tried to get Alistair to take a wee cup o' broth, today?"

"Aye, Ma. But he won't even answer me when I speak to him. He just turns his head away and shuts his eyes. I..."

"Quiet!" some one said in a hushed tone. "Listen!"

Silence gripped the hold. We could hear the unmistakable thundering of Rory's voice.

"Ach, he's a good lad!" a woman whispered. "He's fightin' wi' the Captain for us again."

"Shshsh!"

"As Doctor of this ship, I request, *again*, and I emphasize *again,* that these people be allowed to exercise in the fresh air. Do you realize that some of them have even survived the Dunnottar Castle and Bass Rock Prison and you want them to die in your ship's hold? Do you want to be known as the very elixir of inhumanity? Have you been down in that hold yet, Captain? Do you have any idea how foul the air is?"

"Doctor, there is absolutely no necessity for me to go into that hold," the Captain countered. "They are the offenders, not I!"

I couldn't help smiling. I knew Rory's ways now and I could see him in my mind's eye, making this great effort to control his temper. But his neck would becoming deep red and the veins would be standing out, throbbing with the anger, a dead give-away that he was about to explode.

Rory's voice became louder with the next appeal. "Captain Adams, I'll give you any assurances necessary, in order to persuade you to allow them to have benefit of the deck. Even once in a while. Please!" Rory was actually begging.

A few moments of silence reigned. I knew from experience, now, that the Captain would have hidden behind that granite look, where it was impossible to figure out what he was thinking.

Finally, the Captain spoke; however, the congenial sound in his voice was confusing. "Well, if you can carry out your promises, I'll allow ten at a time on deck for ten minutes a day!"

"...and the men in chains released!" Rory demanded.

"Rory, you're pushing your luck." I groaned out loud.

"...and Lizzie Whitelaw as my dinner companion...tonight!" the Captain shot back. His wicked, evil laugh filled my ears. "Checkmate! You fool!" the Captain gloated.

Rory had no reply. He had been out maneuvered.

"Then, Doctor, I can assume it's settled? Do you have any other requests of me?" The question was riddled with smugness. Without waiting for an answer, he added, "Oh, by the way, Doctor, don't be too hard on yourself. You've done remarkably well by your people. By now, there are usually a dozen deaths and most of the women prisoners would be appreciating the rewards of keeping my crew satisfied. You see? I, too, try to look after my people."

A few moments of strained silence, then Rory and the Captain began speaking in subdued tones. I strained to hear them, but it was impossible. Eventually, the hatch cover lifted. Rory, looking terribly defeated, peered down at us. We squinted up into his face and the bright daylight.

Rory looked very tired, as if the steady, non-stop pace had caught up with him all at once. I wanted to hold him. My "I want to make you feel better" feelings for him startled me.

"What is it, son?" one of the men called up to him. "What's he done tae ye?"

I pushed my way through the tangle of bodies until I was at the bottom of the ladder, waiting for him to descend. "Rory, what's the matter?" I asked, when he was finally standing in front of me. When he didn't answer me, I sensed that it had something to do with me having dinner with the Captain.

"I'll have dinner with him. I don't mind," I assured him.

He looked so deeply into my eyes that I felt uncomfortable. Eventually, he spoke. "Captain Adams will allow ten of you a day on deck until we dock and will remove the shackles from these folks." He gestured toward the line of men who sat side-by-side against the wall of the hold, their ankles and wrists festering under the crude metal bands.

A cheer went up.

But I wanted to know more, "...and?" I prompted.

Rory took a deep breath and blurted out, "If Lizzie agrees to be his dinner companion tonight."

"I don't mind that," I said innocently.

"Lizzie!" Rory shouted at me. "Will ye grow up, woman! He wants you for the whole night!"

There it was...the truth was out!

I was dumbfounded. "I don't believe what you said, Rory!"

"Rory! No!" Ma cried out from the depths of the hold. She was immediately at my side. "I'll go instead!"

I looked at Ma's face, still scabbed from the disfiguring brand on her cheek. Her voice quivered with fear.

"Please, Rory. Not Lizzie. Not this way! She's never known a man. Give him someone else. Anyone! But not my daughter! No more! I can't take any more!" She threw her arms around me.

"Is it goin' to take him a' night tae eat his supper?" a woman's voice asked naively. Her husband groaned.

"Bridget, just shut yer gob, will ye?" he demanded.

"And if I don't agree?" I asked quietly, but I already knew the answer.

"Lizzie. I'll not let ye do it!" Rory stated flatly. "There'll be another way around it! Just give me time to think!"

Fear and panic seized me, again. They were becoming my constant companions. I wanted to run. Anywhere...but where? I looked past those who were crushed around me to the sixty shackled prisoners. Their eyes were on me.

Some were pleading silently. Others dropped their eyes to the floor, rather than meet my gaze. But no one except Ma and Rory had told me that they didn't want me to make this sacrifice. And it was a sacrifice! Everything that I had ever been taught to hold sacred was going to be sacrificed.

"Keep yersel' pure and clean for yer husband," my Ma had counseled me over and over again. I hadn't so much as held hands with a man. Rory was the only man that had ever held me, other than my Da and Grandda!

Sacrifice!

The word brought back the vivid memory of my father standing on the scaffold, head high, smiling at Ma, commending his spirit to the Father. He had sacrificed his *life* for his beliefs...the Covenant. "Oh! God, please, no! Don't ask me to do this. I'm not strong enough. I'm not like my Ma and Da! The words screamed in my mind, struggling to be shouted out loud. I was so confused! Where was the answer!

Finally, one of the shackled men spoke up and offered, "Lizzie, ye dinna have to dae this for me! I've gotten used to sittin' here. Besides, wi' my luck I'd probably just fall overboard, anyway!"

A nervous titter rippled throughout the hold.

"Aye, lass. Don't dae it." Many voices joined in, releasing me from my decision. Ma dropped her arms from around me. She smiled into my face and patted my cheek. There was happy relief in her eyes.

"Rory..." I began, as he put his arm protectively around me. I looked up at him, relishing the feeling of security for the moment and said nothing; although my mind was reeling. We'd only been at sea for two weeks. Another four and then some, to go. I looked at the slopping waste barrels and I didn't have to look down to know that I was standing in human excrement. We will surely die in this muck if we have to live in it much longer.

A shudder ran through my body.

Again, my father's face flashed in front me. He had taught me so carefully about the importance of chastity. "The Lord delights in the chastity of his daughters," he would say and each time I heard his advice, my resolve to never offend Him strengthened. I was grateful that Da was at least being spared watching me agonize over this decision.

I held my hand up for them to be quiet. "You all know that the Captain will have his way, and he certainly won't listen to reason. Remember what happened to Willie when he was thrown into the brig. Well, if the Captain doesn't get what he wants tonight, the same thing will happen to me and you'll all still be in this stinkin' hold!" I realized that I was shouting.

Willie was the immediate center of attention, as we recalled how he had been whipped for hitting one of the crew. A sailor, who had brought down the bucket of gruel for our supper, had made the mistake of poking fun at Willie's harelip lisp. Willie landed on him like a big cat, but was quickly pulled off by another sailor.

They battered him to the ground and he was dragged off to the brig. When he returned to the hold, his back told the story of the inhumane whipping. Leather thongs wrapped around small metal balls had lifted off strips of skin leaving behind raw, gaping flesh. The memory of Willie's screams flooded into my memory and I hid my face against Rory's chest.

"Pray for me. Please, pray for me!" I asked. My decision was made.

"No! Lizzie! Don't!" Ma cried out.

"Ma, I must. Just look around you. If we don't get out of here, most of us will die anyway. I have to try!" I heard myself speaking confidently, a confidence I surely was not feeling. Rory's arm dropped from around me and he took a step backward.

I was standing alone.

"We'll all pray for ye, lass," one of the shackled prisoners called out.

"Aye."

"Aye."

The 'ayes' rippled throughout the hold as they all agreed.

Torture and humiliation were not strangers to Covenanters. The stories of how so many had spent month after month in prisons specifically designated for our people, came to the forefront of my memory. They knew the terror and agony of hearing the dying screams of their kin and friends who had been devilishly tortured by the Royalists. Still others, some right here in this hold, had survived these horrors, only to relive them in ever recurring nightmares.

I looked into their faces. This "pile of human garbage", as the Captain was so fond of calling us, had developed deep bonds—we even took care of the six women who were being banished because they were 'ladies of the street'. They had even began to join us when we knelt in daily prayer, pleading for faith and hope. We received strength from our supplications…they strengthened us and we knew our God lived and that our experiences were for our strengthening; at times, but not often enough, some even found joy in their adversity. feeling that they were being 'refined as gold'.

I knew my people—my 'ain folk'; I knew they could speak words in a way that would cut you up as if you had been knifed, but at their core was a loyalty and integrity and generosity you could rely upon. That I was going to be defiled by the Captain was causing a deep sorrow in most of them. However, I knew 'the six' women prisoners were even envying me my good meal and soft bed for the night.

I was coming to a realistic understanding of human nature and was not about to be fooled by the shallow sounding pleas that I was "not tae dae anything foolish". I was very aware of the hope in their voices. But still, most were genuine in their objections, saying they'd take their chances with the Captain rather than let me throw my virtue away.

Their loyalty touched me. I looked down once more at my feet. My shoes were crusted with filth and, as if on cue, the stink assailed my nostrils, making me want to gag. I turned to the ladder and looked up.

"Lizzie, don't!" Rory bellowed.

I gripped the rung of the ladder with my shaking hand and Rory placed his over it. "Lizzie, please don't! For me—for us!" he said softly; the pleading look in his eyes almost changed my mind.

I gently moved his hand away and began my climb.

"No!" he roared, as he swung at the ladder with his fist.

"Ye'll be ruined! You're mine! You're mine—not that pig's!"

I hung on with both hands until the ladder was steady again. Out of the corner of my eye I noticed the blood spurting from Rory's knuckles. I couldn't turn back now, no matter what. My decision was made.

Ma's voice was dull with resignation. "She's her father's daughter, Rory. She's a Whitelaw, through and through. You'll never change that streak. If they think it's right—they'll carry it out, no matter what! Believe me, I tried wi' her father."

CHAPTER 16

I struggled to keep my hand from shaking as I reached to knocked on the Captain's cabin door.

"Tap...tap."

"Ah! Miss Whitelaw!" he gushed as he flung the door open. "Ahem—you...ah...look a little different than when I last saw you," he sputtered.

I looked down at my dirty shoes and dress. My hands were grey with dirt...dirt that had been there for twelve days. And that awful odor, I realized to my dismay, was me. I watched the Captain's nose curl up involuntarily.

"Come in! Come in! Don't just stand there, my dear." He was using his "charming" voice, as we called it in the hold. "Now, now, now, don't feel shy," he counseled with slippery sounding words. The door closed behind me with a terrifying finality.

Mercy! There was a loud thump on the door. My heart skipped a beat. I was about to be rescued! Oh, thank you Lord!

"Come in!" the Captain sounded annoyed.

Two sailors entered. One was carrying a large oval metal tub; the other toted a pail of steaming water in each hand. "What...?" I stammered, as I watched the water being poured into the tub.

The sailors laughed.

I blushed. From the very tips of my toes to the top of my head, I was glowing bright pink.

"A bath...Miss Whitelaw. A bath. Have you never had a bath before?" The Captain's impatience was surfacing.

A bath! This was going to be far worse than I ever imagined. In my panic I reached for the door to make my escape—into the ocean if necessary.

"Let me out of here!" I wanted to scream. "But I can't!" I reminded myself. My hand dropped from the door handle. I'm trapped! By my own stubbornness, I admitted to myself. I had announced my decision to the others. Now, I couldn't go back on it! I had forgotten the word "sacrifice" and why I was here. My stomach quivered with fear.

"Uhh—Miss Whitelaw, I don't want to seem indelicate but, ahem," he coughed politely, "you do need a bath and clean clothes. Don't feel badly, I always insist that all of my dinner companions bathe first." His efforts at soothing my nervousness failed miserably.

"Stop telling me what not to feel!" I spat at him. "I may be part of your cargo but I've my own mind!" Fear turned to anger and spilled over.

"Ye've a feisty one tonight, Cap'n," observed one of the sailors. "If I wuz you..."

A withering look and, "But you are not!" from his Captain stopped him in mid-sentence.

The Captain, ignoring my rudeness, pulled a beautiful pale green, silk dress from a cupboard. He laid it carefully over the bed. Beside it he placed a delicate, lace petticoat and chemise and pantaloons, which he fondled first. I thought it strange to see a man use his hands in such a way.

"Yer the lucky one!" whispered one of the sailors, as he passed by me to leave the cabin.

"Shut yer trap!" I hissed at him under my breath.

"There, Miss Whitelaw," the Captain was determined to maintain dignity. "That is your bath. You'll find soap and a drying towel on the bench." The Captain pointed at the tub. "And...this is perfume." He smiled as he sprinkled it over the steaming bath water. He was waiting for me to say something and I knew it.

"Miss Whitelaw, are you able to speak, uhh—civilly?" he asked.

I glared at him before nodding my head.

"This certainly has all the earmarks of a joyful evening," the Captain muttered sarcastically. "Please make sure you wash your hair as well. Then put on the clean clothes."

He glared at me so angrily, I was sure he was going to hit me, so I backed away from him which only served to anger him more. "Miss Whitelaw! Why are you being so difficult? The ladies I bring up here from the hold are more than pleased with what I offer them!" He angrily swung his hand toward the bath and the clean clothes, adding "*and* are extremely appreciative!"

"Well, I'm petrified, that's why I'm difficult," I thought, but remained silent.

"Leave your clothes and especially your shoes outside the door. One of the crew will clean them for you," he instructed me. "Now, don't take all day, but do enjoy your bath!" With that, he stepped quickly out of the cabin with only a quick glance behind him.

I flicked the water with my fingers causing the fragrance from the perfume to rise in the steam. It was something I had never experienced before. How delicate! If I closed my eyes, I could imagine a bouquet of flowers and their fragrance wafting up to me. Slowly, never taking my eyes from the door, I undressed.

As ordered, I opened the door a crack and pushed the sorry bundle of my clothing out onto the deck. Then I noticed the bolt—there was a bolt on the door! I slid the protecting piece of iron into its cradle, locking the door and allowed myself a sigh of relief.

Ah! The perfume was like a field of flowers and all in one tub! For the first time in my life I was wet all over, at the same time. Never had I ever had an all-over bath before. That was something for only the queen and the likes of her.

In spite of my anxiety, I was very much aware of the soap's velvet texture. I rolled it between my palms, letting its rich, milky lather slide down my arms. Glancing around to ensure that I was alone, I slipped under the water, wetting my hair.

"Ohhh!" I moaned. Ecstasy!

But the thought of the Captain coming back before I was out of the tub, hurried me. Besides, the bath made me feel that I was making myself clean for a dirty purpose. The contradiction spoiled what could have been a two-hour luxurious respite. As it was, I had just managed to button the dress moments before he was banging on the door.

"I don't want to do this!" I muttered to myself. I slowly moved toward the door in response to the Captain's insistent knocking.

The Captain stared at me in open approval. "That was worth waiting for!" He reached out and held my face between his hands. A feeling of revulsion raced through my body as I looked up at his dirty, crooked teeth and hairy nostrils.

"Your hair—your hair is so—so sensual!" The words came from deep in his throat. He bent down and breathed in the scent of my clean hair. My eyes were screwed shut. I did not want to see what was going to happen. I felt his hands leave my face and lightly touch my shoulders and his fingers began to flutter down my arms. It was annoying! So annoying that I stopped trembling.

This action almost brought me to the point of screaming, but I clenched my teeth shut and stopped before it could escape my throat.

His wet lips found my neck and throat.

I shuddered. "I can't do this! I hate it! I'd rather be whipped!" I pushed him away.

The word "sacrifice" surfaced, almost violently in my mind and, once again, I was reminded of the shackled prisoners. The struggle was pulling me apart. Maybe I can't carry this sacrifice out! Maybe some sacrifices are too much!

A loud knock on the door saved me.

"Captain! Dinner is served."

My relief must have been obvious, because the Captain grabbed me and said, "You're not getting away with this! I mean it!"

"Sir?" came the query from the other side of the door.

"Yes! Yes! By all means, come in!" the Captain growled petulantly.

The sailors hurriedly brought in covered silver bowls, which they placed on a small sideboard while they obviously made an effort to keep their eyes on their work. A white cloth was spread over the table; flatware and china plates were placed carefully on it. It looked so elegant! so regal! The wine goblets reflected the light from the small fireplace and the silver knives sparkled in the candlelight. For a small moment I almost forgot why I was there.

The sailors stepped back to admire their work, but were brought back to reality with a curt, "Thank you, gentlemen." The Captain had brought them up sharply. "Take the tub when you leave."

"Please spill the water! Do something, anything, so you won't have to leave me alone with this man," I silently begged.

They left, carrying the tub between them. Not a drop spilled over.

We were alone again. I moved to the table, anxious to put distance between me and the Captain.

"You are quite right, of course, my dear. We should eat while the food is hot. We have all night for…" and he looked at me hopefully.

"I hate him," ran through my mind. "He must be incredibly stupid! Does he actually think I'm only being shy? That he just needs to coax me a little? Maybe he thinks that I'm being coy. And besides, it's he that needs the bath. Not only that, he's ugly! Oh, Ma!"

"Coy!" The word rolled around in my brain. A plan was forming.

"Come, my dear, please eat. You don't want to let all of this good food go to waste, do you?"

I wanted to scream at the sound of his syrupy voice. Where had I heard that tone before? I strained, trying to remember. Aha! It was Wallace Lauderdale! That same slippery, slimy tone that I detested, and for good reason.

Oh, Ma! Was this what you faced!" The thought was a revelation.

"Eating is an art, my dear," the Captain droned on. "Let me serve you. We will begin with the soup." He lifted the lid from the tureen, releasing the steam. With a courtly gesture, he dipped in the ladle and filled two small bowls. When it was placed in front of me, I couldn't help but respond to the savory fragrance of pea soup with small pieces of salt pork floating on top. I pressed my spoon into its thick center and put it to my lips. Food! It took all of my self-control to not lift the bowl to my mouth and gulp down the contents. Ma had taught us our manners, though. I knew not to gulp! Not to belch! And to use a serviette. The Captain was obviously relieved that I didn't eat as though I was at a trough, as he watched me sip my soup.

"Next!" he announced, as if he were introducing something extremely important. From an oblong silver tray he slid a piece of white fish onto my plate. "Halibut," he said proudly, and proceeded to pour a creamy sauce with small onions over it.

Ohhh, how it melted in my mouth! As I savored that beautiful fish right to the very last morsel, the Captain busied himself by producing and opening a bottle of white wine. With a courtly flourish, he filled my glass and waited for me to taste it. Never before had I tasted or drank any alcohol; although I must admit I'd been curious about its taste. I hesitated, staring at the clear, slightly amber liquid in my glass.

"To cleanse the pallet, my dear...to cleanse the pallet."

Slowly I raised the glass to my lips and took a small sip. It bubbled on my tongue and tasted, I thought, a bit like vinegar. However, I expressed approval which caused the Captain to brightened. "Yes, my dear Captain, two can play this game." I thought smugly.

"Now, for the 'piéce de rèsistance'," he said, in almost perfect French. I understood because Grandda had taught us the language.

"You certainly know how to eat well, Captain Adams," I offered easily.

He nodded modestly and reached for my hand across the table, giving it what I'm sure he thought to be an affectionate squeeze. "Just you wait!" I said to myself and smiled at him sweetly.

A plate, with perfectly layered slices of roast beef and greasy Yorkshire pudding, roast potatoes and mashed turnips was placed in front of me. My stomach, not having had any amount of food for almost two weeks was complaining as it stretched. I ate everything, much to the Captain's surprise.

"Make sure you save yourself for the desserts, my dear," he cooed.

"He sounds like a blessed pigeon", I thought.

"Oh, I can't help myself! It is so tempting!" I lied…well, sort of. Waves of nausea were beginning to wash over me.

"This red wine has come all the way from France," he bragged as he filled my goblet. The fire made it sparkle even more. I sipped it, determined to get it down as well.

"How many trips have you made across the Atlantic?" I asked, trying to make conversation. I hoped he would take the lead in the conversation so that I could concentrate on not throwing up. I didn't want to ruin my escape plan.

"I shall tell you all about them over dessert." His voice trailed off as he rose from his chair and walked around the table. It was a most sickening sight to see his loose, moist lips descend upon me. His mouth was sour with the wine and it took all of my determination to remain motionless.

"I think you need just a little more wine, my dear," he observed, returning to his own chair. "Better still, brandy! Ah, the very best for you! With your dessert, of course. Must keep you from being sick, mustn't we?" he crowed.

I smiled, nodding my head in agreement.

Raspberry tarts, white and yellow cheese, shortbread and large, plump raisins, Kadota figs and dates served on beautiful china plates that 'had come from the Orient', he boasted about.

I ate a bit of everything, along with sips of brandy.

"Would you care for some more, Lizzie?" he asked me. There was a somewhat dubious note in his voice. "Ah, you don't mind if I call you 'Lizzie' do you?"

"Thank you, no. I can't eat another bite." I said this as politely as possible.

Deliberately, I did not answer his question. Of course I minded him calling me 'Lizzie'. I detested his very being! To even hear him utter my name was offensive. "Everything has been delicious and the cakes, so delicious and so sweet! I've never seen such a variety of food!" At least that was the truth, I thought.

"Would you care for another brandy?" he asked politely.

"Aye." Being brought up in the strict Presbyterian faith, I was well warned of the "evils" of drink, and now I was beginning to understand why they called it "evil". I was beginning to lose control of my thinking. I hoped I wasn't becoming inebriated, but I was afraid it was so.

"Well, well," the Captain was purring again, "I must say that I've never seen a lady with as healthy an appetite as yours. Would you care to lie down for a while? To digest your dinner, of course" he hastened to add.

I instinctively knew he was testing the water, so to speak. However, the tone of his voice and his obvious intent; the rich sauces; greasy meat, along with the wine, a liqueur, overly sweet cakes and a sudden roll of the ship combined to create a heaving attack of nausea.

I gagged in a most unladylike fashion. Sitting still, not moving a hair, I stared wide-eyed at the Captain. I could feel myself turning decidedly green, just as I had planned.

The Captain watched me, first in dismay and then in anger as it dawned on him that he was about to lose his dinner companion—who was about to lose her dinner!

My knuckles were white from gripping the table edge and my eyes never blinked as I stared back at the Captain. The ship rolled again…and I heaved again.

Suddenly, Captain Adams jumped to his feet, shouting, "You planned this! You deliberately gorged yourself! Deliberately! Deliberately made yourself sick!" He, too, had been out-maneuvered, and finally realized it. Fortunately for me, he had twigged to it too late.

The shipped rolled once more.

My throat tightened and my tongue felt numb. From past experience, I knew what was about to happen. Clapping a hand over my mouth, I vaulted myself toward the door, which, thankfully the Captain reached before me and was holding it open.

One thought and one thought only was motivating me and that was to get outside and to the railing of the ship. I heard the cabin door slam behind me. The Captain had left me alone to lose my dinner in solitude.

* * * *

"You look so pale! Are ye sure yer alright?"

"She's not pale. She's clean and that's a new dress!" someone noted suspiciously. The women were clucking around me where I sat on the bottom rung of the ladder. I smiled weakly. Rory had stationed himself about ten feet away from me.

"Why are ye shaking'?" someone asked.

"Well," I began slowly. This was the signal that a story was forthcoming. Swallowing hard because my stomach was still queasy, I waited a moment, but I was anxious to tell of my deliverance.

Taking great pains to relate the entire experience, I described in detail the furnishings in the cabin, the bath and new clothes. I lingered over the description of the food.

Again and again I was asked to tell them about the food. The women asked about the tarts and the men wanted to be reminded of the taste of fish, mutton and beef. When they finally allowed me to continue my story, I told them how I escaped the Captain's trap by eating so many rich cakes that I had made myself sick and had to run for the rail!

"What a shame! There it is—floating on the ocean!"

"Tsk, tsk." Ma wasn't happy about the wine and brandy. I hadn't lingered over that part of the story.

Rory was leaning against one of the support posts, arms folded across his chest and his legs crossed at the ankles. A dark frown furrowed his brow. He was protecting himself from the expected blow.

"Ah, Lizzie…ye mean…? I mean…he didn't?" one of the women was stammering, trying not to ask the question that was in all of their minds.

I smiled shyly and shook my head, "No. Thanks be to God! And my weak stomach."

Rory brightened. "You mean he didn't…?"

I smiled a little broader this time and gleefully shouted "No!" and clapped my hands together in victory.

Rory was at my side in two strides. "That's my lassie!" he whispered in my ear as he spun me around and around while the others did their best to dodge my flying legs and feet.

"Let us give thanks," Ma said above the laughter. We immediately sobered and knelt as one, giving thanks for keeping me out of harm's way, meaning the Captain. There were a few seconds of quiet after the prayer and then Alistair put the bagpipes to his shoulder and began playing an eightsome reel. We jammed against one another, trying to find room for a few to dance. The rest of us sang and kept time with the music.

I stared in open astonishment at Alistair and Rory laughed. "And that's my surprise for you, hen," he said smugly and embarked on his success story of "getting Alistair up on his feet".

The music stopped but the pure joy of the moment prevailed. Everyone laughed and talked at once.

"Oh, how I wish my John was here, he would have loved this, crowded as we are and all," Ma said wistfully.

"Aye, but he's not and you are, so you'd better start livin'," one of the older women stated wisely and patted Ma on the arm. Alistair started another reel, but Ma wasn't able to recapture her previous lightheartedness.

"I miss Da, too." I said softly, as I put my arm around her shoulder.

"Oh, aye, Lizzie! I miss him when I cry and I miss him when I laugh. Oh, Lizzie, I miss him so much it feels like my heart bleeds at times. Oh, John, John, my Jo!"

Chapter 17

The day after my "ordeal", as it was referred to, Ma told me what occurred in the hold while I was with Captain Adams. It seems that, as soon as I disappeared through the hatch, Rory plunged into his work like a madman. His task was to attend to the weeping sores of the prisoners as they were released from their chains, as per the agreement with the Captain.

"The ship's blacksmith brought a small anvil down into the hold," Ma said, "and he broke open the prisoners' shackles with a hammer. Ach, Lizzie, I'm glad ye didn't have to see the sores that were under those shackles, all bleeding and festering, they were. It was a sickening sight, doesn't even bear thinking about."

"The women rolled up their sleeves and helped me," Ma continued. "Rory came behind us, checking our work. Hard to see in this dim candle light, but he dusted on the silver nitrate. He told me later, when he had a chance to say it without everyone else listening, that he's afraid the sores on those men are too far gone; too badly infected to heal."

"Jimmy Henderson, there," Ma bobbed her head at the man standing against the ladder, "right off tried to stand up, but his leg muscles had withered and couldn't hold his weight. It was then that Rory called for help. He wanted the rest of us to support the poor things so they could walk. Just one small step at a time—we coaxed them all the way."

"The rest pushed themselves as far back as they could," Ma continued, "making room for our sorry procession. We managed to get the men to hobble the length of the hold and back." She smiled proudly and paused.

"Don't stop, Ma!" I was curious.

"Well, someone started humming a tune. Soon, the others joined in and pretty soon we were all singing, 'Scots, wh' hae wi' Wallace bled, Scots, whom Bruce has of'en led'! You know how that tune stirs us up!"

"Aye," I agreed. Though it always made me cry when *I* heard it.

"We were proud of those men, Lizzie, fighting with everything they had to just stay up on their pins. It was great to feel that pride run through this hold. It made us sing even louder. It's a wonder you didn't hear us up there in the Captain's cabin, yourself. Ach, it felt good!"

"Did the women make mouth music, Ma?" I asked. It was always a pure delight to me when the women would imitate the exact notes played on the bagpipes. Each note had its own word and when strung together was a very pleasing sound.

"Aye, it sounded good," Ma nodded, the memory making her smile. "Eventually, we all settled down," she continued. "That was when one of the shackled men, struggling to stay up on his feet said, "Let us pray for our dear sister; that she might be delivered from th' evil about to be forced on her!"

"And we prayed with all our might and faith, Lizzie, begging the Lord to have mercy on you. And on me. I couldn't live with that, too, Lizzie. The Lord must have known I was at the end of my tether and took pity on me."

She reached out and patted my cheek, then continued in a less strained voice. "It was quiet for a few minutes. We were all thinking our own thoughts. Suddenly, one of the men cried out, 'Gie us a tune, Rory!'" Ma smiled, remembering.

"'Aye! Come on Rory!'" Ma was getting into her story. "'Let Lizzie hear the sound o' the pipes! It might gie' her courage!'" We were grasping at straws. Anything other than just waiting for you to get back down here. Rory didn't feel like playing and he had refused us, when he glanced at Alistair MacCrimmon, who was still hunched over, facing the wall."

"Alistair?" I encourage Ma. I sensed we were finally getting to it.

"It was a flash of inspiration! Rory knew exactly what to do to get his friend going."

"'You're right! We need our music tonight!' Rory agreed, almost shouting out loud and then I heard him mumble under his breath, 'for more than one reason.' And he went to his cabin for his pipes."

"We clapped and sang while we waited for him to come back with his pipes. Ach, it was good to see him put his pipes together, you know how they fit the drones and all?" Ma reminded me. "It was like a wee bit of home, just watchin' him."

"At last he blew them up, patting the bag so gently, as if it were a wee bairn. Then he reached over and tuned the drones until the sound was just right. After a few more practice notes, he was off into a medley of strathspeys and reels. Pretty soon our toes were tapping. Ach, Lizzie, it was food for our souls!"

"But Rory had something else in mind." Ma was now using her 'storytelling voice'. "He immediately changed the pace and broke into a lament and to our amazement, made several mistakes. Eaghh" Ma held onto her ears, "It just grated up and down m'back!"

"The toe tapping stopped and we tried to figure out what was wrong with Rory. Never had we heard such bad piping. Then I wised up. I noticed he was watching Alistair MacCrimmon. One by one we all began to understand what Rory was up tae. So we motioned to each other to keep still and watch while the play unfolded before our eyes."

Ma grinned with pure pleasure.

"Ye know, pet? It's good to be goin' through it again, without the worry I had about you up there with the Captain. I can really enjoy it, now."

"Well," she continued, "Rory's pipes were ringing like bells, in spite of the neglect over the last while and his fingers were strong and true. But it sounded terrible! The lament he was playin' was "MacCrimmon's Sweetheart". Rory told me later that it was a pibroch and had been written by Alistair's uncle, who had taught both Rory and Alistair to play the pipes. You should have seen Rory's eyes twinkle as Alistair wriggled further down on his haunches.

"Another bad note, and another! Oh, it hurt m' teeth! Alistair pulled his plaid over his head and pushed it into his ears with his scrawny hands. It was all we could do to keep from laughing out loud!"

"And then more wrong notes until my teeth fairly ached! Alistair finally let a devil of a roar outta him! 'I can't stand it! What in Heaven's name are ye doin' tae those puir things, and that beautiful tune!' He pushed himself away from the wall and stood up. I thought for sure he was going to go down again, but he only swayed slightly before he caught his balance."

"At that very moment, Rory pushed an awful screech through the chanter and Alistair flew at him, his eyes blazing."

"'Think ye can do better, do ye, laddie?' Rory threw out the taunt and Alistair willingly picked it up."

"'Aye, and ye know it!' Alistair shot back at him. Oh, my! Was he aggravated!" Ma snickered.

"'Well, then, let's hear ye!' Rory handed him the pipes."

"Lizzie, it was a miracle! Just like we'd prayed for. Just to see the life flow through Alistair again. We knew that God had heard us!"

"Aye," I agreed. "He heard you alright." My mind flitted back to my narrow escape.

"Alistair picked up those pipes like they were his own true love and so fondly put them on his shoulder. He played as only a MacCrimmon can play. Then Rory sat down beside me, looking so smug, but I couldn't blame him, though. It had been a wise move and he pulled it off so nicely. It seemed to me that he just put his whole mind into the music. I think he was drowning his worries about you, pet. He has a real liking for you, ye ken?"

I ignored the last statement, only because I didn't know what to say and I was concentrating on not blushing, which my Ma would look on as a dead give away about my feelings for Rory. Besides, I noticed Rory moving toward us.

"You were tellin' her about Alister, Christie?" he asked.

Ma nodded.

"Those old tunes brought back many happy memories," Rory interrupted Ma's story and continued. "I remember when Alistair and I were young boys and Alistair's uncle, Patrick Og MacCrimmon, was the piper to the Clan MacLeod. In those days the festivities were frequent and the piper was always an honored participant. Any skirmishes the Clan found themselves involved in, the piper would be there as well, leading them into battle. I think the music drowns out the fear. At least it does for me."

Ma grinned at Rory and with a nod of her head, let him take over the story. "The competition between Alistair and me was always keen and I simply used this to bring him to his feet. I knew he couldn't sit still long, at least not without showing me 'how it should be done right'. Rory chuckled out loud. "When Alistair finished playing, well, the applause was more like thunder. Just the medicine he needed. When he looked around at the faces of his friends he must have finally realized that the applause was not only for his music, but for him as well, that we wanted him to live!"

Rory was speaking so sincerely that I had to take a second look at him to make sure that he wasn't just being sarcastic.

"Well, I've never seen Alistair so humble before, it was a sight for sore eyes!" Rory crowed. "He thanked everyone for their efforts, 'so tenderly administered', and he said, 'with a heart full of gratitude' that they had pulled him back to the land of the living. But did he acknowledge me? Not on yer life!"

Ma interjected. "Ye know, Lizzie, they all forgot their own troubles for a little while. They were just happy with Alistair coming back to them. Rory and I were the only ones still with a hurt. We were waiting for you," Ma said sadly. "And then someone told Alistair that some of us would be getting a turn on the deck on the morrow."

"But I'll give Alistair this much. He didn't waste any time in speaking up to remind them that it was Lizzie Whitelaw who was paying for that privilege, right at that moment," Rory added.

"The party atmosphere just faded," Ma whispered.

"But it didn't take long for Alistair to be his old crusty self again!" Rory grimaced in a good natured way. "Christie, did ye hear him do his imitations of us. Here we were, so worried about him, all hunched up and looking at the wall, and what was he doin'? Thinking of us? Naw, naw, he was saving up all of our sayings; to come back and torment us with them; and he must have been eating something in order to keep his strength the way he did. He just didn't let us see him eat! That man can get my goat faster than anyone else I know. Faster than even you can, Lizzie!"

Grinning happily, Rory put his arm around my shoulders and hugged me to him.

I didn't move away.

Chapter 18

The ship pitched and rolled for three days, riding out the first storm of the journey. Captain Adams and some of his crew were old hands at this and the others, who were hardened criminals scrambled to learn fast, therefore, the ship itself realized little damage. But, not so, for those of us in the hold.

Only a very few of the prisoners escaped without being seasick, making the stench in the hold even more unbearable.

Those, who were able, helped nurse those who were sick. However, this help was very limited. Rory no longer had access to his cabin, as the hatch had been "battened down" by one of the crew at the onset of the storm.

"Captain's orders!" was the only explanation.

Rory was sure that he was going to lose at least three of our group. The men had complained of fever, sore necks and limbs and had retched continuously until they were spewing up blood. Now they were simply lying limply on the blankets, unresisting against the roll of the ship.

Rory kept brow beating them into surviving. "For cryin' out loud, don't give it up now! You've made it! We're almost there! Think of what ye've been through and to give in tae a little fever—ach, cum' on now!" he pleaded, cajoled and reasoned. With no medicine, only words...he reached into the depths of his own will to live. Humbly, he begged these men to not give up the fight but his only rewards were patient and hopeless smiles. Rory doubled and redoubled his efforts.

I was seeing a different Rory. His high regard for life made me wonder if he wasn't a lot closer to God than he wanted to admit.

"Rory," I said, sitting down next to him, "you'll exhaust yourself. You can't keep pouring all of your strength into them like this! You need to reserve some for yourself!"

"Aye, I know, but how can they give up like that? That is the real sin! The greatest sin!" He was angry, not just agitated, but indignantly and righteously angry. "Not to fight for life. It's God's gift to us, is life, and to not use it, even to the last breath, well," he heaved a great sigh, "to me that is what's unforgivable."

"Da used to get upset, as well, when people just gave up. More than once I heard him say, 'We've tried to give them a gallon of life, but they have only brought a cup to receive it. The rest is spilled, wasted on the ground.'"

"I know what he meant," Rory stated, looking at the men in question.

I quickly realized it wasn't death that frightened Rory. No, he was no stranger to death. What drove him to persist in his efforts to revive these nearly dead men was fear. Fear springing from guilt; a guilt over his lack of medical knowledge.

"Rory, you've done more than any doctor could have," I whispered.

He swung around and glared at me. "How dare ye…" he began, the fire of righteous indignation flashing in his eyes. But I looked steadily into his eyes realizing that I had hit a raw nerve; and his anger didn't frighten me in the least.

Finally, he lowered his eyes. "Yer right, Lizzie. I am scared," he whispered, "for me, more than for them."

I reached out and touched his hand, wrapping my fingers around his. As he lifted my hand to his lips and kissed my palm, I could feel him draw strength from me.

For three long days we had been without food and in addition to that, Rory had been forced to ration out the water in what seemed like useless, little dribbles. At the beginning of the journey, Rory had put a silver coin in the bottom of the barrel which helped keep the water freer of germs. Now, even the last little drops were gone and the silver coin shone back at us.

I rubbed my bruised arms. "I'm so sore from being battered against someone else's bony body. We're like walking skeletons," I grumbled lamely. We could deal with the hunger, but now we were slowly dying of thirst. No one was angry any longer. There was only a dull resignation. We had even lost track of time, not knowing if it was day or night. We slept where we could find a place to lay down, usually by pushing someone else out of the way.

"Death is rising up to claim its victory!" Marion Lesley repeated over and over. When she first began to utter that morbid thought, most of us jumped on her verbally, demanding she stop. But now, there seemed to be quiet agreement.

Only one small candle was still spluttering out a faint light. My mind ran around the thought that all of the darkness in the hold could not put out the light from one tiny, little candle. Somewhere in that thought was a sermon but I couldn't hold onto it. My mind seemed to float around like a feather on a soft breeze.

"Seasickness is something I never had to contend wi' in medical school or on the battlefield!"

Rory's complaint brought me back to the present. We had been sitting at the bottom of the ladder for several moments when Rory suddenly reached out and gripped my arm.

"Quiet!" he demanded and looked up at the hatch cover.

"Something's missing," I thought, then realized I wasn't bracing myself against the roll of the ship.

"Quiet!" Rory shouted again as he continued to peer up at the hatch.

The sound of crashing waves sweeping over the deck had stopped as suddenly as it had begun three days ago. "It's over! I think we've made it!" he whispered, as if he spoke the words aloud, the storm would return.

We listened, holding our breath, straining to hear.

Suddenly, Rory jumped up and pulled himself up the ladder. "Open up! Open up! Is any one up there? Open up!" he yelled.

"Oh, God in heaven, they're all washed overboard!" a woman whined.

Rory was pounding wildly on the hatch cover, yelling louder and louder, over and over, "God help us...and you...if ye don't open up right now!"

The sound of voices filtered down to us, along with the scraping of metal. "They're moving the locking bar," Rory called out.

"Hold it!" yelled one of the crew as the latch gave way and Rory flung the cover open.

"Away wi' ye! Hold it yersel'!" Rory yelled back.

Those of the crew who were near the hatch grabbed at their noses as the stench and Rory escaped from the hold at the same time.

Ever so slowly I struggled, rung after rung, to pull myself to the top of the ladder where I folded over the edge of the hatch way. Huge gulps of sweet, cool, clean air rushed into my polluted lungs. Rory was leaning over the railing doing the same, letting the ocean spray wash over his face.

"Let us up!" they were demanding below me.

"Captain!" Rory called out. "Let them up! Ye've nothing to fear from them! They're more dead than alive!" Rory pleaded for us.

"Ten at a time, Doctor!" was his answer.

"Lizzie, bring them up…ten at a time!" Rory called to me.

A roar of anger burst from the hold. The ladder began to shake as a surge of bodies hit it.

I hung on, shouting, "None of us will get out of here if I get knocked offa this thing!" I threatened.

"Ye hear that?" Rory shouted at the Captain.

"Not my problem," was the insensitive reply. "But before you worry any more about them," the Captain grumbled, "you'd better look after yourself first, Doctor, or your people won't have you around much longer to champion their cause. See the cook and get some food in you before you start doctoring again."

"Later!" Rory shot back as he walked toward the hold.

"Lizzie! Send them up," he shouted to me.

One at a time, they emerged from the hold, gaunt, grey and dirty; squinting against the bright light of the morning sun. Rory and I stumbled along with the first group toward the water pails, greedily inhaling the precious liquid.

"Poor devils," muttered one of the crew. Captain Adams watched from the helm as they struggled up the ladder and onto the deck. The effort sapped the very last drop of everyone's strength.

"Forget about only ten at a time, Doctor. We've nothing to fear from this lot. Let them all come up!"

Rory indicated his gratitude with a quick salute, choosing not to tell the Captain that the order had been given already.

"Captain," Rory called out, "would you let me have some of the crew to swab out the hold?"

"Go ahead," the Captain agreed. "I can spare them for a short while but work fast. I think I see another storm brewing on the horizon."

We all looked in the direction that the Captain was pointing.

"I won't live through another storm," Ma said flatly.

"Where's the First Mate?" Rory asked, losing no time in appointing a clean-up crew.

Mops and pails of sea water were carried into the hold and the sailors soon had the hold cleaned of the accumulated filth. The hold was deserted, except for the three sick men. Rory called me into the hold to help him. I noticed that one of them was deathly still.

"Fetch me that mirror from my bag, will ye Lizzie?"

I returned with the shiny piece of metal. Rory held it under the man's nose, looking for the slight fogging on it, but it remained perfectly clear. He anxiously pushed his ear against the man's chest, then sat up again, shaking his head. "No heartbeat. Nothing," he muttered to himself as he sat back on his heels, resting his hands on his thighs. "He's gone. Just like that. It's always so simple. No drum roll, no pipes, no nothing! One minute yer here and the next yer gone. What's the purpose anyway?"

I didn't answer because all I could think of were long sermons about "learning obedience" and "going to live with God again". I was sure Rory didn't want to hear that just now.

Rory looked intently at the dead man for several moments before he reached out to close the unseeing eyes for the last time. "Maybe John Whitelaw did know something I don't know, yet," he said thoughtfully.

After a few minutes, Rory pushed himself to his feet, saying grimly, "I'll have to tell the Captain." Then he laboriously pulled himself up the ladder, his shoulders rounded by this most recent burden.

I followed, staying close behind.

"Captain Adams," Rory called up to the helm, "one of my men died."

"What did he die of?" the Captain demanded.

"The fever," Rory answered.

"Which one?" The Captain's narrowed eyes never left Rory's face.

Rory look back steadily at the Captain and said, "It looks like Dengue fever. Ye know the one brought up from Havana."

"Havana!" the Captain sounded surprised. "One of my crew is sick. I wanted you to look at him. He complained of a sore neck, sore joints—high fever? That's Dengue, Doctor?"

"Sounds like it," Rory muttered. "If they can make it through the first three days, they usually recover."

"If I remember correctly, this sailor's last trip was from Havana," the Captain said.

"Isn't that wonderful!" Rory exclaimed sarcastically. They were both silent for a few moments. "Well, Captain, suppose you tell me how we go about burying this man?"

"Hmmm," the Captain began. "Well, I suppose you'll insist on a proper burial, won't you?"

"Aye," Rory nodded.

"You know, Doctor, this isn't a pleasure cruise and the man was a prisoner. He should be thrown over the side and that's all there is to it!"

Rory summoned enough strength to plant his feet firmly on the deck and cross his arms over his chest, a stance the Captain had come to know very well and had wisely learned not to challenge.

"Alright, MacLeod! Alright! What do you want?" Captain Adams was tired as well, that was obvious when he capitulated so easily.

"He'll have a proper burial! That's what I want!" was the quick reply.

"Aye, he'll have a proper burial." The Captain agreed wearily.

"Thank you. I'll be getting back to the others, now." Rory said and turned to leave when the Captain called him back.

"Doctor, you've done well," the Captain admitted grudgingly.

"Why say it at all, if you have to say it like that!" I muttered to myself, having overheard the Captain's comment.

"Don't be too hard on yourself," the Captain continued. I was surprised to hear a sympathetic note in his voice. "By now," he continued, "we are usually well on our way to the twenty-five that we generally lose before we get to Jersey."

The look on Rory's face prompted him to continue. "Look at it this way. Have you ever hunted the stag?"

Rory nodded.

"Then you know that the weak get picked off by predators, both two legged and four legged. It just leaves more for the rest to eat and that way the herd is constantly being strengthened. It's the very same when you get a group of people in your situation. The weak will die and the stronger ones who are left will gain more strength. It is just the way everything balances out. And don't make the mistake of thinking that it has anything to do with food or water or warmth or any of that nonsense. No, no, my dear Doctor!" the Captain's laugh had infuriating superior overtones. "It is the spirit that is within a man that keeps him alive. I've watched the skinniest, scrawniest, frailest woman survive a terrible crossing when big, strong men were dropping around her like flies. But she had a purpose; she wanted to live. She was joining her banished husband in the Americas."

Rory listened, quite politely, I thought; especially since he was probably waiting to hear something that he didn't already know.

"Your people," the Captain continued, "will not die from lack of food or fresh water or anything else that is usually blamed. No, no, they will die from fear."

"Fear?" This was obviously a new thought for Rory.

But it wasn't a new idea to me—I often wrestled with the fear of the 'big, black hole' that no one ever returned from—except sailors. I didn't even want to discuss it with the others, it was so—so—unknown to me—America was a punishment—where the Covenanters were sent as a punishment. I never thought I would ever agree with the Captain about anything—but he was right in this case.

"Yes, fear! They don't know where they are going and what will happen when they get there. You are not as functional as you should be, either. Do you realize that you haven't once, not even once, tried to ask me about Jersey or what you can expect to find there?"

"Just you hold on there, one minute! You know I've not just been twiddlin' my thumbs!" Rory was on the defensive.

"Are you willing to be herded along with the rest, with no thought for your future?" The Captain ignored Rory's defense, but looked at him for a long minute. "I think not, Doctor."

Rory acted somewhat embarrassed. He shuffled his feet like a young schoolboy being brought up in front of the Head Master.

"Will you tell me something? Are you really a surgeon?" The Captain was taking advantage of the moment, but Rory was quick with his decision to live out the lie.

"Yes, yes I am," he said, hiding behind clipped and perfect English. "And that is where I must go at this moment, to do some doctoring. But I promise you, I'll be back! And I'll have some questions for you!" Rory looked embarrassed when he turned around to see that we had all been listening.

Ma, Alistair and I were huddled with the others, trying to protect our thin bodies from the stiff sea breeze. Our icy fingers found warmth holding the tin cups of hot gruel, that had been dished out for us.

Rory disappeared into the hold without a word where a sailor was still mopping up. "Will you please prepare him for burial at sea," we heard Rory say.

"We take our orders from the Captain, Doctor!" the sailor informed him.

"Oh, oh!" Alistair grinned. "Thar she blows!"

What a perfect excuse! Rory exploded! "Then go get your orders from the Captain! Now! Unless you want to be the next one on this ship to be buried at sea!" All of his pent up anger was roared at the unsuspecting sailor.

However, the sound of Rory's angry voice booming out once again made us smile and wink at one another, making this the first sign that our lives were about to return to what we now accepted as normal.

I glanced at the Captain. Was that a hint of a smile? I tried to look closer, but that fleeting hint of human-ness had quickly retreated once more behind his granite mask.

The sailor returned—on the double—with help, and he also brought a long bag which they slid the corpse into and then closed and secured the open end. The strongest of the two sailors put the dead man over his shoulder and carried him up the ladder to the deck.

Rory followed close behind and once on deck had found that the Captain had gone into his cabin, leaving his door open. "Captain," Rory said, stepping into the cabin, "we're ready for you to perform the service."

"Aye. And what was his name, Doctor?"

"It was Thomas Thompson."

The Captain nodded and continued to leaf through the small Bible he was holding, while the two sailors laid Thomas out on a plank. We crowded as close as possible to "our Tam".

"That could of been any one of us," Mary Anderson observed. "I don't know right now who is the lucky one, him or me." From the "ayes" that were mumbled, I knew that more than one agreed with her.

We set our cups of gruel aside and prepared to pay our last respects. Tam, besides being our brother in the Covenant, was a friend as well, and we each had memories of him that we held dear.

The Captain began by reading the 23rd Psalm. "The Lord is my Shepherd, I shall not want..."

A beautiful sound—like silver looks—rose among us on the cool breeze. It was the soprano voice of Sheilagh Kirk, continuing the Psalm in song.

"An angel voice," Ma whispered.

When she finished, the Captain gave a nod of his head; the sailors lifted the plank and tipped it over the rail. Thomas Thompson slid to his grave at the bottom of the Atlantic Ocean.

Sheilagh was singing another hymn taken from Psalm 100—"Make a joyful noise unto the Lord."

The spirit was strong with a feeling of peace that seemed to ease our grief. There was a special beauty in the faces of those around me and much to my surprise, even the Captain was singing.

Too soon, it was over and we became silent, wanting to be left alone with our thoughts for a bit. Slowly, though, we began to shuffle around the deck, trying to find comfort in something or someone.

As unthinkable as it was to me, some even returned to the hold. But the rest of us leaned against the railing of the ship to stare into the sea. I wondered about the secrets that lie on its floor. Still others gazed off into the horizon, some looked toward their new home and others, with tears in their eyes, looked back toward our beloved Scotland.

"Doctor," the Captain called, "who was that woman? The one who sang the hymn?"

"Sheilagh Kirk," Rory answered. "A fine young woman. Her husband was hung for not taking the Oath, the same as Christie Whitelaw's husband."

The Captain rubbed his bearded chin and I watched him survey Sheilagh from his cabin door and shuddered, remembering my very narrow escape. Since that time, the Captain had neither spoken nor looked at me. As far as he was concerned, I did not exist, which suited me just fine!

A woman's flirtatious laugh caught my attention. Margaret McKay (one of 'the six') was looking up at the sailor who had taken over the wheel. With his eyes, he was coaxing her to come up and stand beside him. She, very coyly, was shaking her head and giggling. The other five of the 'six' were enjoying private little conversations and laughs with members of the crew.

"They're asking for trouble," Ma whispered in my ear, sounding worried for them; then shaking her head as if to clear her brain, she gave a short "Humphf" before adding, "What am I talking about? That's what they do!"

"Aye," I said, not caring, and let my head fall backward, letting the sun wash my face in its warmth. I didn't condemn them as much as I would have a month ago. Rory's very presence was enough to make me think thoughts that Ma would wash my mouth out with soap for, if she knew. No, I wasn't going to make a judgment about them. I just kept quiet.

"Thar she blows!" cried a sailor from the crow's nest. He pointed excitedly at a great spout of water erupting from the calm sea. Prisoners and crew alike rushed to the railing to get a better look. The whale broke the surface with great energy and crashed his tail on the surface of the water and then swam toward the ship, closer and closer, as his audience watched intently.

"He's tellin' us Tam's happy!" Geordie cried out. Geordie was an old fisherman and he should know. The thought felt good, and we all relished it.

The Captain steered the ship away from the whale that seemed to be playing with us. It circled 'round and around, crashing its tail on the surface again and again. Then it was gone. Just like that! However, within a few minutes a school of dolphins surfaced making us laugh out loud at their playful antics.

"What a performance!" Alistair said as he, too, laughed. "They look like mischievous bairns." The word 'bairns', that he had just uttered so happily, suddenly sobered him and we knew it brought back the memory of his own children.

"We call 'em the "jesters of the sea," a sailor whispered in my ear. His mouth was so close to my ear that it startled me.

"Get away!" I shouted and shoved him, trying to push his lewd, smiling face away from me. The sailor merely stepped back, shrugged his shoulders and moved on. When I turned around to make sure no one else was behind me, I noticed that Rory was watching me from the other side of the ship and that his knuckles had actually turned white from gripping the rail so tightly.

I gave him a small wave, indicating that everything was fine. "That's annoying!" I muttered to myself. I felt flattered, but at the same time I felt somewhat smothered by Rory's protectiveness. However, the atmosphere on board ship had lost its' gloom and had slid into one of relaxation. Everyone seemed to be enjoying the fresh air and each other's company and I determined not to spoil it for myself with petty thoughts.

"Anyone here considers himself a fisherman?" the Captain called from the door of his cabin. "Could be there's some cod around here."

Isaac Miln jumped at the invitation. "I'm a fisherman! I'll reel ye in a nice uin! Just gie me a line!" Isaac disappeared with the First Mate, returning soon with a heavy rod and a trolling reel. Within minutes he had his hook in the water.

"I can taste it already, old son!" encouraged Robby MacVittie.

"Get off! I've work tae do. Ye blind?" Isaac tried to growl, while smiling ear to ear.

"Cum'on, Isaac! Bring in a good uin!"

Never did a fisherman have more enthusiastic support. Our mouths were watering at the prospect of 'a wee bit o' fish' for our supper.

"Doctor," the Captain called, "will you come here, please." The note of anxiety in Captain Adams' voice caught my attention and I noticed that Rory quickened his step, as well.

"Doctor, remember I said that it looked like we had a storm brewing on the horizon? Look at it now!"

There was a large, bright white mound on the horizon. "Is it a cloud? If it is, it's the strangest one I've ever seen," Rory noted.

"Those, Doctor, are icebergs," the Captain said with dismay.

"Icebergs? What are icebergs?" Rory wanted to know.

The Captain shook his head. "I'm afraid you're going to find out the hard way," he said as he continued to peer into the distance with his telescope. "Looks like it's broken away from the main mass of ice with the summer heat. It's floating with the warm current."

"How much time do we have? And what do we do to protect ourselves?" Rory asked in rapid succession.

"That depends upon the current and me. I'll do my best to out maneuver it, but those 'bergs have a nasty habit of popping up just where you don't expect them! Your second question. Get everyone into the hold...and fast. I'm going to need my wits about me and I don't need any panicky landlubbers standing in my way." The Captain immediately turned his attention back to the iceberg.

"Aye, Captain!" Rory didn't argue and neither did he waste any time in herding us back into the hold.

"Aw, Rory!"

"The sun's still high. What's yer game?"

"What's wrong wi' ye man? Have ye gone daft?"

"Aye, he has! There's more of us and only one o' him! He can't make us go into that hell hole again...ever!" William Orr shouted his rebellion.

"Believe me, Willie, ye don't want to be up here right now." Rory said. I don't know whether it was Rory's tone of voice or the firm grip he had on Willie's arm that was the convincing factor, but Willie moved along with the rest of us.

Isaac turned the rod and reel over to the First Mate. I thought both Isaac and Robby were going to cry.

Rory simply ignored the complaints as he shepherded us back into the dark hold. Many resisted his prodding, jerking their arms away from his touch as he pushed them along. I didn't blame them; if I hadn't learned to read Rory so well, I would be objecting as well. But I knew that there must be something afoot.

The smell of the fresh sea air clung to our clothes, but soon it was swallowed up by the strong smell of wet wood. Being jammed against each other so tightly seemed even worse now, after our brief respite on deck. But the appearance of more pails of gruel and large chunks of bread took our minds off our disappointment.

The others crowded around the sailors who were dishing out the food...a rare treat, seeing as we had already had soup while on deck.

It was then that I noticed two of the women were curled up on the floor of the hold. When I reached them, I put my hand to their foreheads. They were both burning hot. "Are you sick to your stomachs?" I asked.

"Naw. It's m' neck! And m' bones feel so sore. I've never felt so sick in m' life!" Marion Rutherford said between clenched teeth. Sarah Knox, the other woman, just groaned.

"Rory!" I called out.

He was kneeling beside me within seconds. "I think we've an epidemic on our hands," he whispered as he stood up. "The Captain said that one of his men had it as well. It is called 'Dengue Fever'. Seems it comes from Havana and that sick sailor probably brought it back with him."

"What do we do, now?" I wanted to know. "And how are the other two men?"

"From what I remember at school, the books said that if they lived through the first three days, they usually made it."

I tried to make the women more comfortable and before long, Ma was beside me, bathing their foreheads with cool water.

"Lizzie!" It was Rory. I rushed to where he was kneeling beside the two sick men.

"Just take a look at these two!" Rory crowed proudly. "Look at the two o' ye! Ach, yer just grand! That's what ye are!" Much to Rory's delight the men had rallied and were actually trying to sit up to take a cup of gruel.

I laughed, thinking I had just had a glimpse of what he would be like over his child taking his first step...or any other accomplishment. It was good. He stood up, arms akimbo, ready to make the happy announcement of recovery when the First Mate came down the ladder.

"The Captain wants to see Sheilagh Kirk. Where is she?" he wanted to know.

"And what does he want with Sheilagh?" Rory asked, although we all knew. "Besides that, can you tell me how the Captain is going to steer this ship, pass that iceberg safely and carry on with...with Mrs. Kirk?" Rory emphasized the 'Mrs.', "Can you tell me that?"

"I don't have tae tell ye anything, at all!" the sailor countered and both Rory and the sailor took a stance that could only lead to an all out brawl.

We all held our collective breath, knowing that this fight could mean the end of our deck priviledges. Unexpectedly, Sheilagh's voice broke through the tense silence as she stepped forward and said flatly, "It's alright, Rory, I'll go."

"No! Ye don't have tae," he argued.

She put her hand on his arm, "Rory, please, I've lost the war...it's beaten me. I can't live down here another minute. I...I'm not as strong as the rest o' ye! I want out!"

"At any price, Sheilagh?" Rory asked her very quietly.

"Aye, Rory. At any price," she said with tears in her eyes. "I'm sorry. Please forgive me."

"It's not for me to forgive, Sheilagh, ye have to ask God for that," he said quietly.

The First Mate looked like he was thoroughly enjoying his victory and took great pleasure in announcing, "Oh, Doctor, there are six of your women still up there." He jerked his head toward the open hatchway.

Rory looked puzzled.

"Yes, yes. They are very willingly bedded down at the moment, with six of my men."

"What do ye mean 'willingly'," Rory roared.

"Just what I said, Doctor. Willingly! Now, excuse me, sir, the Captain's waiting." With those parting words the First Mate turned toward the ladder, calling over his shoulder for Sheilagh Kirk to follow him.

Rory looked deflated. Ma moved close to him and whispered, "Rory, don't blame them. Let them be! That's been their life up to now and they've been alone too long, it seems."

"What do ye mean 'alone'. Look around ye, Christie! How can they be alone when we're packed in here like kippers in a barrel?"

"Ye know very well what I mean, Rory MacLeod!" Now Ma was losing her patience.

Rory's anger quickly turned to self-pity. "Well, I'm lonely, too, but a lot of good it's doin' me!" He looked at me hopefully.

"Rory, don't! You must know how Lizzie was brought up! You knew John Whitelaw and what he believed in!" Ma hadn't missed the look that Rory had tossed at me.

"Aye," was the petulant reply.

By now our conversation had become of interest to the others and I began to squirm. "He's going to bring up my 'ordeal'. I know he is!" Keeping my thoughts to myself, I waited—my jaw clenched—"Well, I have something to say, too." I was ready for Rory!

"Lizzie..." he began, but noticing the open interest on the faces around him, he stopped in mid-sentence, frustrating the would-be eavesdroppers at being cheated out of feeding their habit. He took me by the arm and led me to the ladder where we sat on the bottom rung.

When he was sure that he wouldn't be overheard, he tried to continue in a whisper, but I interrupted him by groaning out loud. "What's gotten into you, Rory? And those up there, for that matter?" I nodded toward the deck, indicating I was talking about the "bedded-down" six women. "Rory," I continued, "under other circumstances we probably would have courted. But you know that it will have to be marriage first before I...afore I..." My embarrassment was taking the form of all-over blushing again.

"Marriage?" Rory said weakly.

It was obvious to me that his needs hadn't brought him to the altar yet.

"Well, I certainly hope that's what you had in mind, Mr. MacLeod!" I saw my escape route and I was quickly wiggling out.

"Lizzie!" he growled, having recovered from the shock, "that's not what I wanted to talk about, but if that's what you want, here it is! Those women up there are nothing but trollops. And worse, because they knelt with us in prayer! And first chance they get they're bedding down with anyone who offers them a trinket! But it's different between us—but that isn't up for discussion right now. Now listen to me, the Captain just told me that he is going to do his best, but we might..." I gripped his arm, waiting for the bad news that I knew was coming, "We just might be encountering icebergs."

Angus Winters had told me about icebergs and their danger. "What...?" I began, but before I could finish my question, a terrible screech brought us to our feet, forcing us toward the sound. It was Catherine Sims.

"What is it?" Rory asked her sister, Agnes, who was kneeling beside her.

"She's in her sixth month. She's losin' the baby," she said flatly. "All I pray is we don't lose her, as well!"

"Yer a midwife?" he asked her.

"Aye, and I know Christie and Lizzie can help."

"Lizzie?" Rory raised an eyebrow.

"It was Lizzie who helped me with Iain. She knows what it's all about," Ma stated firmly.

I knelt down beside Ma and Agnes. "Where's she at?" I asked.

Aggy shook her head. "It's her first time 'round and it'll tak' a long time...at least I think it will," she added cautiously. "Who knows wi' the first."

Catherine moaned and rolled onto her side, asking if someone would rub her back. Maggie MacAdam responded. That relief only lasted a few minutes and Catherine was up on her hands and knees again, rocking back and forth like a child, trying to ease the labor pains that were coming stronger and faster now.

"Here, Katy," Agnes said, calling her by a pet name, "bite on this." She placed a wad of folded cloth between Catherine's teeth but it dropped from her mouth as she screamed with another pain. When it passed, Agnes tenderly rolled her over until she was again on her back.

"Catherine, just stay like that, so's we can help ye. When the pains come, just ye push down hard wi' all o' yer might! C'mon now, push! you can do it, pet—push!" Ma coaxed.

A long agonizing scream escaped from Catherine's throat. A hush fell over the hold. Then I heard a scramble of feet. I stood up to look past the women who were crowded around us to the men who were now bunched together at the other end of the hold, as far away as they could get.

"God, help her!" was a common plea.

Agnes wiped the perspiration from her sister's brow and the rest of us said and did everything within our power to make her more comfortable, but to no avail.

Agnes sat back on her heels, quietly cursing the fact she had nothing with which to help her sister. No herbs, nothing to ease her pain. "I've never felt so helpless in my life," she exclaimed.

For over two hours we watched Catherine, wracked with pain, grow weaker and weaker. Suddenly, she threw her head back and arched her body and Agnes flew into action, ordering Ma and me to hold her legs down.

"It's comin', but she needs help!" Agnes reached inside her sister's body. "I've got the head!" she cried and I watched beads of perspiration spring onto her forehead as she pulled, then let go, and pulled again, and again in concert with the contractions. Another scream and another until one long, piercing, animal-like scream cut into our ears, our minds and our hearts. Catherine had mercifully fainted.

"Thank God!" I heard myself saying.

The baby was so small and so blue and still. It was easily held in only one of Agnes' hands. "It was a boy," Agnes said solemnly. She cut the cord and handed me the baby. "Do what ye have tae, Lizzie." It was more of an order than a request.

I looked down at the lifeless little body and began to cry. Agnes snapped at me, "No time fer greetin', lass! Get outta here with it now. I don't want Catherine tae see it!"

I picked up the skirt of my dress, rolled the baby in the cloth folds and clutched it to my stomach, sensing so acutely the warmth of his still little body touching mine.

The ladder seemed endless as I climbed to the deck. Suddenly I felt weak and the climb seemed too hard; but only because everyone's eyes were on me was I able to muster the strength to force myself to struggle up the ladder, gripping each rung with one hand while clutching the baby with the other.

When I had pulled myself onto the deck, I saw Rory standing by the rail, staring out at the sea. I walked over to him and as I unwrapped the little body, I heard him suck in a long breath. It was so small and so easily fit into my trembling hands. I held the wee one over the rail but hesitated...I could not drop him into the water.

"Ye have to let it go, Lizzie," Rory said.

"I can't. I can't do it!"

"Lizzie...now...ye have to!" Rory whispered firmly.

Somehow, from somewhere, I gained the courage to open my hands and let the little boy drop into the sea.

"Iain! Oh, my Iain" I cried. The agony of the memory rose up to torture me once again.

I looked down at the bloodstains on my new dress and suddenly I was again hiding in the wool, hearing Ma scream as the soldiers jammed the hot eggs under her arms. Iain's face—the red finger marks around his mouth! "I suffocated him!" I wanted to scream to the world—confessing my sin. Da! The rope around his neck! "It won't stop!" I cried and clapped my hands over my eyes. The Lord is my Shepherd...Mr. Thompson's body sliding off the plank! "Stop! Stop!" I cried out once more.

Grief gripped my heart and tightened around my throat. It was strangling me! Frantically, I looked around for somewhere to hide! Solitude! I knew I was about to fall apart and didn't want anyone to see my torture. Nowhere to hide. "Oh, God! There is nowhere to hide!"

"Lassie, cum' here." Rory rescued me from my frenzy. His arms were around me and I fell, ever so gratefully, into the circle of their protection. Protection from my terrifying world.

"Rory? I...I..." The words would not come. They were stuck in my chest and in my stomach and somewhere in my soul.

"I love you so much! It tears me apart to watch your pain," Rory whispered, holding me close to him. The tenderness in his voice was the key. It opened up the door to my grief, allowing it to pour out in a torrent of tears and huge sobs. Sobs that shook my body until I was too weak to stand.

"All hands on deck! All hands on deck!" the First Mate was shouting.

"Into the hold, you two!" he yelled at us.

"Aye, we're on our way!" Rory called back to him as he maneuvered me toward the hold.

"Rory!" I screamed as a huge wall of ice had suddenly loomed out of the ocean on the port side.

"Into the hold!" he shouted at me.

The crew was running onto the deck, pulling on hats and coats and boots. They ran to the railing of the ship, staring at the iceberg that was within an arm's length. Captain Adams was at the helm, spinning the wheel, moving the ship out of danger. A cheer went up from the crew but it was interrupted by a sickening thud. I ran to the starboard railing and stood beside Rory.

The ship was surrounded by icebergs.

The ship creaked as she objected to the force of the ice against her hull.

"Captain..." Rory began.

But the Captain, reading his thoughts, interrupted him. "I don't know how long it'll be. You can never predict what these 'bergs' will do. One minute they're here and the next they're gone."

The ship groaned again, as if to attest to the truthfulness of his words.

"Doctor, you'd better check the hold for leaks! And if you find any, stop them with anything you can find...blankets, clothes. Pound them into any leaking seams. The ship's carpenter can give you tools and tar. Just make it fast!!"

A sailor handed Rory a lit lamp as we descended into the hold.

"What's up, Rory?" the men in the hold shouted.

"Are we goin' under?"

Ignoring the questions thrown at him, he demanded, "those of ye next to the walls, can ye see any leaks?"

"No! Not here!"

"No. We're fine here as well!" came the hoped for replies.

Rory was making a careful inspection of the walls, waving the lamp along the walls, looking for any telltale dampness. "If ever we prayed for deliverance, we had better mean it tonight!"

Finally, Rory said, "We're caught in some ice. It can go one of two ways and if ye want to see Jersey, well..." Rory didn't finish. He didn't have to.

I looked for Ma and found her beside Catherine Sims.

"Are you alright, hen?" she asked me.

"Aye, Ma...and you?"

"Och, aye, I've just given everything over to the Lord. I can't be afraid any longer. I'm too tired. If I'm to live, then I'll live. If not, well, I'll be seein' your Da all that much sooner." She smiled so beautifully. The thought of seeing Da again brought a glow to her face I hadn't seen for weeks.

"Yer Ma's right," Marion MacVittie was nodding her head. "It's fear that'll kill us afore anything else."

"The Bible says that God didn't put the spirit of fear in a man. So, if He didn't, then we've gotta know its comin' from the evil one," Willie Brand stated.

"Aye!" Others nodded as they rolled the advice around in their minds.

Ma smiled. I too remembered the words of the scripture she had taught me and Jenny and Iain on that beautiful day we went back home from Glasgow—that beautiful day after that horrendous day when Grandda was killed.

It was good to hear the scriptures being expounded...so strengthening. I looked around for Rory, wanting to hear his comments. He wasn't in the hold. Within seconds I was scrambling up the ladder and found him speaking with the Captain.

"Aye, she's a good ship! She's been through a lot, but nothing quite like this before!" the Captain was saying.

"Is there anything we can do at this point?" Rory wanted to know. They were ignoring my presence. This was good because I wasn't supposed to be there.

"No, nothing, Doctor. I'll leave a man on watch and as soon as there's a change we'll know it! The ship will either be set free or we'll be crushed."

To realize that it was a strong probability that I would not 'live happily ever after' with Rory, that our lives were about to grind to a halt, settled around and in me like a huge, cold, black enveloping cloud. At that moment, I knew that all I actually wanted was to be loved by Rory and have his babies...and grow old with him. And that might not happen. Out of our whole family, only Jenny would be left to carry on. The sad realization swept over me and all but choked the life out of me.

I inched my way over to Rory and slipped my hand into his as the unforgiving reality of our situation continued to infiltrate my mind.

The Captain smiled wryly and said, "I don't know about you, sir," and he winked at me, "but I think I'll spend what could be my last few hours taking my pleasure with Sheilagh Kirk. Might as well go out the way I've lived...in sin!" He laughed bitterly and began to walk toward his cabin.

His laugh rang in my ears, it was so—so unhappy and so hopeless. For a small moment, I actually felt sorry for him.

"C'mon you, into the hold." Rory smiled faintly as he led me to the hatchway. "Where's yer Ma? We'll find a place beside her."

"Last I saw, she was with Catherine Sims. Rory, aren't you worried?" I wanted to know.

"You will never know, Lizzie—you will never know!"

When we managed to find Ma, she was lying down, and in the flickering candle light, her eyes seemed to be closed. We pushed and shoved bodies, to the tune of much verbal abuse, until we made enough space for ourselves beside her. Just then, the candle light flickered and went out, leaving us in darkness so thick as to not allow a person to see their hand in front of their face.

"What's the matter?" Ma asked sleepily.

"Nothing, Ma. Go back to sleep."

The ship creaked. The sound reminded me of Catherine's screams. Not as piercing, but just as painful.

Suddenly, I was very aware of Rory's body and turned to face him.

"Rory?" I whispered.

"Weesht! Just ye coorie in, now, dae ye hear."

"Rory, are we going to die this time? We are, aren't we? I know it!" The fear I felt crept into my voice.

"Sshh! For cryin' out loud!" he scolded in a whisper. "Ye'll be startin' a panic!"

Forcing myself to lie still, I listened to the ship creak and groan. It was fighting for its' life. "Please don't die!" I cried out to the ship in my mind. "I can hear you fighting to live! Can you hear me fighting to live?"

Rory's lips were on my forehead. He kissed me gently. "Good night, darlin'" he whispered and tucked my head under his chin. Closing my eyes, I waited, knowing in my heart that he was going to kiss me...and I wanted him to...more than anything I had ever wanted in my life.

Gently, with a finger under my chin, Rory tilted my face upward and kissed my closed eyelids, the tip of my nose, my cheek. His lips found my mouth, so tenderly and softly at first. Then his mouth crushed mine as the dam that had held our emotions in check, broke. Easily, so very easily, I melted against his warm body.

"Lizzie, Lizzie..." he whispered into my ear, his hot breath fanning the fire that was leaping inside of me. We lay still, holding each other so tightly. The darkness protected our secret! Our precious moment. Never had I known such excitement before. My heart was beating in my throat and my body was demanding consummation. I kissed him back, deeply and passionately. We moved even closer together. His tongue touched mine! I fought to not groan my need for him out loud.

Rory's hand slipped down my back, pulling me against him. My passion was now greedy desire.

"Lizzie, you alright pet?" Ma asked...her voice had just thrown cold, icy water on my inflamed body.

"Aye," I eventually muttered, when I got my breath back.

Rory pressed his lips against my neck. We clung to each other. His body was like a hot peat fire warming me through and through. I could feel his heart beating against my breast. Slowly, our muscles relaxed. Each one taking its turn to relinquish us from its fiery hold.

Suddenly, Willie McHardy's snoring shattered the quiet. A giggle welled up inside me—from where, I don't know—but it took all my effort to stifle it!

Then, cruelly, the foul body odors, along with the hideous moans springing from the ever recurring nightmares that invaded the minds of the sleeping men and women, infiltrated my world again. I listened to the angry responses of those who were hit or kicked by the arms and legs that were flailing the air in yet another attempt to escape Lauderdale and his dragoons.

Gradually we returned from where ever we had flown. I became aware of someone's foot lying across mine and it felt like a ton weight.

As I rolled over, Rory tucked me into him. He whispered, "Lizzie...Lizzie!" so very softly, over and over again, until it sounded like a lullaby, coaxing our tired minds and bodies into restless sleep.

CHAPTER 19

The swaying of the ship woke us. Rory scrambled to his feet and bounded up the ladder to the deck, with me not far behind him!

"Captain! Where's the Captain?" he shouted.

"Ma!" I yelled into the hold. "Come quickly! Look at this!" But she didn't answer or come up.

The bright sunshine bounced off the ocean creating a million shining diamonds on its surface; the sails were full blown and the Captain? Wonders of wonders! He was actually smiling.

"Doctor! The gods are with us!" Captain Adams made a flamboyant gesture at the sky.

"Aye, Captain, I can see that!" Rory called back as he turned his face upward, allowing rays of the sun to wash him with its warmth.

"If we keep up this speed, we'll be in Jersey in record time!" the Captain boasted as he watched the sails billow in the strong wind.

Rory shaded his eyes with his hands and scanned the horizon. I followed suit but could see nothing but sun glinting off the water.

The Captain said, "They're well behind us now. Not to worry!" He had guessed at Rory's concern correctly. "By the way, Doctor, what were Mr. Barclay's terms when he hired you?" The Captain changed the subject.

"Well, we agreed upon my fee which I will receive when we dock and I meet with his plantation overseer; and then he said that Lizzie and I would be free to either stay in New Jersey with these folks, or return with you."

"Ummm...that was mighty kind of him!" said the Captain, "seeing as how he never discussed that with me! I don't carry free passengers!"

"Do you forget that I am not a prisoner but a doctor on this ship and according to my agreement, I'm entitled to return with you, if I choose!" Rory sounded angry. "And exactly how much are you getting paid to deliver this human cargo?"

"Not nearly enough!" the Captain snapped back. "Do you want to talk about the New Jersey plantation or not?" The Captain's annoyance equaled that of Rory's and after a few moments of electric silence, Captain Adams added, "Thomas Barclay has been paid a specific amount of money to make sure each passenger arrived safely, barring sickness or natural death. He'll be fined one thousand Scots merks for each of the prisoners who might die through his or my carelessness. That's why you were hired. When we arrive in New Jersey, the prisoners will be taken to a plantation that belongs to Barclay. There, they'll work for him for three years at no wage. This will repay their passage."

"That puts the prisoners in the same category as slaves," Rory stated.

"That will include you, and Miss Whitelaw, if you decide to stay with them. But the others are prisoners, and they'll do as they're told for the next three years. I hear that Barclay is pretty tough on his people. He's started five colonies all together but only three are still operating."

"Which one will we be sent to?" asked Rory.

"The one on the coast of Jersey. And they're not a friendly lot, either, so don't expect them to throw you a welcome party," the Captain snickered. "However, it sounds to me as though you've made up your mind to stay on with this bunch and not return to Scotland. Am I right?"

"Aye," admitted Rory, "Aye, I'll be stayin' wi' 'em…or at least close by. I will want to begin my own business."

"Well, it's good you won't stay on the plantation because with that strong back of yours, Barclay would work you like a bloody horse."

"After the three years, then, they can work for themselves? Build their own houses? Plant their own crops? Am I understanding you correctly? That's right, isn't it?" Rory asked as he glanced at me, hope in his eyes. Surprisingly, that same sparkle of hope still shone there, just as when he spoke about "going to the Americas" on the High Street in Edinburgh.

"Aye, but…" the Captain hesitated.

"But, what?" Rory demanded.

"Well, suffice it to say that it'll be a long three years! If they don't have their backs broken with the work…and," the Captain lowered his voice to a whisper, then added, "if the Indians let you."

"Aw, cum'on, Adams!" This last bit of information snapped Rory's patience.

"You asked for it and I'm giving it to you! If you make it through the three years, well, you might have a chance. You can go off right away on your own, but if you intend to stay with this lot, you won't be looking at your own piece of land for three years. And," he continued, "the law says that if any of the prisoners run away before their indenture is up, Barclay's within his rights to shoot them when he catches them! So, for their sakes, make sure they understand that!"

"It's almost as if we would've been better off with the devil we knew in Scotland, than the devil we don't know in the Americas!"

"Aye," the Captain agreed. "You have a choice, but the others don't."

Rory and I returned to the hold. "Make sure you show them a cheery face, lassie!" Rory cautioned me.

Ma's anxious voice summoned us when we lowered ourselves into the hold. "Rory, they're both running fevers again! Worse than last time! Will you look at them?"

She led the way toward the sick men. Ma was right—they were burning up with fever, but their general appearance seemed different, too. Their legs looked detached from the rest of their bodies. They were so still.

"Let me see you move your foot, Jamie," Rory asked. After a moment of struggling, Jamie whispered, "I can't. I can't move my foot."

Rory lifted Jamie's leg. It looked lifeless—a dead weight. He carefully put the leg down and said, "Jamie, wiggle your toes. Cum' on, man, show me—wiggle your toes! Do you hear me? Move your bloody feet!"

"I told ye, I canna dae it!" Jamie cried. His eyes widened with fear. Rory and I exchanged worried glances. Palsy!

It can't be! No! No! I won't even think it!

Ma gripped my arm. "It's palsy," she whispered to me. We were all too familiar with palsy. It left a person crippled, unable to walk. Entire families had been wiped out by palsy. It spread like a peat bog fire; and, like a bog fire, you never knew where it was going to pop up!

"Quick," Rory said, "we have to separate them from the rest. Get me some help to carry them to the other end of the hold. No one is allowed to come near them!" he ordered. "No one, absolutely no one," he repeated, "with exception of myself, is to come near them. With luck...and prayers...maybe we can keep it from spreading!"

"What can I do to help?" Ma asked.

"Christie, yer not as strong as ye should be; I think ye'd better stay up on the deck and away from here as much as ye can." Rory's tone of voice left very little room for discussion.

"Ma, if they really do have palsy—well, I don't have to tell you about it," I reminded her. Ma's sister had died of the disease when she was a young girl.

"Ach, Lizzie. Will it never stop? Here, you're having to take on work like a grown woman and you're still a child yersel'." Ma was worrying again.

"Ma, I'm not a child anymore!"

Ma glanced angrily at Rory.

"No, Ma. No! Don't think that! I finished growing up when I dropped Catherine's dead baby into the ocean. I'm not a little girl anymore, Ma. No matter how much you want me to be, I'm not. Ma, think about it. I've lived a lifetime already and I'm only seventeen—well, almost eighteen."

"Oh, how I wish your Da was here!"

"Even if he was, Ma, he couldn't turn the clock back; not even Da could do that. I still grew up—fast."

Rory picked up the sick men and moved them to the far end of the hold. We watched him in silence.

"I want you all to stay away from these men and remain on deck as much as possible," Rory announced. He no sooner got the words out of his mouth than there was a scramble for the ladder.

"Palsy! They've got palsy!" With a frenzy of commotion, the hold quickly emptied.

"How is Catherine Sims, Christie?" Rory asked. "Can she be moved up on deck?"

"She's weak, but she'll make it. That is, if we can keep her warm and fed.

Rory walked over to Catherine and knelt beside her. He held her hand in his and asked, "How are ye, soldier?"

She grinned backed, "I'm alright, Doctor. Can't get up and dance a jig at the minute—just give me an hour or so..." her voice trailed off as her bit of humor weakened. "Naw, I'm alright. I'll be up and about by the time we dock."

"How would ye like a little sunshine, Catherine?" I asked, peeking at her over Rory's shoulder.

"Oh, that'd be grand! Just to smell the fresh air. I don't care if the sun is shining or not!" she exclaimed.

"Let's get you up there, then." Rory picked her up as tenderly as he would a wee bairn. She clung to his neck as he pulled the two of them up the ladder. Once on deck, Ma, who had followed close behind with a blanket, made a bed for Catherine on the deck and was soon tucking blankets around her.

After seeing to Catherine's comfort on deck, I watched Rory make his way to the Captain's cabin. "Captain," he called, "a word with you, please, sir!"

"By all means, come in! Just leave the door open, please, the sun is as good as medicine, is it not?" The Captain was obviously in a good mood. "A wee drop, Doctor?" I heard him ask Rory.

"Oh, aye, that would go down well, about now," agreed Rory, but his voice sounded flat. He looked at the rum in the glass, rolled it slowly around once or twice and brought it up to his lips and in one long swallow, emptied the glass.

"That's not some magical potion, Rory," I chided him silently, not liking the way Rory enjoyed his drink. "It won't make the palsy go away!"

"What's the problem?" the Captain asked. "If I may say so, you're looking very grim."

"Captain," Rory blurted out, "I believe we have a case of palsy on board."

"We have what?!" the Captain exploded. "Damn! I knew it was going along too good to be true!"

"I suggest that we keep everyone else on deck as much as possible." Rory's voice was almost apologetic.

"...my crew will not be allowed into the hold now. You understand that don't you?" the Captain interrupted.

Rory obviously resented the Captain's tone but carried on. "I suggest that if the weather stays warm, we let the group sleep up on the deck. Can you help us out with extra blankets?"

"I don't really have a choice, do I?" Captain Adams was not amused.

"And neither do I!" Rory snapped back. They glared at each other for a few moments. The Captain regained his composure first, then cursing under his breath, poured them both another drink.

"Ach, why not!" Rory accepted the proffered truce.

"There's no use in adding to the death toll, is there?" He gave the Captain a quick nod as he tipped the glass back. "I'm sick to death of going from one calamity to another! When's it going to end?"

"When you're six feet under, Doctor," the Captain quipped. "Actually, you've had it pretty good. Only one man lost. That's some kind of a record, you know!"

"The way I figure it," Rory said, "we'll need every last body if we're to survive this plantation, and then start our own colony. At least that's what I've in mind."

The Captain growled, "I didn't think it would take you long to come up with some sort of a plan, MacLeod. A couple of weeks will see us dropping you off at a place called Strawbery Bank and then you'll have an entirely different set of headaches, Doctor." The Captain actually sounded pleased at the prospect.

Rory was thoughtful for a moment. Then he thanked the Captain for the drink and turned to leave, his strong, young shoulders slumped forward a bit under the burden.

"Oh, by the way, Doctor," the Captain stopped him. "Sheilagh Kirk will be sailing back to Scotland with me."

Rory looked puzzled. "But she's branded. She can't go back into Scotland. What will you do with her?"

"I'll keep her on board the ship. She'll be better off with me than on that plantation. She won't want for anything and if and when she desires, she can rejoin you after my next trip."

"I can't say I like this! What does Sheilagh say about it? What about Barclay?" Rory shook his head disgustedly.

"Have you heard her screaming or trying to get back into the hold? Take a look at her! She's even gained a little weight! Ask her for yourself what she wants to do. If she doesn't view it as being held prisoner, why should you? As for Barclay, he's my worry—not yours!"

"I'll ask her, Captain, you can be bloody sure of that! Because I want to hear it from her own lips, then I'll know for mysel'!" Rory suddenly looked puzzled, then asked, "Why Sheilagh?"

"High spirited...good lines..." the Captain was tormenting Rory and he knew it.

"Sounds like you're judging horseflesh instead of a woman." Rory was angry.

"Not much difference when you stop to think of it, Doctor," the Captain quipped.

Rory stepped over the sill onto the deck, shaking his head. "The man mustn't have had a mother! Not the way he thinks about women!" he mumbled under his breath. "God help us!" he muttered, as he looked around at our huddled group, "if there are many more like Adams in the world!"

CHAPTER 20

During the next week and a half we greedily soaked up the sunshine and fresh air, living in constant fear of being sent back to the hold again.

The crew welcomed the extra help in keeping everything 'ship shape', and we were pleased to justify our presence on deck. Morale improved by huge leaps and bounds. Why, we even looked forward to what we imagined about plantation life. However, a black cloud loomed on our horizon when, in spite of Rory's diligent efforts, the two palsied men died. He seemed to take it personally, ignoring our reassurances that he had done everything humanly possible to save them. Gloom hung like a wet blanket over Rory and it spread like the plague to the rest of us. Even Alistair couldn't cheer him up. Also, discontent was being created by the six women who were now regularly sleeping with members of the crew.

"Ye see wot Arthur gie me last night?" Fanny shrieked, making sure that everyone heard her.

"Aye, that's lovely, so's it is!" came back the gushing, overly loud reply of her cohorts.

This infamous "six" took great delight in displaying the gifts that the grateful seamen had given them...bits of silk and pretty jewelry from Spain.

"Dae they think those few little baubles they're crowin' over is worth the price they will pay?" Catherine asked disgustedly.

An expectant silence quivered through the hold.

"I wonder how much good that wee bit o' silk will dae ye at the Judgment Bar?" another woman of the Covenant shouted.

"Ah, yer just jealous! Ye just wish they'd picked you instead o' us!"

"No, that's not so!" Catherine struggled to her feet to object. "We're chaste out o' choice! There's not one o' us here that couldn't get bedded down wi' that lot!" She waved her hand toward the crew's quarters. "We have respect for ourselves. But I wonder if ye even know what I'm talkin' about?"

Our nods of agreement gave her encouragement.

"Besides, I still love my husband!" she continued, "even though I don't have him any more! And I love my God!" Catherine was adamant in her declaration. "I haven't forgotten the Covenant or why I'm here! Ye've been bought with a few trinkets. Where's yer stinkin' morals?"

A chorus of "ayes" went up from the women of the Covenant.

The men were quiet. Not just silent but, 'holdin' their breath' kind of quiet. They offered no opinions, in fact, I'm sure they thought that a stotter of a cat fight was about to break out.

"Well, here's something ye should know...and ye would'na found it out here with all yer being so high and mighty. I was told by Simon—the one I'm with—that if we get to Jersey wi' our scalps still intact—well, it will be a miracle. During the last voyage with Captain Adams, Simon said that as soon as the Indians spotted the ship they came out by the boat load and climbed up the rope ladders and swarmed over the ship, taking everything on board and killing several of the crew.

Rory stood up. "That's enough!" he bellowed. "You," Rory pointed at the "six". "Never again tinkle your baubles under their noses and ye know what I'm talking about! And, if what you are saying is true—and I'm not so sure it is—well, we'll cross that bridge when we come to it." Rory was once again on his feet and taking command. Before I could fully enjoy the fact, our battle was interrupted by a shout from the deck.

"Land ho!"

We immediately quieted down and listened. The seaman in the crow's nest called out again. "Land ho!"

A third invitation wasn't needed. We scrambled up to the deck rail. Warm morning sunshine and clear skies had us blinking toward land.

"There it is!" we shouted to each other. Jimmy grabbed hold of Willie's coat just in time to keep him from falling over the railing in his excitement.

"Look! Look!" Willie kept shouting, oblivious to his narrow escape. Nothing mattered now! We had arrived.

Broad smiles, back slapping, hugs and kisses ran rampant throughout the ship. Catherine even hugged one of the "six".

"Captain! Is that Jersey?" I called to him.

"No, no," he laughed. Even his condescension didn't annoy me this morning. "That's not New Jersey yet! That's Newfoundland. It'll take another few days to get to Jersey!"

And the Captain was true to his word; however, the time dragged, to the point of being painful. How I longed to set foot on land once more. Even the unknown seemed like it would be a paradise compared to what I had just lived through—or so I thought...and it didn't look like a black hole.

A day before we were scheduled to dock at Strawbery Bank, all peaceful anticipation that we were enjoying was shattered by a frantic cry from the crow's nest. "Boats! Boats to the starboard! Hundreds o' them!" He was waving his arms in the direction of the shore.

The Captain snatched up his spyglass to scrutinize the horizon. Our eyes flitted from his spyglass to the direction of the coastline and back again.

"What is it?" Rory asked, having lost no time in getting to the Captain's side.

Captain Adams lowered his spyglass, nevertheless, he continued to look toward the shore. "Well, Doctor," he said, "if I was you, I'd say my prayers and hope that those Indians are not after your scalps."

Rory impatiently snatched the glass from Captain Adam's hand. "What the...?" Rory muttered.

"Rory, tell me! What do you see?" I demanded.

He looked at me, his eyes full of disbelief. "They're half naked—feathers sticking out of their heads..." He put the spyglass to his eye again.

"What do you see?" I demanded, becoming more anxious by the moment. "Tell me!"

The others had crowded around him as well. We all waited for his answer.

"They have strange markings on their faces. It looks like paint." Rory seemed confused.

"Captain Adams! What's going on?" Rory wanted to know.

"Those, Dr. MacLeod," said the Captain, "are Indians! And they have a nasty habit of removing the hair off your head...with just enough skin...to hang it from their belts."

"What are you going to do?" Rory asked anxiously.

"I know what I'm going to do! The question is, what are *you* going to do? You're now on your own, Doctor." The Captain grabbed the spyglass out of Rory's hand.

"We're what?" Rory exploded.

"You have to look after your people and I look after mine! It's that simple. My job was to land this lot on shore and I'm giving you the boats to do just that!

Now get going...unless you're coming back to Scotland with me!" the Captain shouted. "I'll not have those savages climbing over my ship again!"

"Then it's true!" Rory gulped in astonishment, "but you said that they'd scalp us or whatever you called it!"

"Right! Those are the chances you'll have to take. I can't help you. You'll have to fend for yourselves, the best you know how. I'll not have them on this ship!" The Captain cupped his hands to his mouth and shouted, "Man the life boats!"

"I'll kill ye, you pig!" Rory lunged at the Captain.

"Try it, MacLeod!" The first mate grinned at Rory, "I'd love an excuse." He slid a long, thin knife out of its sheath and pointed it at Rory's throat.

Alistair suddenly appeared at Rory's side, ready for the fight—frail and incapable, but ready.

The two men glared at each other until the Captain spoke up, his voice once again calm. "It's your choice, Doctor—for the next thirty seconds—then I'll make it for you!"

Rory straightened his shoulders. "Aye! The boats it is!" he barked. With a dark sidewise look at the Captain, he walked toward the ship's railing, the heels of his boots striking the wooden deck like hammers. The crew lowered the large lifeboats into the water and rope ladders were swung over the side of the ship.

"Ma! Where's m' Ma?" I couldn't see her anywhere.

"Move it! Get yersel's into the boats. We'll be rowin' ashore," Rory shouted at everyone in general.

"Aayyeee! Simon was right!"

"But Rory...?"

"There's no time tae blether about it! Just do as I say! Move! Fast! Get down those ladders and into the boats. Lizzie! Go down first and steady them as they land in yer boat. Alistair, you do the same!" Rory was pushing, pulling, coaxing—but we were frightened.

"There's only four boats, Rory," Alistair shouted back.

Rory stood up, arms on his hips, but before he could say anything, the Captain shouted, "That's it, MacLeod, four boats and no more!"

We all heard him. Rory didn't have to tell us. We squeezed and squeezed some more, one on top of the other...again and again. Some were reluctant to leave the security of the ship and had to be prodded on by Rory.

"Where's Ma?" I cried again.

"She's in here wi' us," someone shouted from another boat.

"Rory! Where are you?" I was up again, frantically peering into the other boats.

"Here!" he answered from the deck of the ship. "I'll be right down!"

He ran in the direction of his cabin and immediately reappeared with the medicine bag in one hand and his pipes in the other.

The boats full of Indians were coming toward us...closer and closer...looming larger and larger by the second.

"Rory, hurry!" I was almost in tears. "Oh, God! Please don't let me lose him now!" I begged over and over again, the words running together in my mind.

He swung himself over the railing and managed to climb down the ladder with one hand, the other holding onto his medicine bag and his pipes strapped to his back. He jumped and landed in the lifeboat, throwing it off balance.

"Rory!" we screamed in unison, as the boat rocked back and forth in the water. One more person and I was sure the boat would have gone down. The water was lapping at the rim as it was.

No sooner had he cleared the rope ladder than the crew pulled it up. Captain Adams gave Rory a wave of the hand and a sneering "Good luck...and Doctor, your 'six' are staying with my crew!"

"I'll tell ye what ye can do wi' yer 'good luck,' Adams! I'll get ye for this if it's the last thing I do in life!" Rory screamed at the disappearing Captain. Within minutes the ship began turning around.

We were stranded, abandoned and defenseless.

We turned our attention to the Indians who were bearing down on us—fast!

"Ahhhrrgg!" screamed Aggie. "They'll eat us alive!"

The Indians were covered in blood. We learned later that it was seal blood. And each boat was heaped with bloody mounds of dead seals. "Whooop-a-whoop-a!" the Indians shouted again and again. Each terrorizing whoop found an easy mark as it paralyzed me with fear.

Within minutes, our four lifeboats were surrounded by long and narrow, wooden boats. Some looked like hollowed out trees, while others were covered with what looked like tree bark.

Rory stood up. I frantically tried to pull him back down. "Stop it!" he said angrily and pushed my hands away.

The Indians immediately stopped whooping and stared at Rory, but continued to circle round and around us, glaring into our faces. Finally, a tall Indian, with more head feathers than the rest, stood up in his boat. He and Rory stared at each other, each measuring the other.

I was almost out of my mind with fear. "Get a grip on yersel'" Rory barked at me as I tried to get him to sit down.

The Indian patted his chest and said "Mugwump nia", while thumping his chest.

"What's he sayin', Rory?" Alistair shouted.

"Use yer head, man! How would I know!" Rory shouted back.

"But I think he just told us his name or that he is a chief," Alistair offered.

Rory seemed confused as to what to do next, so he simply mimicked the Indian's gestures and rubbed his chest saying, "I'm Rory MacLeod." Little did Rory know he was using the Indian sign to communicate he was a friend.

The Indian boats continued to circle our lifeboats. Their occupants gawked at us with eyes full of curiosity as we sat still, numb with terror, not daring to move. We could only stare back at them.

"What's going to happen?" I whimpered.

Rory was standing in the middle of the boat with his hands on his hips, continuing to stare at the standing Indian.

"Alistair, where are you?" he called out, ignoring my question.

"To yer left!" was Alistair's quick reply. "Why?" He hesitated for a moment, then added "I hope yer not thinkin' o' taking on this lot! There's a limit to friendship, ye know!"

"Don't be daft! The way I figure it is this, if this is my time to go over to the other side, then by all that's holy, I'm goin' over wi' a good tune!"

Alistair laughed and slapped the man next to him on the back. "Well done, old son! Well done! We'll look for ye over there! Hope ye've got a clean shirt for the journey!"

The rest of us were in shock and didn't realize that Rory and Alistair had just said their farewells and that they fully expected to be dead shortly.

Rory reached for his pipes and slowly put them on his shoulder, filled the bag with air, patted it gently, and brought the drones into tune, then played "Dunvegan's Galley", a MacLeod tune. The notes of the majestic melody floated on the air. Unwittingly, Rory had done the right thing…again.

The sound of the pipes, so foreign to the Indians, stopped them in mid-whoop.

It was their turn to be terrorized. They scrambled for their paddles with shouts of fear and within seconds all twenty of their boats were speeding toward shore.

Alistair's booming laugh signaled a momentary respite, and I drew in a deep, shaky breath. The others were still too frightened to do anything more than sit and stare at the retreating backs of the Indians. Rory stopped playing; his mouth gaped open in obvious surprise.

"I told ye, ye couldn't play! Look, ye scared the livin' daylights outta them!" laughed Alistair from the other boat.

Rory ignored the friendly jibe. "We've no choice, folks. Guess we'd better row for shore and take what's comin'."

The men reluctantly picked up the paddles and dipped them into the water. Slowly, laboriously, they pulled the boats toward the shore. No one spoke as we peered at the shoreline and tried to face up to what was to be our possible and more than likely—death. Finally, the dreaded moment arrived when our lifeboats ground to a stop on top of a reef of boulders not far from shore.

Rory jumped out first. The cold water made him gasp, but with his arms raised over his head and the water lapping at his waist, he shouted for someone to give him his medicine bag and pipes. Holding all his earthly treasures high above his head, he picked his way ashore amid the rocks and accumulated seaweed that danced on each wave. We watched him, but not one of us made a move to follow him.

Rory struggled against the ebbing tide. The weight of his water soaked kilt and jacket, socks and shoes dragged heavily on him. His shoulders swung with every step as he fought to keep his balance. Finally, we watched as he pulled himself out of the ocean to fall, face first onto the sandy beach. About ten feet from him were the beached Indian boats.

After a moment or two, Rory pushed himself to his knees and turned his head from one side to the other; evidently he had expected the rest of us to be beside him.

"Ma! We'd better start. Where are you?" I called.

"Aye, Lizzie—I'm wi' ye!" she said bravely, but I heard the quiver in her voice.

"I might be scared, but I'm not stupid," I muttered to those beside me as I slipped over the side of the boat. I jumped into the water, not wanting to be sitting in the boat when Rory turned around to see where we were.

As the shock of the freezing water hit me, I gasped and stood on the tips of my toes to keep as much of my body out of the water as possible.

A splash—and another—told me that the rest of our sorry group was jumping into the waves. I couldn't see Ma.

"Ma! Are you alright?"

No answer.

"Ma?" I began to panic.

"Aye—just get going, will ye? Afore I freeze!" her voice came from behind me and in trying to turn around to make sure she was there, I stumbled over a rock and almost lost my balance. "Lizzie, just mind yersel' and stop worrying about anyone else!" Ma shouted.

Rory was waving us on, shouting encouraging words. It looked rather comical to see Rory acting so confident, when peeking from behind the trees, at his back, were the Indians.

One and two at a time the ocean waves dumped us onto the sand, exhausted. Alistair, his well honed sarcasm at the ready, commented casually, "I'd keep those pipes on my shoulder if I were you, Rory. See—they're watchin' us from among those trees...might be the only thing we can do to save oursel's is to have ye play again. Ye surely scared the devil out o' those puir savages."

In their haste, the Indians had left their boats on the beach still loaded with seals and fish. That was the reason they were still lingering nearby...I hoped.

Rory asked us if we had any ideas as to how he should ask the Indians to help us find some food.

"We can thank th' Lord that Rory's a typical Glasgow glutton—always thinkin' o' his belly!" someone observed.

"Rònach!" Someone said in Gaelic, pointing hungrily at the seals.

"Let's use one of their seals!" The suggestion came from somewhere down the beach.

"And how long dae ye think they'll let us live if we did?" Alistair shot back wisely.

"The trick is going to be in holding onto my scalp long enough to make friends with them." Rory muttered. "I've got to think of something and fast!"

Much to my horror, he moved toward the trees, patted his chest, as he had done in the boat, and said, "I'm Rory MacLeod," and extended his other hand, palm up, in a friendly way.

No response. He repeated the gesture and waved his hand at us saying, "We are Scots." Only silence rewarded his efforts, however, he continued his gesturing. Eventually, there was a little movement in the trees and the Indian who had stood up before, emerged, appearing as hesitant as Rory.

"Look, Rory, he's just a'scairt as you!" Alistair said mockingly.

The Indian was clad only in a breech clout, bringing forth little cries of astonishment from some of the women, who immediately turned their heads and covered their eyes. However, the more curious just stared at the half naked man. His head was shaved, except for a ridge of hair that ran down the middle of his scalp. Black and white feathers were secured in this ridge of coal black hair at the back of his head and around his neck he wore a necklace, which I learned later was made of bear teeth and claws.

Rory kept a wary eye on the short handled axe the Indian was clutching. "Alistair!" Rory called out, not taking his eyes from Mugwump, "hand me my pipes, will ye?"

"Come and get 'em yersel'...I'm not goin' over there!" was the quick reply.

"Do you want us all killed? Gie 'em to me now!" Rory demanded.

After a moment of deliberation, Alistair muttered philosophically, "Ach, well, in for a penny—in for a pound!" as he walked toward Rory very slowly and handed him the pipes.

Mugwump took two or three steps backward, his eyes opening wide as Rory put the pipes on his shoulder. However, curiosity soon overcame his fear. First he looked at the pipes and again at Rory, then he stepped toward Rory.

Our fear had frozen us like statues.

"Play them! For cryin' out loud! Or we're all done for!" Alistair moaned.

Rory stood his ground bravely, not backing away as Mugwump advanced toward him. He reached out and pointed at Rory's chest, asking "Mugwump?".

"Rory! I think Mugwump means Chief!" Alistair surmised correctly.

"We'll give it a go!" Rory agreed and reciprocated by touching his own chest saying "Mugwump" then pointed to the Indian's chest and repeated the word.

This elicited a nod of approval from the Indian.

"Are ye sure ye didn't just tell him it's fine wi' ye if he took yer hair?" Alistair whispered hoarsely.

"Alistair, shut yer mug!" one of the prisoners cautioned.

The Indian repeated what was beginning to look like a gesture of friendship and nodded his head up and down. Rory mimicked the Indian once again. Slowly and deliberately, the Indian pointed at his boats and the seal meat.

The Chief uttered some words, that Rory, of course, didn't understand.

"Fer cryin' out loud!" Alistair yelled, "gie the man his boats and meat and let him be on his way!"

"Rory, ask him if we can have some of their meat," I suggested, hoping Alistair wouldn't make me feel like the village idiot for my efforts.

Ignoring me, he spoke and gestured to Mugwump, "Aye, take it. Take it all!" Rory said enthusiastically, trying to communicate his meaning while pointing at the boats, bobbing his head up and down so fast it looked as if it wasn't even attached to his shoulders.

The Chief, in turn, waved his warriors out of the trees. They cautiously moved toward their boats, giving Rory a wide berth. The Indians lifted the dead seals onto their backs, anxious to haul their catch away. This was too much for Rory, having to watch a good meal being taken away, right from under his nose, was more than he could handle.

He touched the arm of Mugwump to get his attention and pointed to a seal and then pointed to his mouth while rubbing his stomach.

The Indian stared at him for almost a full minute.

Alistair groaned, "Now he's done it. This is the end for sure!"

Slowly, deliberately, Mugwump grunted something to one of his young braves. The young man brought a seal and dropped it at Rory's feet. He left again, but returned within minutes with several large salmon which he dropped at Rory's feet."

Rory looked at the mound of fish and meat and wondered how raw seal and raw salmon would taste. But, as if reading his thoughts, Mugwump piled little branches and bits of dried leaves together.

"He's tryin' to show us how to make a fire!" said Alistair, who was seemingly beginning to enjoy the experience.

"I don't have a flint to start the fire. Do you?" Rory looked hopefully at Alistair.

"Oh, aye, here's one in my sporran." Alistair said sarcastically and then added, "Don't be daft, Rory!"

I was riddled with misgivings, but Alistair's sarcasm was taking some of the fear out of the situation for me.

When the Chief finished laying the fire, he reached into a leather pouch which hung from his belt and pulled out a large seashell. He seemed to be waiting for something.

"He wants ye to watch him, Rory." Alistair said.

Although we were still at a distance from Rory and Mugwump, we peered at the shell as he opened it up and there, lying in its center was a small, burning ember. He placed the ember on the pile of dry leaves and wood and within seconds a small flame leaped from the middle of it.

Rory and Alistair clapped each other on the back and tried to shake the Chief's hand. This obviously startled him and I feared that our new and wobbly friendship had just been nipped in the bud. Mugwump's expression was stony, but he didn't move away from them.

"I think I'd better learn—and fast—the differences between our customs and theirs," Rory groaned.

"Spread out! Find some dry wood for the fire. I think we're about to eat!" Alistair shouted to the others. We remained still, afraid to move.

The Chief again grunted something and his braves came out of the trees, bringing pieces of wood with them.

Rory shouted at us, "You lot, help as well!"

This time we moved, and fast. We obediently picked up pieces of dried driftwood, all the while keeping a wary eye on the Indians. However, they were just as cautious about coming too close to us. In spite of everyone's misgivings and trepidation, a huge, warm fire was soon blazing.

Mugwump then took it upon himself to show Rory how to save fire. He walked a few paces down the beach, turned around and motioned for Rory to follow him. Then he walked a few more paces and stopped, looked behind him to make sure that Rory was following, and continued his walk. I tagged along, uninvited, and was thankful that the Chief ignored me.

When we reached the edge of the water, the Indian dug into the sand until he found a shell that was similar to the one in his pouch. He put the shell into Rory's extended hand, turned toward the trees and motioned for us to follow.

Further up the beach and closer to the trees, the Indian dug into the earth and scooped up a handful of clay. He lined Rory's shell with it. Off we went again; into the forest this time. I stuck to Rory as if I was his shadow.

Rory watched Mugwump's every move as we traveled further and further into the forest. Every tree stump was examined by the Indian until he finally found one that was rotting and dry. Reaching into its' center, he pulled out a handful of powdery wood rot and poured it onto the clay lining in the clam shell.

Much to my relief, he then led us back to the beach and our roaring bonfire. Mugwump pulled a small ember from the edge of the fire and carefully lifted it into Rory's shell and put one in his own.

Rory closed the shell quickly and carefully placed it in the small pocket of his dripping wet sporran. Hands on his hips, he grinned as he watched the Chief put his own shell into a small beaded pouch that hung from his waist.

"Maybe our customs aren't too different after all," he said.

Once back on the beach with our group, Rory patted Alistair on the back and chuckled, "Well, now, old son, we're not doin' too badly. We've only been here a short time and look! We've a fire, we have a seal, we have fish and I've learned how to keep fire in my sporran!"

Rory was obviously pleased with the state of affairs and this was radiated to the rest of our group, with the exception of Alistair. "Aye, ye've not done too badly," he growled. "Now just learn tae keep yer hair on yer big head and ye'll be alright! Remember what the Captain said about them likin' tae scalp folks? Did it cross yer mind that they could just be fattening us up for the kill?"

"MacCrimmon! Will ye never change?" Rory bellowed at Alistair.

I left them to argue it out.

The women were taking turns pivoting in front of the fire in an attempt to dry their hair and clothes and the men were staring longingly at the fish and the seal.

Ma motioned to one of the Indian braves. He walked over to her slowly, his hand on his short-handled axe. She pointed at the fish and at her stomach, hoping he'd get the message that she would like to eat. She didn't look very sure of herself, but at least she was trying, I thought.

The Indian stood in front of her, folded his arms over his chest and grunted, shaking his head from side to side. It was evident that she had upset this Indian brave.

Rory was amused as he watched Ma struggling to communicate with the brave and was about to intercede when Mugwump stepped forward.

"What did I do wrong?" Ma wanted to know. "All I did was point at the salmon they gave us and rub my stomach. I just want him to gie me something to clean the fish with!"

"The way he's glaring at you, well, you've managed to get his hackles up somehow. Are ye sure that's all that ye did?" Rory queried.

"Aye! I didn't do another thing!" Ma was adamant.

"I wonder if he thinks you're wantin' him to cook it for you?" mused Rory. "Christie, I think that yer supposed to cook the fish, not him."

"Well, I know that and that's what I intend to do!" Ma's pride was hurt.

"Don't ask any more questions and just use your imagination. Maybe they'll help out when they see you doin' it wrong." Rory was making a mess of being helpful.

Ma stood up and turned to face Rory. "Just what do ye mean 'watch me dae it wrong'?"

With her nose in the air, she stomped and stumbled down the beach toward Rory's medicine bag, opened it, put her hand in and came out with his surgeon's knife. She marched right back to the fish, sat down, slit it, gutted it, cut off the gills and tail and washed it in the ocean water.

This is the Ma I knew! It felt so good to see her come back to herself again. I knelt down beside her. "What are ye looking surprised about?" Ma asked sarcastically. I just shrugged my shoulders, knowing from experience when to keep quiet. Besides, my thoughts of America being a gaping black hole were being challenged by what was happening right now. These Indians—so far—were seemingly friendly—but we had only been here, perhaps two hours altogether.

"Yer no help!" she snapped at me.

Ma then sat back on her heels and thought for a moment. "Well, if I could do it in Scotland, I surely can do it here!" she said and slapped her knee for emphasis. "When I went hunting with your Grandda, this is how…" her words were lost in activity as she looked around for a green stick with which to skewer the fish. Propping it between two other pieces of wood, Ma proceeded to bake the fish over the fire.

Alistair grimaced and said to Rory, "Ye'd better be watchin' yersel'. Did ye see the way she handled that knife when she was angry?"

"Aye, I noticed!"

Ma looked up at Mugwump and asked, "How's this?"

We were all relieved to see his nod of approval. Ma's naturally charitable disposition gained her much ground with the Chief, because when the fish was finished baking, she said to me, "If it wasn't for this man, we wouldn't be eating at all. I should offer him the first piece."

Ma cleaned off a flat piece of wood and placed the steaming fish on it. She walked over to Mugwump and offered it to him with a little curtsey, saying, "Mugwump, we thank you for your hospitality."

We held our breath, hoping Ma hadn't overstepped her bounds, but he accepted it as if it was his due and ate most of it.

This prompted the other women to fly into action, quickly cleaning and washing the rest of the salmon.

The Chief spoke to his braves. They immediately disappeared into the forest and just as quickly returned with handfuls of bright red berries, plump with juice. The Indians showed the women how to stuff the fish with the berries and then skewer them closed with slender green twigs. Before long the aroma of baking fish was tantalizing us. Scots and Indians sat down to the first meal of many together.

Ahh, food! What a pleasure it was to feel the tasty morsels in my mouth, and to know there was more! Oh, I'm so fed up with being hungry! Maybe, just maybe, this is a sign that we'll never be hungry again. "Oh, God, thank you," I said, as I munched my way through bite after bite of delicious salmon.

Ma smiled and winked at me. Her smile brought back memories of supper at home in our own little Tigh Sona. She always enjoyed watching us eat our fill. And that same look of triumph was in her smile now.

"Oh, Ma! Keep getting better!" I wanted to shout. But Ma was now eyeing the seal. "I've never cleaned one o' these before," she admitted.

Aggie Burns was at her side. "Aye, its usually up tae the men folk tae clean these uins," she advised.

"I don't think that's how it's done here, Aggie," Ma said.

"Well, then, where dae we start?" Aggie asked, as she rolled up her dress sleeves.

"Ohh!" shouted Ma. Mugwump had startled her by trying to take the knife out of her hands. Thinking quickly, she ran to Rory's medical bag and searched quickly for the shiny metal mirror. As soon as she had found it, she ran toward the Chief, offering it to him.

As he took it from her, he glimpsed his reflection and again jumped back. He looked again; this time he pointed at the mirror and laughed. Once more we all breathed a sigh of relief and Ma slipped the knife into her pocket.

"Whew!" Ma muttered under her breath and taking advantage of the moment, she pointed at the seal. Mugwump nodded his head in agreement.

Ma whispered to me, "And what is he saying 'aye' to?" as she watched the Indian nod his head. She stood in front of him with a puzzled look on her face. He was nodding his head "yes" alright, pointing to the seal and to Ma.

"Right! I should have guessed!" Ma finally said. Ma and Aggie, in unison, squatted down by the seal and tried to open up its belly with Rory's surgeon knife. The hide was too thick for the slender instrument and it bent, almost to the point of breaking before Ma stopped.

Rory stood back and watched with an amused look on his face. Ma caught him smiling and snapped, "This is not amusing! Not at all, Dr. MacLeod! I'm not even sure that we started at the right end."

"And I don't blame ye for being cranky. It's about time that daughter of yours helped out! Lizzie," he called.

I heard him but was studiously ignoring him.

"Lizzie, come on, lassie, it's your turn."

Alistair tried to come to my rescue. "I imagine it would be the same as cleaning a fish, Lizzie."

"Then do it for me, please!" I whined.

"Uh uh! Sorry, not me! Besides, we'd lose face in front of these Indians. That's women's work!"

"Alistair!" I complained, finding myself the butt of his teasing. I walked over to the seal and stared at the huge mammal. "Well, Ma, I know we can use the skin. I know we can use the fat and I know we can use the meat." I continued to mutter to myself as I circled the seal.

"Lizzie! You are stalling! Come and give us a hand!" Ma ordered.

My 'stalling', not only irritated Ma, but had made the Indian Chief nervous, too. He began gesturing to Rory, then to his braves and back to Rory again. Rory and I stared at him in an effort to understand what he was trying to say. I squatted down in front of the seal, looking it over, trying to figure out how to cut through the hide and how to get out of helping with the cleaning. The whole idea was making me feel sick to my stomach.

"Rory," I called out lamely, "I'm gonna be sick!"

"Lizzie!" he said impatiently, "ye can't go through life, vomiting every time ye don't want to do something!"

A crashing noise in the trees startled us. An Indian brave emerged, dragging a woman behind him. "She must be his wife," Aggie whispered to Ma. "He wouldn't treat anyone else like that! Aye," she continued, "men—they're all th' same!"

The brave had pulled the poor woman over to the seal and grunted some words at her. She stood motionless in front of us, silently looking from Ma to Aggie and then to me.

We stared back.

I had never seen such luxurious black hair. She was clothed in soft, brown leather that had been beautifully decorated with shells and small animal teeth and something else I couldn't identify. On her chin were four vertical dark blue lines, running close to one another, ending at her neck. Her cleanliness and beauty made Ma aware of her own dirty body and dress. She tried to smooth out her wet and tattered dress and then looked embarrassed as she pushed stringy, filthy hair away from her face.

My dress had a row of little round buttons down the front and the Indian woman openly stared at them. I pulled one of them off and handed it to her. She smiled shyly and immediately dropped it into a fringed leather pouch that was tied around her waist.

Out of that same pouch, she produced a long white bone which we learned later was the shinbone of a deer. It had been honed to a razor sharp edge and with no effort at all, she slit the belly of the seal open, spilling the innards onto the sand. Then two fingers were carefully inserted under the hide. We could see that she was separating the flesh from the fat that was just under the skin. Quickly and easily she was beginning to remove the hide and had our undivided attention.

The Chief spoke. Immediately the woman stopped working and handed the instrument to me. With the crude knife gripped in my hand, I said over and over again, "I can't get sick...I won't be sick...I can't get sick...I won't be sick!"

With determination to do this task correctly, I bent over the seal in the same manner as had the Indian woman; inserting two fingers under the skin fat I proceeded to separate it from the hide. This wasn't as hard or as sickening as I had imagined it would be. Before I knew it, the rest of the skinning was done.

"Just look at the cocky wee uin, will ye?" Alistair said, smiling broadly at me.

The Indian woman indicated she wanted to take over and I happily handed the instrument back. When the hide was entirely removed, the woman cut the flesh into strips and laid them on green striplings that the braves had quickly and expertly made into a drying rack for us.

Ma, and some of the other women, joined us and we worked side by side, appreciating the fact that we were actually working at something important and especially enjoying each other's company. All this happened in spite of not being able to communicate verbally with the Indian woman.

'Many hands made light work' and the job was soon finished. And none too soon, the sun was going down.

"If ye want some roasted seal meat, get yersel's a green stick and lace the meat around it." Rory demonstrated as he spoke, and then thrust his seal meat over the red hot embers of the fire.

I had thought the seal work was finished, so turned to join the others at the bonfire. But as I walked away, the Indian woman caught hold of my hand and pulled me back toward the seal, motioning me to watch her.

She picked up a big rock and with all her might brought it down on the seal's skull, cracking it open. To my horror, she scooped out the brains with a shell and piled them inside the seal skin and folded it into a neat parcel.

"I have no idea why you wanted me to watch you do this, but it has absolutely ruined my appetite," I said quietly. She smiled at me, believing, I guess, that I was admiring her work.

I turned toward the bonfire where my people were sitting when I heard 'ooos' and 'ahhhs' of approval coming from them and looked up to see four Indian women coming toward us, carrying buckets of water. The buckets looked like they were made of bark and to everyone's delight, we were given a refreshing drink of water, which we gulped from a dipper made of bark.

"They're good people!"

"Aye!"

"The Lord be thankit!"

"Aye!"

Our fear of this new land and the Indian people was beginning to melt away...and for me, the black hole was shrinking.

Shelaigh Kirk, who had decided to stay with us rather than with the Captain, began singing and coaxing the rest of us to join her. Soon, the early evening air was filled with our songs.

Before long, Rory had his pipes out and as he tuned up, the Indians beat a hasty retreat into the forest, but he continued playing. His instincts told him they would come back; and as we tapped out feet in time with the music, the Indians did return—but very slowly, mind you. And it wasn't long before they, too were moving in time with the music.

When Rory was tired of playing and had carefully laid his pipes down on a log, Mugwump approached him cautiously, hand out, wanting to touch them. There was still a little bit of air left in the bag and as the Chief pushed it, the air squawked through the drones and chanter reed, sending him reeling backwards.

Everyone laughed, but the Chief was not amused. Rory, sensing the man's loss of pride did not laugh but busied himself, taking the drones apart and blowing on the reeds and then screwed the chanter out and blew on that reed. His actions took the attention away from the Chief's embarrassment, which was quickly replaced by curiosity.

While all of this was going on, I was uncomfortably aware of the brave who had brought the woman to help me; he had been staring at me for some time now, hardly blinking. Striding over to where I was standing, he motioned to the Indian woman to leave my side.

Suddenly, he grabbed my wrist. I twisted, trying to free myself but his grip was like an iron vise. "Rory!" I screeched. "Hellllp!" He was dragging me toward the forest.

Rory came on the run, catching me by the other arm. I was stretched between the two of them. "Lizzie, I know you're not ready for this, but I'm going to tell him you're my wife and you'd better act like it!" Rory whispered through clenched teeth.

Rory waved his arm, pointed at me and pounded his chest, and motioned for Mugwump to come over. The Chief said, "Behanem—Behanem," pointing to me. The Indian brave stared at me, then at Rory, who was maintaining his hold on my arm waiting for the brave to drop my other arm. Finally, he almost threw my arm at Rory, who quickly gathered me up in his arms and we stood there, clinging to each other.

The brave spoke to his Chief, using hand signs, pointing to the Indian woman and then to Rory. It didn't take Rory long to figure out the gist of the conversation. The Indian brave wanted to trade wives! Rory laughed as he watched my horrified expression when it dawned on me what was actually being negotiated.

And I certainly didn't miss the fact that he was thoroughly enjoying how I was clinging to him.

The others looked on in astonishment as Rory held up one finger to the Chief and pointed at me shaking his head as he looked at the Indian woman. The Chief nodded his head in understanding.

It wasn't long before the Indians began to disappear into the forest and Mugwump gestured toward his boats lying on the beach. Finally, we understood he was going to leave them there. Rory, nodding his head, indicated that the boats would be safe with us.

I was anxious to return to the fire and tugged at Rory until he accompanied me. More than a little shaken by my narrow escape, I was shivering uncontrollably.

Thankfully, the fire was still burning brightly and I turned around and around in front of it, warming myself. Ma stayed close by my side, not saying a word, just watching; her concern for me evident on her face.

Rory climbed onto a wooden stump that was near the edge of the forest and called for everyone's attention. "The Lord has dealt with us mercifully..." he began, much to the surprise of the group. Never had they heard Rory express an opinion about religion, either pro or con. Alistair didn't even try to mask his astonishment. Rory continued, "the Captain of the ship could have been much worse and now these strangers...well, we all still have our scalps and they did feed us. I, for one, want to give thanks to the Lord for His help!"

"Aye!" "Aye!" we all agreed.

Humbly, we bowed our heads as Rory offered thanks and pleaded for continued mercy allowing the warmth of spiritual unity to create an even stronger bond between us. When the prayer was finished we hugged each other, responding to the feeling of indescribable love and joy flowing between us.

Suddenly, a cool breeze blew in from the ocean, forcing us to pull our still damp shawls and blankets around our shoulders, surrendering the warmth the fire had given our bodies to the cold cloth. The men had hauled large pieces of driftwood from further up the beach and laid them on the fire. The heat of the fire drew us close as we prepared for our first night's sleep in this new land.

Excited chatter soon gave way to a comfortable low hum, until I cried out in astonishment, bringing everyone to a sitting position, and some of the more valiant men to their feet. I had taken one more look into the trees and was startled to see two small, bright coals of light blinking at me.

Rory laughed, "'Tis simply the eyes of some little animal watching us. We'll be safe as long as the fire keeps burning."

I moved closer to my mother and eventually fell asleep, watching the stars and listening to the lulling sound of waves breaking on the shore.

Chapter 21

The morning air jangled with the sound of raised voices. An argument was raging between the men over what should be our next move. The women were a little further down the beach, milling around, wondering how to find something for breakfast.

The sun was hot, making the heavy woolen dresses and kilts or trousers and jackets very uncomfortable. It wasn't long before the men began peeling off their jackets and the women loosened the necks of their dresses. Shawls and the few blankets we had managed to bring off the ship were carefully folded up and stacked after they had dried.

What was in the forest became a curiosity I found difficult to contain. I had to see what was in there. Everyone was busy with their own thoughts and affairs, so I took this opportunity to explore—just a little. With only one step into the trees, it seemed as though I was in another world; a world so dense and green and made even more beautiful by the sun beams that struggled through the leaves of the huge branches, giving the undergrowth a lacy appearance. Another step. The coolness of the shade was a welcome respite from the hot sand and sun. So refreshing....

"Aaeeyy! Rory!" I screamed, running as fast as I could toward the beach and safety.

Only when I felt safe, did I turn around to see, standing at the edge of the trees were what looked like human forms, but they were painted in strange colors. My screams brought the others on the run. They, too, stopped in wide-eyed astonishment, staring at what seemed like apparitions emerging out of the forest.

Six people, obviously women, stepped onto the beach. They were naked under several coats of paint. One of the women motioned for me to follow her. I resisted, until I recognized her as being the one who had helped me skin the seal the night before. She, and the others with her, were covered in a greasy, deep blue paint. We learned later it was used by this particular tribe to protect themselves from the burning rays of the sun. The paint was made from fruit and vegetable juices mixed with eagle fat or the fat from some other animal. This concoction was then smeared over their entire body.

My instincts told me that I was safe in following this woman, but I beckoned for my Ma because I didn't want to go alone. The Indian woman seemed to understand and waited for Ma to follow as well. She pointed at the other women, as if she was inviting them to join us as well and then turned and disappeared into the forest.

"Ma?" I didn't need to ask the question.

"I'll go with you, I think we are safe," Ma answered. A few of the other women quickly decided to come along, as well. We cautiously stepped into the trees. I could see our beautiful Indian friend ahead of us. As hard as we tried to keep up, however, our clothes kept catching on the twigs and branches, slowing our progress until we were finally brought to a stand still. We had altogether lost sight of our Indian guides.

Bewildered, we did not know where to turn; we were lost. How would we get back to the beach? Thankfully, we didn't have to wait long, because within moments, an Indian woman appeared, seemingly out of nowhere and without a sound, to lead us once more.

One moment we were in dark forest and then, quite suddenly, we were standing at the edge of a lake…a most beautiful lake. Sunshine made the water sparkled as though it had been covered in diamonds. The deep blue surface rippled with little waves as several Indian women bathed themselves in it. Those who weren't bathing themselves were bathing their babies and small children.

Their laughter sounded like music. It cascaded gently and naturally, much the same as the small waterfall that fed the lake. The Indian woman pointed at me and then at the lake. I finally understood that she wanted me to go into the lake.

"No," I said and took a step backward, shaking my head vigorously from side to side. But the Indian woman was not to be dissuaded; she again gestured toward me and toward the lake. And the scene was repeated as I said, "No! Absolutely not!"

She was still for a moment, then waved her hand toward the beach and then at the lake and said, "Sanoba—nda."

Ma brightened up, "Lizzie, I think she is trying to tell you that there aren't any men at this lake." Ma then looked at this beautiful woman and gestured toward the lake, asking, "No men?"

In exasperation, the Indian woman pointed once more at me and at the lake, but this time she held her nose. I understood *that* and so did Ma. Not having ever undressed in public before—not even in front of women—it took all of my courage to start removing my clothes. Timidly, I peeled my dress off—but that was as far as I would go—down to my petticoat.

The other Scots women, who had been brave enough to go along with us, stood firm in their denial to join me, shaking their heads, arms folded across their breasts, ensuring that their clothes would be staying on their bodies.

"Not me! Ye won't be findin' me in there!" they said to each other.

I stood in front of them, saying, "I think we'd better go along with them just now. We need their help and if we smell that foul, well, I wouldn't blame them for not coming near us...and I'm hungry. I don't know about the rest of you...but I am going to trust that there are only women allowed in this lake...and I'm going in there in my petticoat!" Immediately I plunged into the water before I could change my mind.

The small waterfall appealed to me and I made my way toward it. Standing under the falling water was absolutely luxurious. It was deliciously cool and I let it spill through my hair, removing the weeks of dirt and grime. The water swirled around my body, cleansing and invigorating it.

At the sound of someone approaching, I opened my eyes ; it was the Indian woman and she had what appeared to be a handful of berries and leaves. She rubbed them together, making a lather, which she put into my hands, pointing at my hair. I rubbed the lather into my hair and thoroughly enjoyed its delicate scent and the feeling of the dirt and grime being washed away.

Eventually, some of the other Scots women, including Ma, were shyly emerging out of their tattered and dirty dresses...and slipping shyly into the enticing beauty of the lake.

Reluctantly, I walked out of the water, my petticoat dragging me down with its weight; but that was a small price to pay for the exhilarating feeling of being clean!

The hot sun soon dried my hair and freshly washed dress. I relaxed and watched the others splashing and laughing, clearly enjoying themselves.

The Indian woman once again approached me, seeming to be hesitating with each step. So I smiled, encouraging her to advance. Ma, who was sitting beside me, looked up at her and smiled warmly as well and said, "Thank you—thank you!" Then Ma pulled some of her hair under her nose and exaggerated breathing in deeply and smiling, indicating that she liked being clean.

"My name is 'Christie'" Ma continued and pointed at herself.

"What is yers?" Only a shy smile in response. Again, Ma pointed to herself and said, "Christie." After several attempts, the Indian woman's face lit up with understanding and she pointed at Ma and said "Rrrrstee."

Proud of her accomplishment, she repeated it over and over, much to Ma's delight. Then, the smile faded; she pointed to herself and slowly said a word that was extremely long but Ma managed to pick up bits of it that sounded like "Beauty" and said it aloud, to the Indian woman's delight. The Indian woman laboriously repeated, "Rrrstee" gesturing at Ma and then with both hands patted her breast, repeating her name.

Ma repeated her interpretation of the name as "Beauty". They looked at each other and smiled, obviously approving of the other's attempt at her name. "Here, Ma, give her this." I had taken the little leather pouch from around my waist, and much to Ma's surprise, took out one of the precious pearls Da had given me."

"Oh, Lizzie! I had forgotten about these—have you had them all of this time?"

"Aye, Ma, but I do believe she deserves one of them, don't you?"

"Aye, Lizzie, she does." Ma took hold of Beauty's hand and turned it over so the palm was up and dropped the little black pearl into it. Beauty's eyes widened with surprise before she wrapped her fingers around it, holding it to her breast. Tears had filled her eyes and we came to know later that a pearl was highly prized among this tribe and a great treasure. We were both touched by her expressions of thankfulness.

"If only we could tell her how much her kindness has meant to us," Ma said gently.

"I think we just did, Ma," I said gently.

By this time some of the other women, both Scots and Indians, were gathered around, smiling and nodding their heads in approval at this simple attempt at friendship.

"Ma, I'm hungry!" I found myself whining like a wee bairn.

Ma looked at me and then at "Beauty". She patted my tummy and pointed to my mouth, trying to let the woman know that I was hungry. Beauty's eyes lit up with understanding and gestured for Ma to follow her. Not to be left behind, the rest of us tagged close behind.

To our very audible delight, we found ourselves back on the beach. But when we glanced around the beach we realized that very few of our men were there.

"Where's Rory?" I wanted to know.

One of the men motioned for me to look out to sea where several boats were bobbing around on the waves. Eventually, one of the men spoke up, "Hopefully they're goin' tae bring us back some breakfast!"

My anxiety melted into a smile of relief.

"And just where have ye been all o' this time?" Alistair asked Ma.

"I'll tell you about it later. I'm going with Beauty just now..."

"Who in heaven's name is "Beauty?" growled Alistair, emphasizing 'Beauty' sarcastically.

"My new friend! That Indian woman over there." Ma pointed to where Beauty was standing near the edge of the forest. "You know, the one who showed Lizzie how to clean the seal last night! Well, Lizzie said she was hungry and Beauty understood, I think, 'cause she wants us to follow her."

Ma turned to leave and then tossed back over her shoulder, "Please tell Rory where we've gone if he gets back a'fore we do."

"Oh, aye. Leave me tae tell him yer goin' off wi' one of these savages."

"Alistair, I feel safe with her. And besides, we have no choice right now but to trust them," Ma said, trying to reason with him.

"Cum' on now Alistair, we have to start somewhere!" Ma said as she took my hand. "Save us some of that fish...mind ye don't eat it all!" And we were gone, following Beauty into the forest once more.

Chapter 22

During the following days and weeks, friendship blossomed into trust between the Indians and the Scots, allowing a perfect blend of teaching and learning to evolve. The Indians did their best to teach us the skills we would need in order to survive the coming winter; and of course, we were more than willing to learn.

Ma surprised us all with her ability to learn the Indian language. She was constantly being asked to interpret for both the Indians and Scots. In the beginning, only Ma and I had been invited into their village, however, it wasn't long before Rory was invited to visit Mugwump; and soon the rest of our group were making friends and enjoying each others' company, as well.

The Indian village was surrounded by a fence made of sharply pointed wooden stakes which were inclined outward over a deep ditch; and inside were several small huts that we learned to call wigwams. There were three types of wigwam; one was round or domed, the other was conical and the other was conical but longer. All of them were made with a framework of poles and covered with bark or mats of woven wood fiber, or both. The domed wigwam was about fifteen feet across with fur covered benches placed against the walls which served for sitting on during the day and became beds at night. In the center was a shallow pit for the cooking fire and it was placed directly under the smoke hole in the roof. It was very reminiscent of our black houses in Scotland.

"Poor blokes have tae grip the floor like we did until the supper's cooked!" Alistair commented when he saw the Indians crouched down to avoid the eye watering smoke.

The larger wigwams were used as council lodges or as sweat houses for their purification rituals or for the medicine man to be able to commune with the spirits. The men put up the framework of the wigwams but the women took great pride in covering them with closely woven and beautifully decorated wood fiber mats or with large pieces of bark and sometimes with animal skins.

Beyond the village lay several acres of land. These were subdivided into family plots and separated by banks of earth. Corn, squash and beans were grown in the same mounds, making use of each square inch of the plot. We learned that during planting season they would put two or three fish in a hole and put three seeds in that hole, and the plants would grow beautifully with the good fertilizer.

One of the many things that puzzled us at first, was that quite a few of the birch and elm trees surrounding the village had been stripped of their bark. Later, we learned the reason for this.

Each family consisted of parents, grandparents, aunts, uncles and cousins and they occupied one house. In time, when Ma and I had a better understanding of the language, the Indians were able to teach us that they were of the Abeneki tribe; they also called themselves the people of the light, meaning that they were where the sun rose first. Most interesting was their clan system. It was the women who voted in the "heads" of the tribes and if these leaders were found to act inappropriately, well, the women voted them out.

Each clan had a symbol they called a "totem" and this totem was adopted by the entire clan. It was always the name of an animal; the clan and its members were known by the name of that animal. It could be the wolf, the bear, the beaver, the deer, the snipe, the heron or the hawk.

A woman could only marry into another clan; they could never marry someone from their own family or clan. When a man married, he left his own home to live with his wife's family, but he did not become a member of his wife's clan.

His children belonged to his wife's clan as well, and not his own. Although he was treated with respect and affection, he was never actually accepted as a relative in the official sense. In fact, an absolute stranger of the same clan could come in and be accepted as a member, whereas this man, who had married into the group, was not accepted as a brother.

All inheritance was from the mother, and a son only inherited property from his mother's brother rather than his father. It was easy to understand then, why Beauty's brother was training her sons, instead of their own father.

We found the similarity between some of the Scottish customs and those of the Indians quite remarkable. For instance, many women in Scotland kept their maiden names so that they would still be eligible to inherit from their father.

However, how they disciplined their children was different to the Scottish ways. They never hit their children; but when the child misbehaved, his face would be blackened with charcoal and he or she was made to sit outside the wigwam for an appropriate amount of time...in shame. I much preferred that custom to our own, which was a lightening fast back hand before you knew you had even done wrong.

The Indians patiently taught us as many of the survival skills as we Scots were willing to learn. One of the first skills the women taught us was that of making pots and utensils from birch bark. Much to our surprise, these birch bark pots or mocucks, as the Indians called them, did not burn when placed over the hot fires—as long as they were filled with water or some other liquid.

We learned how to cut out a mocuck from a pattern they showed us and then we sewed it together with basswood fiber. We learned how to shape the bark into drinking cups, spoons and other utensils needed for cooking. And it wasn't long before we had also learned the knack of taking the bark from the trees in one strip and were soon making our own canoes; of course, still under the expert tutelage of the older Indian men.

Our first shelter for each of us was a cedar bough lean-to, which we built on the beach. All of this activity was accomplished against a background of Alistair's never-lagging, sarcastic wit. The day his lean-to fell in on him, brought forth loud peals of laughter as we enjoyed watching him get his "cum' uppence"!

However, we were learning very quickly how much we needed each other in every respect, to simply survive, never mind anything else. With this dependence, a healthy respect and caring for one another surfaced. Even those who were initially reluctant about accepting the new situation allowed themselves to be drawn toward the warmth and good spirits of the others.

Rory and the other men held a council and decided that more permanent and stronger lodgings were required—and soon—before the onset of winter. This sense of urgency was sparked by the report Ma and I brought back from the Indian village.

We had been told that there would be more snow than usual this winter. When Ma asked how much that was, Beauty had raised her hand above her head, as high as she could reach. The worried look on her face made us feel even more concerned.

I wanted to ask her how she knew that, but by now I had learned not to doubt her wisdom about such things. We would have to have proper clothing and shelter in order to survive, and all of this must be done very quickly, along with growing more corn and beans. Our hope was in harvesting enough of it before it froze.

The Indians had shown us where to gather nuts; they also showed us how to dry berries into a delicious tasting fruit leather. And, very kindly, they shared some maple syrup with us that they had gathered in February. It tasted so good when it was drizzled over corn cakes.

Another council was held and it was decided that we would build a longhouse and stay in it until the following Spring, when we would head out to look for a suitable site to start building our own settlement.

However, Rory was apprehensive about inadvertently walking into Thomas Barclay's plantation and ending up at his mercy, which could very easily include being executed for 'escaping', as we were very sure that Captain Adams would not have told him the truth about how he had forced us to go ashore.

"Adams probably thinks that the Indians killed us and he is free of any responsibility!" Rory had surmised. He felt sure that the long winter would give him enough time to scout around and formulate a good plan for our people. His leadership went unchallenged and even the Indians called him Mugwump Rrrry.

We divided into groups in order to get our work done more quickly. Those men who had worked with wood "back hame" supervised the building of the longhouse. Those who knew how to hunt went along with the Indians to learn how to trap the animals we needed for food and clothing. The fishermen brought back large catches of salmon, cod and seal, which was cut into strips and dried.

We adhered to a very simple philosophy: those who were able to work and didn't pitch in and help, would not eat nor would they have shelter. There was no time or room for those who would not carry their own weight thus, everyone worked according to their individual capacity.

On our diet of fish, berries, nuts and the vegetables the Indians shared with us, we glowed with health and strength.

Although our men weren't able to keep up with the young Indian braves who could actually run down a deer to kill it, they were able to join in some of the games that the Indians played. These were always contests of strength and in some instances the Scots actually emerged as the victors; especially when it came to the Scots game of "tossing the caber". They won because they had learned in Scotland how to balance a long pole (a skinned tree) and run with it and with the proper flick of the wrist and arms, they would try to send it end over end. Whoever managed to do this, was of course, the winner.

The women were busy all day long learning new ways of cooking and fashioning warm clothes out of animal hides. We learned to bake bannock on flat rocks that were placed at the edge of the hot fire; or by putting the dough between two large leaves and cooking it in the hot ashes.

The animals trapped by the men were welcomed for their meat and hides, which we tanned. The fresh hide was placed hair side down on a slanting log and the remaining flesh, fat and membranes were scraped off with a sharpened animal bone that was shaped like a half moon. When it was thoroughly cleaned, it was left to soak in a brine solution for three days. The hide was then wrung out and the hair easily removed, leaving it smooth and clean. It was at this stage of the tanning we learned why Beauty had kept the brains of the seal.

"She says that we should stew the dried brains in a little fat," Ma instructed us after listening carefully to Beauty. "Then we rub the brains into both sides of the damp hide. Next, we sprinkle the skin again with water and roll it up tight overnight to absorb the 'braining'." Ma smiled, pleased with her ability to interpret.

The next day I helped to wring out the hide. We wrapped it around a tree, leaving room to insert a stick, three feet long. With this stick, we twisted the hide, squeezing out all of the moisture. This accomplished, we shook it out and pulled it onto a stretching frame made from a couple of saplings placed about seven feet apart. Two poles were lashed across the saplings and adjusted to the size of the hide. Beauty punctured holes in the edge of the hide and showed us how to lash it to the frame with strips of bark fiber which we laced through the holes, pulling it as taut as possible.

The next step was called "beaming" which stretched and softened the hide. It took all of our strength to wield the long handled tool which had a working end of stones or horns set at a right angle; with this we rubbed the leather until it was dry. When the beaming was finally finished, the leather was pliable and nearly white.

Now, only "smoking" the leather remained in order to finish the job. We were shown how to shape the hide into a cylindrical bag and place it over a smudge fire made of green or rotten wood, and, of course that special wood that gave it a wonderful fragrance. This could take from ten minutes to an hour, depending upon the thickness of the hide. The smoking turned the hide a tan colour and sometimes they could obtain the coveted grey.

The Scots women became very competitive about the quality of their dressmaking abilities as they turned out beautiful buckskin dresses, moccasins and gloves, trousers and jackets. Even seal skin coats appeared with the skins very carefully and artistically arranged, bringing forth ooh's and ahh's from an admiring audience.

By nightfall we were all more than ready to drop, totally exhausted onto our beds of moss. The exhaustion was actually another gift with our new life—making us far too tired to find fault with each other. Our fight was with the oncoming winter which was looming like a threatening thunder cloud in our minds, forcing us into a deadly race with it.

Gradually, we brought order to our lives, including deciding which day was Sunday, as we had lost track. The decision was made and we eagerly looked forward to the Sabbath Day, our day of rest, as it had been in Scotland.

It was necessary to call upon our memories for scriptures and hymns as we didn't have books or Bibles. After Donald MacDonald had given us our first Sunday sermon, he said that we would be given time each Sunday to tell the others of our experiences of the past week where we "plainly saw the hand of the Lord in our lives."

"Here was my perfect chance!" I thought excitedly. I had been waiting to tell my story because I knew it was the Lord who had saved me and I wanted the whole world to know it. I waited patiently for my turn. Finally, Donald pointed at me, indicating it was my turn. I clambered up on the big stump we used as a speaker's platform and began.

"I had been gathering berries and nuts with some of the older Indian children. My second bucket was full and I went back to pick up the first one which was also filled to overflowing. To my surprise, a huge bear had his snout stuck in the pail eating all of my berries! 'Git! Git outta there!' I shouted at him. I was so angry over losing all of my berries I picked up a stick and tried to scare him away. But instead of running away, the bear reared up on his hind legs with his forepaws clawing at the air and roared!"

"I wasn't angry any more—I was just plain scared! So scared that I couldn't move and just stared at the beast. My feet wouldn't move and I couldn't shut my mouth—it just hung wide open! It was almost as scary as Captain Adams' dinner!" I paused, shuddering over both of the memories.

"Lizzie! Ye just stop teasin' us! What happened next?" demanded Alistair.

"Well, you know the big Indian boy?" and I reached a hand high over my head and they all nodded. "He shouted to me to stand still. I was able to do that just fine—my legs were frozen with fright...why, I couldn't even talk! Anyway, he told me that he was going to throw a stick at the bear and when he did, I was to run for the beach. I could see him out of the corner of my eye as he slowly bent down and picked up a branch that had fallen from a tree."

"The bear opened his mouth and roared and then everything happened so fast! Buck threw the branch and the bear hugged it to him with his big paws and before he could let go of it...I was off! But, when I looked back to see where the bear was, I tripped and fell. Before I knew it though, Buck pulled me to my feet and was dragging me along with him. I could hear the bear growling and crashing through the trees—right behind us. I never stopped praying that the Lord would save me...and He did," I whispered reverently.

"When we got to the beach, with the bear still crashing behind us, Alistair was playing the pipes. The crashing behind us stopped and when Buck and I looked back, we saw the bear running in the other direction."

"Now, just a wee minute, lassie!" Alistair complained, but he was smiling.

The congregation was quiet for a moment and then Ma whispered, "Ye never told me, Lizzie."

"Aye, I didn't want to worry you, Ma," I defended myself. Thankfully I was spared any further scolding when someone else stood to tell of their experience. I looked across at Rory who hadn't taken his eyes from me. He looked pale and slowly shook his head from side to side.

Later that day, when we found ourselves alone, he took me in his arms. "Lizzie, I could have lost you!" he whispered. He seemed very subdued and thoughtful as he looked deeply into my eyes. His lips found mine in an arousing kiss. I hungered for more, but instead I moved away from him, afraid of my beating heart and remembering the fire that had exploded inside me when I lay next to him on the ship. It had been too painful.

"I know, lassie, I know." We didn't have to speak to understand we shared the same passion for each other. Rory dropped his arms to his side, and we walked back to the beach and the others, in silence—words were not needed because a wonderful golden cord was drawing us closer and closer.

Chapter 23

"A party! That's what we need! A party!"

"Isn't it grand?" Ma almost crowed she was so proud.

Oh, yes! The longhouse was the grandest house I'd ever seen. We all crowded around it, waiting for Rory to say his few words and then to give us the grand tour.

"Not a bit too soon, we didn't finish!" That was Alistair with his usual gloom, although, coming from him, we could call it high praise and enthusiasm. The men had cleared the site for the longhouse, and used the logs to build it.

"Gentlemen and ladies," Rory began "I wish to say..."

"Cum' on man!" Tam complained, "get on wi' it! Let us in!"

"Aye, Rory! Ye've said enough."

"No couth! That's what ye've got! No couth at a'!" Rory complained. "Here we have our first home in this new country and ye won't even let it be done right and proper!" He glared at us for a few moments, standing in the doorway with his arms akimbo before he relented with, "Well, in ye come then!"

We pushed our way past Rory and through the door. The carpenters had insisted on keeping us out while they did the "finish up work" and we were anxious to see what they had done.

Oh, what a grand sight it was, too!

"Look Aggie!" Sheilagh cried, "real beds! offa the floor and a'!" We were oblivious to the fact that it was only rough hewn lumber lashed together with vines. It couldn't have been more palatial—at least in our eyes.

Dividers between the "beds" had been made. We could hardly imagine privacy or any semblance of it! What more could we ask? They were primitive, to say the least, being woven out of thin vines, but velvet drapes would not have brought forth more praise.

Shelves had been made from tree branches and pieces of birch bark and hung above the beds. These served as a place to store dry corn and fur pelts and anything else we had acquired.

"Thanks tae Alistair, we're in here a lot quicker than if we'd only used the axes!" Willie patted Alistair on the back, as did some of the others, making Alistair shuffle his feet in embarrassment, but he gruffly accepted his due.

At the outset, the logs for the longhouse were felled with axes made of hand honed flint which broke very quickly. Alistair's patience had been sorely tried as his ax kept breaking, so it wasn't long before he had learned another and better way from the Indians.

Someone had made the observation that if you give a lazy man a hard task, it wouldn't be long before he made it an easy task.

Alistair had ignored the jibes and kept repeating, "Necessity is the mother of invention," as he plastered a band of wet clay around the tree, a couple of feet from the ground, to act as a fire stop. Then the space below the clay was ringed with fire, which was fueled and fanned until it had eaten through the tree trunk. As it burned, he chipped away at the charred wood and this hastened things a little.

For a smaller tree, he cut a small groove in it big enough to slide a birch bark rope into it. Then he lit the rope and it burned slowly, severing the tree. He was ecstatic over his success and of course went on to fell another tree and another, using these same methods. Once in a while, he lost control of the fire and the whole tree would burn, bringing everyone on the run with birch bark buckets of water.

The rest of this day was spent in moving into our allotted spaces, arranging our winter clothing on the shelves, along with other acquired treasures. It was good just to catch our breath after the long, hard days of preparation.

Several days passed in sheer laziness as we reveled in our new and warm longhouse. But it wasn't long before the old familiar whining began. With all of the work done, we had time to notice each other's faults once more.

Rory took this time to meet with the Chief and get a better understanding about the sound of drums we had been hearing lately, in the distance. He learned that a neighboring tribe was rattling its' sword—so to speak. But Rory wasn't able to understand why.

Also, it was not a rare sight any longer to see a man and a woman pair off, taking long walks along the beach, their heads together as they shared intimate stories of their lives—getting to know each other better.

I felt a pang of jealousy when I saw them and I knew very well that Rory was watching them as well and wondered what he was feeling. Was he having the same longings? Daily, my yearning for him grew.

Ma and I slept together in one bed and Rory slept in his bed against the opposite wall. One night, long after the small, flickering oil lamps had gone out, my fantasies overcame my good sense and I crossed over to Rory's bed.

"Rory," I whispered.

"Wha...?" came the sleepy answer.

"Rory, it's me...Lizzie." I waited for him to pull me in beside him.

"What's the matter?" He sat up, trying to see my face in the darkness.

"I...I..." I stammered, losing my courage.

"Lizzie, I know," he rescued me, "but think about tomorrow morning. I want ye as well, but, I can't yet. I just can't hurt yer Ma and Da."

I felt crushed—rejected—humiliated. "Oh..." I whimpered and scampered back to my own bed.

"Lizzie!" he called softly, but I was again in my own bed, covering my head in shame. The next morning found me up and out before anyone else even stirred. How was I going to face him? Where could I hide? I walked as far down the beach as I could, making sure I was out of sight of the long-house and sat alone by the water and mindlessly tossed pebbles into the foamy surf. I suffered my humiliation over and over—oh, it was so embarrassing!! I knew I would never—no, never—speak to Rory again—in fact I would never even look at him again—*never.*

However, in spite of my agony, by the time the sun was high in the sky, hunger had overridden my pride and I found myself back in the longhouse sitting by our cooking fire, waiting for Ma to dish up the stew.

We had copied the Indian's longhouse, leaving enough room down the center to accommodate one fire for every two families. Because the longhouse was filled with smoke whenever anyone was cooking, we were most comfortable lying down or sitting, keeping our heads below the level of the smoke that filled the upper half of the longhouse before it escaped through the small holes in the roof.

We had one large, cooked meal a day, and this was eaten at midday; during the balance of the day we ate berries or nuts or dried meat whenever we were hungry. On this particular day, Ma was stewing some venison along with beans and squash. The aroma was so tempting that I almost forgot my humiliation as I waited for the moment when she would announce it was time to eat.

Rory sat quietly on the other side of the fire.

"Ye know, Lizzie," Rory said, "don't you think it's time you were doin' the cooking—and give yer Ma a rest?"

"What're ye talking about?" I snapped, forgetting my resolve to never speak to this man. Never!

"Well, I think yer old enough to be having yer own fire." Rory continued.

"I don't care what you think!"

"Lizzie! What's gotten into you?" Ma demanded to know.

I hung my head. "I'll not say another word to anyone—not anyone!" I thought, almost on the verge of tears.

"I think the two of you might have something to settle between yourselves—before we eat." And she took the pot from the fire, covered it and left.

"Well, will you?" Rory asked.

"Will I what?" I pouted.

"You know what I'm saying! Now, will you?" he was getting angry.

"Will I what?" I shouted back at him, fully out of patience.

Rory's expression was a mixture of anger and anxiety. "Will you marry me?" he shouted back.

"Fer cryin' out loud, Lizzie! Say 'yes' and marry the bloke and put him outta his misery!" Alistair shouted from the end of the longhouse.

"Aye!" the others chimed in impatiently.

Rory's face had turned red, and then purple; he looked like he was going to explode.

I was shocked. Was he actually proposing to me? "Well, you don't need to shout, Rory MacLeod! And you could ask me properly. Yes, I'll marry you!" I couldn't believe what I had just said!!

"You will?" It was Rory's turn to be surprised. "You will?" he repeated as he stood up and reached for me.

"Rory! Don't..." but he lifted me off my feet and spun around, kissing me, not letting me speak. It was hopeless to stay angry with this man. I let myself melt into his arms. That familiar flame engulfed me once more and only when the sound of applause thundered in our ears did we remember the others.

"Well done, old boy!"

"Finally! What did ye have to promise her?"

We were surrounded by well-wishers. A wedding! A party! How soon, everyone wanted to know? Excitement swept through the little settlement like a bush fire; but eventually we all calmed down enough to think of practicalities.

Now, I was really nervous. I wanted to back out when I heard Ma ask, "Who is going to perform the ceremony?"

"Well, I've been thinking about that. What's wrong wi' handfasting? If it was good enough for us in Scotland, it should be good enough for us here!" Rory stated.

"What's 'handfasting' Ma?" I wanted to know. I wanted to talk to my mother, alone. "Ma? Can we talk?" I asked quietly.

Rory looked worried as he let go of my hand.

"Aye," she answered and led me outdoors. We walked along the beach in silence for several minutes before we sat down on a log that had been tossed up by a recent ocean storm.

"This is the biggest step ye'll ever take, Lizzie," she began. "Are ye sure that Rory's the one for ye?"

"Ma, I've known no one else. He's the only one who has ever kissed me," I confided.

"...on that night we were stuck in the icebergs?" she asked with a sly smile.

"Oh, no, Ma! Were you awake the whole time?" I asked sheepishly.

"Aye."

"Ma, did Da make you feel like that?"

"Aye," she said quietly and when I looked closer, I saw tears glistening in her eyes. "I miss him so much, Lizzie! And when you were with Rory that night, it brought back so many good memories." She continued, her voice soft and dreamy, "Aye, yer Da had me in the palm o' his hand, and he knew it. Ach, I'd fight—just so's he'd not take me for granted, but he knew...he knew! And that's how yer supposed to feel. Don't let any of those old biddies tell you any different, either! Many o' them don't know what it's like tae have a good man!" She bobbed her head toward the longhouse.

"Oh, Ma! I don't know so much!" I cried. "And I've not the courage you have. I couldn't go through what you did with Da."

Ma sat up straight. "You mean...?" she was genuinely surprised. She really had made herself believe that I didn't see Da's hanging.

"Ach, Lizzie! Until this moment, the only comfort I had was that my children had been spared having to see their father lose his life at the end of a rope."

After a long silence, Ma spoke again, "Your Da made his sacrifice willingly. He was happy to serve God, even with his life."

"Ma," I ventured. "Do you think you could ever marry another man—like Alistair MacCrimmon—let's say." I had noticed that Ma and Alistair looked out for one another and seemed to enjoy a good laugh together.

Ma was thoughtful for a moment and then she said quietly, "It's too soon, Lizzie, for either of us. We're just happy to care about each other—for now, anyway."

"Oh, Ma! I don't know if I can be happy, yet!" I confessed, "I'm still grieving for Da. I feel like I'll grieve for him all of my life!"

"No one will take the place that your father has in your heart, Lizzie, but we must make the best of what the Lord gives us and at this moment He is providing you with a good husband. And he'll be a good father, too, if ye give him a chance." Ma suddenly brightened up. "You know, I'd love to be a granny."

"Ma!" I objected. "I'm not even married yet!" But we giggled like young lassies.

"What's 'handfasting', Ma?" I asked.

"Well now, "handfasting" is a way of marrying when there wasn't a minister around to do it and folks were too far away from a Kirk. First, a special festival day is announced for all of the couples who want to be married.

Next, we prepare food for days before the festivities because folk from other villages came to join in and...oh, my, what a lot of dancin' and singin' and good laughs we can have!"

Ma smiled at the memories and I mellowed under my mother's gift of storytelling. "Finally, when the big day arrived," Ma continued, "the lassies always looked so bonnie: and the men, well, they always looked so nervous!" She giggled happily.

"At two o'clock sharp in the afternoon they lined up on either side of a wee burn, the brides on one side and the grooms on the other, joining hands over the running water, while the rest of the villagers watched and witnessed the act. Then, a cord is laid across your clasped hands and if you both still want to be married at the end of the year, well, the same cord is laid across your arms and a knot is tied, making you married for all time."

"What did they say to each other?" I wanted to know.

"They made up their own words, but always promised to be true. And when the minister did get around to the village, he performed the marriage but as far as the villagers were concerned, the couples were legally married."

"And that's how Rory and I will be married?"

"Aye, Lizzie," Ma smiled.

I flung my arms around her, feeling more like a little girl than a woman who was about to be married. Suddenly I felt overwhelmed by how much I didn't know! The step seemed too big for me. I wanted to cling to Ma for the rest of my life, warm and secure. I was afraid to have babies! I didn't know how to cook like Ma! I felt so anxious—no, I was afraid!

"It's a big step, Lizzie. But one we all have to take. And thankfully, we don't have to do it all at once." We were now arm in arm, walking back to the longhouse.

Rory came toward us, smiling broadly. "And how's my bride-to-be?" he asked, trying to sound light hearted but I didn't miss the questioning look in his eyes as he glanced at Ma.

"She's just fine!" Ma said confidently. "Now, how about a bit o' that stew I was cooking. Unless, Rory...naw, you didn't eat it up on us, did ye?"

"Christie, now, would I dae that?" He grinned mischievously as he put his arm around my waist and led me back to the cooking fire.

There was an air of excitement in the longhouse and before long we learned that several other couples had decided to handfast along with us.

Our wedding day was to be on Saturday—only four days away. My stomach knotted at the thought. "So soon!" I felt panicky; however, the excitement was contagious, and soon I was caught up in it.

When Ma told the Indian women about the forthcoming marriages, they immediately started baking bannock cakes. Corn was popped for decorations and the men disappeared to fish and hunt.

Precious deer hides were produced and the women made kilts for the grooms, which were copies of the "dress up" outfits the Indian men wore for special occasions.

Christie hurried to finish a light grayish-white piece of buckskin that would do beautifully for Lizzie's wedding dress.

Alistair MacCrimmon busily repaired the bagpipe reeds with Rory's scalpel and was off to the woods to compose a special tune for the festive occasion. He was not getting married because his heart was still with his "bonnie Mary" in Scotland.

Beauty brought a lovely beaded headband to me as part of my wedding outfit. With so much to do, there wasn't any time for my initial worries.

Somehow, amidst the flurry of activity, our Handfasting Day arrived. It was a crisp but sunny October morning. I slipped out of the longhouse before the others were awake so that I could enjoy my bath in solitude. The women's bathing lake was like a jewel—an emerald—shimmering ever so slightly in the morning breeze. I shivered as I stepped under the waterfall so that the cool water could careen through my hair.

"Oh, the luxury of it!" I crooned aloud, smiling into a ray of sunshine boring its way through the trees. What a difference between this morning and the bath that Captain Adams had forced me to take!

Today—now—this moment—I had never felt cleaner. Marriage is good! Standing under that waterfall, a sense of peace enveloped me and I knew for sure that what I was doing was right and pleasing to the Lord. For the first time in my life I was experiencing what I had only read about in the scriptures—peace—heavenly peace. So this is what it is like to live in peace. I remembered asking the Lord for this blessing—it was the only thing I had ever wanted and prayed for from my earliest childhood.

"Thank you, my dearest Father in Heaven! Thank you for hearing my prayer and answering it!!" I sang the words out loud, startling the birds and squirrels.

I felt so loved! Ummm...what a beautiful day! My heart was full of love for God, for my husband-to-be, for Ma and for the whole world.

Jenny! My sister's face came into my mind and for a brief moment I longed for my sister to see my wedding—and Iain—no! I pushed their memories from my mind. I will not let anything spoil this day!

Wallace Lauderdale's cruel, monstrous smile and ugly face invaded my mind and that too was forced out—along with the memories of his heinous acts toward those I loved. I ducked under the water, letting the cold water bring me back to the present—and to what should and will be the happiest day of my life.

"Life! I love you!" I sang out loud again, and this time the birds and squirrels had the cheek to chatter back, scolding me as though I was invading their territory.

"Enough!" I chided myself, "Hurry yourself, Lizzie."

Reluctantly I waded to the shore and once there, shook the water from my hair and body before dressing. As I walked back to the longhouse, I combed my hair with the seashell comb Rory had made for me.

Anxious for the day to begin now, I ran toward the longhouse. Smoke was curling through the holes in the roof of the longhouse, signaling that breakfast was being made—and I was hungry.

"And here I thought that ye'd run away on me, lass!" Rory scolded when I sat down by the fire.

"No, I'm afraid you're out o' luck. You're stuck now, like it or not!" I tossed back at him.

"What's going on? Listen to all the clatter in here!" I nodded toward the others.

"It's sounds like a hen house, doesn't it?" Rory agreed. "Everyone's trying to dress themselves and each other at the same time. I'll tell you, some of them will be splittin' the blanket before they're even married!"

Suddenly, Alistair stomped past us. "Ach, they're goin' outta their minds in here! I'm away tae play m' pipes!" and he stalked off, shaking his head and tossing black looks at everyone in his path of retreat.

Rory and I laughed and then with no other alternatives immediately in view, joined the melee. As Rory had predicted, there were a couple of spats where phrases like "I wouldn't marry ye, not now…not ever!" and "I must'a been outta my mind tae ask ye in the first place!" were hurtled through the air.

"Ach, now, ye don't mean it—just let me fix that and ye'll see—everything'll be alright!" Aggie, and others of experience, soothed ruffled feelings and kept the love-boats from completely overturning.

The sun, in spite of us, made its way to the two o'clock position and everything and everyone was ready and waiting. The pipes sounded, sending a thrill through me; and Rory offered me his arm.

He looked so handsome in his own kilt and buckskin shirt (he had refused to wear a buckskin kilt for his wedding).

The men had erected a small rounded bridge over a narrow neck of a stream for the ceremony.

"How beautiful they are!" I thought, as I watched each bride take her turn at standing on the bridge with her groom, clasping hands over the running water. Tears ran down my cheeks as I listened to them speak their carefully chosen words to each other, vowing to be faithful.

"Ye'll be a mess by the time it's yer turn, lassie! Better quit yer bubblin' now," Aggie warned me.

Rory and I were the last to exchange our vows. I was nervous, and horrors of horrors—I felt like I was going to be sick!

"Elizabeth Whitelaw," Rory's booming voice stilled my fears and the warm strength of his hand steadied me. "My wife forever—even death will not take ye from me. I will love you, honor you and protect you with my very life—always—eternally. I promise this before God and these witnesses!"

I looked at the wood fiber rope laying across our clasped hands and then beyond him into the faces of the witnesses, Scots and Indians, standing together. And then I looked up into my beloved's eyes. "Rory MacLeod," I heard myself saying, "I love you and I will do only that which will allow that love to grow and grow. I will honor you and care for you all of my life. I promise my love and faithfulness, as God and these others are my witnesses."

I was married!

Rory continued to hold me with his eyes, speaking beautiful, silent words—filling my heart to overflowing with love. Then I was in his arms and he picked me up and carried me across the little bridge to the lilt of the pipes. The very air seemed to sparkle with music and happiness and I knew that everything in my life had led me to this very moment.

"An eightsome reel! Let's have an eightsome reel!" someone called out and within minutes we were dancing. In rapid succession we danced a quadrille and then a schottische! And before they knew it, our Indian friends had been drawn into the dancing as well.

Laughing and enjoying with us, the Indians gave vent to high pitched "whoops". Not to be outdone, we hooted our own Scottish "whooock"s as we closed our circles in the dances.

We had learned that 'micida' was Indian for 'let's eat' and when the call came we quickly put a stop to the dancing and Scot and Indian sat together and ate. Out of deep pits in the earth came roasted venison and salmon; wild turkey and duck had been done to a turn on spits over red hot coals of hardwood. Nuts, berries and maple syrup trickled over bannock cakes was the delectable finish to the banquet.

The Indian children noisily chased each other, adding happily to the festivities. At this point of the festivities, Mugwump produced a dark brown liquid, which was carefully measured out and offered to each man.

"A toast!" Rory cried. "A toast tae the lassies! Bless them all, and especially those here in this land, in this place!"

"And tae those back hame in Scotland!" Alistair added, making a visible effort to curb his anger. His "bonnie Mary" was never far from his thoughts.

They lifted their birch bark glasses and toasted each other with the arrogance of self-confident men and then drank the contents in one traditional gulp.

"Och, aye—that was a good wee nip!" croaked Willie as he grabbed at his throat. The others could only gasp, being rendered speechless by the firewater.

"What in the name of all that's holy, was that?" Alistair eventually choked out, his eyes watering.

Then came the lip smacking and back slapping and good natured kidding and before long, the men seemed more aggressive than usual. Actually, that was an understatement, to say the very least. I knew something was wrong when old Bobby tried to pinch Aggie's bottom. She squealed and gave him a look that should have sunk a ship, but Bobby wasn't even bothered by it and went on his happy way, looking for another bottom to pinch. Old wives, new wives and women who weren't even wives yet, were forced to sidestep their advances...but the men carried on, seemingly determined to get a woman—any woman.

I noticed that Ma and Beauty were talking and Beauty was shaking her head and shrugging her shoulders. Ma kept gesturing with her hands, looking as though she was trying to coax Beauty to do something, but Beauty continued to shrug her shoulders.

It was years later we learned the truth about that special "man's" drink; it was considered to be a potent aphrodisiac which was composed of powdered animal horn and fermented berry juice. It seemingly had worked! And it was Ma who had twigged as to what was happening and was prevailing upon Beauty to put a stop to it. But she couldn't and wouldn't...it was tradition.

The women coaxed the men into more eating than drinking and the dancing lasted long after the sun had set. First, the Indians performed their dances for the Scots, using their drums and hollow gourds for music. Then the Scots crossed two long thin pieces of wood and danced the Sword Dance and then the Highland Fling, much to the delight of the Indians. Back and forth, long into the night they competed, dance for dance.

Again, the dark brown liquid was poured into the small cups and the more the Scotsmen and Indian braves drank, the greater the frenzy of the dances.

Gradually, the newly handfasted couples made their way to the longhouse, doing their best to slip away unnoticed. At this point, I saw Beauty whisper something in Ma's ear, to which Ma nodded her head in agreement.

"Let's go for a quiet walk on the beach first; I have something to show you," Rory whispered in my ear. I readily agreed, as I wanted to delay going into the longhouse, for what would be our very 'unprivate' wedding night.

We walked slowly along the beach, enjoying the sound of the waves breaking on the shore; the moon was full and touched each wave with its magic. Tonight it seemed larger and more yellow as it hung over the ocean, outlining the whitecaps on the waves.

Rory was happy and relaxed, and only slightly inebriated. I was happy and nervous...at the same time. As we neared the end of the sandy beach, I turned around, expecting to walk back to the longhouse, but Rory took me firmly by the arm and led me onto a small path in the underbrush.

About twenty feet into the forest, he came to a halt not far from an outcropping of rocks and asked me to wait. I watched while he removed some cedar boughs, which were cleverly concealing the mouth of a small cave.

"Come closer," he whispered. Within seconds he was lighting a small fire that had been laid at the front of the cave and its light revealed several thick fur hides that were spread on the cave's floor.

Rory held his hand out to me, inviting me to come to him. "Lizzie," he said softly, "I didn't want to share our first night with the rest o' that mob!"

"Oh, Rory! How beautiful!...and thank you!!" I pushed my fingers through the soft fur rug...and blushed.

Rory reached out and touched my cheek so softly and his lips found mine. An orange glow from the fire filled the cave with warmth. My skin, my body, my mind tingled with excitement.

His mouth was on my neck, rekindling the fire he had ignited that night on the ship. The hungry blaze within us grew and grew until the heat of our passion exploded into blue velvet.

"My own! My love!" he whispered and trembled as he crushed me to him.

Our desire for each other was satisfied, only to be awakened again and again, stronger and sweeter.

Our souls felt such depth of understanding and soared to the heights. Ours was a joyful, sacred beginning.

CHAPTER 24

Screams!

More screams!

Blood curdling screams of terror ripped through the early morning air!

We struggled to surface from our deep sleep and freed ourselves from each other's arms, pulled clothes over our bodies and crawled on our hands and knees to the mouth of the cave.

"It's the longhouse, Rory!" I said anxiously. "The screams are coming from the longhouse!"

"Stay here, Lizzie. Don't ye move 'till I come back for ye! You promise me?"

"Aye! Oh, Rory! Find my Ma—don't get hurt!" My mind was spinning.

Rory cautiously pushed aside the cedar boughs. Just then, muffled screams and groans came to us from a short distance away. Rory quickly backed into the cave again, pulling the boughs around the mouth of the cave. We waited, peering through the boughs. A painted Indian burst into our view, dragging a woman by her hair and stopped immediately in front of the cave. Three other Indians were whooping wildly, right behind him.

I gasped...quickly Rory put his hand over my mouth.

As the woman twisted and fought for her life, her face flashed past us with horrific terror grotesquely distorting her features. Oh, God! No! It was Catherine Sims! Rory took his hand from my mouth and tensed his muscles, ready to leap into the fight.

"No!" I cried, trying to stop him. My cry was drowned out by Catherine's screams of terror—the Indian had slowly raised his tomahawk in the air—enjoying her horror. Then, in one swift downward movement, he had scalped her.

I gasped. The Indian's head snapped around. The others were yelping and dancing drunkenly, but this one looked up, glancing slowly and cautiously all about him. He straightened up from his gory task and listened. His body paint and the decorations on his breech clout were now mixed with spatters of Catherine's blood. A string of animal fangs hung about his neck and a band of wampum beads was wrapped around his arm; his moccasins looked as though they were made from one piece of hide and were gathered around his ankles.

He peered at the cave, his black ringed eyes not seeing us. We watched as he replaced his hatchet in the belt at his waist and looped the hair of Catherine's scalp around the other side. Again he motioned for the others to be quiet, but they were obviously anxious to be on their murderous way again and ignored him.

The Indian stood still a while longer, cocked his head to one side and listened for a another moment and finally gave a slight shrug of his shoulders before turning to run off in the direction of the longhouse.

I felt sick with fear. Fear for my friends...for my mother.

The thought of Ma sent a surge of energy racing through me. I made a move to leave the cave but Rory held on to me.

"Lizzie, we can't help them right now! Use your head! As soon as these savages leave, we'll be able to help...if we are still alive. Otherwise, we'll lose our scalps as well! Now, wait!"

I glared at Rory in defiance...a defiance that quickly evaporated when three more whooping Indians ran past the mouth of the cave, jumping over Catherine's body. Now, I crouched down in fear for my own life.

Ferocious war cries from the attacking Indians rang in my ears. A whirrr of running feet past our cave kept us still. Then, just as suddenly as it has all began, it stopped.

The silence was deathly still.

It seemed like an eternity before Rory whispered, "Wait here!" He didn't leave any room for argument before he cautiously crept out of the cave. When satisfied that the Indians had left, he waved to me to come out.

I ran to Catherine. She was dead. Her face, a twisted mask of horror; her eyes—wide and staring; but very little blood was coming from her scalp—it was the wound in her arm that had bled. The Indian had removed her scalp so cleanly that it might have been done with a surgeon's knife. He had taken only the very top layers of skin, Rory noted, as he closed her eyes. She hadn't died from the scalping—she had died from terror.

Rory tenderly picked up Catherine's body and I led the way to the longhouse. As we approached it, there, where we had danced only a few hours ago, was a bloody scene of butchery.

Rory put Catherine's body down and I clung to his arm as we slowly—unbelievingly—walked around the mutilated bodies of our friends.

The sight made me gag, over and over again, but we kept walking, stepping over bodies as if we were in a trance.

The door of the longhouse was ajar. Rory tightened his arm around my shoulders and pushed the door open.

Carnage! Bloody carnage!

Bodies were strewn over the floor, some still in their beds.

"Rory!" I screamed, "where're their heads?"

He shook his head from side to side. "Don't look, Lizzie!! Don't look!!"

"I don't know them without their heads, Rory!!" I cried, not hearing him. My grip on his arm tightened when I realized that it was the men that were without their heads and the women had been scalped.

"Ma? Ma!" Panic twisted inside me as I ran toward a body crying "Ma!" and to another and another, turning them over, madly peering into the faces, trying to recognize my mother. Some of the women were headless as well and I pulled at their hands—looking for my mother's hands.

Somewhere in my agony, Rory pick me up and I laid my cheek against his—his tears mingled with mine. I clung to his neck as he stumbled out of the longhouse door, into this, the first day of our marriage.

I don't remember our walk to the Indian village, but when we arrived I became very aware of the sounds of confusion and shouts of anger coming from behind the log walls. We walked through the narrow passage way that was made by overlapping the walls of logs and we banged at the barricade to the compound. Finally, Rory kicked at it, demanding to be let in. "It's Rory! Mugwump Rrrry!" he shouted. "It's Rory and Lizzie!"

Eventually we heard the sound of the heavy wooden poles being lifted away, giving us enough room to squeeze through. We lost no time in helping replace the logs behind us.

"They took us by surprise!" Our Indian friends stated flatly, adding only one word, "Iroquois!"

"How do you know?" Rory queried them.

"It's their war tactic to surprise...strike...and run...at night!" we were told. A hatchet, painted red and decorated with red feathers and black wampum made from quahog clam shells, had been struck into the war post in the center of the village. Mugwump, who had become Rory's friend, began battle chants and a war dance around the post.

I was numb. But the noise, confusion and unspeakable grief managed to twist into a terrible knot somewhere deep in my body. It was so familiar—Scotland—Iain...Da!

"Whoooppp!" The Indian braves jumped into the dance with angry energy. Rory didn't have to have anything explained to him. He knew what was happening and pulled away from my tightening grip on his arm.

"Rory, you're not going!" I was crying.

"Lizzie, listen to me. I have to. Please understand. I'll be back, I promise!" And he walked toward the war party.

I was alone. Suddenly everything seemed unfamiliar. I was alone in a foreign country—without my own people, and I felt sure that Rory would not come back to me. My courage failed me—my strength drained from my legs and I crumbled to the ground. Helplessly, I sat and watched Rory, not knowing what to think or how to feel. The center of my life—Ma and Rory—was gone!

Da's words floated back to me. "Make the Lord your only choice and His love your delight; for if it be not so, you will soon faint in your own hour of trial".

"He was right," I thought limply and with only shreds of strength left in my soul I began to pray...for Rory, for Ma—and for myself.

Rory stood a little way from the circling Indians, watching, but didn't join in the war dance. The Mugwump noticed him and stopped dancing and walked to where Rory was standing. He put his hand on Rory's shoulder, grasping him tightly, then he spoke to one of his braves who disappeared into the longhouse, returning within moments with a hatchet, flint knife and war club. The Chief handed the weapons to Rory, and I watched as he reached out and grasped them firmly. The very sight of them terrified me because I knew that all weapons were meant to deliver death—or at the very least—wounds.

The club was made of a dense, heavy wood and was about two feet long with a five inch ball on the end. The weight of it alone made it deadly. Rory tested it, lifting it with both hands.

"Aye, this'll do just fine!" I heard him say.

Rory was looking for revenge and I knew he would be satisfied or die trying. "Oh, God! Save my...husband." The word was so new I stumbled saying it.

The women had packed parched corn and maple syrup for their men folk, giving Rory a share to carry as well. The braves had whipped themselves into a frenzy and Rory seemed to flow along on the tide of it. I had never seen this anger in him before—this unrelenting anger that seemed to burn so coldly within him. I did not know this Rory.

The drums stopped, signaling that the war dance was over, and it was time for the men to run out of the compound in single file. I stared, dazed, at their retreating backs.

A hand slipped into mine, childlike, and Ma's voice, thin and high, whispered, "Lizzie, yer not dead?"

I couldn't speak.

"Lizzie? That's you?" she asked again, squinting into my face.

"Oh, Ma! Ma! I thought you were dead!" I stammered through my tears. We clung to each other, not daring to let go. Finally, we released our hold on each other and stepped back to search each others' face again.

"Ma, I was so afraid! When I saw the others...how...how did you get away?" I stared into her eyes and face, sensing that there was something basically wrong with her.

"Ma? Are you alright? Ma!"

A frightening realization washed over me as I looked into her eyes and I remembered where I had seen that far-away look before. It reminded me of Jenny—that one step away from reality that had dulled her eyes—and now Ma!

My joy at seeing Ma turned into despair. Ma was only half here—as Maggie had explained to me about Jenny—her mind had closed down, not able to take in any more hurt.

But she *was* here and I wasn't alone any longer. "I will take care of you for the rest of your life, Ma. Don't you fear any more!" I promised. "Oh, Ma, Ma. It's not been fair! You've had too much!" I whispered as I kissed her cheek.

She laid her head on my shoulder and cried, "My Ma! Ma, oh, please, I want m' Ma!" I held her close to me and rocked her like a child...again.

CHAPTER 25

Rory on the Warpath

The path had obviously been used many times before; it was a deep rut trodden out by numerous war parties and the Indians were traveling over it at a breakneck speed in single file. Rory was toward the front of the line, not far behind their Chief.

Anger was the whip that lashed at them until they were running at their top speed; but suddenly, the pace slackened. Rory noticed Mugwump hail another group of braves, as friends. As the newcomers fell into line with them, Rory loosened his grip on the war club, thinking, "Not any different than in the Highlands." He remembered help coming the very same way when Clan MacLeod was on cattle raids or heading for a battle.

Without any warning, the Chief raised his arm and the line halted, but Rory, not aware of the signals, clumsily ran into the man in front of him. The entire war party stood perfectly still, not making a sound; within moments of stopping, the Chief circled his arm over his head and the warriors spread out, moving soundlessly over the floor of the forest. Mugwump signaled again, and Rory glanced at the man beside him and copying him, dropped onto his belly. They began to advance, crawling through the trees until the enemy's village was in view.

"Oh, God! No!" Rory groaned.

Mounted on posts around the village were the heads of the Scots—his friends. "Willie! Tam! Ach, no—Aggie!" Rory agonized as his eyes swung from one post to another. He closed his eyes—screwed them tight—not wanting to see anymore.

But when he opened them again, there, about a ten yards away was the unmistakable head of Alistair MacCrimmon, his red hair and beard flapping defiantly in the wind.

Rage boiled in his gut. Rory, with hatchet gripped in one hand and war club in the other, waited for the signal to attack. And it was not too soon for Rory. Chief Mugwump, fist clenched, finally waved them forward. Rory charged with the rest of the warriors with equal ferocity, swinging his war club and hatchet with a mad will to crush, mutilate and kill.

In the midst of the battle, Rory spotted the Indian who had killed Catherine Sims; her scalp and blonde hair were still swinging from his belt. The Indian looked up just in time to see Rory raging toward him and crouched, war club in one hand and hatchet in the other, ready to spring. The two men circled. Rory cursed as he glared at the painted Indian. Suddenly, with the strength and agility of a mountain lion, the Indian sprang, gripping his hatchet and aiming it at Rory's skull.

Rory sidestepped and swung his hatchet. The blow connected with the Indian's back, knocking him flat on the ground. Rory landed on him and planting one foot firmly on his enemy's back, he raised the club with two hands, high over his head and roared, "Aaeyyyah!" like a wild animal.

Swinging the war club down with enormous strength, borne of immense anger, he crushed his hated enemy's skull. He stood over him, the anger draining out of him as the blood seeped from the dying Indian. Rory had his revenge. Empty and suddenly very tired, he left the field of battle, abandoning it to those who were bent on annihilating the entire village.

He found a place a short distance from the massacre and slumped down to the ground, grateful for the support of the huge tree trunk. Sadness began to reign where anger once boiled. Deep, gut-wrenching sadness. With reluctance, he summoned the needed strength, once more, to perform his last duty for his friends.

He found a soft patch of ground and with his hatchet, loosened the dirt and scooped it out with his hands. Thankfully, the earth gave way easily. As he worked, he tried to make sense out of the efforts that his friends and he had made to survive and just to end up like this? Why?

One by one, the braves appeared at his side, tired and covered in blood and gore. But wordlessly and without invitation, they stooped to help dig the grave.

The moment arrived when Rory was forced to face the gruesome task of gathering the heads of his friends from the posts, to lay them in the shallow grave. It was agonizing to hold in his hands the heads of those whom he had come to know as a brother or sister; with whom he had worked, fought, lived and had come to love.

Pain! Such pain he had never known before! It cut through his heart as nothing he could have ever imagined! Gentle, loving words were spoken to each one, as he lifted their head from the post, telling them of his love for them.

However, the most difficult task of all was still to be carried out—to remove Alistair's head from the post. He tenderly lifted it from the post, speaking his love for his friend—but suddenly stopped. Rory knew it wasn't possible, but as he carried Alistair's head to the grave, he was sure he could hear his guttural laughter. "That bugger is laughing at me! He's had the last laugh!" Rory said to himself, surprised at the chuckle that was welling up in him. Somehow, hearing that laugh took some of the pain away and made it bearable to place his head in the grave. Oh, how he was going to miss his life long friend!

Alistair's was the last head to be carefully placed in the grave. Rory gently pushed the earth over them, saying his last good byes. The Indians wisely did not interfere with his grieving but waited patiently while he gathered stones and built a small cairn over the grave.

Rory stood before the cairn, his head bent in prayer. When he was finished he looked toward the sky, saying, "John Whitelaw, ye're right, ye know. If a man hasn't made Christ the main thought in his life, he surely will faint in his own time of trial. I have fallen short in the past but You gave me the strength to do what I had to do for my friends today. I'll mend my ways—Oh, God, I'll mend my ways—please forgive me—please help me!" Rory cried.

His friend, Mugwump, put a hand on Rory's shoulder.

"Aye, I'll be right wi' ye," Rory said, wiping his face on his sleeve. He turned to see the warriors ladened with the food they had retrieved; he picked up his share of the load before he joined the line.

Five prisoners had been taken and they too were forced to carry back the sacks of food that they had just stolen so few hours ago. Night had dropped its black cloak over Rory and the Indians before they finally straggled into the village.

* * * *

"What's happening?" I wondered as noise and the excited chattering of the Indian women woke me. I tried to move without waking Ma. How long had I been asleep? From the stiffness in my back, I guessed it had been too long.

Thankfully, Ma was finally sleeping peacefully on a fur rug that Beauty had given her.

More chattering and a sense of excitement! What was happening?

Some of the women were running toward the barricade while others were lighting torches that cast eerie shadows over them. Could it be? I didn't move—waiting and watching as each warrior entered the compound. First one—then two—then another one…

"Rory! It's Rory, Ma!" I screamed as I crawled and stumbled toward him. "You're alright! Are you hurt?" I touched his face, his arms, looking for signs of wounds under all of the dried blood.

"Aye…and no!" he smiled. "Ye weren't worried, were ye? I told ye I'd come back."

"Oh, Rory! Rory! I love you!" I cried over and over again while leading him to where Ma was sleeping.

Without another word, he sat down on the ground ready to sleep where he had dropped. Exhaustion had etched cruel lines on his face. I covered him, grateful to be tucking the blanket around him, grateful that I had my husband back…back where I could wrap my arms around him.

"Oh, God! Thank You! Thank You for bringing him home safe!" I had now joined the ranks of the wives of warriors, offering prayers—the same prayers that had been offered through countless ages by countless women.

Ma was awake now. She looked from me to Rory and memory faintly flickered in her eyes. I dropped down between her and Rory, wrapped a fur rug around us, and began my vigil. I would not let myself sleep. My hand gripped Rory's hatchet. If the enemy attacked again, I was ready.

Dawn broke, finally, streaking the sky with ribbons of orange and pink. Rory stirred and groaned. He pushed himself to a sitting position and looked at me through bleary eyes and asked, "Lizzie, ye've not been up the whole night, have ye?"

"Aye…didn't want any more surprises."

He loosened my fingers from around the hatchet. "Ach, lassie…" he began, but then looked carefully into my eyes. "Ye would've used it, wouldn't ye?"

"Aye. No one…and I mean *no one* will ever hurt you or Ma—not if I can help it!"

"Cum 'ere," he said as he pulled me to him, kissing away the tears that ran down my cheeks. "Ye're some woman, Lizzie!" he paused, then added with a sparkle in his eyes, "all woman, as I remember!" I melted easily into his arms.

Ma stirred and woke up. Rory greeted her but Ma only stared at him with a puzzled look.

"What's happened to your Ma?" Rory whispered.

"Same as what happened to Jenny." I answered, forgetting that Rory knew nothing about my sister, or brother, for that matter.

"Lizzie, what's going on?" he asked. "Where are the rest? I know there couldn't be many, but surely..."

I didn't want to tell him. "Ma slept here..." I began, evading his question.

"How did Christie...?" he interrupted.

"Ma stayed with Beauty's family on our wedding night—I guess to give us a chance to be by ourselves."

"Thank God for that! It saved her!" Rory exclaimed. "Why did they attack us?" I led him away from his question, trying to keep the answer from him as long as possible.

"Christie," Rory said to Ma, "do you think you could find out why that other tribe attacked us?"

"Rory, Ma...she's not..." I faltered.

Rory held Ma by the shoulders and looked into her beautiful eyes, looking for answers, but only a blank stare was his reward.

"Ahhh, good God!—Christie! Christie! It's just been too much—too much!" and he cuddled her as he would a child. Ma didn't resist. She was simply limp with no response, no giving back—nothing.

"You wait for us here, Christie. Don't move, you hear me?" Rory said, raising his voice.

"I don't think she's deaf, Rory. She just doesn't comprehend anything."

"Let's go," he said. "I want to know why that tribe attacked us."

As we searched for Beauty, we came to the five prisoners. They had been tied to stakes in the center of the village compound. Women and children danced around them and poked them with sticks and knives, until blood was drawn; jabbed the point of a heated flint arrow in their eyes; rammed long thin pieces of wood under their finger nails. Still, in the face of this intense anger and cruelty, the prisoners maintained emotionless expressions. Not one flicker of feeling was visible.

We had watched the young boys of this tribe deliberately inflict pain upon themselves by rubbing their foreheads against another's until one of them gave up. This was how they taught themselves to develop a tolerance for pain. To show any form of emotion in front of strangers was, for Indians, to show weakness.

"Beauty!" I called her from the circle of women dancing around the prisoners. "Beauty," I began, "why did they..." I pointed to the prisoners, "attack us?"

We struggled for a few minutes, but Beauty finally understood me. Now it was my turn to try to understand. She made the sign for "us"—us? No? Oh, "white people". Next she showed me her brother—yes, brother...of the Chief? Killed. Who killed him? Rory struggled to understand as well. After much gesturing, we at last understood that some white people had killed the brother of the Chief of the enemy tribe. They took revenge on us, being white people, and also on this tribe because they had befriended us.

Beauty continued, using words that we had taught her along with hand signs and her own Indian words. She laid three sticks on the ground and pointed to the sun, "three days walk from here...to the south...white people live there and killed the Chief's brother."

Rory nodded his understanding. "I wonder if it was any of Barclay's people?" Rory muttered aloud.

Beauty continued, "Five of our Indian braves...killed yesterday in the massacre...five prisoners brought back here...women and children will torture the prisoners...if they show no sign of pain, they will be allowed to live, but will have to work for this village for the rest of their lives."

Rory thanked Beauty for her help and we returned to where Ma was still sitting in the same place we had left her.

"Lizzie...Christie," Rory said, "these people have suffered too much for us! We have to leave before we bring more harm to them. I know that there are white settlements to the north of here." He paused, his face grim, "Now, tell me, Lizzie, how many of the Scots survived?"

I shook my head, dreading to tell him the truth.

"Lizzie!" he raised his voice, "don't aggravate me! How many are left?"

I could hardly get the word out. Finally I whispered, "None."

"What do you mean, 'none'?" he demanded.

"Rory, no one survived the attack, except you, me and Ma...'cause we didn't sleep in the longhouse that night." I added lamely, searching for words to soften the blow.

"No! It can't be! Not everyone!" His eyes blinked rapidly as he shook his head from side to side. He didn't think that everyone's head was on the posts. Surely, some escaped!

"I looked all over for Alistair..." I began.

"No! No more!" he shouted and stood up. "Don't say any more!" And he walked away from me.

I waited for him to return, not knowing what to do or how to comfort my husband. I did not have long to wait. Within minutes he was back and sat down beside me.

"You know where he is?" I asked quietly, trying to understand the pain in my husband's eyes.

"Sshh," he nodded, holding my face in his hands. "I'll tell you sometime, but not right now."

A shout went up from the vicinity of the five prisoners. We scrambled toward it, trying to see what had happened. "What the...?" Rory's question was soon answered. Ma had come with us and we worked our way to where the prisoners were being held and tortured. The Indian women and children, whom we had come to know and call friends, had finally broken one of the prisoners by putting hot rocks in his armpits. Another prisoner was tied so that he was bent over, his buttocks bared. He had buckled under barbarous anal tortures.

Without any warning at all, Ma began to flail the air with her arms as if she was fighting off an enemy. Rory picked her up in his arms and carried her back to the blanket where we tried to calm her, sooth her; but we knew what she was remembering...the thought seared my mind, as well—of Wallace Lauderdale's inhumane demand that Duncan torture her with the blackened eggs in her arm pits.

Beauty had heard Ma's scream and came running. "Beauty," Rory asked, "please stay wi' her while Lizzie and I talk to Mugwump."

"The Chief?" I asked.

"Aye! Cum' on!" He pulled me by the hand to the longhouse and Mugwump, who was sitting in front of it, his face impassive as he puffed on a long pipe sending, at regular intervals, spirals of smoke over his head. He was hunched under a thick fur rug that was drawn tightly around his shoulders, looking very tired.

"Mugwump," Rory greeted him, after the usual formalities, "we would like to bury our dead, then we'll leave as soon as we're finished. We want to go north." Mugwump listened to Rory and watched me as I struggled to interpret. In time, I was able to make him understand what Rory was trying to say.

The Chief was thoughtful for several minutes before he reached for a nearby stick and said, "Kina!" We obediently watched as he drew a map in the soft earth. There was a long, winding line that looked like a river. Mugwump pointed at it and said, "Kennebec". At the head of the river he drew the outline of a lake and some distance away he drew another lake which flowed into a river the Chief called "Allagash".

Rory pointed out to me that we would have to portage the canoe and supplies over land between these two lakes.

"Uh uh," the Chief grunted and shook his head from side to side. He then drew a line, which told us there would be a river flowing out of the second lake and into another river. Suddenly, the Chief jammed the stick into the ground and pointed to it.

"Is this a white settlement?" I asked. I struggled to understand him. After many gestures on my part and his, I understood that, yes, this was a white settlement—where he had jabbed the point of the stick in the ground.

The Chief studied my face, and when he saw that I understood, he continued. He picked up the stick and began to draw again. This time he drew what looked like a wide, long river running from west to east, emptying into an ocean. "What is the name of this river?" I wanted to know, but the Chief just shrugged his shoulders, which I interpreted as he didn't know. We learned later that it was called the St. Lawrence River.

Rory gathered up several little sticks and laid them end to end and pointed at the sky, asking how long the journey should take.

"Many moons," we were told.

"That means we'll be traveling during the winter, Lizzie," Rory said.

Mugwump raised his hand, indicating that he was going to speak again. He pointed to Buck, my friend who had saved me from the bear and who was his son. Buck was to be our guide as far as the Kennebec River.

Rory was enthusiastic in his thanks and wanted to shake hands, but the Chief pointed at a seat beside him and invited him to sit down. The Chief offered Rory the long pipe. Rory drew on the pipe, and then passed it back to the Chief. No words were exchanged between them and it didn't seem necessary. It was obvious to me a bond had been formed between these two men, beginning when they had stood in their boats, struggling to communicate with each other. Respect flowed between them, one chief for another. I sensed they both shared an understanding of the responsibility and pain of leadership.

"I want to tell him I'm sorry for what he has suffered for us." Rory said to me, looking for me to explain what he was feeling. Before I could begin, the Chief struggled to his feet and stood squarely in front of Rory. He pushed a finger at the big Scotsman's chest, saying, "Mugwump RRRory" with a beautiful Scottish accent, his 'r's' rolling expertly off his tongue. The Chief endured Rory's spontaneous brotherly hug.

As soon as he could escape from Rory's bear hug, he motioned for us to follow him. We walked toward the barricade and as we moved through the village, the Chief motioned to his braves to follow.

Once outside the village, Mugwump pointed at the boats and at the corpses which were still strewn on the ground. Rory nodded. He understood the Chief was telling him he should carry the dead out to sea in boats.

Rory and the tired warriors gathered large rocks and with long strips of rawhide, attached them to the stiff, cold and decapitated bodies. Body after body was loaded into the canoes, similar to the dead seals.

I watched the Indians paddle far away from the shore and when they stopped, I knew the bodies were being thrown into their ocean grave, just as I had thrown Catherine Sims' baby into the ocean.

"Go back tae yer Ma, Lizzie!" Rory ordered. "You don't need to see this!"

I didn't argue.

Inside the Indian compound, I sat down by Ma and waited for him, never taking my eyes from the huge barricade gate. Ma whimpered and whimpered until I put my hand on her head, saying, "I know Ma. I know. It's almost got the best o' me too!"

Beauty had moved us into her wigwam to share the warmth of her fire and a meal. She was trying to coax Ma to eat when Rory appeared at the door. Drained again, he staggered to my side and sat down. Beauty offered him meat and vegetables. He shook his head, staring at his hands in the light of the fire. They were crusted with blood.

"Lizzie, come wi' me, please!" He demanded this more than 'asked' and pulled me to my feet. Ma cried out, grabbing at my dress. Beauty took Ma's hands in her own and smiled calmly into her eyes, quieting her. We left the wigwam.

"Where's your lake? I have to wash this off!" he shouted, waving his hands in my face.

"This way…but it is the women's lake—but—ach, well, what does it matter now?" I said and ran, as fast as I could, through the forest, over the familiar path.

The lake was beautiful and calm, reflecting the last rays of the setting sun and the golden hue of the trees.

I collapsed on its bank, gasping for breath. Rory pulled at his blood stained clothes and heaved them into the lake, jumping in after them. He pushed with all of his might against the water as he waded around the edge of the lake to the waterfall. Once under the cold, cleansing water, he opened his mouth and roared the most agonizing sound I had ever heard. It was not human, nor was it animal. It was pain! Ugly, soul searing pain erupting from the center of his being!

He held his hands under the careening water, scrubbing them against one another. His mouth twisted…I knew he was crying.

Slowly I slipped my buckskin dress off and waded into the cold water, too, and made my way toward the waterfall. I reached for Rory's hands, which he was still angrily rubbing against each other. He pulled away and turned his back to me. I held his arm and walked around to where he had to look at me. Before he could push me away again, I put my arms around him, pressing my body against his.

"Oh, Lizzie, Lizzie, Lizzie…" he sobbed and clung to me as if I was life itself. How long we stood like that, I don't know, but when we climbed out of the lake, it was dark.

"Let's get you into something dry, Rory," I said after I had pulled on my clothes and wrung out his. We quickly traveled to the edge of the forest, where I left him, hiding his nakedness in the foliage. After taking a deep breath, I plunged through the door of the longhouse, thankful that the darkness had hidden the bloody signs of the massacre.

Jumping from bed to bed, I searched the shelves for dry buckskins and found some! Immediately, I turned around and wasting no time, ran back to Rory with my treasure. I found him, clutching his precious, dripping wet kilt around himself.

We spent the night inside the village, it being the safest place. The next morning, Rory was up early to look over the canoes our men had built, seeking the best one. Ma and I found him on the beach, inspecting each pitch sealed seam.

"Does it look good, Rory?" I wanted to know.

"Aye, it looks water tight, alright. See?" He pointed at the black, sticky seams.

I gave the canoe more than a cursory glance; our very lives depended upon it being watertight.

"What do think, lassie?" he grinned at me.

"How heavy is it?"

Rory's muscles bulged as he gripped the sides of the canoe and swung it over his head.

"Light as a feather!" he bragged, and swung it back down on the ground. "Now, listen you two," he looked from Ma to me, "be careful how much you bring, 'cause the two o' you will have to carry the supplies if I'm to carry this canoe."

To our delight, Ma moved her head up and down, as if she understood what he had said.

We tied up our bundles of fur rugs and buckskins. Birch bark pots were stuffed with herbs and medicines, which Beauty had taught Ma and me to use. One of the most precious herbs to Ma, personally, was a potion made of animal fat and the roots of several different plants. Until three days ago, every morning and night Ma followed a careful ritual of applying this potion to her scarred face, desperately trying to coax new skin over the brand mark on her face.

"Are ye takin' your pipes, Rory MacLeod?" I asked, remembering that Alistair had been the last one to play them.

"Aye!" he answered, astonished that I would ask such a question.

"And who's gonna carry 'em?' I teased as I walked into the longhouse.

"Ye can just strap them to m' back!" he shouted, "'Cause if I go down, they go down wi' me!"

"Rory MacLeod! I swear you love those things more than you love me!"

"Well..." he said, not committing himself one way or the other.

Beauty unknowingly rescued us when she appeared, carrying a bundle of parched corn to add to our already large supply of dried venison and fish, shelled nuts and dried fruit. A small birch bark pot with a tightly lashed lid held some precious maple syrup.

Close on Beauty's heels was Mugwump, the Chief and our good friend. He handed Rory a fish hook he had made from the wish bone of a bird; attached to it was a long strand of twisted birch bark fiber. Rory was properly appreciative.

My Highland husband insisted on wearing his kilt, which wasn't quite dry yet, and a deer skin shirt. On his feet were the moccasins I had made for him. Ma and I wore buckskin dresses and long moccasins that covered the calves of our legs.

Beauty produced another parcel. It was a second set of moccasins for each of us. I happily noted that she had lined them with rabbit fur, which she had taught us would keep out the winters' cold from the 'wazoli'—snow.

Buck—our nickname for him—was ready to guide us to our first stop: the Kennebec River. Beauty showed us how to lash bundles together and place them on our backs so the weight was distributed evenly, at least as much as possible. Eventually, we were ready to leave.

My eyes swept past the longhouse to the ocean—it was still early morning and the sun was still pink in the sky. I peered at the ocean. Somewhere out there, under the white capped waves were my friends...and beyond that was my beloved Scotland—Da, Iain and Jenny. Tears welled up in my eyes. I forced myself to turn my attention to saying goodbye to the Chief and Beauty, and others who had gathered for our final farewell.

"Olibamkanni!" they repeated over and over, wishing us a good trip.

Rory lifted the canoe over his head and rested it on his shoulders—our signal to move.

I helped Ma into her pack and shrugged into my own. "Aye! We're away!" I called to Rory and stepped in front of him, following close on Buck's heels with Ma falling in behind me.

Thankfully, it wasn't long before Buck had us on the banks of the Kennebec River and was helping Rory push the canoe partly into the water. It was a blessed relief to have Rory lift our bundles off our backs and pack them into the canoe. I perched myself on those he had put in the middle and Ma sat in the bow of the canoe.

The two men grunted as they pushed the heavy canoe into the water. Rory jumped into the stern of the canoe and picked up the paddle, using it to push the little craft out into the river.

We waved good bye to Buck, who was standing by, silently watching us.

"Ye know, I think he's sweet on ye!" Rory said.

"Rory!" I scolded and blushed. I felt my face turn what I knew was a bright red.

"Aye, I think I've a rival there! Good thing were movin' on!" He laughed with delight at my discomfort. However, it wasn't long before Rory's teasing was lost in my insatiable curiosity that had me turning this way and that, while I tried to see everything at once.

"A deer! Look!" I shouted and spun around to get a better look. "Ma, do you see it?" I turned toward her. "Ma? Oh, Ma!" She was clutching the sides of the canoe so tightly that her knuckles had turned white. Her face reflected the terror she seemed to be enduring. But not one word did she speak.

Rory pulled hard on the paddle, having to fight against the flow of the river. Beads of perspiration stood out on his forehead and the muscles in his arms bulged under his shirt.

"Christie! Are ye gettin' used to it yet?" he called to Ma. She didn't answer, but I noticed that her face had relaxed a little. "And, how about you, Lady Elizabeth MacLeod? Are you ready to take a turn at paddlin'?"

"Who...me?"

"Aye! You!"

"Well, I've never..."

"Well, you are just about to then, aren't you?"

"You don't need to be so cocky wi' me!" I stood up in the canoe, ready to change places with Rory. Ma made a choking sound and once again was gripping the edge of the canoe as if her life depended upon how tightly she held on to it. And maybe she was not far wrong.

I picked up the paddle and stuck it in the water. Grunting and groaning, I pushed the river water behind me, moving us backwards. We were losing some of the ground that Rory had gained for us.

Suddenly, I felt the canoe rock and looked over my shoulder. It was Ma, on her hands and knees, coming toward me. She sat down beside me and took the other paddle.

Delighted with this turn of events, Rory shouted "pull!" at us until we were pulling on the paddles at the same time and had stopped both zigzagging or going in circles. I was pleased to point out to Rory that at least we weren't moving backwards and were even making progress and issued the warning, "If you expect your supper tonight, Rory MacLeod, don't you say a thing!"

He grinned and made a show of choking back his laughter at my observation.

"Ah, Lizzie—I'm only teasin' ye!" He turned his attention to admiring the beauty of the forest, commenting on the trees that hung lazily over the banks of the river, dipping their long branches into the water. All was peaceful and yesterday seemed such a long time ago.

I noticed smoke rising above the tree tops. "Must be an Indian village," Rory guessed. We tensed, watching the bank carefully for any sign of danger and were grateful to pass without any trouble.

When the sun was high overhead, we pulled the canoe into the bank. "Don't ye be wanderin' off, now, you two!" Rory warned as Ma and I left his sight to 'refresh' ourselves.

"No fear," I tossed back at him. Within minutes we were back at the camp site where Rory had pulled out some dried meat and we made a meal of that along with some nuts we found growing along the river.

"No time to waste!" Rory rushed us back into the canoe and we were off again. Day after day, we followed the same routine and each night, in spite of his bone-weary fatigue, Rory left us to build a fire while he caught our evening meal. Sometimes it was a fish or bird or rabbit, but always he returned, smiling triumphantly, with supper in hand.

The aroma of meat cooking would fill the air, making my mouth water. How we loved to eat!

We slept when the sun went down and rose when it came up again. At night, Rory built a lean-to that not only kept the dew off us but kept away curious animals or birds. He always stoked up the small campfire before we slept, giving us more protection.

Soon, our fear of the forest left us as we became familiar with it. It was no longer our enemy, but our friend. Even the Indians, who watched as we paddled by, seemed friendly. At least they didn't make any attempt to hurt us. Toward the end of the second week we noticed that the river was narrowing and becoming very shallow and before long we were in a maze of tall marsh grass. Now we could paddle no longer and the canoe kept rubbing against the mud at the bottom of the stream.

"I'll have to pull it by hand," Rory said as he jumped out of the canoe into the cold water. It was up to his knees. "Ahhhch! you heathen, freezin'…" he roared at the icy water.

"Rory!" I scolded. "Don't swear!"

"Well, at least we know now there's nothing wrong wi' yer Ma's ears!" he shouted back. "Look!"

I turned, and there was Ma, her hands over her ears. I couldn't help but laugh.

"If ye think it's so funny, you get out here and pull!" Rory was not amused as he grunted and pulled us first in this direction and in that. Eventually he looked up at the overcast sky and admitted that we were lost. "Where's north?" he asked. I didn't know—I was turned around as well.

The canoe suddenly rocked from side to side. We both looked back at Ma who was struggling to stand up in the canoe. I tried to pull her down but she pushed my hands away and stretched up on her toes, looking over the grass.

"What do ye see, Ma?" Rory asked.

Ma pointed to our left, making a big circle with her arms. We were puzzled at first, then Rory asked, "It's the lake, Ma?" She smiled, pleased with herself, and sat down.

We were only about twenty feet from the lake, but the tall grasses had grown over that part of the mouth of the river that divided it from a huge lake. Rory jumped into the canoe and soon we had escaped the confusion of the maze and burst out into the lake.

It was such a welcome and beautiful sight! Especially since I had thought we would never find it!

Rory pulled in the paddles, laid them down beside him and just let the canoe drift on the mirror-like surface. After the noise of our confusion, the silence was a wonderful respite.

Ma patted me on the shoulder and waved her hand where she wanted me to look. On the bank at the far end of the lake stood a huge moose—head up and very aware of the strangers who were trespassing on his territory.

A loud crack startled Rory into action. He gripped one of the paddles in both hands, ready to fight...but only silence again. We listened, nervously looking around. Again, that same loud "crack!" as if something was slapping the water. The canoe had drifted toward a pile of logs and there, peering from the center of the pile was the little brown face of a beaver.

Slap! Slap! He bravely tried to scare us away by smacking his big round tail on the water.

"We won't hurt you!" Rory called to him, "but don't get too cocky, wee boy. We just might have you for supper!"

Not far past the beaver's dam we found a good site for making camp. The bank sloped into the lake and the overhanging trees were dense enough to help protect us from the wet weather which was on its way, judging from the dark clouds gathering overhead.

As usual, we talked over the events of the day as we ate. "Ma and you did well, Rory, getting us outta that mess of grass," I told them. Ma smiled shyly. Then we talked about Scotland and told our stories. Rory's stories about his boyhood had me curled up with laughter.

I could see him in my mind's eye, running from one mischief making to the other, always with Alistair by his side, grumbling, being sarcastic—but always there.

Ma responded to the laughter, silently, her eyes lighting up and crinkling at the corners.

"Rory, what happened to Alistair...?" I began, but he cut me short.

"Not now, Lizzie, not now!"

The fun drained from the evening, leaving us silent. I vowed never to speak about the massacre—no, not ever again! Another pain to be jammed down with the others. I'd never told anyone about wee Iain's death; I never spoke about my father's hanging; and now I couldn't talk about the massacre—about the loss of friends whom I had learned to love like family. That part of me was full to overflowing with sewage...and sadness.

"Why won't he let me talk?" I thought, feeling angry at the unfairness. "I held him while he screamed and cried like a madman under the waterfall!" Finally, I just pushed the anger down—down—down.

Rory picked up his pipes and went into the forest and played where the trees absorbed the sound of the music. Never, though, did we hear him play Dunvegan's Galley, the tune that he had used to get Alistair up on his feet during the ocean crossing.

I turned my attention to Ma. Here she'd lost her voice from one shock too many, but she was carrying on…no choice, really. She must be really missing Da, now. Well, she has us but it's not the same as having your own husband. It was amazing to me how quickly I had evolved into 'married' thinking. The fact that we were good friends, as well, was an extra blessing and as with good friends, we didn't need talk at all to feel comfortable with each other.

The days offered plenty of time for peaceful meditation. During this time I often wondered about the effect the events of the last five months had on me. Ma couldn't speak but groaned a lot and held her armpits and I knew she was reliving the ordeal Wallace Lauderdale had put her through. Rory suffered terrible nightmares, thrashing the air with his arms and legs. What was my affliction? Did I even see it? Maybe the others were tolerating mine as I was theirs? My mind flashed back to Iain and Jenny, time and time again. "Would I ever see my sister again?" I wondered sadly.

I learned that Ma liked to hear about Maggie and Angus Winters taking care of Iain and Jenny. I kept up the lie, not ever telling her that Iain was dead. It was hard to speak about Iain, and when I'd come to that part of the story, I couldn't look Ma in the eye and would look anywhere except at her. Once, when I was avoiding Ma's eyes, I noticed Rory watching me with a puzzled expression, but he didn't say anything.

We worked hard, sharing the paddling and the chores and the adventure of living in the forest. The sounds became recognizable and we learned to identify the various bird calls and even came to recognize the difference between real bird calls and the Indians imitating the birds; they were probably sending messages to each other, we decided. Every day we learned something new about the forest—it became our teacher.

This particular day, we tied up the canoe earlier than usual because Ma was tired. After making sure that she was settled, Rory took me by the arm, saying that he wanted 'tae have a wee talk' and we walked into the forest. I had a sense of foreboding—I felt strange, like a little girl and this was my Da, instead of my husband. Rory had to ask me twice to sit down but I remained standing. "What do ye want?" I asked suspiciously.

"Lizzie," he began, "you know when you tell your Ma the story about Iain and Jenny? Why is it that I get the feeling that yer telling something that isn't quite true when you come to the part about Iain?"

He had taken me by surprise and I didn't know how to respond. Quickly, but gently and firmly, he pulled me down beside him on the log and with a reassuring arm around my shoulders coaxed me in low, tender tones to "go ahead, you are safe—you can tell me".

With the reassurance of his love and the security of his strong arm around my shoulders, my courage began to manifest itself. From somewhere deep within my being and with each passing moment the desire grew and grew, to rid myself of all the hurt that had been so carefully buried. Words wanted to erupt—to explode in a frenzy to be free and to bring with them the tangle of emotions. To not scream my story at the top of my lungs took immense control.

"I'm lying about Iain!" I began.

"Aye—aye—go on" he coaxed.

"Oh, Rory—I killed my brother!!" I wailed into his shoulder. I felt his arm jerk slightly and then tighten again around me.

"Tell me, sweetheart—my little sweetheart—tell me everything!" he crooned into my ear. "Why don't you tell me all about it, then? I'll keep your secret," he reassured me.

I couldn't find the words—they wouldn't come. Tears came, but not the words.

"Lizzie, this could be a wee bit too big for you to be carryin' all by yourself, don't ye think? You can tell me," he coaxed patiently.

"Aye," I whimpered, but continued to struggle for several minutes. "I'm goin' to hell!" I finally blurted out.

As I flung my arms around his neck, I noticed his eyebrows shoot upward in surprise—but this was immediately lost to me as the entire horrific ordeal came tumbling out—from beginning to end. How Da was wounded and taken by the soldiers; how Ma was tortured with the blackened eggs; how Jenny and I found Iain dead—with my finger marks around his mouth—ohhh, the pain of that memory seared through my mind—the Winters—the prison—Da's hanging—Ma—the massacre—oh, it hurt so much as it ripped its way out from the center of my being. I cried and cried—great huge sobs shook my body. But during the entire regurgitating of these painful memories, my husband wisely only held me close, allowing me to experience my grief again to the point of where I could let go of it.

When I had finished, I lay limply in his arms—exhausted. Confessing that I was ready for whatever punishment God had prepared for me.

"For what, Lizzie?" There was a tinge of anger in his voice.

"I told you! I killed my little brother! I killed my little brother!" I repeated. I wanted to shout it from the tops of the trees—I wanted to confess it to the whole world. I needed to be cleansed of this sinful thing that I had done.

"Sshh!" Rory whispered, "you'll wake yer Ma. Besides, lassie, I think you're takin' a wee bit too much guilt on those shoulders o' yours."

"No! It's true! It's true!" I again reached back into the dark memory, into the terror of that night and repeated every detail. How the soldiers wounded Da—holding Iain still while Ma screamed—Captain Lauderdale and his soldiers ramming the black eggs into her armpits—the sound of the soldiers' boots as they left the cottage—the dark red marks around Iain's mouth—that they were my finger marks—that black moment when I realized that I had killed him—the fear we felt as Maggie opened the door. Finally, the pain of leaving—leaving Jenny behind!

It all tumbled out again, all of the ugliness and the pain—the terrible pain that had wrapped itself around my heart and clung there, almost choking the life out of me.

"I killed my brother! I killed my wee Iain!" I cried over and over again. I felt Rory take a deep breath and he took me by the shoulders, forcing me to look at him.

"No, you didn't, lass!" he said. "No! You did *not* kill him! Wallace Lauderdale killed your brother, don't you be takin' on that guilt. It wasn't you! Do you hear me?"

His mouth was close to my ear, his cheek pressed against mine. His words poured salve over my burning guilt and slowly calmed the whirl in my mind and I could feel that terrible load being lifted from my heart. My sobbing again gave way to relief, as the icy torment I had endured since that life altering night gradually melted before the fire of my husband's love.

"Will God forgive me, Rory? Do you think He'll ever forgive me?" I asked between the now quieter sobs.

"What are you feeling right now?" Rory asked.

"I'm...I feel quiet...sort of..."

"Peaceful?" he coaxed.

"Aye," I answered after a few moments of searching.

"Is peace a gift from God?" he asked gently.

"Aye, at least that's what we're told."

"Well, do you think God would give ye peace if He hadn't forgiven you?"

Slowly, the wisdom of his words infiltrated my feverish mind. Could he be right? Is he telling me a truth? "Oh, Rory! Rory! I want you to be right! I—I—I think you are...I feel you are! Oh, Rory!" I cried, flinging my arms around his neck. I kissed him. I kissed his mouth, his eyes, his cheeks. My kisses rained over his face! I began to allow myself to feel the pure joy of release. "Oh, Rory! I love you!" I sobbed.

Then I had a sobering thought. "Rory, what should I tell Ma?"

"Right now, I think it would push her over the edge to know that her Iain's dead. You've told me—can that be enough for now?"

"Aye, the load is lifting."

"Well, you'll know the right time to tell her. Just keep it between us th' now," he advised.

"Rory?" I suddenly felt the need for my husband, an overwhelming desire borne of the love with which he had enveloped me. But I wished that I didn't feel so shy about it, though.

"Aye?"

"Rory, when do you think we'll get a chance to be alone—ye know—like..." I hesitated to speak the words out loud.

"Yer Ma isn't here—she's probably asleep..." Rory grinned.

Before I knew it, he had me in his arms, whispering his longing for me. The forest floor of pine needles made a soft bed for our love making. We were one again! Not only in body, but in spirit as well. The golden cord had tied us ever closer...again.

Chapter 26

"Where did ye put the map?" Rory called to me from the canoe.

"It's rolled up in that fur rug," I said impatiently. "Why don't ye keep it in one place so's you'll always be able to find it?"

Ma touched my arm and shook her head. I knew she was telling me to not be cranky. But every morning Rory checked the map the Chief had given him, looking for the designated landmarks and would put it away in a different place, sending me looking for it.

Each time he studied the map, he would ask "I wonder what all those little circles are—in the middle of the river?"

"Is it just marks in the deer hide, or did the Chief actually draw circles on it?" I asked, trying to be helpful and repent of my impatience with him.

"Lizzie, it looks as if we must tangle wi' another river soon; maybe even today," he continued, ignoring my suggestion.

"Aye," I agreed absentmindedly, as I tried to fit our gear into the canoe. I kept the fur rugs unpacked as it was chillier now and I didn't want Ma comin' down with the cold.

"Everyone in?" He was making a show of stuffing the map inside his shirt.

"Aye."

Once more, Rory pushed the canoe into the lake and after jumping in, took up the paddle and we were off, gliding smoothly and silently over the lake. Rory seemed to get stronger every day and was handling the canoe as if he had been doing it all his life. His bulging muscles, under the deer skin shirt I had made for him, delighted me.

Suddenly, I was aware of a sound that wasn't familiar. It sounded like thunder, but it didn't stop—just a constant roar in the distance.

"Look at that!" Rory pointed at the distinct line in the water between the clear, deep blue lake and the dark brown murky water of the river. I was looking where he was pointing when, just as the bow of the canoe passed over the line, it was snatched by the river's current and we were spun around and around.

"Paddle!" Rory yelled, the urgency in his voice catapulting me to his side where I snatched up the other paddle with both hands. Only by using all our strength were we able to wrestle the canoe from the river's greedy grasp. Taking a deep breath we relaxed, only to be whipped away again by the river's current. Suddenly, out of nowhere, a wall of jagged rocks loomed before us.

"It's a waterfall!" Rory shouted. "The circles! That's what he meant! Pull yer paddle in, Lizzie! Hold on! Ma, get down!" His words were lost in the roar. The canoe was tossed around like a toy in the white lather of the angry river.

I know I was screaming but I couldn't hear myself—it was lost in the thunder of raging rapids. The canoe shot forward into midair, then landed with a spine jarring thud, narrowly missing a huge rock. We were at the bottom of the falls, the water boiling around us.

"Rory!" I screamed as I realized we were being hurled toward yet another solid wall of rock. "Ohhh!"

"Grab the paddle! Help me!" Rory held his paddle upright in the turbulent water, fighting to keep the canoe from capsizing. The muscles in my arms burned as I tried to balance Rory's efforts. We were oblivious to the icy water that was drenching us.

"Paddle!" Rory yelled. "Paddle!"

In one last frenzied effort, we pulled on the paddles—pulled, and pulled hard; the canoe turned and ran along side the rock wall! We had swerved just in time, missing the rock wall by inches. We pulled on our paddles once more, pulling away from the rock wall and shot around the bend in the river!

Just as suddenly as it had started, the commotion stopped. We were floating on top of a calmly flowing river. It was as if we had been shot out of a cannon and had landed in a soft feathery pillow. The white water had smoothed out just as quickly as it had started. Rory and I pulled in our paddles and slumped over them, exhausted.

"Ma!" I whimpered lamely and in a child's voice, "Ma, I think I wet mysel'"

"Darlin'," Rory gasped, "if that's all I did, I'll be lucky!"

He struggled to sit up and paddle toward the river bank where the canoe ground to a halt on the river bottom.

Still shaking, we sat without speaking for several minutes. I turned to glance at Ma who was sitting bolt upright, still gripping the sides of the canoe with white knuckled fists. With a great deal of effort I slowly climbed out of the canoe, my legs trembling beneath me, onto blessed terra firma. When Ma scrambled out behind me, she crumpled onto the ground—patting it affectionately. We both agreed with her—it was a blessed relief to feel something solid under our feet.

"What happened?" I asked, looking backward toward the waterfall, which was no longer in view.

"Did you see that rock wall? I thought we were done for that time!" Rory asked.

"And when we shot into the air?" I added. We both looked at Ma who was nodding her head up and down as fast as she could. We burst out in nervous laughing; but what a relief to have that behind us!

"Oh, no! My pipes!" Rory gasped as he reached for them. He had strapped them to his back and his brow furrowed with worry as he shrugged out of the straps and tore away the leather covering. Just as a mother inspects a newborn baby to see if all its fingers and toes are there, Rory checked the drones, the chanter, the reeds. Eventually, he looked up, smiling proudly, "Ach, they're bonny! Not a mark or a drop of water on them!" Rory carefully wrapped them up in the leather bag and tied his precious bagpipes onto his back again and called out, as he stepped into the canoe, "Let's go, the pair o' ye!"

Ma and I were apprehensive about getting into the canoe again. Although Rory wasn't very fond of coaxing—coax he must, this time.

The river became a narrow strip of water, allowing us to pass with only a few feet between its banks. Eventually, after a short time of uneventful paddling, I found myself relaxing a little and looked back at Ma, who had finally released her grip on the rim of the canoe.

"Isn't that beautiful?" I marveled at how the leaves had turned into brilliant oranges and yellows which gave the forest a sunny glow and when the wind ruffled the leaves, a body could swear that the forest was on fire. Around each bend in the river we were greeted with another scene of breathtaking beauty, making the anticipation of what was next exciting and exhilarating. However, this excitement was always mixed with just enough anxiety to keep me from relaxing completely.

I don't know who was more surprised, the six Indians or us. We almost ran into them as we rounded the next bend. Ma moved closer to me, rocking the canoe as she did so. "Ma!" we both shouted at the same time, "sit down!"

The Indians were gesturing wildly, staring wide-eyed at us.

"Lizzie, what're they saying?" Rory wanted to know.

"I don't know, but" I answered, "I don't think we'd better stop to find out."

Rory kept paddling past them. How I wished that Ma would get her voice back so she'd be able to talk to them. I listened, trying to understand. I caught one word that I understood and then another. "Ye know, I do believe they think we're ghosts. I'm not sure, but they seem to be afraid of us."

This gave Rory a bit of courage and he stopped paddling the canoe, beaching it just beyond the precipice where the Indians were fishing.

Cautiously, we stepped from the canoe, Rory taking the lead. The Indians dropped their fishing lines and ran into the forest. "Maybe you're right at that, Lizzie," Rory commented, trying to see where the Indians had gone.

Rory, thoroughly enjoying this turn of events, winked at Ma and said, "let's do this up right!" He took the pipes from his back, removed the leather coverings and connected the drones. As he blew up the bag, he grinned and said between breaths, "This should finish them off properly."

Rory played so beautifully, making his music ring throughout the forest with true, bell-like tones. After several minutes, a young Indian boy appeared, probably driven by curiosity more than bravery. I made hand signs, letting him know that we were friendly which encouraged him to advance a little closer to us—but only timidly at first.

His trousers had fringes up the side and his moccasins were made from one piece of hide. The wampum beads around his arm had a different design from that of our Abeneki Indians, but he appeared friendly and ready to talk, and before long he and I were exchanging signs and words.

Ma wouldn't come anywhere near him. She hung back, ready to jump into the canoe at any sign of trouble.

Eventually, I understood what the Indian boy was trying to tell me. "Rory, Ma,—it seems that the Indians had watched our canoe go over the falls. They thought we were dead, so we scared the livin' daylights outta them when we came around that bend." I giggled at the thought.

"Hold it!" Rory warned us. "They're coming back!" He pulled both Ma and me close to him, putting a protective arm around us. Ma pulled away and immediately began tugging at us, trying to pull us into the canoe. Her face was twisted with fright.

Rory said, "If it's bothering ye that much, we'll go Christie, but I really don't think we have that much to worry about wi' these ones."

Ma shuddered, and kept tugging at us.

"Alright! Alright! We're leaving!" Rory said impatiently, "but don't act as if ye're afraid, Christie, or we *will* have trouble." Rory sounded annoyed.

We stepped into the canoe just as another Indian joined his brothers. The sight of a blonde haired scalp hanging from his belt horrified us as it swung back and forth in time with each of his steps. Without another word, Rory paddled away, pulling on the paddle with all of his might. The sight of the scalp brought back too many, still fresh, painful memories.

We traveled in silence for many miles, each wrestling with his own thoughts. Rory paddled longer than usual and before we knew it, darkness was closing in—we had left it too long to make camp. Now, we had to strain our eyes, peering into the darkness for a suitable place to tie up the canoe and build our lean-to for the night. Eventually we spotted a clearing on the bank and beached the canoe.

Rory built a bigger than usual campfire that night and the three of us slept a little closer together.

"Lizzie, did ye notice that scalp was fair haired?" Rory asked as we settled down to sleep.

"Aye, it was short hair so it must be a man's," I answered, then added my sympathy, "Poor bloke!"

The next morning Rory was up early, trying to catch a fish for breakfast. I watched as he stood in the cold water, motionless, waiting for a fish to swim by. He was as quick as any animal as he grabbed the unwary fish in both hands and threw it onto the bank.

I took out my flint knife and slit the fish, cleaned it, washed it and gave it to Ma, who was heating rocks in the fire on which to cook it.

Rory caught another fish; this one was larger than the first. Ma shook her finger at him, letting him know we had enough.

"Aye, Ma!" he grinned.

The aroma of breakfast lingered around the campfire, enveloping us in contentment as we cleared away our cooking and eating utensils. But just as we were ready to get into the canoe, we were startled by a loud crash behind us and there, not five feet away, a huge bear reared up on his hind legs, thrashing the air with his forepaws.

We were frozen with fear...until the bear roared and that sent Ma and me scrambling into the canoe at the same time, with me shouting, "Hurry! Rory! Hurry up!" Later, when thinking about this incident, I realized it was a ridiculous thing to say to someone who was facing a bear.

Rory threw the lean-to branches at the bear first and then jumped into the canoe. The bear wrapped his forepaws around the branches, giving Rory time to push the canoe away from shore and jump in and he paddled as if the devil himself was chasing us. We watched the bear disentangled himself from our lean-to branches and lumber into the water, roaring his disappointment.

"Go faster! Go faster!!" I shouted. I was on my knees, trying to help paddle with my hands because I couldn't reach the other paddle; while Rory, expertly swung from side to side with the one paddle, moving us quickly into the center of the river.

Ma clapped her hands to get our attention. When we looked at her, she pointed to the river bank where the bear was lumbering out of the water and thankfully giving up his chase.

"Thank the Lord!" Rory said, and pulled his paddle in and slumped over it. We drifted for a few moments, catching our breath, then I giggled. "Ye should have seen the look on yer face, Rory!"

"My face? What nerve! Ye should have seen yer own!"

Our laughter echoed back to us from the hills on either side of the river and we allowed ourselves the luxury of relaxing into the beauty of it all.

Before long we found ourselves gliding into another huge lake. By now, I was becoming stronger, so we could paddle faster and by late afternoon, we had almost crossed the entire lake. That evening, Rory studied the map by the campfire.

"Take a look at this, Lizzie!" The excitement in his voice moved me to his side quickly. "This lake leads into another river and," he grinned triumphantly, "that will take us to the white settlement. Our trip is almost over, lassie!"

Ma and I looked over his shoulder at the map, studying the lines and marks made by the Chief. I scrutinized it carefully for circles—there weren't any.

"We must get to the settlement before the winter gets serious about setting in! That means we don't stop as much...or as long, because we'll never survive without proper shelter!" His big grin had evaporated and was replaced by worry lines in his brow.

The next morning, Rory had us up and away before streaks, heralding the dawn had even appeared in the sky. By mid-morning we entered the river we had seen on the map. In spite of my pleading to stop, he kept paddling.

"Rory! Yer cruel!" I complained. Then suddenly I called out, "Look!" and pointed to a spiral of blue smoke rising above the trees. "Let's stop, please!!"

Ma shook her head and Rory asked, "How do ye know that isn't an Indian fire?"

"We don't," I answered, "but we are getting closer to white settlements and it just might be one of our own!"

Under protest, Rory beached the canoe. I jumped out quickly to disappear and 'refresh myself', but Ma hung back, still hanging onto the canoe, shaking her head, "No."

"Look, Ma," Rory said patiently with a big grin, "if it's a bear, I want tae check out just what kind of fire he builds. Maybe he'll gie me a pointer or two!" Rory took Ma's hand, ignoring her "No's!" and lifted her out of the canoe and put her down on her feet on the bank.

We walked cautiously toward the smoke. "For cryin' out loud!" Rory and I stared in amazement. Here, in the middle of nowhere, was a clearing around a small log cabin. We hung back in the trees, waiting...for what, I wasn't sure.

"Ach, I'm not going tae skulk around like this! I'll see if anyone's home," Rory said impatiently and made a move toward the cabin. I tried to hold him back, but he pushed my hands away.

Rory didn't exactly bound up to the cabin. He approached it slowly, warily looking around the clearing and into the trees. When he was about ten feet from the door, it suddenly opened and there, filling the door way, was a huge man with a grey, wiry beard and tousled hair. He was wearing a thick woolen tartan shirt tucked into heavy twill trousers, which were tucked into long leather moccasins. His mouth fell open in surprise at the sight of Rory.

"What the...?" he spluttered. "Where in the devil did ye come frae?"

He was a Scot! Never had I heard a sweeter sound in all of my life. "Ma!" I cried out and looked back at her. She was grinning from ear to ear.

"The name's Rory MacLeod!"

The big man slapped his knee and laughed, "Will ye just look at ye? A sight for sore eyes, ye are!"

Rory looked down at his kilt, "Nothin' wrong wi' me!" he said and laughed.

They walked toward each other, hands outstretched, greeting the other as a long lost brother. They were both talking at once, shaking their heads and laughing—nothing and everything they said made sense. The big man ushered Rory inside the cabin, but Rory immediately reappeared, looking sheepish for forgetting about us. "Cum' on! He's a friend!" Rory waved us forward.

Ma and I held hands tightly and timidly walked out of the trees, toward Rory and the cabin. "My wife and her Ma," Rory introduced us. I felt shy and could only smile.

Suddenly, the big man remembered his manners. "Well, let's not stand out here! Cum' in, cum' in!" He pushed the door open wide and invited us into the warmth of the small cabin.

The cabin was about fourteen feet square but it looked like a palace to me. A narrow bed stood against one wall and a rough hewn table and chair stood against the other wall. Metal traps and snowshoes hung from the rafters. In the center of all the clutter stood a small, potbelly stove and a kettle, full of boiling water, whistling its steamy invitation into the air. Ma and I were drawn to it like moths to a flame.

"Missus MacLeod, sit here," he motioned to me to sit on the bed. That was the first time anyone had called me "Mrs.". I obediently sat down while he bustled around and pulled the one and only chair closer to the fire, indicating that Ma should sit there. Then our new acquaintance rushed outdoors, returning within seconds with his arms wrapped around a huge stump of wood which was to be his chair. Rory sat on the edge of the bed next to me.

The man pulled the stump a little closer to Rory, saying, "Now, by the looks o' ye, there's a story here for the tellin'!" But before Rory could answer, our host interrupted himself. "Where are my manners!" he growled at himself and stood up. "I don't get visitors out here and I forgot mysel'. By the way, my name's Hector...Hector Murdock. I'm from around Glasgow way. What a treat tae have one o' my ain folk tae talk to!" He bowed before Ma and me and shook hands, once more, with Rory.

Hector turned and started rustling through piles of this and stacks of that, muttering, "I know there's some cups somewhere! Ye've got tae have tea! I've been savin' it special—for just such an occasion!"

Ma rescued him by fetching our own bowls from the canoe. Rory had carved them from maple wood burls. She put them down in front of Hector. He nodded and picked them up, his finger tracing the beautiful wood grain. "Ye've been living among the Indians, have ye?"

Rory nodded, "Aye." But Hector acted as though he hadn't heard him, so Rory repeated himself, saying, "Aye, we have."

Hector turned around and said, "Were ye speaking tae me? I'm sorry! I have a little difficulty hearing with this ear." He laughed grimly and added, "As a matter of fact, I don't have one. It was lopped off."

Ma's hand flew to her cheek. Hector's quick eyes caught the movement and he walked over to her. Sitting on his haunches in front of her, he gently pulled her hand down and turned the branded cheek toward him. Very lightly, he traced the 'C' with his finger, his eyes speaking his sympathy.

Ma didn't pull away from him; instead, she gently pushed his bushy hair away, once again revealing the ugly lump of tangled scar tissue where an ear had once been.

Sadly, she shook her head from side to side. Hector took Ma's hand and very tenderly kissed it. They seemed to be saying so much to each other without speaking a word—knowing that each had suffered for the Covenant, told them so much about each other. I felt a tear rolling down my cheek as I viewed the tender scene before me.

Finally, Hector forced a smile and almost shouted, "Well, I think this calls for something a little stronger than tea!" From the depths of a fur robe he produced a tall bottle of clear amber liquid and poured a small portion into our bowls. Ma pushed it away, vigorously shaking her head.

"This is different times and a different country," Hector explained to her. "Besides, this is just to keep you warm," and he winked at Rory as he filled the cups to the brim.

"To Scotland! God bless her!" Hector said almost reverently and held his bowl up in salute.

Rory and I replied, "To Scotland!"

"Slante!" He wished us good health in Gaelic and we replied.

He waited for Ma before he took a drink. She opened her mouth, trying so hard to speak, but finally just nodded her head.

Hector studied her closely before continuing, "And to those who have had the courage to stand by her and the Covenant!"

"Aye." Rory agreed and the men quaffed down their drink.

Ma and I were more timid. We weren't used to liquor.

"Cum' on now," Hector encouraged us. It's medicine—it'll keep the cold away!"

"I don't want to waste—it's good, but I've had enough." I tried to not be rude, but gave my bowl to Rory. Ma did the same.

"Then it's a cup o' tea for you and yer Ma!" Hector laughed, not at all offended. "I'll make it right now!"

By the time Rory had downed his drink, mine and Ma's, he was talking and laughing with ease. I realized at that moment how much I didn't know about my husband. I had never heard him laugh and talk this way before.

But our new friend was not to be outdone. He told Rory how he'd worked his three years on a plantation in the Carolinas and had come north to find his own land. "This place, here, is the farthest from the settlement—the way I figure it, it takes me less time to walk to my traps." He was obviously pleased with himself.

The drinking and story telling lasted all afternoon, speeding the hours by until dusk arrived with its responsibilities.

"It's time we ate!" Hector announced. He put a large cast iron griddle on the stove and disappeared outside. When he returned he was brandishing a knife and a chunk of venison, which he sliced into thick steaks and threw them into the pan where they sizzled and smoked, oh! so deliciously!

Ma was not afraid of this man. In fact, she seemed happier than I had seen her in a long while. She went back to the canoe for our own supplies and returned, carrying cornmeal, which she shaped into cakes, thus taking over the preparation of supper. Hector happily turned the chore over to her.

The venison fairly melted in our mouths and the cornmeal cakes were more tastier than ever with the gravy from the venison poured over them. We ate, and ate. No cold wind chilling us, no smoky camp fire, no bears! What luxury!

Before long I felt my eyelids drooping and I couldn't stay awake any longer. The good meal, the fire crackling in the stove—singing out a familiar lullaby. I simply couldn't resist any longer and curled up on the bed, ready to drift into a contented sleep. Ma covered me and then laid down herself.

One time when I woke during the night, it was to hear the men telling each other of their "crossings" and the various outrageous acts of the ships' Captains and about Wallace Lauderdale. Their voices dropped to a whisper and I drifted off to sleep again.

"I've learned that Lauderdale is in and out of Quebec City—he's drumming up business with the natives—trying to arrange to buy furs. But the Hudson Bay Company started up a few years ago—around 1679—and they are cornering the fur market. I don't know how he thinks he's goin' tae get around them—big company—big company." Hector paused and thoughtfully scrutinized Rory for a few moments before continuing, "Rory, I have a score to settle wi' that man—and I will settle it!" he said firmly, leaving Rory with no doubt that it would be settled—to Hector's satisfaction. "I have someone on the lookout for him—I want to know when he's in Quebec."

"Hector," Rory told him quietly, "whatever it is you have planned, can we keep it from the women? They are petrified of that man—and with good cause."

Another time when I awoke, Rory was explaining that Ma hadn't always been like this, that he figured she was shocked by the massacre and lost her voice. Hector's face was full of compassion when he looked in Ma's direction.

So, the whole night passed and by morning they were talking about their plans for making a living in this new land. Hector was a fur trapper and it was his aim to establish a fur trading post somewhere along the St. Lawrence River. He offered Rory a job working for him, but Rory turned it down explaining that he would like to strike out on his own and work for himself.

"Well, sir," Hector said matter-of-factly, "that might be a little more difficult than ye think. First of all, ye'll need a trading license and ye'll have tae get that in Quebec City."

"How far away is that?" Rory asked.

Hector tried to hide his smugness. "Well, let's see. In the summer ye could make it in about a week. But the snow isn't far off, so ye could triple that for winter traveling."

Rory looked dejected and Hector let him stew in his disappointment for a few minutes before adding, "Tell ye what I'll do! You want your own business and I need help. How's about joining up wi' me and we'll build a trading post on the St. Lawrence River?"

"But ye already have *your* start: money and a license. I haven't anything to offer, yet."

"Ye have something more valuable than money tae offer, MacLeod. Just take a look at the size o' ye. Ye'll dae fine as a trapper. And there's yer wife and Christie. They can take care of the trading post while we're away trapping. And Lizzie'll be a great help wi' speaking Indian and a'!"

I watched Rory mull over Hector's offer for a few moments. Before long he mumbled, "Ye're right about me not being afraid of work, and I know that both Christie and Lizzie have the good sense to run a trading post while we're away and they're both good wi' the Indians..." A few more minutes passed in thoughtful silence.

Hector sat back, his hands clasped behind his head, waiting patiently with a smile on his face.

"Aye. It's a fair offer, Hector! I accept." Rory slapped his knee and laughed happily.

Hector poured them both another whiskey and they raised the bowls to one another...again.

"To our partnership!"

"Aye! To our partnership!"

The bowls were set down on the table with a firm thud and they shook hands—sealing the contract. Rory nodded toward the door. "That's not the birds, already, is it?" he asked.

"Aye, it is," Hector grinned. "It's been a good crack, hasn't it—long time since I've done that—aye, a good chin wag!" He got up and opened the door.

I snuggled further into my blanket as a cold blast of air filled the room, bringing with it the birds' early morning melodies. Hector opened the door wide and sucked the fresh air into his lungs. "Sun's almost up!" he reported.

"Feels a little crisp out there," Rory noted.

I drew the blanket up over my head because I knew what was coming next!

"A new day! Lizzie!" Rory exclaimed, as he pulled my fur rug away. "A new life! Get up, lassie! Ye can't lie there a' day!" He leaned over Ma to kiss me, but I rolled away. His breath was sour with whiskey.

"Just see the sass o' her!" he said to Hector, laughing loudly. "Ach, well, tell ye what! You get these two up and I'll go and get our breakfast."

Hector, sitting again on the squatty stump with his chin in his hands, smiled contentedly and nodded. "Aye, and I'll stoke the fire."

"Wait for me!" I called out to Rory. "I'm coming with you!"

We walked to the river where Rory removed his moccasins and proceeded to wade into the chilly water. Standing perfectly still, he waited for breakfast to swim by. A long, plump, unsuspecting trout came within arm's reach and Rory had him, grasped tightly in his two hands. He threw it up onto the bank where it landed, wriggling and flopping at my feet.

"Ye have more bloody Indian in ye than any white man I've ever known!" Hector's voice startled me.

Rory acknowledged the grudging compliment with a broad, boyish grin and went back to his task. He had but to wait a few moments before he scooped up another, and another, tossing them triumphantly onto the bank after each catch.

Soon, he climbed out of the river, pulled on his moccasins and we were on our way back to the cabin.

"Ye'll be needing warmer clothes soon," Hector observed.

"Aye!" Rory said through chattering teeth. "And I'll be using a hook and line from now on, too!"

The tantalizing aroma of the fish frying began to fill the cabin. Ma tugged at me, indicating that she wanted me to follow her. We walked back down to the river bank.

"Ah, Ma—it's too cold!" I objected when I realized that she wanted to wash herself. But Ma was so much like her old self that I didn't want to dampen her spirits. So I just followed her example. We didn't dawdle—in and out and dressed again. When we returned to the cabin, our skins glowed, invigorated by the cold river water. Ma sparkled—there was life in her eyes again.

"Ohh, that smells so good!" I exclaimed.

"Then the two o' ye sit yersel down and eat up!" was Hector's reply. While we ate, Rory asked, "What do ye think of me goin' in partnership with this man?" He nodded his head at Hector.

"You've already agreed, why are you asking me?" I thought to myself, but out loud I asked, "What would we be doing?"

"Running a fur-trading post. The Indians bring their furs to the trading posts and trade off for blankets, food, guns—right, Hector?" Rory looked at him for help.

"Aye!" Hector said enthusiastically.

"You and Ma will run it while Hector and I are out taking care of our own traps." He glanced up at the traps hanging from the ceiling.

"It sounds fine," I said, warming to the prospect. Actually, I was excited. My imagination was already flirting with the adventure of it.

Ma wasn't as happy, though, and was looking apprehensive. Hector must have seen the worried look as well, because he pulled his stool close to her and took her hands in his, saying, "Don't worry, you and yer lassie'll be safe. There's lots o' white folk around." He paused, then added, "that's not much consolation, though, is it?" Ma smiled into his eyes and he patted her cheek. "That's a good lass. It won't be as lonely as it is out here, Christie," Hector continued to explain. "Ye'll have neighbors close by and good men around who'll keep an eye on ye for us."

Hector and Ma seemed oblivious to us. Rory seized the moment and whispered to me, "Lizzie, let's go for a walk, hen." He held his hand out to me. I slipped my hand in his and we walked toward the canoe. When we were out of earshot of the cabin, he asked, "Does this sound right to ye, Lizzie? How do ye feel about it? Do ye think it'll work?"

"Aye," I said slowly. "I think it'll work—but you'll be away a lot, right?"

"Aye, at first I will, until the business is built up. But Lizzie, I can support us this way, and maybe even better than we knew in Scotland!" His voice was full of hope.

"Aye, Rory, I believe ye will at that!"

"You're wi' me, then? 'Cause I could'na do it wi' out ye."

He watched me carefully, looking rather anxious for a moment, before relaxing into a relieved smile when I said, "Aye, I'm wi' ye!"

CHAPTER 27

"What th'?" Rory bellowed as we entered the cabin...there was Hector, clumsily trying to look at his precious pipes.

"I couldn't help mysel', Rory," Hector explained. "I had to take a wee peek at them. Will ye gie us a tune?" Hector immediately sensed that he had just walked on sacred ground and it was going to take Rory a few minutes to settle down.

Finally, Rory murmured "Well, no harm done, I suppose. What do ye say, Lizzie? What dae ye want to hear?" he asked as he put the pipes on his shoulder and began to tune up.

"Westering Home," I answered.

"Ach, it's been so long!" Hector whispered, drinking in the sound. Rory played tune after tune and Hector's toe was tapping so fast and hard I thought he'ld work it right through the wooden floor. Without any warning at all, he reached over and lifted Ma to her feet and they both whirled their way through dance after dance.

Suddenly, Rory changed the tempo and the notes of a lament sobered us. Rory's mood had changed. Hector looked at Ma, an unspoken question in his eyes. She put a finger to her lips and shook her head. No one spoke. Soon Rory left the cabin and walked toward the edge of the clearing and into the forest.

I recognized the lament—it was one that Rory and Alistair MacCrimmon had played for each other so often—the one that had brought Alistair to his feet in the ship. The slow, deep, sad notes hung in the air, filled to overflowing with Rory's grief.

Hector tenderly wiped a tear from Ma's cheek. "Beautiful lady, ye don't have to speak, do ye? Yer eyes say it all," he whispered.

I suddenly felt uncomfortable. What was this man doing to my mother? I felt the hairs on the back of head bristle. "Stop it, Lizzie! It's Ma's turn—you're just jealous of him! Stop it, now!" I scolded myself silently. I forced a smile and walked out of the cabin to wait for my husband. "Why can't things ever stay like they are—just once in my life?" I grumbled to myself.

The words, "There's no growth in that," filled my mind. "Aye, Lord, I know it! It's just that I can hardly keep up with all of it at times. I know I've a lot to learn, but..."

A prayer filled my mind and soon a warm peacefulness wafted over me, rescuing me from the turmoil of my emotions. When Rory emerged from the forest, drained and pale, I was ready to be his friend; to hold his broken heart in my hands and help it heal as he had done for me.

And heal it did. Never again did he suffer the agonizing nightmares that had wakened us, night after night.

* * * *

"Ye'll never make it tae the settlement now," Hector said. "It'll be crowded, but yer welcome to stay wi' me, here—until spring break-up." He actually looked happy about the prospect.

"We can't just drop in on top o' ye like this," Rory objected politely.

"Well, we can manage," Hector said, then added hurriedly, "I could use the help on the trap lines".

"Well...aye, that's right! We could get started at that right away!" Rory brightened at the prospect of earning his way. "And I wouldn't mind catching one of those blasted wolves that keeps howling all night, either. How do you manage to sleep through their racket, Hector?"

"Ach, well—a body gets used to them, I guess," he answered with one eye on Ma and me as we looked over the cabin.

"Hardly room to swing a cat," I said under my breath. Ma nodded and shrugged. I knew that meant, "Let's make the best o' it."

How I longed to hear my mother's voice again. Rory and I thought that once she had relaxed she would speak again, but it hadn't happened so far.

"We'll need two more beds and some chairs," I heard Hector say, as he and Rory inspected the wood around the cabin.

I picked up the pail and walked down to the river for some water...and to be alone. My stomach was upset. I didn't feel well, not well at all! I reached the river bank just as everything began to spin in front of my eyes, making me lose my balance. Only by hanging onto a tree, did I narrowly escape falling into the river. Never had I felt quite this nauseated before.

When everything stopped spinning, I dipped the pail into the river water and trudged back to the cabin. Ma had stoked the fire and was making bannock. Putting the pail of water down, I got ready to start washing up the dishes but the smell of the grease in the pan brought my stomach to my throat again and forced me to run from the cabin.

"What's wrong?" I wondered as I sat on a stump, inhaling great gulps of air.

Ma waved to me from the cabin, wanting me to come in. I took a deep breath and walked back, determined to control my heaving. Ma held me by the shoulders, furrowing up her brow with a question.

"I'm fine, Ma...just my stomach's queasy, that's all." She felt my forehead and then held me at arm's length, peering into my eyes, checking my tongue to see if it was coated...all of the things she did when I was a child.

"Honest, Ma, I'm fine. It's going now, I don't feel sick anymore!" That was the truth, the nausea had passed and she seemed satisfied.

Ma heated some water on the stove and we washed the bowls, cups and bone spoons, trying to create some order out of the mess. We hauled in the fur robes, deer hides, and food supply from our canoe. Every inch of wall space was used to store something. Hector built a narrow little bed for Ma and a bit wider one for Rory and me. Rory chipped away at blocks of wood he had cut with Hector's saw and produced three chairs. Ma took over the cooking and my job was to clean and find storage space. Soon, the cabin was as comfortable as possible.

Snow began to accumulate on the ground. One morning, when Hector went through his ritual of opening the door to take deep breaths of the fresh air, he was met with a bank of snow that had blown against the door during the night.

"MacLeod!" he shouted as he kicked away the snow, "it's time to lay out the lines."

Winter had arrived!

Ma and I helped pack the gear and we also double checked all of the seams in their clothing, making sure they were secure. I wished that Rory had a jacket as warm as Hector's but he promised he'd bring home some pelts so I could make one for him.

The men spent the day stacking up a good wood supply and strung the meat on a tree limb so wolves couldn't steal it from us. My head spun with all the instructions Rory gave me about keeping safe in the cabin.

Finally—thankfully—they left. The cabin seemed so quiet and big without them in it. Ma smiled and slumped back onto the bed. I laughed and followed her example.

What a relief! We simply relaxed and enjoyed the rest of the day, just puttering, without interference or instructions as to how to do it better. The day was sweet—just Ma and me.

That night the wolves seemed to howl longer than usual and I missed the security of Rory's protection. And I missed him, which made me laugh at myself; here he was just barely out of the door and I was missing him already!

Our days were spent in keeping the fire stoked and cooking for ourselves. When our chores were finished, Ma brought out Hector's little Bible that he had given her and I would read to her. At times I would stop and state my opinion regarding some point of doctrine. I watched for Ma's nod of approval to let me know I was on the right track, then would continue.

Nearly two uneventful weeks had passed and we were anxiously looking for the men to return. Ma and I had just snuggled down into our beds when a loud thump on the roof brought us to our feet. We listened. Something was clawing at the roof—and then at the door! I walked to the door, unlatched it, and opened it a crack to peek out.

"Ma!" I screamed as a huge wolf threw himself at the door. Ma was instantly at my side. Bump! Bump! The wolf was throwing himself at the door, growling and clawing to get inside.

"Ma! Sneck it! Sneck the lock!" I yelled, pushing against the door with all of my might. Ma struggled to slide the heavy wooden bar into place, locking it against the hungry and very determined wolves.

"Good! that's good!" I cried and slumped against the door. Ma spun me around, looking into my face for an answer.

"It's wolves, Ma! A pack of them. I saw one big one, right at the door, and I don't know how many were behind him!"

She pointed to the clawing on the roof. I nodded, "Aye, they're up there too!"

Suddenly, the clawing stopped. There wasn't a sound! Only the quiet night around us. We waited. Then an eerie howl broke the silence—the wolves threw out their warning. With that signal, they began their attack once more. All night long we listened to their clawing and scraping on the roof and at the door and walls. The only thing between me, where I was lying, and one of those blood thirsty creatures was the cabin wall. The wolves knew, as well, that we were that close and growled and scratched all night, trying to reach us. Throaty growls, so close to my ear, ran chills down my back.

"Ma, will you sleep wi' me?" I asked. She slid in beside me, drawing me into her as she did when I was a child.

By morning there was silence. Had they gone? How could we find out? I walked toward the door, but Ma pulled me back. "Ma, we have to get wood and water," I argued. "I think they've gone—they have to sleep sometime!"

Ma picked up a long piece of wood and raised it high over her head ready to brain any wolf that tried to jump in. I opened the door a crack, bracing it with my foot. I could see nothing but trampled snow. I opened the door a little wider and peeked around. Not an animal was in sight. I lifted my foot to step over the sill when Ma yanked me back into the cabin.

"Ma!" I cried impatiently. She shook her head as she began to wrap me in fur rugs. Ahhh! I immediately understood her thinking. The wolves would have a harder time of getting to my skin if I was covered with fur rugs.

"I also have to be able to move, Ma!" I complained as she wrapped me and wrapped me in hides and furs.

Again, I opened the door and ventured outside. The snow around the cabin had been trampled down but the wolves were gone. By the size of the paw marks, I knew we wouldn't have a chance if they ever managed to get to us. The woodpile had been knocked down and as quickly as I could, I picked up an arm load of wood. Ma was at my side helping to pile the wood into the cabin. We each took a pail and ran for the river. The river had begun to freeze over. With a long stick, I smashed the new ice and broke a hole big enough in which we could dip our pails.

As with every other morning, a wave of nausea washed over me and I had to sit down, gagging, trying not to throw up. Ma sat down beside me, all thoughts of the wolves gone out of our minds. Ma put her arms together, as if she were holding a baby.

"Aye, Ma. I think so. I think I'm having a baby," I said, suddenly feeling shy. She hugged me and kissed my cheek and her eyes sparkled with tears.

Ma picked up a stick and wrote in the snow, "Pray I will some day sing to the wee one."

"Oh, Ma, I pray every morning and every night that you'll get better!" I picked up the pail of water and said, "We better get our work done, in case those beasts have woken up again!"

The wolves had clawed at the bottom of the covering Hector had wrapped around the venison but they couldn't jump up to where it was hanging from the tree limb. Ma and I untied the rope and let the carcass down; then we cut off a large chunk of the almost frozen meat and pulled it back up, higher than before.

Finally, we were safely locked in the cabin again, breathless from all the activity. "At least we know that they can't get in here, Ma! Thank goodness Hector made the door strong enough!"

Ma nodded proudly.

"Ma, do you like Hector? You know, like the way you felt about Da?"

She dropped her gaze to the floor and shrugged her shoulders.

"He's nice?" I coaxed.

Ma didn't look up.

"He has a way about him that reminds me a bit of Da."

Ma nodded.

"Ah, Ma! Would he make you happy?"

Ma shrugged again and picked up her Bible. I knew the discussion was over.

For the next four nights the wolves stalked the cabin, clawing at the door and leaping onto the roof. Surprisingly, we actually got used to their howling and snarling and could even sleep, knowing that with the sun, they would disappear into the forest.

It was around noon. Voices! I could hear voices, getting louder and louder. "Rory!" I yelled and ran to open the cabin door. Rory and Hector were standing at the edge of the clearing, grinning from ear to ear. Rory dropped his pack and opened his arms and I flew to him! The fact that he smelled bad and his beard was frozen didn't make any difference. My husband was home!

"Get inside afore ye catch yer death!" Hector shooed me back to the warmth of the cabin. We tumbled into the cabin, anxious to hear each other's story. Ma gave Hector a shy smile and turned her back to take up her post at the stove and fried the fresh deer liver Hector presented to her as if it was a prize trophy—and it was!

After we ate, Hector again made an elaborate presentation. This time he gave Ma some beautiful muskrat skins, "To make a warm coat for yersel'!" he said. He held one of the dark brown pelts against her honey colored hair, that was now streaked with grey, and stood back, admiring what he saw. His head moved from side to side as if he was judging an exquisite painting.

"Beautiful lady!" he smiled, not at all embarrassed to express himself. "Just look at those green eyes, Rory. Lizzie, look!"

Ma smiled shyly. But there was a twinkle there I had not seen for a long, long time.

"Well, the lines are laid!" Hector announced, reluctantly changing the subject. "It's going to be a good winter for trapping! We'll all have new coats and much more before it's over!"

Rory told us how he had learned to lay a trap line. He and Hector had spent a week running the line toward the north west and then turned around and, following the markers they had left on the trees, returned home, checking their traps along the way.

"Fast learner, this man o' yers!" Hector told me. "He can skin as good, if not better, than most old-time trappers. Not one pelt was ruined!" Rory basked in the warm praise.

"At this rate, we'll have the money to open our trading post in the spring!" Hector announced.

"We can use some warmer mitts—dae ye think ye can make them for us?" Rory asked.

Ma nodded.

"Rory, we've got something to tell you!" I began.

"Aye?"

"For the last four nights we've had wolves around the cabin. They clawed at the door and jumped on the roof, and put up such a racket!"

"They what!" Rory exploded. He looked at me more carefully. "Yer not hurt?"

"No, but it sounds like the devil himself trying to get in here. I'm glad you're home!"

"That's strange," Hector thoughtfully rubbed his bearded chin. "I've never heard of them attacking a cabin before. I wonder what's got them riled?" And after a moment of deep thought, he said "We'll fix those beggars!" and he reached for some traps that were still hanging from the ceiling. "These need fixin' but they'll do! We'll have us some wolf skins by mornin'!"

"I'll mend the snowshoes while you do that," Rory said and again the cabin was a hive of activity.

That night, the wolves appeared again, howling and scratching, but I felt safe now that I was in Rory's arms.

"Yelppp! Yellppp! Yelllppp!" rang out in the night.

"One!" Hector stated quietly into the darkness of the cabin.

A few minutes later, "Yelllppp!"

"That's another!"

All through the night, the wolves sniffed out the meat with which Hector had baited the traps, and snap! they were caught.

Next morning, Rory and Hector, knives in hand, killed and skinned the wolves, carrying the carcasses away from the cabin and into the forest.

Ma and I cleaned the skins and worked them the way Beauty had taught us. It wasn't long before I had fashioned a coat of wolf pelts for Rory and had trimmed the edge of the hood with the soft belly fur. Also, we made the requested mitts from the soft hides and had lined them with the soft belly fur, as well.

"How long will you be gone this time?" I asked, as we prepared food for their packs.

Rory looked at Hector for the answer. "Around a month this time. We'll have a lot more skinning to do, but we'll be back as soon as it's done," he smiled. "I won't keep yer husband away any longer than I have tae!" However, he didn't look at me when he said that, he was looking straight at Ma.

She blushed and turned away.

I rolled strips of dried venison and fish into a piece of tanned deerskin and tied it securely with a leather thong. Ma parboiled the dried corn to soften it before putting it into a birch bark pot.

"Let's take a wee treat wi' us this time, MacLeod—uh, how about two wee treats?" he winked at Rory and dove into the corner of the cabin, digging behind some small barrels.

"Ah ha!" he exclaimed and produced a bucket—maple syrup he had gathered last Spring—and another bottle of the amber colored whiskey. "Just tae keep us warm—uh, it's medicine!" he grinned.

After our goodbyes, we waved them on their way and began our wait for their return...but this time we had much work to do. The days flew by as we shaped jackets of muskrat and wolf fur, sewing the large and small pieces together with the sinews Hector had pulled from the wolves bodies. Ma had brought bone needles and the knife-sharp deer shinbones Beauty had given her.

We used them very carefully, treasuring our tools.

At the end of each day when we put our work away and had eaten our supper, Ma handed me the Bible. As I read, she worked on her muskrat pelts, matching each one to the other until there was a perfect blend, with not one seam showing—a work of art.

And so the winter passed. Hector and Rory laid four trap lines, fanning them out from the cabin like spokes of a wheel. The men constantly checked their traps, bringing home the pelts. These were weighted down with heavy rocks and then the compressed furs were bound into tight bales with strips of leather.

Each time the men came home, they were a little more tired. The hard work was telling on them. When they returned in mid-February, after being away for six weeks, Rory, as usual, swept me up in his arms and spun me around. But Ma stopped him and made him put me down. She locked her arms together, like she was holding a baby and pointed to my belly.

"Oh, Ma!" I cried, "I wanted to tell him!"

She shook her head as she made circles with her hand. I wasn't to let Rory spin me around anymore.

Rory looked doubtful. He patted my stomach and asked, "Really?"

"Aye!" I suddenly felt shy and looked down at the floor.

"When...?" he stammered.

I shrugged and stood on tiptoe and whispered into his ear, "the cave? Or the forest? Or..."

"No! G'wan! Really?"

"Aye!"

"Here, put something on ye! I want to talk tae ye!" He helped me pull a fur rug around my shoulders and we left the cabin.

"Lizzie, are ye sure? When will it be born? Will I have time to fix a house for ye?" he asked in rapid succession.

"Aye, I'm painfully sure," I assured him.

"Yer in pain?" he worried.

"No. I'm just sick to my stomach every morning, but that's easing off now."

"When will he be here?"

"He?" I smiled. "*He'll* be here around next August."

"Ach, well, I've time. We'll be well on our way by then!" Immense relief eased the worry lines in his face. "Cum' on, now. Let's get you back into the warmth."

"Rory," I said, "I love you. There's nothing I want more than to have your bairn."

"Oh, Lord! I don't deserve ye!" he cried as he took me in his arms and kissed me. When we walked into the cabin, Ma and Hector were waiting for us, smiling as though it was they who had really accomplished something. I realized at that moment that my baby belonged to them as well. Ma had already started making a papoose carrier out of the softest of the furs and when she offered me food, she was thinking of the baby—and I knew it.

"Well, done, old son!" Hector patted Rory on the back. It was Rory's turn to feel shy, but that only lasted a moment before he was throwing his chest out, proudly grinning from ear to ear.

There was an air of urgency about the activities, now. Everything seemed to revolve around August, "when the bairn comes".

Winter literally melted into Spring and the runoff swelled the river until it was raging with broken ice and muddy water. Spring break-up was long, soggy and muddy! I detested it and Ma hated it even more! There was mud everywhere and on everything!

Eventually, though, the big day arrived when we were able to load the pelts into the canoes and begin the last leg of our journey.

Leaving our cabin—and it had become 'our' cabin—made me feel a little sad. I walked through it, touching the potbellied stove, our bed, the chairs, saying goodbye...and thank you!

"Lizzie, will ye come! Now! Not next year!" Rory called from the canoe. I was to ride with him and Ma with Hector. The pelts had been divided between the two canoes.

Hector took the lead, guiding us safely around the river's hidden dangers. So many times we could have been upset but he always managed to keep us in safe waters.

Toward the end of the second week of canoeing, Hector pointed out that the forest was thinning and announced that the settlement was just around the next bend.

"Yayyy!" I shouted, overjoyed at the thought of not having to sit in this cramped position any longer. My belly was beginning to get in the way.

Hector's canoe was the first to round the bend and we were startled by a woman's high pitched voice greeting us. "Hec-torr! Hec-torr!" she screeched happily and waved frantically as she ran along the river bank, keeping up with the canoe.

Hector turned and looked very sheepishly at Ma, who was looking more than a little disgusted.

"Damn!" we heard him mutter as he paddled even harder.

Soon there were more people on the bank—white people, dressed in clothes made of cloth, not of animal skins. I looked down at my buckskins. I felt ashamed of how I was dressed. Suddenly, I wished the canoe wasn't traveling quite so fast. I didn't want to get out and face those people with their fancy dresses.

"Oh, Ma!" I moaned, as Rory and Hector jumped out and tied the canoes to the small dock.

"Lizzie, we've made it!" Rory sounded exuberant. "Lizzie, are ye alright? Here, let me help ye, hen?" he said as he offered me a hand.

Ma was holding back as well, trying to straighten her hair and brush the imaginary wrinkles from her buckskin dress. But Hector had her by the hand as well, pulling her from the canoe.

"Hec-torr!" The woman on the river bank persistently repeated his name. She breathlessly ran toward him, obviously expecting to be swept off her feet.

"Nicole!" he said, holding her at arm's length.

"You beeeen gone for so long!" she scolded in broken English.

"Just listen tae you! Who's been teachin' ye English?" he asked.

"We 'ave a new school teacher," Nicole said proudly. "I do her washing and she—uh—how do you say? she teach me English! Da priest brought her from Quebec City."

Ma gripped my arm at the word 'priest'. The gesture wasn't missed by Hector and he reached out and put his arm around her saying, "Don't upset yersel', Christie, it'll be alright! Here, the Papists and us live together in peace."

"Who dees woman?" Nicole demanded, pointing at Ma.

"Christian Whitelaw," Hector answered casually.

"She your woman now? Not me?" Nicole was angry—very angry—and she stood in front of Hector with her hands on her hips and fire in her flashing black eyes.

Hector hesitated. He took a deep breath and said, "Aye!" He glanced at Ma, and then back at Nicole. Defiance was written all over Ma's face. She stepped closer to Hector and put her arm through his and glared back at Nicole.

Nicole stamped her foot. "Mon Dieu! Mon Dieu!" she screamed. "I wait for you! I learn thees stoopud English!" She made a show of spitting on the ground. "Ahhh...you dog!"

"Enough, Nicole!" said one of the men, as he not too gently led her away from the group.

"I even learned about that man—the one in Quebec—you wanted me to find.......!" But her words were lost as she was pulled away.

"Whew!" muttered Hector.

"A woman scorned and a' that!" added Rory. "I think I'd rather face a wolf!"

"Remember that!" I warned him.

Rory and Hector turned their attention to the furs and fully enjoyed the sincere praise from Hector's friends. The bales of furs were soon unloaded and carried into what was to become our trading post.

A friendly woman by the name of Mrs. Buchanan had taken Ma and me in hand. "Hector," she said, "I'll take the two lassies wi' me, gie 'em a chance to rest in a bed! Especially this wee uin!" she said, patting my stomach affectionately. Just to hear her sweet Scottish brogue and feel of her hospitality—oh, what good memories it brought back. What comfort! She reminded me of Maggie Winters.

Rory and Hector decided to sleep at the trading post, "Just tae keep an eye on things." What that meant was that they were taking no chances of losing their furs.

Mrs. Buchanan clucked over us, never asking questions, but waiting for us to tell our story in our own time. I explained about Ma losing her speech. "Ach, shame! Shame!" she sympathized as she flung her arm around Ma's shoulders, and then gave my protruding belly a motherly pat asking, "How long now, hen?"

"I figure sometime in August," I answered.

"Ach, well, then you've got the worst over. Only three months and a bit and it'll be in yer arms! Looks like a good size wee uin, though!" she smiled.

Not far up the road we stopped in front of a large house made of logs and stone. Windows were cut into the walls and wooden shutters stood open; the lace curtains fluttered a cheery welcome when the door opened. I learned later that Mrs. Buchanan had wrapped them about her body during the trip from Scotland and with great difficulty had preserved them from ruin. When her husband told me about the great pains she took to keep them from ruin, I nodded sympathetically and told him about Rory and his pipes.

Ma and I stepped over the doorsill onto an oval braided mat. "Look Ma!" I whispered. "It looks like Grandda's." On the opposite wall was a large stone fireplace and hearth, which housed a cozy, blazing fire. "Oh, Mrs. Buchanan!" I exclaimed, "you can't imagine how good that looks to us!"

She nodded her head knowingly and led us to a rough hewn table; it was set with pottery dishes and cups—cups with handles. Good silver knives and forks were placed at either side of the large, round plates. Ma ran her finger around the edge of one of the plates with such longing on her face and tears sprang into her eyes. I knew she was homesick for Tigh Sona and Da and our happy times there, though always overshadowed by fear—we were happy.

"Halloo!" a small girl bounded into the house, smiling broadly. Three others bounced in behind her, bringing bubbly laughter with them. I thought of Jenny. They were dressed similarly to Mrs. Buchanan, who wore a clean dress covered with a huge white apron and a white bonnet was tied under one of her chins. She was a comfortable, congenial, plump woman.

"That's a fine dress ye have there, Mrs. Whitelaw," exclaimed Mrs. Buchanan. Ma looked down at her dress and brushed away imaginary dirt. "It feels so soft. Did ye do the beading yerself?" Ma nodded shyly as she slowly relaxed under the approval.

We didn't have long to wait before Mr. Buchanan strode into his home and welcomed us in the same congenial manner as had his wife.

He had been helping Rory and Hector unload the furs. "We need that trading post of Hector's," he exclaimed after he had offered a prayer of thanks over the food.

"Aye, my husband and Hector have formed a partnership and Ma and I will help tend it," I informed him.

Ma smiled. To be needed, was important to her.

Dinner was delicious, especially the potato! We hadn't tasted an honest-to-goodness potato for so long. And the squash and beans! I scooped up every last morsel on my plate.

At the end of the meal, one of the girls jumped up and carried a huge pie over to Mrs. Buchanan and set it down in front of her.

The aroma of berries wafted through the room. I grinned at Ma, but suddenly felt guilty about Rory and Hector, left alone at the trading post.

"I've had more than enough, Mrs. Buchanan," I said, refusing still another helping of pie. "But...would ye mind if I take this to my husband?"

She laughed heartily, saying, "Only if ye want tae insult Mrs. Hamilton! She's feedin' yer men folk." I had learned my first lesson in pioneer hospitality. The familiar customs had been brought with them from Scotland to this new settlement. Same customs...new land. The berry pie beckoned me and I did eat, much to the delight of the others. Mrs. Buchanan kept urging me on with, "Yer eating for two, now, lassie!"

After the meal was finished, the girls cleared the table of the dishes and were off, playing in the last rays of sunshine. Mr. Buchanan lit his pipe and lifted down a musket from its hangers above the fireplace. He sat down in the rocking chair by the hearth, musket in his lap, and was soon carving more whirls into the intricate design on the wooden stock.

"His Da was a tinker—taught him the meaning o' these Celtic designs."

"Aye," Mr. Buchanan agreed, "this one'll keep the user o' this musket safe." He was quiet for a moment, then pulled up a chair beside him and invited me to sit down.

"Lizzie," he continued, "how are things back hame?"

I thought for a moment, not knowing where to begin. "We came over on the 'Henry and Francis'," I offered. Mr. Buchanan let the musket fall into his lap. "Yer not the bunch that Adams dropped in the water—wi' the Indians comin' at ye?"

"Aye," I said simply. Ma's eyes were wide as she waited for me to continue.

"Did ye hear that, Marion?" he asked his wife, not taking his eyes from me. "Mind what they were telling us in the town about it?" I learned later that Captain Adams had sailed the St. Lawrence River to Quebec and the crew had told our story when they came ashore.

"Where are the others?" Mrs. Buchanan asked gently.

"Weesht, woman," her husband scolded, sensing a tragedy.

They waited for me while I was took time to choose my words carefully, not really knowing where to begin. It was so hard to speak about it—we never had, so far. However, in spite of my hesitation, the words began tumbling out just as though they had a life of their own and I was just a bystander. Finally, mercifully, the whole story was told. Ma's face looked as cold as granite when I finished and I was exhausted.

Mrs. Buchanan patted Ma's knee. "Shame—what a dreadful shame, and waste! Can I get ye a bite tae eat?" she asked. "Ye'll feel better!"

The kettle was on the hob before we could answer; tea made from chamomile and a piece of lovely cake was in front of us within minutes. "Just tae warm ye afore yer bed," she explained.

"My wife thinks that food'll fix everything!" Jimmy Buchanan said with an apologetic smile.

I glanced at Ma, knowing she was remembering when Da said those very same words to her.

Mrs. Buchanan was right. I had forgotten how comforting a cup of hot tea could be.

The Buchanans were kind and tried to sooth us with warm words of kindness, but eventually, it was time to retire.

The Buchanan girls had been sent scurrying up the ladder to the loft and Mrs. Buchanan pulled back the curtain that had hid their bed from view.

"Dae ye mind sleeping in the loft? I think ye'll be comfortable there," Mrs. Buchanan asked.

"Aye," I said for both of us. We were anxious for our beds. I felt drained from the day's activities and especially reliving the events of the past months spent my emotional strength.

Up the ladder I went, with Ma behind me, thinking, I'm sure, that she would catch me if I fell. Several beds lined each wall of the loft, each one covered with a thick down comforter and huge square pillow. The pillowcases were embroidered and edged with hand made hairpin lace. A basin and pitcher of water was on a stand at the end of the loft and Ma and I were allowed, as guests, to wash first. That in itself was a luxury but sliding between the clean sheets was pure ecstasy. Oh, what a grand feeling! The candle flickered its shadows on the gabled roof, casting a warm glow over us and as I glanced at Ma in the next bed, I noticed she was trying to say something to me. Carefully she shaped each word with her mouth, "I think I've died and gone up to Heaven!"

"Aye, Ma! He hasn't forgotten us after all!" We both slipped into a healing, refreshing sleep—not to wake until several hours.

It was the warm morning sun, streaming through the shutters covering the glassless window at the end of the loft that woke me. For a few moments, I wondered where I was and then, with a sudden rush of memory, quickly sat up.

"Ma, wake up!" I called out quietly, not wanting to wake the girls. Ma sat up with a start and glanced around her, looking lost as well.

"It's alright Ma, we're at the Buchanan's. Remember?"

Her face relaxed into a smile as she rolled out of bed and onto her knees. To watch Ma say her prayers was to see a sermon. The spirit that hovered about her was so reassuring—that God lives. I waited, enjoying the peace it always brought to my own spirit.

The aroma of baking biscuits wafted up to us. We could hardly wash and dress fast enough to get downstairs.

"Here, I've made a basket for yer men folk; thought ye might like tae take yer breakfast wi' them," Mrs. Buchanan said, when we were once again in the big, cheery kitchen. "They're likely a wee bit peckish by now!" she predicted.

"You couldn't be more right, Mrs. Buchanan—my husband can always eat!" We laughed together and Ma was also smiling when she took the basket and I thanked her again for her hospitality.

As we left, she instructed us "tae bring the four o' ye back for supper the 'night."

Our feet flew over the road to the trading post and soon, it was in view. Rory was walking around the unfinished building, inspecting it.

"Rory!" I called.

His face lit up. "Ah, ye didn't desert me after a'!"

"Rory!" I bubbled with enthusiasm, "you should see their house! It's so clean and there are real sheets on the bed and they eat from pottery dishes with knives and forks—and Rory, you should just see it! Oh, ye will!" I remembered, "she's invited us all back for supper!"

"Take a breath, lassie!" he laughed. "What's for eatin'?" His eyes were on the basket that Ma was opening.

"Hector, get outta there! Christie, stop him, he's got the whole lot o' biscuits!" Rory shouted.

Ma playfully smacked Hector's hand and took the biscuits from him, much to Rory's pleasure. Warm biscuits with butter and honey, strips of bacon and a jug of milk! What a feast! We each defended our share from Hector who had an enormous appetite—bigger even than Rory's—and enjoyed the many good laughs and joshing that accompanied the meal.

When we eventually finished, Rory took my hand and led me slowly around the building. "Ye'll have more than a house like the Buchanan's, Lizzie. You are going to have a mansion and live like the lady you are!" He spoke in the unfamiliar perfect English.

"Oh, Rory!" I flung my arms around his neck. "I don't need a mansion! Just a house and clothes made out of cloth, not animal hides."

"I mean it Lizzie...it'll be a mansion I'll be givin' ye!"

He's serious, he's not just talkin', I finally realized.

"Were ye cold last night?" I asked, trying to change the subject without hurting him. "Where did you sleep?"

He took me inside the roofless building and there was the pile of furs where they both slept. Absentmindedly, I lifted one of the pelts. I was taken back at the sight of the war club and flint knife the Chief had given Rory.

"No one'll catch me napping either, Lizzie!" he said solemnly.

I stood, staring at him—remembering my thoughts the night Rory had returned from being on the warpath with the tribe.

We were rescued by Hector's booming voice, saying to Ma, "there's a lot of work to do in a short time."

And Rory enthusiastically added his opinion with, "But it's goin' to be good for us here! I can just feel it!"

"The Indians won't attack us here, will they?" I asked.

"I don't know for sure—they haven't so far, but who's tae say," Hector answered. "We can expect many more white people to settle around here once the trading post is operating. And I guess that'll mean less chance of attack, at least from the Indians. Right, Rory?"

"Aye, makes sense. But now, we need shelves, doors..." Rory's voice trailed off as he looked around.

"And just think what a difference a roof would make!" I teased, as I looked at the blue sky overhead.

"Just for that, yer sleeping wi' me tonight...here!" Rory stated with a grin.

Chapter 28

Spring flew into summer on wings of activity. The long, hot days rippled with the thrill of discovering new friends and coming to understand the politics of the country.

It seemed that in 1682 King Louis XIV of France had recalled Quebec's Governor, Count Louis de Frontenac and the Intendant, Jacques Duchesneau, as a result of their constant quarreling and jealousies of each other. Because their official positions sometimes overlapped—to hear the locals describe it—they were 'butting heads' constantly. We were told that Frontenac did enforce peace with the Iroquois and for that everyone was thankful. And the Intendant, who was to take care of the financial affairs of the new territory, such as collecting taxes which, because there wasn't much money and really no need for it up to now, received payment in chickens, produce and furs. The Indendant made sure that each Seigneur (a noble who had been granted land by the King) provided his habitants with a flour mill. This was acceptable to everyone and in general, the people were satisfied with their government.

It was early July and today was the big day!...the day we had worked toward for months. The roof was to be put on the Murdock & MacLeod Trading Post!

The entire settlement turned out for the celebration. Everyone had taken part in helping build the "Post", as they called it. And now, finally, it was time to put the roof on and, of course, what better reason to have a party?

Beginning in the early morning, folks from miles around arrived on horseback, in wagons and even walking, hauling huge baskets of food with them. Rough tables made of planks had been set up to receive the heavy baskets that were gratefully plunked down with gasps of relief. While the women began cooking and arranging the food on the tables, the men hauled logs onto the roof and before long a shout went up, letting everyone know it was finished!

What a thrilling moment! To know that a new life was at last beginning—for us and our little family. However, my magic moment was shattered by Hector's shout, "Let's eat!"

"First, we give thanks, Murdock!" Rory reminded him soberly, and proceeded to lead us in prayer, giving thanks to God for his bounteous mercies. All of us had experienced, first hand, His love and goodness and were more than anxious to acknowledge it.

"Amen!" we all agreed.

"Let's eat!" Hector cried out again, this time through cupped hands and actually strutted as he led the way to the feast. Every imaginable kind of food, cake, pie, meat, fowl, fruit and vegetable, had been loaded onto the tables. Two men were turning the spit, roasting a suckling pig. Oh, my! that porker was being roasted to a turn! And Mrs. Buchanan kept dousing it with her secret sauce. Our mouths were watering, waiting for the first taste!

"Just look at that, Lizzie!" Rory had pulled me aside to inspect the building. "It's only the beginning, hen!" he said proudly. There were counters and shelves and storage places; in the back was our living quarters with a separate bedroom for Ma.

I stood on the floor of wide planks, surveying our kingdom. "You and Hector are off to a good start, Rory!" I said, feeling proud of my husband's accomplishment.

"Aye, he was a Godsend, alright!"

"Is it really happening to us?" I could hardly believe our good fortune and there wasn't a cloud on our horizon. Rory kissed me lightly and put his hand on my bulging tummy, giving his "wee son" an affectionate pat, before we joined the others at the table. We enjoyed and benefited from each and every one of our friends' personalities. Nothing better than good food and good company.

And now—good music—the time for dancing had arrived. One of our French neighbors brought a fiddle and soon we were learning French country dances. A call for Rory and his pipes went up. The Scots now showed the French how to dance Scottish quadrilles and reels. The fiddler soon picked up the tunes Rory was playing and "enjoy" was the rule of the day.

I sat out most of the dances, now that I was among the 'expecting' lassies. I chatted with two other young women who were also expecting their first babies and we exchanged symptoms and pains and referred to tales told us by midwives of the settlement. Everything seemed so mysterious. Here it's my own body and I really didn't know what was happening to it, and no one would tell me what I wanted to know. It was as if it was dirty or something—to be only spoken about behind closed doors. My thoughts were interrupted as a woman asked, "Missus MacLeod! Did ye get that new cloth in yet?"

"I'll be making the trip across the river after my little one arrives." I answered. "Only a couple more weeks!" I grinned at her and put a protective hand on my baby.

Hector and Rory had promised me that I could choose and buy the laces, buttons and bolts of cloth for the ladies' dresses. The women were most anxious to get on with their sewing and kept requesting the materials they needed every time they came to the Post.

All of our supplies were bought in the city across the river from our own little settlement called "Quebec".

The tedium of ordering supplies, receiving the goods and at times even selling the wares before they were properly unpacked held a certain charm for me. I loved visiting with the folks as they came into the Post. And Ma...well, she was in her glory. The customers were even learning to read her lips and hold conversations with her.

Word about my interpreting skills spread quickly and now, many of the Indians made their way to our Trading Post. But that wasn't the only reason they came; it was Rory's and Hector's reputation for fair dealing that brought them. Never did they feed the Indians liquor in order to rob them of their furs when they were drunk.

Unfortunately, many of the white traders did just that—cheating the Indians out of a fair trade. As Hector and Rory became financially successful, our neighbors began to look to them for advice, so it wasn't long before they had earned reputations in the settlement as "good men".

Murdock and MacLeod were now respected names in our small community.

The Scots and the French had all fallen very easily into the custom of helping each other; raising barns and building log homes and planting crops. We were already making plans to help each other with the harvesting. "Survival dictates that we work together," Hector explained to us. "No one family, at this point in time, is strong enough to exist by itself."

Ma and I worked hard at stocking the shelves, making lists of what our neighbors needed and wanted and pushing barrels and pails around to make things more convenient. After one particularly long day, I fell into bed exhausted, only to be awakened during the night with the first of the long anticipated labor pains. "Rory!" I shook him awake. "Rory! Get Ma!"

"Wha...?" he asked sleepily and then, realizing what was happening, flew to Ma's door, banging on it and yelling, "Christie—it's time—it's Lizzie—it's the bairn!!"

Within minutes she was dressed and had Rory building a fire and boiling water.

The next pain had me grabbing onto the bedstead. "Ma!!" I screamed. Another pain and another! Too fast, it's coming too fast! I bit on my lip, trying to keep on top of the pain but it rolled over me again...and again! "My hips...are breaking apart...Ma! My hips! Ooohh, my back!"

For hours I rolled back and forth with the pain. Was this never going to stop? Mrs. Buchanan appeared, seemingly out of nowhere and sang out encouraging words. "Yer fine, lassie. Rest if ye can!"

"OOOhhhh" another pain and another until, finally, I heard, more than felt, a loud crack and pushed with all my might. My water broke and the baby was push out by my contractions and me!

"I can see the head!" Mrs. Buchanan shouted. "Cum on, lassie! Another push—that's a good girl!"

Ma was smiling encouragement and trying to pat my head with a cool cloth, while Mrs. Buchanan was giving me a loud progress report.

"Christie!" Mrs. Buchanan shouted, "get your wee grandbaby out of there! Another pain, another push and Ma actually caught the baby in her hands, it had come out with such force. Immediately, she laid it on my stomach—and I looked down at its red and blue mottled body, so firm and warm against my skin.

"Rory!" I cried weakly, trying to tell my husband that he had his son but another pain immediately ripped through my body before I could say anything.

"Eeeyahhh! Ma!!" I screamed. Mrs. Buchanan spun around and reached between my legs, crying out, "Push, Lizzie! There's another wee uin cum'n'!" I pushed and pushed, spending the last ounce of strength in my body.

"It's here, Lizzie, it's here! One more push and it's done! There ye are, there ye are! Well, for goodness sake! Well, for goodness sake! Look at this will ye Christie—a bonnie wee lassie!"

I fell back on the pillow, utterly exhausted. In the distance I heard Mrs. Buchanan telling Rory he could come in and then I felt his hand on my forehead and cheek.

"Lizzie, Lizzie—I love you!" he whispered over and over again. I couldn't open my eyes yet or even talk. I just smiled, letting his words touch me.

"Mr. MacLeod, meet yer bairns," Mrs. Buchanan said proudly. I opened my eyes and saw that Ma was holding one of the babies and Mrs. Buchanan, the other. Rory stared at them in open-mouthed amazement.

"Lizzie! Look what ye've done!" he cried.

"She had some help, ye ken!" Mrs. Buchanan laughed.

"Twins! Heaven help us! A laddie and a lassie!" Rory shouted, startling the babies into crying again.

"Hector!" he shouted. "Hector! It's twins!" And he was off to wake up the settlement with his news.

Ma and Mrs. Buchanan cleaned me and the bed and soon the babies were laying at my breast, trying to suck.

"They're so wee, Ma," I noted.

"Aye, not more than four and half pounds a piece!"

Mrs. Buchanan agreed. "They'll take some special carin'! Yer lucky yer Ma is here tae help ye!" Without taking a breath, she changed the subject. "Ye'll follow the Scottish way of namin' them, won't ye?"

Ma smiled shyly.

"Aye," I answered. "The boy will be Douglas after Rory's father and the girl will be Christian after my Ma...probably will end up being called 'wee Christie'."

The next few days were filled with visitors bringing gifts for the first twins born in the settlement. Ma ran herself ragged, caring for the babies and me. Thank goodness for Mrs. Buchanan; but unfortunately, she loved to wield her power over Rory and Hector as she helped out with the house chores.

I sensed a storm brewing in that area, so, as quickly as I could, I was up on my feet again, trying to meet the demands of being a mother and a wife.

My milk came in, swelling my breasts painfully, but I lived through that as well, and the babies thrived. Rory laughed happily whenever he saw their rosy "apple cheeks", as he called them.

Toward the end of August, Rory very gently broke the news to me that he was leaving on a trip to Europe, in order to secure a new market for our furs. He had been told it was now fashionable in Europe to wear beaver-skin top hats.

"We need a part of that market, Lizzie and I want to go around the Hudson Bay Company—they are becoming a monopoly!" He sounded adamant regarding his business reasons but apologetic for leaving us. "And I've heard the ship I'm booked on makes the crossin' in four weeks. I'll be home by the end of October. I'm sorry, Lizzie, tae leave ye now! But if we don't sell these furs, we can't keep on going...well, we would make it but Hudson Bay will take a big chunk away from us. Ye understand?"

"Aye," I said, "but don't expect me to like it!"

"That's my lass. Hector is staying so's I know you'll be safe. Just don't let him sweep yer Ma off tae the altar before I get back!"

What I didn't know was that Hector's old lady friend, Nicole, had managed to keep him informed about Wallace Lauderdale, who was in Quebec, working now for the Hudson Bay Company. Had I even had a hint that he was in the area, I would have been a nervous wreck and for that reason, the information was kept from me and Ma.

Evidently, Nicole managed to become Lauderdale's 'evening companion'—which wasn't very difficult—and she prospered both ways for her efforts. Lauderdale paid her services and Hector paid her for the information as to his whereabouts and his business.

Little did I know that Hector was planning to 'repay' the man for all of the hurt he had caused. Nicole reported to Hector that 'Walleece' was leaving immediately on a trip with Grosseliers, a trapper and explorer, to buy furs for his company. Evidently, Hector then put into play a long standing plan he had concocted some time ago for Lauderdale to be 'disposed' of on that trip. Because Lauderdale was in Quebec, is why Rory and Hector kept putting me off when I wanted to go on my shopping trip. But now that Lauderdale was off with the trapper, it was evidently safe for me to go.

"Why can't Hector go to Europe?' I pouted.

"He figures that I'll do better than he would at securing our market...besides, ye know he is marked with that ear."

"When will you go?" I asked, but the sight of the hangman slicing off ears and throwing them into a bucket flashed back into my mind's eye, making me shake my head to chase it away.

Rory hesitated before answering me. "Day after tomorrow," he said quickly and looked away.

"Day after tomorrow!" I cried and was silent for a few more moments. "Ach, well, the sooner you're away, the sooner you're home!" I tried to not make our separation any more difficult than it was going to be.

Rory left on the small river ferry that would take him to Quebec, where his ship was docked. I stood on the dock, waving until he disappeared into the river mist. "This is going to be worse than when he's off trapping!" I complained to myself as I made my way back home to my little ones.

The next day Hector came to me with a proposition. "Would ye like tae 'cross the river to Quebec on that wee buying trip we promised ye?"

I knew he was trying to make me feel better about Rory being away, and I was tempted to pout, but the thought of finally getting to see Quebec—where all the fashionable ladies lived—was too much to resist. "Oh, yes! I'd love it, Hector. But what about the babies?"

Later that day I walked over to Mrs. Buchanan's house and explained what I wanted to do. "Well, Mrs. Campbell, down the road, there," Mrs. Buchanan nodded her head in the direction of the Campbell house, "she's just lost her wee uin and I'm sure she won't mind wet nursin' yours for a day or two. Yer Ma could go wi' them and look after them there. They have the room, too."

I explained to Ma what Mrs. Buchanan suggested and asked her if she would agree with the plan. Ma looked down at the twins, sleeping in their cradles, and smiled. "I would like to see anyone keep her from tending them," I thought.

The date for my little excursion was set for mid-September. Oh, the preparations that had to be made and Hector complained loudly over my fussing. Finally, the big day arrived and Ma and Hector accompanied me to the small ferry dock on the bank of the river. I kissed them both good bye, giving last minute instructions for the twin's care.

"For goodness sake, woman! Yer only goin' for two days! Yer bed won't even get a chance to get cold 'fore yer back!"

With an exasperated smile on his face, Hector carefully handed me over to the ferry boatman. Ma and he dutifully stood on the shore waving good bye until I couldn't see them any longer.

I turned around to watch the approaching dock on the other side of the river. Quebec! I could hardly believe I was here! I took hold of my deer hide satchel and walked up the stone steps to the streets of the town. Beautiful women in fine dresses and men wearing velvet trim on their coats passed me by, all rushing somewhere.

After locating the inn where Hector had told me to stay, I deposited my small piece of homemade luggage in my room. I didn't linger for the stores were beckoning me to hurry...and I didn't want to keep them waiting!

Each supplier displayed his boxes of buttons and thread to match a wonderful array of gingham, silks and woolens (the calico was dutifully appraised as well). Choices, choices! Oh, it was all so tantalizing!

I decided to not make any decisions today; I wanted to think about it—sleep on it, as I explained to the suppliers, promising to be back tomorrow.

The next day, I had made up my mind. My gloved hand moved quickly from one box of buttons to another, matching their colors to the bolts of cloth I had chosen. The owner was at the end of his patience, but I stubbornly insisted on matching buttons with fabric—a time consuming task, as any woman knows. I felt annoyed at being rushed and was trying to hold my temper when a voice—a purring, oily voice—tore open the almost healed wound in my memory.

I looked up to see Wallace Lauderdale staring at me.

"No," he smiled lasciviously, "it can't be—it's not Christie, not with that red hair, but..." He rubbed his chin thoughtfully before his face lit up with recognition. "You must be her daughter! Of course, those eyes and that mouth. Of course! You are her daughter!"

The annoying voice hadn't changed a bit and brought the scene in our cottage—Ma being tortured, Da wounded—flashing in front of my eyes.

"How well you look, Miss Whitelaw," he purred. "You have your mother's complexion, you know!"

Three thick, rope-like scars ran across his eye and down his cheek. The scar tissue had twisted his eye and face so grossly, that he was almost unbearable to look at and I couldn't help but shudder at the sight. Was it really my angel mother who had disfigured him like that?

My reaction, I realized too late, had caused him to fly into a quiet, cold rage. "It was your mother who did this to me!" he hissed at me.

"Why is scum like you allowed to live while good men like John Whitelaw have to die?" I threw back at him, equally angry.

He recovered his composure and smiled smugly, saying, "I swore I would have my revenge—even if I had to follow her to the ends of the earth! And where you are, your mother is not far behind! Who would believe my luck? And to think I was disappointed in not being able to go with Grosseliers on his exploring trip." He laughed bitterly as he touched his scarred face.

It served to remind us both of a grim memory. With the same evil smile I remembered, he leered at me and then quickly turned on his heel and left the store.

I, too, was finished. "Please send these on the river ferry to Murdock and MacLeod's Trading Post," I instructed the supplier, making sure that Captain Lauderdale was not where he could hear me.

As quickly as I could gather my luggage and pay for my room, I was at the ferry dock, waiting for the next ferry. The flat bottomed ferry boat crossed the river quickly...but not quick enough for me. I wanted to get home to my family. Meeting Wallace Lauderdale had shaken me to the core, letting me know that my fears and wounds were not yet healed completely and that he could still be a threat to us.

"Should I tell Ma?" I wondered. "If I do, she'll make herself sick with worry. How would he know where we lived?" I reasoned, trying to quiet my fears, while constantly turning around, making sure that he wasn't behind me...that he hadn't followed me.

"No," I decided, "I'll keep this little encounter to myself."

Once again at the Post, I was able to relax with my babies, Ma and Hector. Thankfully, Wallace Lauderdale began to fade in my thoughts.

Hector was pleased with the pipe tobacco I had brought him. And Ma! didn't she enjoy the sweets I gave her. I showed them the book of prose I had bought for Rory.

"How much longer will he be, Hector?"

"Oh, only about another month or so."

"Only?" I whined.

"Aye, I miss him, as well," Hector agreed.

About a week before Rory's return, Ma and I were resting in front of the fire. It had been a hard day and the twins had been cranky, which seemed to wear us out even more than the physical work of the Post and babies.

A loud knock on the door brought me wearily to my feet as I went to open it.

Before I reached the door, it burst open and Wallace Lauderdale filled the doorway. "Get away!" I shouted and tried to close the door. But I was no match for Lauderdale's brute strength. He pushed his way inside and bolted the door—the only door, and then swaggered toward us with drunken bravado. Ma flew to where the twins were sleeping and positioned herself in front of them, ready to fight for their lives.

Lauderdale grabbed me by the arm and slurred, "Your neighbors are very friendly, and talkative, too! Why, just a few drinks and they were ready to tell me everything. Oh, pardon me, it's Mrs. MacLeod now, am I right? No wonder you were so upset with me at our last meeting when I called you 'Miss Whitelaw'. Forgive my mistake."

I smelled the unmistakable odor of whiskey on his breath, this no doubt being the reason why his eyes were glassy and not focusing properly.

My arm throbbed painfully in his grip and at my cry of pain, Ma jumped toward him, trying to free me. But he just threw both of us off as if we were annoying bugs on his arm. He pulled off his coat, gloves and hat and laid them carefully over one of the barrels and then looked around saying, "Well, well, well; your God has been very good to you...at last."

We stood very still, not wanting to make any sudden moves, trying to understand what was on this demented man's mind.

I didn't even see it coming! "Ohh!" I cried out again from the pain, as he dragged me by the hair and threw me onto a crate of muskets. Lauderdale was towering over me screaming, You...think...you...are...so...perfect, don't you?" He emphasized each word with a barrage of stinging slaps across my face.

I tried to cover my face with my hands, which only served to anger him more. My only consolation was that if he was hitting me he wasn't hitting my babies or Ma.

The door opened but Lauderdale didn't notice. He was intent on carrying out his sick mission. Ma had left with the babies. I was now alone with this madman!

Lauderdale walked backwards to the door, shutting it with his foot, never taking his eyes from me. He kept calling me "Christie"—announcing every blow by screaming out, "Christie!"

Shrieks of laughter filled the room as he enjoyed my terror and my frantic attempts to hide from him. I was trapped. He knew it...and so did I!

With one hand, he pinned me down and doubled up the other into a fist and shook it in my face. I knew by then I must not even flinch. Any movement on my part angered him to the point where I knew he could easily kill me.

Smash! His fist crashed against the barrel, about an inch from my ear. I forced myself to look into his insane face and watch him sneer at my fear.

"You cheated me, Christie Gray! And you're going to pay for it tonight!" he screamed over and over.

My mind was in a whirl! When did Ma cheat this man—this man who was responsible for all of the pain we had known during the last six years.

"For once, tell the truth, Christie Gray! Say it! Tell me how much you want me! Because you really do want me, don't you?" And he doubled up his fist again, smashing it against the crate; oblivious to his bleeding knuckles. "Don't you?" he screamed. "Admit it!" he screamed again.

I could see the blood pulsing through the veins in his temples; foam dripped from his mouth. He was a ranting, raving lunatic. "Admit it!" he repeated. "You do want me! Say it, you filthy trollop!"

I remained silent. He snatched my hand and twisted it, squeezing it until the silver ring on my little finger almost flattened...with my finger still in it. He wrenched my hand and wrist until I screamed with the pain. Suddenly there was a snap and a light flashed in front of my eyes—my wrist had given way and the bone had snapped.

Lauderdale dropped my arm; it hung limply over the side of the crate and he smiled that ugly, all too familiar smile that was actually a grimace, as he watched me wince with the pain. "Cry! Do you hear me? Cry, you stinkin' trollop!" he screamed over and over.

His hand was suddenly around my throat and he ripped off my dress with his other hand. I grabbed at the remnants of my dress with my one hand, desperately trying to cover my nakedness. My sudden movements antagonized him and I again felt his venom as he slapped my face with his open hand. Blood trickled into my mouth.

His glazed and rage filled eyes spotted a wine bottle on the shelf and he reached for it, dragging me by the throat as he did so. With one crack against the shelf the neck of the bottle was snapped off and he laughed crazily as he poured the wine over my body.

"Trollop!" he growled in his grotesque enjoyment.

Again he looked around the room, wild-eyed. This time he found Ma's Bible and with a heinous laugh he picked it up and threw it at my head with all the force he could muster. "That's all you've ever loved, isn't it? Isn't it? You don't know how to love anyone or anything else! Isn't that right?" He smashed the Bible against my head again and again.

"On your knees! Tell me you worship me, not Him!" he hissed and pulled me to the floor.

"Dear God! Dear God!" I prayed over and over.

He shrieked with delight, yanking my face toward his as he poured more wine over me. Once more he reached down and pressed against my throat as his insane laugh rang in my ears...then warm blackness wrapped around me...

* * * *

I woke with a start! It was Ma! I struggled to push away the blanket she was tucking around me. "My babies...my babies!!" I cried.

"Weesht, weesht, now, pet! The bairns are safe and he's dead...he'll not hurt anyone...anymore!" she said, crying and talking at the same time.

I turned to look through the bedroom door to where she was pointing and there, lying on the floor beside the wooden crate, was Wallace Lauderdale, his body twitching as life ebbed out of him.

Hector stood over him, holding Rory's war club in his hands.

"With him goes all that's been painful in my life!" Ma said angrily.

"Ma..." I began, "where are the babies?"

"Mrs. Buchanan's," she answered.

Suddenly, the realization of what was happening here penetrated my poor tortured brain.

"Ma!" I tried to sit up, "you're talking!" I looked from her to Hector for an explanation and then the blackness came again. When I awoke this time, I was in my own bed and my wrist was bandaged. Ma had washed the blood and wine from my face and body.

"Ma, what did you do? How did you get Hector?" I wanted to know.

"Yer Ma ran over to my place, the bairns in her arms. She tried to tell me what was wrong. I couldn't make out what she was saying and asked her to slow down so's I could read her lips. Well, she opened her mouth and screamed like a banshie, saying that ye were being killed! She ran wi' the bairns to the Buchanans and I picked up Rory's war club—been itchin' tae use that thing for a long time, anyway—and galloped over here and that's when we found that devil chokin' ye! The rest ye know."

Actually, I didn't know as I had fainted.

*   *   *   *

The day of Rory's homecoming finally arrived. Most of my bruises had disappeared and I had made a new dress to wear from some gorgeous yellow linen fabric I had chosen in Quebec. The whole settlement turned out for his arrival and for the party we had planned for him.

Hector let us all know when the big ship had docked at Quebec, across the river. And soon, the small ferry boat could be seen as it made it's way toward the dock on our side of the river. We strained to see if Rory was on the ferry.

"Oh, my goodness! It's him!" I cried out to the others when I saw him stand up and wave. I nearly stopped breathing with excitement. But who was that with him? It looked like a young girl. Curiosity and impatience had me stamping my feet.

"Row faster!" I called out to the boatman. I never took my eyes off Rory...but who was with him? My curiosity had me almost beside myself.

"Ma, who's that with him?" I asked. Ma didn't answer me. She was strangely quiet—and we hadn't had much quiet since her voice came back!

As the boat neared the dock, I looked again, squinting into the boat. "No! It couldn't be!" I looked at Ma.

She was rooted to the spot. Hector was smiling, as though he knew who it was and stepped closer to Ma, putting his arm around her shoulders.

The boat was about thirty feet away, then twenty, and ten—finally! it bumped into the dock—it was here!

"It's Jenny!" Ma cried out and ran toward the docking boat.

Rory lifted Jenny onto the dock and jumped onto the dock after her.

"Ma! Ma!" Jenny cried and ran up the dock toward her mother.

"Oh, my baby, my baby!" Ma cried over and over, hugging Jenny close to her heart.

"Rory! When did you...how did...Hector, did you know?" I cried.

"Sshh," said Rory, as he put his arm around me. "We're all together. That's all that matters. I'll tell ye about it later."

THE BEGINNING

BIBLIOGRAPHY

The Martyr Graves of Scotland by J.H. Thomson

Men of The Covenant by Alexander Smellie

Scots Worthies by John Howie

Ladies of The Covenant: Memoirs by Rev. James Anderson

Traditions of The Covenanters by Rev. Robert Simpson, D.D.

Martyrs, Heroes and Bards of The Scottish Covenant by George Gilfillan

The Makers of the Kirk by Barnett

A Cloud of Witnesses by Rev. John H. Thomson

The Covenanters of Ayrshire by Rev. R. Lawson

Fair Sunshine by Jock Purves

Fathers of the Kirk by Ronald Selby Wright

Light of the North by Jay D. Douglas

The Scottish Covenanters by Ian B. Cowan

The Covenanters by James King Hewison

The Covenanters: The National Covenant and Scotland by David Stevenson

978-0-595-39706-8
0-595-39706-9

Printed in the United States
81372LV00003B/82-84

9 780595 397068